The
BURNING
POINT

The
BURNING
POINT

MARY JO PUTNEY

BERKLEY BOOKS, NEW YORK

THE BURNING POINT

A Berkley Book / published by arrangement with
the author

The Penguin Putnam Inc. World Wide Web site address is
http://www.penguinputnam.com

ISBN: 0-7394-0788-0

BERKLEY®
Berkley Books are published by The Berkley Publishing Group,
a division of Penguin Putnam Inc.,
375 Hudson Street, New York, New York 10014.
BERKLEY and the "B" design are trademarks belonging to
Penguin Putnam Inc.

PRINTED IN THE UNITED STATES OF AMERICA

To Ruth, an agent who has always gone
"above and beyond"

"Love is the burning point of life . . . The stronger the love, the more the pain."

"But love bears all things."

—Joseph Campbell and Bill Moyers,
The Power of Myth

ACKNOWLEDGMENTS

I'd like to thank the Loizeaux family of Controlled Demolition Incorporated for their help with the technical aspects of this book. Needless to say, they run CDI in a far more enlightened, not to mention less accident-prone, fashion than my fictional explosives demolition firm.

In particular, I want to thank Stacey Loizeaux, third-generation member of CDI and clear proof that there is no reason why a woman can't blow things up if she wants to. Any errors are my own.

It takes a lot of feedback from friends when an author is cautiously making her way from one genre into another. Profound thanks for insight and support go to (in no particular order) Binnie Braunstein, Kate McMurry, Laura Resnick, Jeri Wright, Suzanne Kelly, Mary Kilchenstein, Denise Little, Laurie Miller, Val Taylor, Jaclyn Reding, Barbara Ankrum, Chris Ashley, Shannon Katona, Brad Clark, and Mary Shea. Not to mention Loretta Chekani, Marjorie Farrell, Alison Hyder, Julia Kendall, Carol O'Hanlon, Ciji Ware, Nic Tideman, Peggy Wyne, and most especially the indomitable Pat Rice.

I also want to thank Colleen Faulkner for the feral cats, but I really can't take one of the kittens.

The
BURNING
POINT

PROLOGUE

Twenty-five years ago

A piercing wail shattered the dawn air. The waiting crowd, safely restrained behind barriers, began to buzz with anticipation. In the command post, Kate Corsi danced excitedly from foot to foot. "Now, Papa?"

Sam Corsi laughed. "Not yet, Katie. That's just the two-minute warning siren."

She tried to stand still, but two minutes seemed like forever. She'd always known that her father's business was blowing up buildings, had even seen movies of his work. But this was different, her very first live shot. She tugged restlessly at the ribbon that held back her blond hair. "Can I push the button?"

"If you're good, someday I'll let you set off the blast, but not this time." Sam Corsi ruffled her brother's dark hair. "The business will be Tom's, and he has to learn what it's like to control so much power."

Tom put one arm around Kate in an apologetic hug. "Your turn will come, short stuff."

The countdown by Luther Hairston was progressing. When he saw Kate watching, he closed one dark eye in a wink without stopping his steady counting.

"All right, Tom," Sam Corsi ordered. "Put your finger on that button and wait for me to say 'now.' Don't push it before I tell you to."

Looking a little sick, Tom set his finger on the button. But Kate knew he wouldn't make a mistake. He was the smartest big brother in the world.

Seven, six, five, four, three, two . . .

"Now!" her father barked.

Tom pushed so hard his fingertip whitened. Nothing happened, and for a terrible moment Kate's heart stopped.

Then machine-gun-sharp bangs rattled from the tall building across the street, and clouds of dust rolled from the empty windows in the lower floors. Next came deep, deep booms that shook the bones. Walls pitched inward and the huge structure collapsed into its base. Kate shrieked with joy.

Her father swooped her up to his shoulder for a better view. "Take a good look, Katie. This is Phoenix Demolition at work, and we're the best!"

Kate bounced in his arms. "Someday I'll blow up buildings, too."

Sam chuckled. "Demolition is no place for girls. Tom will run the company. If you ask nicely, maybe he'll let you work in the office."

"The times are changing, Sam," Luther said. "That lively little girl of yours might make a fine PDI engineer when she grows up."

"No daughter of mine is ever going to work demolition."

Kate sniffed. Papa was stubborn, but so was she. She'd make him let her into the business.

Because Katherine Carroll Corsi wanted to blow up buildings.

1

Present day, outside Washington, D.C.

One hour until detonation.

Dawn was still a long way off. Donovan entered the warmth of the Phoenix Demolition site office, a construction trailer parked near the shabby apartment building that was PDI's current project. His boss, Sam Corsi, poured a cup of coffee and handed it over without being asked.

"Thanks." Donovan swallowed a scalding mouthful. "Damn, but it's cold out there. Hard to believe in global warming."

"Everything in order?"

Donovan nodded. "In order, and even a little ahead of schedule. The only thing left is the final walk-through. Want me to do that?"

"Hell, no. I didn't spend all these years building PDI so that punk kids like you could have all the fun."

Donovan grinned, not having expected any other answer. The last sweep through a structure on the verge of demolition had a special kind of excitement, and Sam pulled rank shamelessly to do the job whenever he could. No way would he let his right-hand man take his place, even on a night that could freeze fur off a bear.

Sam's daughter, Kate, had shared that Corsi capacity for exuberance. Kate, Donovan's long-gone-but-not-forgotten ex-wife.

Sam knocked back the last of his own coffee, his gaze on the dark hulk of the Jefferson Arms, silhouetted against the lights of Washington, D.C. Closer to hand, police lines kept spectators at a safe distance. Because of the early hour and the bitterly cold January weather, not many people had come to watch the implosion. Voice brusque, he asked, "Ever thought of getting back together with Kate?"

"Jesus, Sam!" Donovan choked, strangling on his coffee. "What the hell put that in your head? It's been ten years since Kate and I split up, and as far as I know, she hasn't set foot in Maryland since."

Sam shrugged, his gaze still on the Jefferson Arms. "Yeah, but neither of you has shown any signs of hooking up with anyone else. You married too young, but there was something damned good between you. Besides, Julia'd like some grandkids to spoil."

Donovan winced as the conversation moved onto dangerous ground. "You're right that we were too young. But even assuming that Kate was interested—and frankly, I think she'd see me in hell first—there is the small matter of her living in San Francisco. Not exactly dating distance."

"Things change." Sam glanced at the clock, then put on parka and gloves in preparation for the walk-through. "Maybe I'll give Tom a call one of these days."

That remark was even more of a shock than the wacko suggestion about Kate. Remembering Sam's unexpected trip to the emergency room the month before, Donovan asked uneasily, "Did the doctors find something wrong with your heart that you haven't told me about? I thought they said it was just indigestion."

"Nothing wrong with my heart, and I've got the cardiogram to prove it." Sam shoved his hard hat onto his salt-and-pepper hair and picked up a big-beam flashlight. "But I'll admit that getting hauled off to the hospital got me to thinking. Nobody lives forever. Maybe it's time I knocked a few heads together."

Seeing Donovan's expression, Sam grinned and lightly clipped the younger man's shoulder with his fist. "Don't worry. If I do any head cracking, it will be for your own good." He headed out into the freezing night.

Wondering what the hell that had been about, Donovan did radio checks with the other members of the team. A perfect shot didn't happen by accident, and PDI's flawless safety record was a result of painstaking care at every stage of a job. This implosion was pretty routine, if there was ever anything routine about reducing a massive building to ruins in a handful of seconds. Soon the structure would be swept away, not with a whimper but an almighty bang. Then something better would rise.

A moving beam of light marked Sam's progress through the Jefferson Arms. Inside the echoing structure, he was meticulously checking the explosive charges, the wiring, and even the flour the crew had scattered in the stairwells to reveal if a homeless person or animal had taken refuge in the building.

Twenty minutes until demolition. Restless with the adrenaline of an impending shot, Donovan picked up the microphone of the radio base station again. "How's it going, Sam?"

"Everything's fine," his boss boomed. "This dump might've been a lousy place to live, but it's going to make a great pile of rubble. I'll be out in ten minutes."

Donovan was about to switch off the mike when Sam muttered, "That's odd."

"What have you found?"

"Not sure. Just a second . . ."

Suddenly the quiet of the night shattered. A series of explosions ripped through the Jefferson Arms, engulfing the building in thunder and flame. Walls pitched inward and the structure majestically collapsed as gritty clouds of dust spewed in all directions.

"Sam! *Sam!*" Donovan shouted in horror, instinctively hurling himself out the door of the trailer.

But it was too late. A thousand tons of concrete had already crushed down on the man who had been boss, friend, and surrogate father for half his life.

Three days later

Funerals were hell, and the postburial gatherings weren't much better. Reaching the limits of her endurance, Kate Corsi slipped away for a few minutes to collect herself before she broke down in front of dozens of friends and relatives. Since the first floor offered no privacy, she made her way through the grand house and up the lushly carpeted stairs, ending in the back bedroom her father had used as a home office.

Everything in the room spoke of Sam Corsi, from the souvenirs of demolished buildings to the faint, lingering scent of cigars. Kate lifted the century-old brick salvaged from the implosion of a derelict factory complex in New England. It was the first PDI project to be featured in a Hollywood movie—an invasion-from-outer-space flick— and Sam had been over the moon. Since then, a number of the company's implosions had shown up on the big screen.

Putting the brick back on his desk, she took a cigar from the walnut humidor and pressed it to her cheek. The tangy vegetal scent reminded her of her father in an intense, primitive way. He'd done most of his smoking in this room, but the faint odor of cigars had followed him everywhere.

She replaced the cigar and crossed to the window, hot tears stinging her eyes as she rested her forehead against the icy glass. Life had been surreal for the last three days, ever since she'd been yanked awake at four A.M. by a ringing phone. If she lived to be a hundred, she'd never forget the timbre of her mother's shaking voice as she broke the news that Sam Corsi had been killed in a shot that went wrong. In the space of a heartbeat, Kate's estrangement from her father had vanished as a lifetime of love welled into devastating grief.

By mid-morning she'd been on an airplane from San Francisco, flying back to Maryland for her first visit in almost ten years. By the time she landed, her father's body had been found in the rubble and the funeral had been scheduled.

Ever since then, she'd been caught up in chaos as she helped her mother with the decisions and arrangements that surrounded a sudden death. Sam Corsi, like his business, Phoenix Demolition International, had been one of a kind, and his death in a premature explosion was front-page news in *The Baltimore Sun*. Now he lay in the ice-hard earth, after a graveside service that had been rushed because of the bitter winds of the coldest January on record.

She still had trouble believing that someone as stubborn and generous, likable and maddening, could be gone. Unconsciously she'd thought her father would live forever. Or at least long enough for their estrangement to fully heal. She should have worked harder at reconciliation. Now it was too late. Too damned *late*.

Warned by the tap of high heels, she hastily straightened and brushed at her damp eyes as another woman entered the room. The dark window reflected an image that could almost have been herself. Her mother, Julia, had bequeathed Kate her own height and lean build and fair hair. Only Kate's chocolate-brown eyes were a visible legacy from her Italian father.

Turning, Kate went straight into Julia's arms for a hug, needing to give as much as she needed to receive. "How are you doing, Mother?"

"Enduring." Julia clung to her daughter, brittle to the breaking point. Kate held her close, aching that she couldn't do more.

Tension eased, Julia stepped away, but lines were sharply etched around her eyes and her complexion was grayed by grief and fatigue. "I saw you leave, so I came up to say that after the guests have gone, Charles wants to talk to us about your father's will."

No doubt her mother had also been glad for an excuse to briefly escape the chattering crowd. "I thought reading the will to the assembled family was only done in Victorian novels."

"This won't be quite like that." Julia's gaze shifted away. "But there are . . . things that need to be discussed."

Before Kate could ask what was so important that it had to be dealt with tonight, her mother dropped onto the edge of a wooden chair and wrapped her arms tightly around herself. "I do hope everyone leaves soon. I don't know how much more of this I can take."

Kate placed a gentle hand on Julia's shoulder. "Mother . . ."

Julia clasped her fingers over her daughter's. "It's good to hear people talking about Sam and how they remember him. But it hurts, too. I've spent all day fighting tears."

"No one would mind if you cried."

"I'd mind, because I don't know when I'd stop."

Kate tightened her grasp on her mother's shoulder. Blue-blooded Julia Carroll had been very different from Sam Corsi, an East Baltimore boy and proud of it, but that hadn't kept them from a good marriage. She had the right to grieve in her own way. Kate understood, because she shared her mother's need to face the world with composure.

Julia closed her eyes. "I'm so glad you're here, Kate. Visiting you in San Francisco just isn't the same as having you home."

The reason Kate hadn't visited Baltimore for almost ten years was downstairs, handsome as sin and twice as dangerous. But today, Kate's problems paled next to her mother's loss. "Of course I came. Dad and I had our differences"—an understatement—"but we've been on better terms the last few years. Not like Dad and Tom."

"I wish Tom was here." Julia opened her eyes, her expression wry. "I'll bet you asked him if he would come, and he said that since he wasn't welcome during Sam's lifetime, he didn't think he should come now."

"That's pretty much what happened," Kate admitted. "Are all mothers psychic?"

"It's part of our job description." Wearily Julia rose to her feet. "I can't blame Tom for not coming to the funeral, not after the way Sam behaved. That man could be so impossible . . ."

Her voice trailed off. Kate guessed that she was remembering the fracturing of her family, an event so searing that even a decade couldn't ease the pain. Wanting to avoid that subject, Kate said, "When things settle down, you must visit us in San Francisco. Tom and I would both love to have you for as long as you want to stay."

"He invited me out for a visit when he called last night. Perhaps I'll take him up on that." Julia brushed back her hair with shaking fingers. "It will be nice to . . . to get away."

Kate considered suggesting that her mother not return to the gathering below, but Julia would never abandon an event in her own home. Inspiration struck. "Didn't you always say a hostess should be able to make all her guests feel utterly welcome, and then get rid of them when she's had enough?" Kate gestured toward the frost-patterned window. "This is Maryland—all we have to do is hint that it might snow and people will vanish quicker than you can say 'white terror.' "

Her mother's expression lightened. "Let's do it."

Kate gave her mother a thumbs-up sign. Julia returned it, managing a faint smile.

Together they left the office, Julia wearing the calm expression Kate saw daily in her own mirror. The lines in her mother's face brought her maternal grandmother to mind. Kate had a swift mental image of a chain of mothers and daughters going back through the generations, sharing stoic strength and support and inevitable conflicts. Someday, if she was lucky, Kate would have a daughter of her own.

But that was another subject too painful to contemplate. Emotions firmly under control, she followed her mother down the sweeping stairs.

2

Kate had returned to the living room—Donovan could sense her presence. Awareness of her had prickled under his skin all day. A good thing he'd been run ragged dealing with the aftermath of Sam's death, so he hadn't seen her until the funeral.

Ending his conversation with a teary Corsi cousin, he topped up his ginger ale and surreptitiously watched as Kate made the rounds of the room. She had the same effortless grace and welcoming charm that distinguished Julia. Relatives and longtime family friends beamed at having her among them again.

He toyed, briefly, with the idea of approaching her and saying something pleasant and casual. After all, it had been almost ten years. They'd both gone on to full, productive lives. Kate was an architect in San Francisco, and he had found emotional and professional success as Sam Corsi's second-in-command.

Then Kate glanced in his direction. As their gazes met, a jolt ran through him. He whipped his head away as if he'd been caught stealing. Better to let sleeping dogs, and ex-wives, lie. His resolution was reinforced when he saw Val Covington speaking with Kate. Of Kate's close school friends, only Val still lived in Baltimore and had been able to attend the funeral. He was glad for Kate's sake, since she needed all the support she could get, but Val and Kate together were a combination he would avoid at any price.

The crowd thinned rapidly, speeded by rumors of snow.

Donovan was considering leaving himself when he turned, and saw Kate bearing down on him with a determined, let's-get-this-over-with gleam in her eyes. He stiffened, no longer sure he wanted this encounter, but it was too late to escape.

He felt a curious duality. On the one hand, Kate was utterly familiar, the woman he'd loved with the total abandon possible only for the very young. At the same time she was a stranger, shaped by a decade of events and people he knew nothing about.

But he would have known her anywhere, despite the years that had passed. Her coiled blond hair set off by a somber black suit, she was even lovelier than she'd been at eighteen. Of course he noticed—it was a biological reaction. They'd gotten married because of roaring mutual lust, and that hadn't evaporated merely because the marriage had ended in an explosion more devastating than dynamite.

Halting a yard away, she said coolly, "Don't worry, I'm not armed. I thought it was time to be terribly, terribly civilized and say hello. How are you, Donovan?"

"I've been better. The last few days—" His voice broke as he remembered the moment when the Jefferson Arms had collapsed in front of his eyes. "I'm so damned sorry about Sam, Kate. Losing a parent changes . . . everything." As he knew from hard experience; he'd lost both his parents before he turned seventeen.

"I'm learning that." Her lids dropped over her shadowed eyes for a moment, concealing any vulnerability. "But you're as entitled to condolences as I. You saw him every day. His death will leave a much larger hole in your life."

She was right; Sam had been probably the most important person in his world. He stared at the glass in his right hand. "Hard to imagine PDI without Sàm. He wasn't just the founder, but the heart and soul of the place."

She took a sip of white wine. "How did the accident

happen? I thought that caution was the official religion of Phoenix Demolition."

"Damned if I know, Kate. We were taking down an old apartment building outside of Washington. Strictly a routine job. Something triggered the blast when Sam was making the final sweep."

"Any idea what set off the charges?"

He shook his head in frustration. "I really don't know. Some stray electricity, I suppose. That's always a danger when there's a cold, dry wind, but even so, it shouldn't have happened. The state fire marshal is investigating, but so far no conclusions."

"I'm sorry, Donovan. Both that he's dead, and that you were there. It must have been a nightmare."

The image of the collapsing building seared his mind again, as it had repeatedly done for the last three days. "I keep wondering if there was something I could have done."

"Maybe it's better not to know." She glanced down at her wineglass, subtle highlights shimmering across her glossy blond hair. Several heartbeats passed before she raised her head. "You're looking well." Her gaze went over his formal suit. Quite a bit different from the jeans she'd usually seen him in. "You've made the transition from wrecker to executive very nicely."

"Don't let the outfit fool you. I'm really just a construction worker." He offered a tentative smile. "Or rather, destruction worker."

So politely that he wasn't sure if it was a dig, she said, "Quite in line with your natural talents." She started to turn away. "Good to see you. Now if you'll excuse me, there are some other people I must talk to."

"Wait." He raised a hand, suddenly unable to let her go without acknowledging the abyss that lay between them. "Ten years ago you left so fast that I never had a chance to say that . . . that I was sorry."

Her brown eyes turned black. "Don't worry, I knew that. You were *always* sorry."

He flinched as if she'd slapped him. There was a long, tense silence. Then she bowed her head and pressed her fingers to the middle of her forehead. "Sorry, Patrick. I shouldn't have said that. But I do *not* want to talk about this, now or ever."

She turned and walked away, her slim frame erect and unyielding. He drew a slow breath. Kate had only called him Patrick when she meant business, so the subject of their ill-fated marriage was permanently closed. He supposed he should be grateful.

Yet his mind could not be stopped as easily as the conversation. How many times had he dreamed of seeing her again? Even after she walked out on him, he'd been sure that if they could talk, if he could apologize, explain, everything would be all right. He'd searched for her with increasing urgency even after she filed for divorce.

Not until much later did he learn that she'd left immediately for San Francisco. He'd never had a chance of changing her mind once she decided the marriage was over. Typical Kate—a long period of tolerance and good nature until she reached the breaking point. Then she'd slammed the door shut forever.

Once he realized that, he'd shattered into bleeding pieces. If not for Sam, who'd treated him like a beloved son, he might not have survived. He probably would have ended by crashing his car into a lamppost at ninety miles an hour, like his old man had.

Now Kate was physically within touching distance, and emotionally further away than ever. His gaze followed her through the room as she moved from group to group, giving people the chance to tell her what Sam had meant to them.

Her black tailored suit was the exact opposite of what she'd been wearing the night they met. He'd been parking cars at the Maryland Cotillion Ball, where young ladies of good breeding were presented to society. When the job was offered, he'd been incredulous that such events still existed. He accepted because his college scholarship covered only tuition, and he worked as many hours as he could spare to earn book and spending money. Besides, he was curious about how the other half lived.

The ball was held at a historic theater in midtown Baltimore. Though the location wasn't particularly glamorous, the guests made up for that. He got a kick out of watching proud fathers and anxious mothers arriving with their daughters. Since the evening had been mild for December, the debutantes didn't have to swaddle up like Eskimos. Even the plain girls glittered like diamonds in their pristine white dresses. He hadn't known Maryland had so many natural blondes.

That is, if they *were* natural blondes. He knew damned well that none of them were as innocent as they appeared. Most were college freshmen and there probably wasn't a virgin in the lot, but he enjoyed the illusion of a simpler, purer age.

The Corsis arrived in a limousine. Julia was all aristocratic elegance, while Sam radiated the confidence of success and wealth. And Kate knocked him for a loop from the instant she slid from the limo, her blond hair swooped up, her slim neck decorated with pearls that had to be real, and wearing a smile that warmed the winter night. Grace Kelly at eighteen and wearing a frothy, snow-white dress.

She was tallish, maybe five-foot-seven. A good height for him. He was so dazzled that he almost forgot to close the car door. Then Kate glanced over, not like a rich girl looking through a menial, but at *him*.

"Thanks." And she winked. For that instant he felt as if they were the only two people in the world.

He'd have followed her into the theater like a moth after a candle if her mother hadn't asked, "Did you remember your gloves, Kate?"

Kate stopped and stared at her bare hands with dismay. "Sorry, Mother, I left them at home. I'm just not cut out for Victorian formality."

Terrifyingly elegant but with an amused glint in her eyes,

her mother murmured, "Why am I not surprised?" as she pulled a pair of gloves from her beaded handbag.

Kate laughed. "For the same reason I'm not surprised that you came prepared."

Donovan watched in fascination as she worked the white kidskin gloves over her hands and up to her elbows. They fit like a second skin. As her mother fastened several buttons at each wrist, Kate glanced at him, her expression saying, You and I know this is kind of silly, but I have to humor my parents. Then she glided into the building like a royal princess, her mother and father a step behind.

As the next car in the line pulled up, he sent a last yearning glance after Kate, wanting to imprint that laughing image on his mind forever. Girls like her were not for guys like him, who parked cars and worked construction to earn college money.

His imagination hadn't been good enough to guess the way the night would end.

But that was then, and this was now. He turned away, hoping no one had noticed him staring at his former wife. The old Kate had been something special, opening her arms to embrace life with a blend of innocent trust and intelligence that had entranced him. Now she wore the same impenetrable calm that was so characteristic of Julia.

Not that resembling Julia was bad—he loved his former mother-in-law. Despite her reserve, she had been a warm, supportive presence in his life. Not precisely like a mother—more of a wise aunt who accepted everything about him.

But where Julia had reserve, Kate had wariness. And most of that was because of him. Oh, no doubt she'd experienced her share of ups and downs since their divorce, but he knew damned well that he was the one who'd destroyed that innocent openness. Over the years he'd done his best to fix his flaws, but nothing could change the past. Kate was a beautiful, excruciating reminder of the worst time of his life.

Thank God she'd go back to San Francisco in a few days.

• • •

The rumor of snow had produced a general exodus. The last to leave was Kate's cousin Nick Corsi and his quiet, dark-eyed wife, Angie. Nick had worked for PDI for years until leaving recently to start his own demolition business. His face was somber, and Kate suspected that like Donovan, he was wondering if it would have made a difference if he'd been at the fatal shoot. Death and guilt were natural partners.

After giving her cousin a farewell hug, Kate closed the door against the piercing cold. With Sam dead and Nick out of the firm, Julia was the owner of PDI, and Donovan was the obvious choice to run it. He'd do as good a job as Sam. Maybe even better, because he was less volatile. Most of the time.

She thought with a flash of bitterness that Donovan had done a lot better from their ill-fated marriage than she had. He'd acquired a second family and an exciting career, while she'd ended up three thousand miles away in a profession that hadn't been her first choice. It had taken death to bring her back to Maryland, and not only because she hadn't wanted to see Donovan. The greater reason was to avoid seeing how much she'd walked away from. Yet if she had to go through the dissolution of her marriage again, she'd probably make all the same decisions, so there was no point in self-pity.

She returned to the living room, pausing in the doorway. Even with empty plates and cups littering every flat surface, she was soothed by the timeless elegance of her mother's lovingly polished antiques and the richly colored patterns of the Persian rugs. The design of the room was pure Julia, yet Sam had loved it, too, as a sign of how far he'd come from East Baltimore.

Seeing Kate, Julia emerged from the temporary refuge of a wing chair. "Since Janet will be cleaning in here, Charles suggested we meet in the family room."

Kate sighed. She'd forgotten that the lawyer had wanted

to talk to them. As she and her mother crossed the sprawling house, she asked, "This won't take long, will it? Surely
most of the estate goes to you. Given his disapproval of
Tom and me, I assume that neither of us will get so much
as a shilling for candles."

"You should know better than to try to predict your father. Though it was hard for him to accept some of your
actions, he never stopped loving you and your brother."

Kate didn't really doubt that her father loved her, though
he'd never forgiven her for divorcing Donovan and leaving
Maryland. Over the years of her self-imposed exile, they'd
made their peace. There had been visits in San Francisco
and regular phone calls. Though their discussions didn't go
very deep, they had become friends again.

But Tom was a different matter. Sam hadn't spoken to
him in almost ten years. Kate uttered a fervent prayer that
he'd left her brother something—anything—as a gesture of
reconciliation.

The lights in the family room were restfully low, and
Oscar Wilde, the elderly family sheltie, lay dozing in front
of a crackling fire. This was the true heart of the house,
and a more interesting showcase for Julia's homemaking
skills than the formal living room. The solid, comfortable
furniture she'd chosen when her children were small had
survived years of bouncing, television watching, and Sunday newspaper readings. The pile of large colorful pillows
in one corner had accommodated endless sprawling young
bodies, since Julia had welcomed all of her children's
friends.

The wall around the fireplace was the family photo gal-
lery, with dozens of pictures highlighting decades of living.
Kate's gaze went from snapshots of Tom as an altar boy
and playing lacrosse, to Kate and her mother working in a
garden glowing with spring flowers. Julia had the greenest
thumb in Roland Park. Flanking the garden picture was a
handsome portrait of Sam and Julia taken the night they
went to a White House dinner, and a shot of Sam helping

his mother move into the house he'd bought for her in East Baltimore, aided by at least twenty other Corsis, including Kate and Tom.

Her gaze stopped when it reached her wedding picture. Lord, she and Donovan seemed young, and so happy that it hurt to look. It was characteristic of Julia not to remove that picture, or the ones of Tom. Good and bad, the history of the Corsi family was written on that wall.

Kate blinked back stinging in her eyes as she remembered the good times. They all had a share of blame for shattering what had once been a happy family.

As they entered, Charles Hamilton was closing the fireplace doors, his craggy face illuminated by the flames. In his late fifties, he had the same kind of lean, aristocratic build as Julia, and exactly fit the image of an establishment lawyer. The stereotype did Charles less than justice. Once, long ago, he and Julia had been engaged. It would have been an eminently sensible alliance between two blue-blooded Marylanders. Then Julia kicked over the traces and broke the engagement when Sam Corsi swept into her life. Instead of languishing from unrequited love, Charles had dismayed his relatives by swiftly marrying Barbara Kantor, a smart, tough, warmhearted Jewish lawyer.

Traditionalists predicted that both marriages would fail. Instead, both flourished, producing two children each. The families had always been close. Tom and Kate had been friends with the Hamilton daughters, Sandy and Rachel, almost from the cradle.

Kate felt a pang as she thought of Barbara, whose down-to-earth directness had made her more approachable than Kate's own mother, who was sometimes too . . . perfect. Barbara had been killed by a drunken driver two years before, leaving Charles well qualified to offer Julia sympathy for the sudden death of a spouse.

Oscar rose from his warm spot by the fire and trotted over to greet the newcomers, tail wagging. Kate bent to stroke the silky fur. Old Oscar seemed to remember her,

even after so many years. Then she straightened and saw a
fourth person pacing restlessly at the far end of the room.
Donovan.

She froze, her pulse spiking. A good thing she'd broken
some very thick ice by speaking to him earlier. Otherwise
this unexpected meeting would be unbearable.

He gave her a casual nod, but he was fidgeting with a
half-empty glass, less relaxed than he pretended. She in-
clined her head as if expecting him, and took a seat as far
away as possible. Actually, his presence made sense. Sam
had probably left his former son-in-law a piece of the company, since Donovan had been a much more satisfactory
"child" than either Kate or Tom. He'd stayed and worked
in the business, providing the affection and companionship
that Sam had wanted.

For the thousandth time she thought that it was a great
pity that neither of Sam's children had turned out as he'd
hoped. It was an even greater pity that he hadn't been able
to accept either of them as they were.

After Julia and Kate settled themselves, Charles said,
"It's late, we're all dead tired, so I'll get right to the point."
His brows drew together as he ordered his thoughts. "Sam's
will is unusual. Julia's financial security has already been
assured, and of course she'll get this house. A substantial
sum has also been designated for charity, and there are
bequests for several other relatives. The rest of Sam's financial assets are to be divided equally between you, Kate,
and Tom, while Phoenix Demolition will go to Donovan—
but only if certain conditions are met."

Kate stiffened, amazed that her father had made her and
Tom heirs. This would mean so much to Tom, and not
because of the amount of money involved.

She glanced at her former husband, who looked startled
and pleased, but also wary. His expression gave her second
thoughts. There had to be more to the will, or Charles
wouldn't have called this meeting. "What conditions?"

The lawyer gave her a level look. "That you and Donovan live under the same roof for a year."

3

"Jesus, Mary, and Joseph!" The paralyzed silence was broken by the sound of smashing glass as Donovan dropped the tumbler he'd been holding.

Kate sprang to her feet as waves of horror swept through her, coming from so deep inside that she almost blacked out. "No!" she said in a choked voice. "That's *crazy*. Not in a million years!"

Her gaze whipped over to Donovan. His stunned face mirrored her own shock.

They were supposed to *live* together? The thought made her blood freeze.

"The will is entirely legal," the lawyer said. "Including a provision to disinherit anyone who contests it."

Kate closed her eyes, feeling the hammer of blood in her temples. Her father hadn't known why she'd divorced Donovan, of course, and whose fault was that? She had chosen silence over public scandal. Talk about no good deed going unpunished! She began to shake as the swift fury that Sam had called an "Italian moment" swept through her. Opening her eyes, she glared at Donovan. "Did you put Sam up to this?"

"Do you think I'm *insane*?" His voice rose incredulously. "I'd sooner share a den with a wolverine."

Much as she wanted to rip at him, it was impossible not to recognize his shock, or a revulsion equal to her own. Kate spun to face her mother. "Did you know about this?"

"Yes. And really, Kate, do try to control yourself. You're making a spectacle."

"Good! I want to make a scene." Kate's fists knotted at her sides. "How could you have allowed Sam to draw up a will that's so . . . so outrageous?"

"Sam was a devout Catholic who believed in the sanctity of marriage," her mother said. "Though you're not Catholic, Donovan is, and you married in the Church. Since the marriage was never annulled, to Sam it still existed."

"Sam could be pretty medieval, but even he knew that divorce was a fact of life," Donovan retorted. "He couldn't possibly have believed that a damned will could resurrect a marriage ten years dead."

Kate couldn't have agreed more. She should have insisted on a Catholic annulment. Donovan had never asked for one, and she hadn't wanted to initiate anything that might require communication between them. Her failure to force the issue gave Sam an excuse to claim the marriage was still valid.

Not that her father needed an excuse. Despite his very real faith, he hadn't married in a Catholic ceremony himself because Julia had wanted the rites of her own church. Nonetheless, he was quite willing to use his daughter's Catholic marriage as a bludgeon to get his own way one last time. Bitterly she said, "What if Donovan or I had married elsewhere? Would Sam have expected us to get divorced?"

"I insisted there be alternative provisions in case there was a change in marital status between the time he drew up the will and his death," Charles said. "However, that's moot since you're both single and able to comply with the conditions if you choose."

"*If I choose.*" Kate's seething gaze returned to Donovan. It had been hard enough to speak to him in a roomful of people. The idea of living with him was . . . unthinkable. "Sam didn't know what he was asking."

But Donovan did. From his refuge by the fireplace, he

watched her as if she were a ticking grenade. Reluctantly Kate recognized that he had been betrayed as badly as she. Instead of inheriting the business that by right of dedication and hard work should be his, Donovan was being victimized by Sam's last ghastly whim.

Pulling herself together, she said through gritted teeth, "Well, be damned to the money and Sam's attempt to control us from the grave." She headed toward the door.

"Wait," Charles said forcefully. "I know this is a shock, Kate. But remember that if you refuse to comply, it isn't just your own inheritance you're throwing away. Tom will also be cut out entirely, and Sam specified that PDI would be sold to Marchetti Demolition."

Donovan swore when he heard that, and Kate came to a halt. Bud Marchetti was an old friend of her father's and had regularly tried to buy PDI and turn it into a division of his conventional wrecking firm. Sam had always laughed off such offers, but obviously he'd reconsidered.

"I don't blame you for being upset," Julia said quietly. "As you said, the will is outrageous, but Sam never gave up hoping that the two of you would get together again."

Kate's eyes narrowed. "Surely you didn't share his delusion."

"No, but I thought his idea had merit." Her somber gaze went from Kate to Donovan. "Not because there is any chance you two will reconcile. I don't know what went wrong with your marriage, but it obviously left deep scars or you wouldn't both be so determinedly single ten years later. Maybe if you spend a year together, you can come to terms with whatever happened, and get on with your lives."

Restraining the urge to swear violently, Kate bit out, "Never!"

"Note, the condition is living under the same roof, *not* sharing the same bed. In effect, you'd merely be housemates." Charles spoke as calmly as if they were discussing tax strategy. "Sam went into some detail about what is acceptable. In a hotel, a suite can be used rather than a single room."

Kate's jaw clenched at this evidence of how carefully Sam had plotted. He must have spent the last ten years figuring out ways to force his daughter and former son-in-law together again.

Charles finished. "Incidentally, Sam also specified that you would live in the home you shared during the marriage, the house Donovan still occupies."

Absurdity piled on insanity! Sensing her distress, Oscar trotted over and began rubbing against her ankle. She stroked his head, her chilled fingers warmed by his small furry body. Straightening, she pointed out, "I'm not the only one who would have to agree to this. Donovan can't be any more willing to cohabit than I am."

Instead of the instant agreement she expected, his expression became troubled. "Kate, we need to talk."

"An excellent idea." Julia rose wearily. "Charles, let's go find something alcoholic. I could use a drink. A large one."

Before following her, Charles pulled a letter from inside his suit coat and handed it to Kate. "Your father left this for you."

She stared at the letter, then jammed it into her jacket pocket. Julia and the lawyer departed, leaving Donovan alone with Kate. She stalked to the window and gazed out, her back rigid.

What the *hell* had gotten into Sam? Donovan wondered. To the extent that he'd thought about it since Sam's death, he assumed that Julia would inherit the company and put Donovan in charge. Even if Nick Corsi hadn't already left to start his own company, Donovan would have been the best choice. He'd worked endlessly to master demanding technical skills until he was as good as Sam, maybe better. He'd developed new methods to drop structures that at first glance had looked impossible, and spent much of what spare time he had earning an MBA.

He sure as hell hadn't worked his ass off to end up as

one of Bud Marchetti's employees. But because of Sam's whim, the firm would be lost, and Kate would have still more reasons to hate her ex-husband.

Breaking the silence, she said without turning from the window, "It's starting to snow. Time for you to go home."

"You can't get rid of me that easily," he said, trying to lighten the mood. "I have four-wheel drive."

She wrapped her arms around her waist, shivering. "Surely you can't want to take part in this . . . this travesty, Donovan. It would be sheer hell."

"At first," he agreed. "Still, maybe . . . maybe we should at least consider doing it."

She spun around, horrified. "You can't be serious!"

Starting with the one thing he was sure of, he said, "I want Phoenix Demolition, Kate." He began to pace about the room, keeping his distance from her. "I've given PDI most of my time and energy for a dozen years. We're the best in the world at explosive demolition. With Sam gone, no one can run the company better than I."

"I also have a business that I've sweat blood over, and it's three thousand miles away," she shot back. "I can't just walk away from that, or let down my partner, Liz."

"It's a bitch, Kate, and far more disruptive for you than me." He stared into the fire. "But forget PDI, forget the arrogance in what Sam is trying to do. The real issue is exactly what Julia said—the fact that you and I are still hung up on the past." He glanced at her, hoping she would understand what he couldn't bear to put into words. "At least I am. You probably are, too, or you'd have settled down years ago. You . . . you were good at marriage."

"Maybe my mother has a point. But if I ever decide I need help, I'll go to a good therapist, not move in with *you*. We almost destroyed each other before, Patrick. We'd be mad to get so close again."

"Not necessarily. Through most of our marriage, you and I were good friends. What broke us up was all related to the fact that we were also mates. Man and wife. This would be different. If we can become friends again, maybe we can get beyond what happened. It's worth thinking about."

Dear God, Kate thought. Yes, they'd been friends, sharing laughter and cooking and the creation of a home. But did he really think they could spend a year falling over each other and not end up in bed? Had the red-hot frenzy they'd called love died in him?

As she studied the sharply planed face of the man she'd loved and hated, adored and feared, her mind slid back to the night when it all began.

4

"Did you see that gorgeous guy parking cars?" Laurel Clark, the only one of Kate's high-school friends to share the debutante game, rolled her eyes meaningfully as she freshened her lipstick in the ladies' room.

"Mr. Tall, Dark, and Handsome?" Kate replied with a grin. "I told my parents that I wanted him washed and fluffed and brought to my tent. Dad was not amused."

Laurel chuckled. "He's taking this debut business more seriously than you are."

"It's a symbol of worldly success. Not only has he done well with his business, but he married a woman from the Baltimore Blue Book. He loves the fact that his one and only daughter can be presented to society. Not bad for a guy from Little It'ly." She dug into her silver handbag for her compact. "Not that I expect society to be impressed, but now that I've buttered Dad up by being a good little deb, I think the time is right to ask for a summer internship with Phoenix Demolition."

"What if he says no?"

"He won't. Ever since I was a tyke, I've known I'd work there when I grew up."

"I do *not* understand your desire to blow things to bits."

Kate hesitated. "The buildings are going to come down anyhow. Isn't there more dignity in going with one last, glorious bang rather than being slowly smashed to bits with a wrecking ball?"

"When you put it that way, it does sound more interesting. But better you than me. I hate loud noises." Laurel turned and peered over her shoulder to check the back of her gown. "In these fancy white dresses, we look like wedding cakes."

"Speak for yourself." Kate powdered her nose, then snapped the compact shut. "When I get married, my cake will be chocolate."

"I want two slices when the day comes. Still, there's something to be said for tradition. This particular ritual—presenting young people to society—is centuries old. It survived the revolutionary sixties and swinging seventies, which is pretty impressive."

"To tradition, then, even if the 'Baltimore bachelors' we're introduced to tonight are old enough to be our fathers!" Kate caught up her full skirts and curtsied deeply. "And now it's off to sweet-talk Dad into giving me that summer job."

Laughing, they left the ladies' room and were presented to the crème de la crème of old Maryland society. As the evening progressed, Kate had to admit that even though the tradition was archaic, it was also fun. By the time her father collected her for the father-daughter dance, she was bubbling with confident good humor. As they moved into the music, she asked, "Does the cotillion live up to your expectations, Dad?"

He gave her the high-voltage smile that could charm a

stone statue. "I know you're just humoring me, but yes, it's what I hoped for. I read about this ball in the newspaper when I was a kid, and it was like . . . reading about Versailles. I never thought I'd have a daughter who would be part of this world." He brushed a kiss on her forehead. "You look gorgeous, *cara*. Just like your mama."

"And you're the most distinguished-looking father in the room." It was the honest truth; he'd always been handsome, and the gray at his temples only enhanced his appearance. She felt a rush of pride. In a room full of men who maintained their fortunes by shuffling papers, Sam Corsi actually *did* things. He'd invented a business, and was the best in the world at it. Even the King Louis who built Versailles couldn't have said that.

Time to make her pitch. She fluttered her lashes, half teasing and wholly in earnest. "Dad, I want to be a field intern at PDI this summer. It's time for me to start really learning the business."

His smile disappeared. As he spun her around to avoid hitting another couple, he said, "I thought you'd given up that foolishness. You haven't mentioned it in years."

"I was biding my time," she said cheerfully. "I understand why you didn't want me doing fieldwork when I was in high school—high explosives aren't to be taken lightly. But now that I'm in college, you can't say I'm too young. You couldn't have been much older than I am now when you learned blasting."

"That was different. I was in the army corps of engineers. I was also a man, and demolition is a man's business. That's why the company will go to Tom eventually."

She'd known he'd say that. "Tom doesn't want to spend the rest of his life wrecking buildings. He's only working for you this summer because he can't resist the prospect of computerizing the office. Since he doesn't want PDI, the company should come to me. I'm as much your child as Tom."

Ignoring what she'd said about her brother, he said, "Demolition work is dirty and dangerous, and I won't have my daughter doing it."

She felt a stab of exasperation, but kept her voice even. "Times have changed, Dad. Women do just about everything but play professional football. I've hung around PDI long enough to know there isn't a job in the company I can't do. Heck, I'm better qualified than Nick, and you're taking him on this summer."

Her father's jaw tightened. "Your cousin is male, a qualification you'll never have. Be grateful I'm letting you study architecture. Frankly, I don't approve of that, either, but you need something to keep you out of trouble until you get married."

Kate stopped stock-still in the middle of the dance floor. As other couples hastily changed course to avoid hitting them, she sputtered, "Good God, how Victorian! Since when is a penis required to make calculations and load explosives? I didn't choose architecture as a way of killing time until I trapped a husband—I'm doing it because it's great training for PDI."

"Watch your tongue, young lady!" His expression changed to that of a tough businessman. "No way in hell will you work for PDI, and I don't ever want to hear about this again. Is that clear enough for you?"

She stared at her father, her whole body going cold with shock. This couldn't be the end of her dreams—she *knew* she belonged in the company as surely as that the sun would rise the next day. It was the future she'd craved her whole life. "Working for PDI isn't some whim, Dad," she said, her voice shaking. "I may look like Mother, but at heart I'm like you. I love the crazy mixture of projects, the challenge of getting all the details right, the excitement of a flawless shot. Just give me a chance to prove—."

"Enough, Kate! The only way you'll work at PDI is over my dead body."

Her shock transmuted into rage. "Then I'll do demolition

somewhere else! PDI may be the best now, but I can learn to be better. And I *will*!"

"You will *not*!" he snapped. "Dammit, I'm your father, and you'll do as I say."

She jerked away, eyes blazing. "This isn't the nineteenth century, Sam, and my life belongs to me, not you. To hell with you and this damned, artificial ball!"

She whirled and stormed across the ballroom, colliding with dancers as tears stung her eyes. It was a family joke that she could always persuade her father to give her whatever she wanted, and she hadn't really believed he'd turn her down now. Oh, she'd expected him to huff and puff a little, but she'd been so sure that he'd be secretly proud that she wanted to follow in his footsteps.

But now he'd issued a public proclamation, and being Sam, he'd never change his mind. Kicking herself for having succumbed to anger, she stalked through the lobby of the theater. Maybe he would have said yes if she'd chosen a better time, or asked differently. Or maybe she shouldn't have mentioned that Tom didn't want to work at PDI. Her brother had quietly made that clear for years, but her father had resisted the truth, as if denial would make Tom's distaste for demolition go away.

No, a different time wouldn't have helped. In retrospect, she saw how badly she'd underestimated her father's conservatism. He was great in most ways, but at heart he was an old-world Italian traditionalist who thought that the measure of a man's success was having women who didn't need to work. He'd indulged her in the past because she'd never really asked for anything that conflicted with his view of the way things ought to be. If she wanted to sit at home and . . . and do needlepoint until some suitable man married her, he'd be delighted.

No way, Kate thought. She wanted action. Challenges. She wanted to blow up a ravaged old building in one beautiful, terrifying instant, and do it with such precision that there would be no need to clear the parking lot next door.

She was her father's daughter, and by God, she would prove it!

Ignoring the staring people who'd noticed her fight with Sam, she flung open the front door and marched down the stone steps. The chilly air gave her pause. Now what? She didn't even have her handbag.

There was no way she'd meekly return to the ball for the rest of the evening. Her heart cried out for a grand gesture, even if she froze to death in the process. She wrenched off the tight kid gloves, popping the tiny pearl buttons, and crushed them in one hand before hurling them into the wall. Then she strode down the street. She should have cooled off by the time she reached home. No, not home, she'd go to Rachel's house. It was a small rebellion, but the best she could think of at the moment.

She'd walked only a few steps when a male voice with an East Baltimore accent said, "Can I help you, miss?"

She turned and saw the gorgeous parking valet, Mr. Tall, Dark, and Handsome himself, wearing a gold-trimmed jacket and a frown. The streetlight illuminated vivid blue eyes and crisply chiseled features that could give him a career in modeling if he wanted it, though he might have to cut the dark hair pulled back in a neat little ponytail. Loose, it would make him look a little too much like a Hell's Angel.

Under other circumstances, she would have stopped to admire the view. This time she just said curtly, "I'm fine, thanks," and continued walking.

He fell into step beside her. She guessed that he was about her age, but seemed older. Tough and a little edgy, he also looked sharply intelligent, like a man who could handle himself equally well talking or fighting.

"You shouldn't be walking alone in this neighborhood." He glanced at her bare, goose-bumped arms. "Especially without a coat."

His words made her aware of how much the temperature had dropped in the last two hours. She told herself that it wasn't really cold, probably not much below forty degrees. "By the time I get to Ruxton, I'll be warm."

"Ruxton! All the way out in Baltimore County? You'll freeze to death."

"Then I'll hitchhike! Look, I appreciate your concern, but beat it. You've already gone above and beyond the call of duty. Go park a car or something."

He caught her wrist, his grip light but uncompromising. "Honest, this is not a good idea. A smart-ass cousin of mine used to hitch home from school every day, until she got raped. Go back inside and I'll call a taxi." He glanced at her empty hands. "And lend you the fare."

"I am not going back to that blasted ball!" An involuntary shiver went through her. "I'll take my chances with rape and pneumonia."

Exasperated, he unbuttoned his elaborate jacket and dropped it over her shoulders. "At least wear this."

The garment was warm with his body heat, and scented with some nice, piney aftershave. She slid her arms into the sleeves gratefully. The jacket fell halfway down her thighs. "Thanks. This will stave off deathly illness. Don't worry, I'm quite capable of walking to Ruxton."

"Not in those shoes," he said with a glance at her high-heeled satin slippers. "They're cute, but no good for hiking."

"I'll manage." She fastened the brass buttons on the jacket. "What's your address so I can send this back?"

Instead of giving it to her, he said, "I can't let you do this."

"I've had quite enough of men telling me what I can't do! I wouldn't take it from my father, and I darned well won't take it from a perfect stranger."

"I'm not perfect." He gave a smile that invited her to join in. "And my name is Donovan, so I'm no longer a stranger."

Trying to resist the power of that smile, she asked, "Donovan what? Or rather, What Donovan?"

"Just Donovan." His smile faded. "Fighting with parents is a bitch. What did your old man do that was so bad?"

For a kid who looked like he'd be more at home in a bar brawl than at the cotillion, he had remarkably kind eyes. Needing to tell someone, she said, "All my life, I've wanted to go into the family business. It's the only thing I really want to do. And tonight . . . tonight"—she blinked hard as she felt the blow again—"my father said that the only way I'd ever work in the company was over his dead body."

He pursed his lips in a soundless whistle. "That's rough."

"I've never been so furious in my life." The seething emotions settled into her stomach as a hard, aching knot. Kate didn't like being angry—but her whole life had just been turned upside down.

"How do you and your father usually get along?"

She wiped her eyes with one wrist. "Really well. In a way, that makes this worse. It's a . . . a kind of betrayal."

"I see." He rocked back on his heels as he considered. "Since you won't go back, I'll take you home myself, if you don't mind riding on a motorcycle."

She hesitated before deciding that she would be better off accepting his offer than risking the streets and the cold weather. He wouldn't be parking expensive cars at the Maryland Cotillion if he wasn't responsible. Besides, all her instincts said she'd be safe with him.

Or at least, as safe as she wanted to be. With a slow smile, she held out her hand. "It's a deal, Donovan."

He shook her hand, his clasp warm and strong around her ungloved fingers. She felt a surprising tingle, almost like an electrical shock. Telling herself that her imagination was working overtime, she released his hand and began walking back to the theater. "By the way, my name is Kate Corsi."

"Pleased to meet you. You're not what I expected in a debutante."

"I was faking it earlier."

In front of the hall, the two other parking valets were

sheltering from the wind in the corner by the steps. Like
her new escort, they were college age. Donovan said,
"Sorry to cut out, but I have to take Miss Corsi home."

"Ms.," she corrected.

"Ms. Corsi," he agreed. "If anyone comes looking, tell
'em she's fine."

One of the other valets, a lean redh. d, made a face.
"With only two of us, it's going to be a zoo when everyone
leaves, but you're right, we can't let her walk." He smiled
winningly. "I can take you home, Ms. Corsi, and I have a
car, not a bike."

She tugged the uniform jacket closer. "Thanks, but I've
never ridden on a motorcycle before, much less in a ball
gown. How can I pass up such a great offer?"

Donovan led Kate around the hall to the crowded parking
lot behind the building. His bike, not new but well tended,
was parked to one side. As he pulled his keys from his
pocket, he cast a dubious glance at her gown. "Your dress
might get wrecked."

She looked down at the froth of satin and lace, then
shrugged. "This sort of gown is only meant to be worn
once, and after tonight, it's history."

He flipped up the kickstand with one heel. "I've only got
one helmet with me. You wear it." He tried to hand the
helmet to her.

She refused to take it. "You're the driver. You need it
more."

"Maybe, but I don't like carrying passengers without helmets." He thought a moment. "I know—we can go by my
aunt and uncle's place in Hampden. It's only a couple of
miles, and in the right direction. I'll borrow Uncle Frankie's
car to take you out to Ruxton. It'll be a lot more comfortable than the bike, especially if it starts snowing."

"Fine. This is turning into a real adventure."

He gave her a devastating grin as he slid off the rubber
band that held his ponytail in place. Dark hair fell silkily
to brush his shoulders. Then he straddled the motorcycle,

turned the key, and hit the kick start pedal. Raising his voice over the roar, he said, "Make sure your skirt is tucked in—I don't want you to do an Isadora Duncan."

Where on earth had an East Baltimore guy picked that up? Laughing, she swung onto the saddle behind him and stuffed voluminous folds of fabric under her thighs and knees so her skirt wouldn't blow out of control. Then she wrapped her arms around his lean waist. His shirt was a crisp white that crackled with starch and emphasized his broad shoulders. He radiated a male magnetism that would cause a riot in a nunnery. She wanted to rub her cheek between his shoulder blades like a cat.

He glanced back. "You're going to feel real exposed. Have faith in inertia, centrifugal force, and the sissy bar behind you."

"Yes, Captain," she said meekly, more interested in the warm, solid feel of his body. No wonder motorcycles were so popular. This had to be the sexiest way of traveling since damsels rode pillion behind knights. And she was sharing the bike with a guy who knew about both Isadora Duncan and centrifugal force!

He pulled the helmet shield over his face and took off. They went down the alley at a relatively sedate pace. Then he turned the bike into the street and hit the gas. She gasped and clutched Donovan's waist as her knees locked around the bike. He wasn't kidding that she would feel exposed! It felt as if the bike was going to shoot out from under her. They were probably only going about the speed limit, but it felt a lot faster.

She tensed when they whipped around a corner and the whole bike leaned. After a moment of panic, she remembered what he'd said about trusting inertia. This was just physics in action. Since Donovan was obviously in full control of his vehicle, she began to relax and enjoy the speed, the intimacy of the two of them slicing through the night.

As the wind whipped through her hair, she called over the roar of the engine, "What a terrific way to travel!"

"Except when it's raining," he yelled back. "Or in a cicada year!"

As the wind destroyed her elaborate hairstyle, she threw back her head and laughed with giddy delight. Her legs were freezing from the knee down, but who cared? She was doing something outrageous with the most gorgeous guy she'd ever met.

Her distress about the fight with her father began to fade. In her bones, she was sure that someday she would work at PDI. She could *see* herself there. If she couldn't go in the front door, she'd sneak in the back. For now she'd lie low and study architecture. After she graduated from college, she would just show up at the office and work wherever help was needed. Sam might never publicly retract his opposition, but he'd get used to having her around. Eventually, she'd become part of the company.

Feeling better, she gave herself up to starry night and icy wind and warm embrace.

5

To Kate's regret, it wasn't long until they slowed to enter a rowhouse neighborhood with parked cars lining every street. Donovan turned right, then left, before coasting to the curb between two cars. He turned off the engine and lowered the kickstand in the sudden silence. "A great thing about bikes is that there's almost always parking space where you want it."

Kate surveyed the brick rowhouse. The owners were the first on the block to put up their Christmas decorations, and cheerful multicolored lights outlined the roof, windows, front door, and the iron railing that ran up the steps. The bushes hadn't been neglected, either. In fact, she saw with delight, there was a shrine to Mary in the corner of the yard and the Blessed Mother wore a crown of sparkling white lights. "Shall I go in, or would you rather I skulked out here?"

"Too cold for skulking." He hesitated. "I'd better warn you, my relatives can be pretty . . . overwhelming."

"I'm not easily whelmed," she assured him.

A smile tugged at his lips as he took off his helmet. "Don't say I didn't warn you." He shook out his hair, and she wanted to touch it.

As she swung her leg over the saddle, her skirt slid up to mid-thigh. His gaze locked on her bared leg with laser-like intensity. It was worth half freezing to see that expression in his eyes. She shook her skirts out, then finger-combed her wind-tangled hair in a vain attempt to make it behave. "I must look like the Wicked Witch of the West."

"Nope. Glinda the Good Witch after a Kansas cyclone."

Helmet under one arm, he guided her up the walk with a hand at the small of her back. His touch was light, but it left her quivering with awareness. She felt . . . cared for. Though Donovan couldn't be more than a year or two older than she, he seemed more mature than anyone else she had dated. More man than boy, despite his sexy delinquent appearance. She asked, "Where did you go to school?"

"Poly."

"Aha! An engineer. I'll bet you took the Poly A course."

"Yep. My uncle Frankie says that Baltimore is the only place he knows where people in nursing homes are still asking each other where they went to school, and they always mean high school."

"Of course. It's a great way to figure out a person's neighborhood, social class, and mutual acquaintances." Donovan was a perfect example of that kind of analysis.

His accent and appearance said blue collar. The Poly A course said that he was very bright, and hardworking. Her father had graduated from the Poly A course. "The next step is for me to think of anyone I know who went to Poly, then ask you about him. In a matter of minutes, we'll have established some connection. It's the Baltimore way."

He sorted through his keys, chuckling. "So where did you go to school, Ms. Corsi? Bryn Mawr? Garrison Forrest? I've heard every girl there is blond."

"Could be, but not all blondes go to Garrison. I went to Friends."

He found the right key and unlocked the door. "Educated by Quakers. Earnest. Socially committed."

She grinned. "Close enough. What are you doing now?"

"I'm a sophomore in engineering at Loyola." He opened the door for her. "And you?"

"I'm a freshman in architecture at Maryland."

They stepped inside to be greeted by a tall, balding man. "Donovan, you're back early. Who's your friend?"

"This is Kate Corsi," Donovan said. "She needs a ride out to Baltimore County. I hoped you'd let me borrow your car. Kate, meet my uncle Frank Russo."

She gave the older man her best smile. "It's a pleasure, Mr. Russo."

"Call me Frank," he said in a booming baritone as he waved her into the house. His face showed a faint but unmistakable resemblance to Donovan. Kate guessed that his sister had been Donovan's mother, which explained why Donovan's complexion was a little darker than his mostly Irish appearance suggested. Probably he was an Irish-Italian blend; Baltimore was full of kids born to mixed ethnic marriages. Russian married Greek, Lithuanian married Irish. Sometimes, even, WASP married Italian.

Frank raised his voice. "Connie, come meet Donovan's friend."

A cheerful alto replied from the kitchen, "He's brought home a girl?"

"Did I say it was a girl?" Frank said with mock surprise. "You wouldn't have called me if it was a boy." A round, attractive woman with salt-and-pepper hair appeared and scanned Kate's smudged satin pumps, white evening gown, and borrowed jacket. Not even blinking, she remarked, "This one's even prettier than that German shepherd that followed you home last year, Donovan."

"Oh, I don't know. It was a really good-looking German shepherd." A mischievous glint in his eyes, Donovan introduced them. "Concetta Russo, Kate Corsi."

Kate guessed that he wanted to see how a debutante would react to a household of exuberant Italians. Little did he know. She took Connie's hand in both of hers. "Hello, Mrs. Russo. I'm really not an escapee from Sheppard-Pratt. I had a fight with my father and was starting to walk home, and Donovan rescued me from turning into an icicle."

His aunt nodded approvingly. "He's a good boy. Frankie, let him take the car, Kate isn't dressed for a motorcycle even if it wasn't starting to snow. But first come eat. We're just about to test a batch of marinara."

Donovan looked at Kate. "Are you hungry?"

"Ravenous." Nothing like a family fight to work up an appetite.

The Russos' kitchen was large and shiny clean, obviously remodeled and expanded from the original kitchen. A real-estate agent would say the house was overimproved for the neighborhood, but no sane person could not love such a warm, welcoming room, full of oak cabinets and enticing smells.

Connie poured a generous quantity of gnocchi into a pot of boiling water, then stirred the steaming kettle of marinara sauce on the other front burner. "This batch is turning out pretty good. Want to taste it, Katie?"

"I'd love to." Kate blew several times on the spoonful of chunky red sauce Connie offered, then swallowed. "This is great! You use red wine, don't you?"

Connie beamed. "You got it. Nothing like wine to deepen the flavor."

"My mother always puts Chianti in her marinara, even though my grandmother Corsi claims no true Italian ever uses wine. Of course, Nonna is Sicilian, so who knows?" She glanced at Donovan. He was watching her with warm amusement.

"Depends on the family. My mama used wine, my grand-mama used wine, every woman in my family since Caesar was in diapers has made her spaghetti sauce with wine." Connie gestured toward a bottle with a handmade label. "I put in some of Cousin Giuseppe's best Chianti, that's why the flavor is so rich."

The chat continued while Connie set the kitchen table, drained the gnocchi, then poured steaming marinara over it. With chunks of bread and glasses of Cousin Giuseppe's wine, it was a feast fit for the gods. Connie gave Kate an amiable grilling as they ate—starting with asking where she went to school.

They were eating Christmas cookies when a toddler pattered into the room, a bedraggled stuffed rabbit trailing from one hand. Connie gave a doting smile. "Meet my granddaughter Lissie, the party girl. Her parents left her here for the weekend in the hope that with a little peace and quiet, maybe they could start a little brother for her."

As the adults laughed, Lissie went over to Kate and looked upward with huge dark eyes. "Princess?"

It took Kate a moment to realize that the question was inspired by her billowing white ball gown. "I'm sorry, Lissie—I'm not a princess."

Lissie looked so crestfallen that Kate decided that honesty was not always the best policy. Dropping to one knee beside Lissie, she said, "At least, not all the time. But every girl can be a princess on special occasions."

Lissie perked up at that, so Kate took off her slightly crushed corsage, removed the straight pin for safety's sake, and gave the lace-trimmed flowers to the child. "Whenever a man gives a girl flowers to wear, on that night she's a princess."

Lissie took the corsage and buried her small nose in it.

"Now that we've settled that," Connie said, "it's to bed with you, young lady."

She was starting to rise when Donovan got to his feet. "I'll take her back to her room, Aunt Connie. I have to get a coat anyhow."

He scooped up Lissie, who shrieked his name happily. The open affection on Donovan's face made Kate melt. He was half-Italian, all right. Adoring babies was in the blood. He was starting to carry his cousin out of the kitchen when Lissie waved the flowers in protest, her gaze fixed on Kate. "Kiss!"

Kate took the child from Donovan's arms, loving the sweet little-girl scent and incredibly soft skin. How could anyone *not* love babies? She kissed the gently curving cheek. "May you be a princess many, many times, Lissie."

Satisfied, her lids already drooping, the child went trustingly into Donovan's arms and he took her away. He returned a few minutes later wearing a dark parka dusted with snowflakes. "I just covered the bike. Now it's time to get you back, Kate."

She rose and put on Donovan's uniform jacket again. "Thanks for supper, Mr. and Mrs. Russo. It was lovely to meet you both."

"Come again, Katie," Frank said. "Anytime."

They trailed out to the front porch. Lacy snowflakes were drifting down and frosting the world with a delicate white haze. Connie gave Kate a hug. "This is a nice girl, Donovan. You should keep her."

"I'm just driving her home, Aunt Connie."

Frank tossed him a key chain. "The blue barge is around the corner."

"Thanks. And don't worry, I won't be out too late." After the door closed behind the Russos, he said, "Don't blame me because my aunt and uncle want to adopt you."

"I wouldn't mind being adopted by Frank and Connie. They're terrific." She looked at him sideways. "You live with them?"

"Sometimes. At the moment." He was silent for a half-dozen steps before saying in a voice that didn't invite comment, "My parents are dead, so I kind of shift around between relatives. I always leave before they get tired of having me underfoot."

Kate was taken aback. How horrible it must be not to have a place of his own, where he'd always be welcome. Wordlessly she slipped her hand into his. He threaded his fingers between hers in a warm, intimate clasp. For the second time she felt tingles.

They left dark footprints in the snow as they walked around the corner to an enormous, white-frosted car. "The blue barge at your service." Donovan unlocked the passenger door and opened it for Kate. "When you said your name was Corsi, I thought it was something WASPy like C-O-U-R-S-E-Y. Obviously not."

"Hell, no, *paisano*." She slid into the car. "I'm half-Italian, just like you."

"Corsi. Is the family business Phoenix Demolition?"

When she nodded, he said in an awed voice, "PDI does fantastic stuff. Hell, your father practically invented the whole field of explosive demolition. He's like Red Adair is for oil well fires. Now I understand why he doesn't want you working for him."

"Don't you *dare* say another word about that! I've had quite enough bossy men for one night."

"I didn't say a thing," he said with a grin.

He closed her door and circled to the driver's side. After getting inside and shutting the door, he turned to look at Kate. The windows were covered with a translucent layer of snow, transforming the glow of the streetlight halfway down the block into a dim, pearly luminescence.

All levity vanished, replaced by a tension as old as Adam and Eve. The expression in his eyes made her feel hot and breathless and a little alarmed. Not in fear of him, but of an attraction beyond anything she'd ever experienced. This was happening too fast. She fumbled nervously for her seat belt.

"Don't buckle up yet." He reached out and gently rubbed her cheek with his knuckles. "You're so pretty. Radiant. Not quite real."

The skin-to-skin touch made her heart beat faster. How could something so simple be so arousing?

He slid across the seat until the hard length of his thigh was pressed along her leg. "Your hair looks better down." His fingers caressed her head with a tenderness that was both soothing and erotic.

She felt fragile, ready to crumble under his touch. She really should tell him to stop. A single word from her would prevent this from going any further. He would start the car, drive her to Rachel's, and that would be that.

She didn't move. Scarcely breathed, her gaze locked on his.

"I've wanted to do this ever since you shimmied out of that limo." He lowered his head and kissed her. His lips were warm and soft, gentle in pressure yet sending hammer beats of excitement through her veins.

She kissed him back, sliding her fingers into that silky, sexy dark hair. Who would have dreamed that a high-IQ Hell's Angel type could be so irresistible?

Hesitant exploration dissolved into fire and desire as reality narrowed to his taste, his touch, his closeness. Every sensation was shockingly heightened. She wanted to devour him, absorb him, learn him so deeply that they would become one.

Her sensual haze was pierced by an internal voice that said very clearly, *You will marry this man.*

The words shocked her. She broke the kiss and drew her head back to stare into Donovan's shadowed eyes. Marry him? But they scarcely knew each other!

The voice repeated, *You have just met your future husband.*

She would have laughed, except that her sensible mother claimed to have experienced the same flash of inner knowledge when she'd met Sam Corsi.

But marriage? She didn't even know his whole name! Yet her certainty was utterly convincing, and surprisingly plausible. Under the biker facade he was intelligent and kind, responsible, with a sense of humor that matched hers. Not to mention liking babies and being drop-dead handsome. Exactly what she would want in a husband—when she got around to looking seriously in ten or twelve years.

But maybe her life wasn't going to run according to her master plan. Silently she raised a hand and caressed Donovan's cheek. Warmth and a faint, alluring rasp of whiskers caused flutters deep inside her.

He turned and pressed a kiss into her palm. "Kate," he whispered. *"Carissima."*

Dearest one. She'd heard the Italian endearment from her earliest days. Desire and tenderness pulsed through her with disorienting force, along with a clear knowledge that he would not always be a comfortable companion, that there was darkness as well as kindness in him.

Struggling for sense, she murmured, "Is it my imagination, or is this something . . . something special?"

"No. It's not your imagination." He kissed her again, one hand undoing the buttons of her oversized jacket until he could slide his hand inside and cup her silk-covered breast. Mental clarity vanished in a torrent of sensations—and the certainty that her life had changed forever.

6

"You don't have to make a decision tonight."

Donovan's low voice—deeper than when they'd met a dozen years earlier, and with no trace of East Baltimore left—snapped Kate back to the family room and her ex-husband. She took a shaky breath as she tried to reconcile the excitement and wonder of that first meeting with the murderous strain between them now. "I'm not the only one who has to make a decision, Donovan. Would you agree to this nonsense?"

He exhaled roughly. "I . . . don't know. If you decide you're willing, I'll have to think long and hard about whether I am. I want PDI. I want it a hell of a lot, but maybe not this much. If I'm forced out, I can always start my own demolition firm."

She thought of the long-term PDI employees. Some would follow Donovan to a new firm, but others would stay with Marchetti, fracturing the family that had been Phoenix Demolition. "That wouldn't be the same."

"No. It wouldn't." He rubbed the back of his neck. "Which is why I'm at least considering whether it would be possible to comply with Sam's crazy will."

She thought of the home they'd once shared, and shivered. "I can't imagine living in the old house again. It's so small. We'd be on top of each other."

As soon as she heard the words, she flushed. For most of the three years they'd lived on Brandy Lane, they *had* been on top of each other. Sometimes Donovan above, sometimes her, in every room of the house.

Mercifully ignoring the double entendre, Donovan said without inflection, "For what it's worth, I've done some remodeling. There's more room now. How about if I pick you up in the morning and take you out to Brandy Lane? It might help you decide if you could bear to live there again."

Visit the home they had worked on together with so much love and laughter? Come face-to-face with their past?

Knowing she had no choice, she said, "Ten o'clock?"

He nodded, then said good-bye.

Relieved to be alone, Kate sank into the sofa opposite the fire. For a long time she stared at the flickering flames, too numb to think.

She needed to talk to someone from her normal life. One of the house's dozen telephones sat on the end table, so she punched in her brother's number. He picked up on the second ring. "Tom? It's me."

"How are you doing, hon?"

Tears stung her eyes as he used a Baltimore endearment from their childhood. She kicked off her shoes and burrowed into the sofa. "Lord, what a day it has been."

After a silence, he said painfully, "I should be there."

His doubt and guilt pulled her up short. This was a hard time for him, and she hadn't called to make it worse. "Forget I said that. Mother and I are doing fine. Everyone has been so kind. The cathedral was packed. Lots of dignitaries, including the mayor, the governor, two congressmen, and a senator. Sam would have loved it." She'd always referred to her father by his first name when she was irritated with him, so he'd been Sam ever since she'd left Baltimore a decade before.

She described the events of the day and passed on good wishes of people who'd asked after Tom, but with a sure instinct for noticing what wasn't being said, he asked, "What about Donovan? I assume he was there."

"He was a pallbearer. We chatted a bit at the open house. Very civilized." Her brother had been spending much of his time at a hospice with a terminally ill friend, which gave her a good excuse to change the subject. "How is Randy doing?"

"He went into a coma this morning. He's not expected to last more than another day or two." Tom sighed. "He was afraid of dying alone, poor kid. At least that won't happen. Half a dozen of us are taking turns sitting with him."

She heard grief in his voice, but also acceptance. Years of volunteer hospice work had deepened his spirituality, enabling him to accept that death was as much a part of the great dance as life. Yet she selfishly wished he were here so she could take refuge in his arms as she had ever since they were toddlers.

Deciding to concentrate on the positive aspect of what had happened, she said, "Tonight Charles Hamilton told us about the weird will Sam left, and there's some surprisingly good news. You're one of the major heirs."

"Good God, Sam put me in his will?"

"Mother said that he never stopped loving you."

"You don't know what this means to me." Her brother's voice broke. "No, that's not true. You're the only one who *can* know what it means."

"Sam couldn't admit he was wrong when he was alive," she said quietly. "I think this is a belated apology for being such a jerk where you were concerned."

"He was what he was, Kate. I'm glad he was finally able to make some kind of gesture toward me. I only wish it had happened when he was alive."

She gave her brother time to absorb the wonder of Sam's posthumous overture before she moved on to the difficult aspect of the legacy. "Though Sam finally made the gesture, don't start spending your inheritance. You and I will receive major money and Donovan will get the business, but only if some very strange conditions are fulfilled."

"What kind of conditions?"

"He wanted Donovan and me to live in the house on Brandy Lane for a year. Otherwise, you and I don't get a penny, and PDI will be sold to another demolition firm."

"Sweet Jesus!" After three beats of shocked silence, Tom said, "Impossible. You can't live with Donovan. I assume you said so immediately."

"Not yet. I'm . . . thinking about it."

"For God's sake, Kate! It's only money. You and I are getting along just fine as we are, and you don't owe Donovan a damned thing."

Tom's concern was comforting, but as her protective big brother, he lacked objectivity. The situation had too many ramifications for her to make a decision quickly. "Mother thinks sharing a house for a year might be good for both of us."

"She wouldn't say that if she knew the whole story! Don't even *think* about doing this, Kate. Please."

Tom cared little for money, but she knew that he could use Sam's legacy. Though he was a first-rate computer consultant, he took on only enough projects to pay his bills. More of his time went into his volunteer work at the hospice and tutoring kids who were at risk. As his sister, Kate wanted him to have more security. With Sam's money, he could buy a place of his own. She'd love to rehab an old San Francisco town house for her brother.

Sam, damn his conniving soul, had known she might do for Tom what she wouldn't do for herself. "There's a lot to consider, Tom. If I agree to Sam's conditions, Donovan and I would just be housemates. We'd hardly ever see each other."

"That may be the theory, but can you guarantee it would be like that in practice?"

"Life doesn't come with any guarantees beyond death and taxes."

"Okay. Think it through. Weigh the pluses and minuses. *Then* say no."

"We'll see." Kate suppressed a yawn. "I'll start by sleeping on it."

"Do that. Give Mother my love. I'll call her tomorrow."

"Will do. Take care, Tom." Kate hung up, weary to the bone and ready for bed. But she doubted that she'd sleep.

An advantage of old friends was that it wasn't necessary to speak. Julia was grateful for Charles's undemanding silence. Even small talk would have been too much.

Kate entered the living room to say good night, dark circles under her eyes. As she headed off in her stocking feet, shoes dangling from one hand, Julia thought how nice it would be to have her daughter in the same city, or even in the same time zone.

After Kate left, Julia said, "Another of the same, bartender."

Charles rose and topped up her Chardonnay. "If you want to get seriously drunk, you'll have to switch to something stronger."

"Then I'd just get sick. Very undignified." The phone began to ring. She ignored it, and the ringing stopped abruptly. "The answering machine is on. I'm at the point where one more kind, warmhearted condolence would make me scream."

"No, you wouldn't. You'd be completely gracious." He refreshed his own drink, then sat again. "As Barbara used to say, you're a credit to steel magnolias everywhere."

She thought sadly of Charles's wife, who had been one of her closest friends. "Barbara overestimated me. Not steel. Iron, and rusting fast."

"A little rust doesn't mean the underlying structure isn't sound," he said quietly. "Are you going to tell Kate your suspicions about Sam's death?"

"Not yet. She has enough on her mind." Julia stroked Oscar, whose head was on her lap. "Maybe never. After all, there's no real proof."

"Given her reaction to Sam's posthumous manipulations,

I'm surprised that she isn't on the way to the airport already." He swished the Scotch and water in his glass. "Do you think she and Donovan will give it a try?"

"I have no idea. Neither of them has ever said why they split up, but I've always suspected that Patrick had an extramarital fling, and Kate left when she found out."

Surprised, Charles said, "I thought he worshiped the ground Kate walked on."

"He did, but that doesn't necessarily mean fidelity." Julia tried without success to keep a caustic edge from her voice. "The double standard will never go out of style. Not when so many men enjoy it."

Reading between the lines, Charles said, "Good God, Julia, did Sam—" He stopped abruptly.

Knowing he would not pursue such a personal question, Julia said, "Once or twice, early in our marriage, when he was on a business trip. Even though I was pregnant with Tom, I almost left him when I found out. Sam truly didn't understand how much his infidelity would hurt me—after all, his straying had just been sex, it was me that he loved. How come I was taking it so seriously? I stopped packing long enough to ask him to visualize me in bed with another man. He looked sick, and swore he'd never be unfaithful again. As far as I know, he kept his word."

Charles whistled. "The things one doesn't know about other people's marriages."

"It wasn't something that either Sam or I wanted to advertise." She closed her eyes and pressed the cool wineglass to her forehead. "We came from different worlds, and a lot of the initial attraction was because of those differences. Problems were inevitable. People are quicker to divorce now. If Kate and Patrick hadn't been so young, maybe they could have worked things out, perhaps even had a stronger marriage for it."

"That could still happen."

"I doubt it. Too much time has passed." She sipped her Chardonnay, remembering. "Did I ever tell you that the first time Sam and I met was when he came to my parents' house as boss of a crew remodeling the basement? He was just out of the army and working construction while he decided what to do next." It had been lust at first sight on both sides.

"I didn't know that. You were mercifully light on details when you gave my ring back and said that you hoped we'd always be friends."

"Lord, did I say that? The oldest cliché in the book for ending a relationship." Despite her well-intentioned words at the time, several years had passed when there had been no contact between her and Charles, though she'd noted the announcement of his wedding, and hoped he'd be happy. But Baltimore was a small town in many ways, and they moved in the same circles. Eventually their paths crossed at the wedding of a mutual friend. Barbara and Sam had adored each other with Mediterranean gusto, which made it easy for Julia and Charles to pick up the threads of their lifetime friendship again.

Soon the four of them had developed the special bond that exists when each member of a pair of couples truly enjoys every other person. That bond had only been strengthened as they raised their children together. When Sam needed an attorney, he'd retained Charles, who had ended up knowing most of the Corsi family secrets, except for the painful one of Sam's early infidelity. Barbara, cut off from her Orthodox family for marrying a gentile, had treated Julia like a sister. In her turn, Julia had found Barbara's company exhilarating in something of the same way she enjoyed Sam.

Thinking of all the happy years, she said, "I've given thanks often that we became friends again. You and Barbara and your girls enriched our lives immeasurably."

"The same is true of you and Sam and your children." He finished the last of his drink and set the glass aside. "I'd had a very clear mental picture of you and me happily growing old together, so I was stunned when you broke things off. But . . . relieved, too. For an engaged man, I was finding the sexy brunette who had the office next to mine entirely too attractive."

"Barbara, I assume?"

"Yes. The fact that you were brave enough to defy expectations and marry someone who 'wasn't our kind' gave me the courage to do the same. I never regretted it."

Nor had Julia. Grief, total and overwhelming, flooded through her. "Charles, how long does it take to accept the finality of death? I'm still in denial. I half expect Sam to come bounding in here, glowing with energy and trailing demolition dust."

"I wish I had an answer. Even after two years, sometimes it's a shock to walk into the kitchen and not find Barbara throwing together one of her instant gourmet meals." Charles regarded her with compassion. "One thing I do know, Julia. It will get worse before it gets better. But in time—it will get better."

She buried her face in her hands. "God damn Sam Corsi. God damn him to *hell*."

The wipers slid intermittently across Donovan's windshield as he drove north on Charles Street. Wet snow had iced the pavement and chased most Baltimoreans inside. Controlling the vehicle took concentration even with four-wheel drive, but it wasn't enough to banish thoughts of Sam's insane will. The idea of living with Kate, seeing her every day, was paralyzing. Terrifying.

Horribly tempting.

It had been snowing like this the night they'd decided to get married. Donovan hadn't thought marriage was possible when they were both still in college. Then, over pizza after a movie date, Kate produced a businesslike sheet of calculations. She'd totaled up his scholarships at Loyola College, the income she got from a small trust fund, estimated wages from summer jobs, then balanced it against projected expenses to prove they could afford to marry.

He hadn't liked the idea of relying partially on her money, but was ready to accept anything that meant they could be together. Privately, he recognized a profound desire to secure her as his own before she woke up and realized she could do better elsewhere.

On the way back to the Corsi house, as the knowledge she was his forever sank in, he'd spun his uncle's car in circles in the slippery snow of empty intersections, whooping like a maniac. Kate had alternated between laughter and alarm, afraid that the police would arrest them, or a huge and unforgiving truck would flatten them into the pavement.

But he'd gotten her home safely. Outside the front door, they kissed so long they'd both had snowflakes caught in their lashes like stars when they went inside to announce their engagement.

Though the Corsis liked their daughter's boyfriend, they'd been startled and none too pleased since Kate and Donovan were so young. But Kate had produced her calculations, adding that her parents were in no position to protest when they had also married young and with blinding swiftness. In the end, the Corsis had given their consent and arranged a magnificent wedding, as if they'd never had any private doubts.

Had Sam and Julia felt the same desperate hunger to be together? Probably. Donovan had ached to be with Kate, and not only for the sex, phenomenal though it was.

The sex . . . His whole body tightened as he remembered the first time. He tried to push the thought away, but couldn't. Memories that had been dammed up for almost a decade raged through him like a spring flood.

Mind churning, he turned left onto Bellona Avenue, almost skidding off the narrow road. He swore and pulled onto the shoulder, knowing he wasn't fit to drive until he had himself under control again. But control was not easily come by as he stared into the blowing snow, remembering the night Kate had swept into his life.

Introducing her to his aunt and uncle had been a deliberate attempt to underline how different their worlds were. Instead, the visit made things worse because she'd been as much at home in a Hampden rowhouse as she'd been at the cotillion. Finding out that she was half-Italian, just like him, made her seem more attainable.

His original intentions had been honorable; underdressed girls should not walk or hitchhike through city streets on December nights. But after they got into Uncle Frankie's car, she looked up at him with those huge dark eyes and he couldn't stop himself from kissing her. The first kiss was followed by more. Instead of withdrawing from his increasingly intimate caresses, she had responded with soft, rapturous sighs, intoxicating him with her utter openness.

Though he burned to make love to her, he managed to find the willpower to pull away before reaching the point of no return. That moment of retreat was engraved vividly in his brain. Snow-covered car windows steamed into a seductive privacy. Pale light filtering through the translucent snow to burnish her fair hair and the elegant curves of cheek and throat. The floral delicacy of her perfume mingling with the richer scents of passion and Cousin Giuseppe's wine.

He got as far as reaching for the key in the ignition. Then Kate whispered, "Don't stop," and he was doomed. Her words were like gasoline on flame. He was crazy with wanting her and she wanted him, too, so why not? Maybe the rich were different from the kind of girls he'd dated. Or maybe he was dreaming all this and any minute the alarm would jerk him awake and he'd have to get up for his eight o'clock math class.

While he was debating, she slid across the front seat and nuzzled his throat, her breath warm and unbearably arousing. "What's your first name?"

If this was a dream, he didn't ever want to wake. "Patrick. I've never liked it, so I go by my last name."

"Patrick. A pity you don't like that. I do."

"I like the way you say it." The name had never sounded better than now, with the sexiest girl he'd ever met purring the syllables into his ear.

Then her hand crept hesitantly down his body, and rational thought ended. Instinct exploded into hungry kisses, hammering blood, frantic hands stroking and probing and pushing away inconvenient clothing.

Such intensity could not last long. She was incredibly responsive, and within seconds of his first intimate touches she dissolved into convulsive shudders, clinging to him as if he were her one hope of heaven. Then it was his turn. Luckily he had a condom in his wallet, and even, barely, the sense to use it.

She was slim and lithe beneath him, so lovely, so giving, that he couldn't quite believe she was real. Too late he realized that she was a virgin. She gasped with pain when he entered her, but he was too far gone into mind-searing pleasure to retreat.

Within moments it was over, leaving him panting and shaken, with the horrible conviction that she had been playing him for a fool. His raw, helpless distress swiftly transformed into anger. He released her and pushed away. "Was giving your cherry to a parking valet a way of getting back at your father? You should have warned me. It would have been easier for you."

A lesser female might have burst into tears at his harshness. Not Kate. "This had nothing to do with my father," she said huskily. Her hands roamed over his chest and arms, as if she could not get enough of him. "It just seemed that . . . that tonight was the right night, and you were the right man. Was I wrong?"

He'd thought his childhood had left him tough and unsusceptible, but her sweet honesty cracked through all his defenses, and he tumbled headfirst into love. *Here is my heart,* carissima. *And my life, my body, my soul, if you want them.*

His emotions were so raw, so powerful, so terrifying, that

all he could manage was to catch one of her wandering hands and press it to his cheek. "I think you probably were wrong, Kate." He turned his head and pressed his lips into the center of her palm. "You deserve champagne and satin sheets and rose petals, not me and an old Chrysler."

She laughed, a joyous sound that drew him into a place he'd never been. For the first time in years—maybe ever—it occurred to him that happiness might be possible.

"I'm not sorry," she murmured, her eyes like dark stars. "I hope you aren't."

He hadn't been. Not then, not even now, despite all of the pain and guilt that love had brought them both.

7

Donovan returned to the present gripping the steering wheel so tightly it was in danger of bending. No wonder he'd kept those memories securely bottled up for so long. Releasing them was almost as disorienting as the original experience had been.

The brutal truth was that he'd stolen Kate's life. He was the one who'd ended up with the exciting job in the family business, the warm, supportive relationship with her parents. Not that he'd deliberately tried to cut Kate out. In fact, he'd resigned from PDI the morning after she left him, sure it would be impossible to keep working there.

He'd been sitting in his kitchen grimly lowering the level of a bottle of Irish whiskey when Sam marched into the house. After pouring the whiskey down the sink, he'd asked his son-in-law to come back to PDI. Sam had looked like hell—a man torn apart by irreconcilable forces. He had too much pride to beg Donovan to change his mind, but it had been clear that he desperately needed to salvage at least one relationship from the family disaster.

Though Donovan had tried to confess, Sam hadn't wanted to hear it. Apparently his father-in-law assumed that his split with Kate was one of the repercussions of the blowup that had broken the Corsi family in half. Kate had sided with Tom, while Donovan, as always, stood with Sam.

The truth was far more complicated than Sam's guess, but because Donovan and Sam needed each other so much, the next morning he'd been back at PDI, doing his best to bury his misery in sixteen-hour days. Stoically he gave Kate the uncontested divorce she requested. But it was no accident that he'd never sought an annulment from the Church. He hadn't wanted one, because in the Catholic corner of his heart she was still his wife. As long as that was true, he would never take another. It was the real reason his dating relationships had stayed casual. Though he'd been plenty busy over the last ten years, he could have found time for a courtship if he'd wanted one. But he hadn't.

It was Kate he had wanted. Only Kate.

Yes, the sex had been intoxicating, but it was Kate's essence that had captivated him. Though she could play the role of cool aristocratic blonde to perfection, most of the time her disposition was as sunny as her glossy blond hair. Just being near her had made him happy. If they were working in different parts of the house, he regularly sought her out for a hug to reassure himself that she was real, not the enchanting subject of a dream.

Not only had she been a miracle in herself, she had opened so many doors for him. Effortlessly relaxed with all kinds of people, she had helped him become equally at ease. With her, he had found a real home. Not that his relatives hadn't been kind. His assorted aunts and uncles would be hurt to know that he'd never felt that he really belonged with any of them. He hadn't belonged anywhere, until Kate.

It was his own damned fault that their marriage had ended. He knew it, Kate knew it, though they'd both stone-walled everyone about their breakup. After Sam refused to hear his confession, it had been impossible to tell anyone else. As for Kate, she'd always been very private about the things closest to her heart. Her friends and family knew better than to pry about a subject she had posted as off-limits.

Because he and Kate had kept the secrets of their marriage, Sam had brazenly decided to try to throw them to-gether again. It felt like a betrayal of the years of trust and affection between Donovan and his former father-in-law.

Or was it? As he stared into the blowing flakes, he re-alized that Sam had trusted Donovan with his daughter once, and he'd wanted to again. The will wasn't an act of betrayal, but of deep faith. A charge laid by a dead man onto the living.

Though Donovan had only seen Kate for an hour today, it was clear how much she had changed from the girl he'd fallen in love with. Much of her openness was gone, and in his heart, he was sure the blame for that rested squarely him.

Yet he would always care for her deeply. Maybe not in the same way as when they were young, but he'd walk through fire for her. He owed her more than he could ever repay, and Sam's will was offering a chance to try to make amends. If Donovan was wise enough, maybe he could undo some of the damage he'd caused.

He would have to act with great patience and care, or she'd be back in San Francisco like a rocket. He must win her trust. Be her friend again, as they had once before been each other's best friend.

Because even more than he wanted her for himself, he wanted what was best for her. And the best would never be him.

After he sorted things out, he pulled the Jeep back onto the road and headed for home. Sam's funeral and meeting Kate had already made this one of bitch of day, and the situation was sure to get worse. But now, at least, he had something to work for.

Expiation of his sins.

Kate's bedroom had changed little in the years since she'd left, and she winced every time she entered. Not that her mother had kept the place as a shrine—Julia was far too sensible for that. But the bedroom still held a lot of Kate, because she'd consciously decided to travel light when she moved into her married life with Donovan. They had needed to start together as equals. Since he had few personal possessions beyond clothes and books, she hadn't wanted to fill their new home with objects from her parents' house.

So her old bookcase still held beloved children's books that Kate had vaguely assumed she would retrieve when she had her first child. Bright Scandinavian rya rugs she'd chosen under her mother's guidance warmed the floor, and the prairie-star quilt on the bed had been made by the two of them during Kate's twelfth summer. A lot of conversation and family stories were stitched into that quilt. It had been the last summer of her childhood. By the next year she was a teenager with other interests. No doubt Julia had seen that coming, which was why she'd suggested the quilt project.

Sleeping in her old room took Kate back to a simpler time, when she'd believed in happy endings. Feeling ancient and cynical, she turned on the electric blanket, curled up in the armchair, and called San Francisco again for another dose of reality.

Her partner picked up immediately. "Chen and Corsi. May I help you?"

"You're working late." Kate leaned her head back and closed her eyes. "Speak to me of mundane things, Liz. Tell

me how the Tanaka project is coming, and what new outrage his brother-in-law the plumber has perpetrated. Feed
me the trivia of normal life."

"Things are that bad?"

"Not really. I'm only tired."

It was impossible to fool Liz. "Sounds like you need a
friend. Want me to fly to Maryland tomorrow? The clients
can wait for a few days."

"You get a gold star in heaven for the offer, but that's
not necessary. It's just that today has been really . . . drain-
ing."

"Of course it was," Liz said gravely. "When my mother
died, I—" She cut off the sentence. "You asked for dis-
traction, not reminiscences. A pity you weren't here today.
Jenny Gordon called this morning. She was just downsized
from her job in Chicago, and decided it was time to come
home. So I took her out to lunch and we caught up on the
gossip."

Jenny had been a good friend of both Kate and Liz when
they were all studying architecture at Berkeley. In fact, they
had daydreamed about working together someday, but
Jenny had followed a boyfriend to the Midwest. He hadn't
turned out to be any better a long-term prospect than her
job. "I'm sorry I wasn't there, but at least we'll be seeing
her more often. Considering how Jenny hated Chicago win-
ters, she must be ecstatic to be back in California. Does she
have a job?"

"Not yet. You know how hard it is to find architectural
work, and Jenny doesn't want another giant firm. Somewhere between the nachos and dessert, I had the genius idea
of asking her to help here for a few days. It will take the
pressure off while you're away, and get Jenny out of her
parents' house. She's finding that a strain."

"If Jenny likes, she can house-sit at my place until I come
back," Kate suggested. "It will save Tom having to stop by
every day to feed Ginger Bear."

"I'm sure she'll be ecstatic to take on house-sitting and

cat care. I'll give her a key to your place tomorrow." There was a rustling of papers. "Will you be back at the beginning of the week?"

Kate didn't have the stamina to go through the story of Sam's will again. "I might be here longer than expected. I'll let you know when I'm sure."

"Stay as long as you need to. I miss you, but with Jenny's help, I can hold out indefinitely." More rustling paper. "Where did I put my list of questions? Ah, here. The bathroom tile for the Jackson job. Do you want me to go ahead and place the order, or wait to see if they change their minds again?"

"Better wait. The Jacksons always change their minds at least three times, and it's only been twice so far."

Liz went to the next item on her list. Kate found the conversation immensely relaxing. This was reality—her business, her friends, her home, her cat.

"If you need me in person or to listen and make soothing noises, I'm here," Liz said when she finished with business. "Phone. Fax. E-mail. Any time of the day or night. And remember that it's okay to cry."

"Thanks for . . . for everything, Liz." Kate said good-bye and hung up, feeling a prickling at the back of her neck. The sudden appearance of an old and trusted friend—one who had the right skills and needed a job and place to live—was so timely that it seemed like fate.

Though the rational side of her brain scoffed at the idea of divine intervention, on a deeper level she more than half believed that there were underlying patterns to life. When a door opened with such dramatic timing, a wise woman had to consider whether she was supposed to go through it. Or to use a good California term, "Hey, ho, go with the flow." The universe had sent her this kind of message once or twice before, and she'd seen similar patterns in the lives of friends.

God help her, did this mean she was supposed to go

along with Sam's will? Or was fatigue making her see omens in what was mere coincidence?

Later. She'd think about all this *later*.

When she took off her jacket, crinkling paper reminded her of the letter from her father she'd stuffed into the pocket. She pulled out the envelope, wincing at the sight of her name scrawled in Sam's impatient handwriting. She was too tired to face a message from him tonight.

But curiosity won over fatigue. She ripped open the PDI envelope, then perched nervously on the edge of the bed and scanned the lines of the last message she would ever receive from her father.

My darling Kate, it began.

> *I don't know when you'll read this, but it's a safe bet that you'll be mad as hell at me. Just as well that I'm dead.*
>
> *Take it as given that I'm a meddling old fool, but I swear on Nonna Corsi's grave that I want only the best for you. I've always believed I was at least partly responsible for you and Donovan getting divorced. I knew how much you wanted to work for PDI, but he was the one I hired. I've never been sorry about that—a man couldn't ask for a finer employee, or friend, or son-in-law. Still, I should have brought you both into the firm, despite my reservations, because hiring him and not you had to have caused problems.*
>
> *Well, I can't keep you out of PDI now. Nick's job is open, and you and Donovan would make a hell of a team—just like when you were married.*
>
> *But I'm hoping for more than an office partnership, which is why I said you had to share the house with him. Living together, seeing each other over break- fast, is different from working together. Whenever your mom and I visited Donovan at Brandy Lane, I'd think how happy you two were when you refinished furniture together, or shared the kitchen to put on a*

*terrific dinner, or just sat on the sofa holding hands
when you had company. Maybe you can be that way
again.*

*It probably looks like I'm trying to run your life
from the grave, and with some justice, but even I have
to admit that I can't force either of you into a relationship you don't want. What I can try to do is give
you both a second chance. I know what it's like to
be young and hotheaded and talk myself into a corner
I couldn't get out of. You and Donovan probably said
and did things that seemed unforgivable, but it was
a lot of years ago. Maybe it's time to look at what
you had, and decide whether it's worth getting back.*

So when you get over being furious with me, carissima, *maybe you'll forgive my heavy-handedness.
After all, I'm Italian, I can't help it.*

And I hope you'll remember how much I love you.

Always,
Dad

By the end, her eyes were so full of tears that she could
barely read his signature. She wrapped her arms around a
pillow and began to weep. If he hadn't died in that accident,
she probably never would have seen the letter. Obviously
he'd written it just after her cousin Nick's departure, when
he was feeling abandoned and wanted more family around
him. Eventually the will would have been changed, when
she or Donovan remarried, but because of the terrible coincidence of her father's death so soon after he'd written
that impulsive letter, there was a poignant immediacy to his
words. She could hear the echo of his gruff voice in her
head as she read.

Damn the man, why did he have to remind her how close
she and Donovan had been? If he was here, she'd wring
his neck.

Oh, God, if only Sam *were* here.

Clutching the damp pillow, she finally drifted into the
sleep of utter exhaustion.

8

Kate cuddled the dog on her lap as Donovan turned his vehicle onto Bellona Avenue. She'd been insane to agree to visit the house they'd shared. The best and worst times of their marriage had taken place there, and the closer she got, the tenser she felt.

She gazed out the window at the wooded hills of Ruxton. Though the neighborhood lay within the Baltimore Beltway, the narrow winding roads and towering trees made it feel like deep country. This morning every tree and dormant shrub sparkled with brittle, crystalline snow. A perfect setting for a dead marriage.

Years in California had made her wary of icy roads, but she had confidence in Donovan and his Jeep Cherokee. His competence at just about everything had been part of his allure. At eighteen, she'd believed this was a man she could trust for anything. Clear proof that instinct wasn't worth a damn.

Oscar raised his head and gave a bark of recognition as they turned into Brandy Lane, the twisty dead-end road that led to the house. The dog had often stayed with Donovan when Julia and Sam traveled, and had insisted on coming today.

After bracing herself for the first sight of her old home, Kate was relieved to see that the modest structure of her memories had changed dramatically. The site sloped away from the road and was heavily treed, which made it difficult to evaluate the extent of the alterations, but at the very least a new wing had been added, with what looked like a three-car garage tucked underneath and entered from the side.

Donovan pulled up in front of the house, then cut the ignition and unbuckled his seat belt. "I thought you might like to use the formal entrance."

"Lay on, Macduff, and damn'd be him who first cries, Hold, enough!"

"Is this really Shakespearean tragedy?"

"Actually, it's more like farce," she admitted.

He climbed out and circled the vehicle to open her door. Oscar leaped from her lap to the ground and dashed to the house, one very fast furball in flight from the cold. He whizzed past the azaleas she'd planted by the entrance. She'd picked them specially because the blooms were a rare shade of magenta. They'd grown a lot in ten years.

Glad that Donovan knew better than to offer his hand to help her down, Kate stepped from the vehicle, then gasped as a blast of icy wind knifed through her. "Good grief, has Baltimore moved closer to the North Pole since I left?"

"So far, this January is the coldest on record." He shut the passenger door and escorted her to the house. She felt brittle as glass as he unlocked the front door.

Inside, she felt relief again. The house had changed out of recognition. To her left, she saw that the small kitchen and dining room had been combined into a large, inviting country kitchen. It was an appealing space filled with sunshine and handsome oak cabinets, but it wasn't *her* kitchen.

On the far side, a broad arch led into a new formal dining room. It appeared pristine and seldom used. Not surprising; if she lived here alone, she'd always eat in that friendly kitchen. She unbuttoned her raincoat and handed it to Donovan.

He hung it with his parka in a closet that hadn't existed ten years before. "Coffee? Cappuccino?"

She walked into the kitchen. "Cappuccino in Baltimore, the city where trends come to die?"

"Clear proof that cappuccino has become mainstream. Would you like some?"

"Regular coffee would be nice."

While she admired the handmade ceramic tiles on the backsplash, Donovan pulled a bag of hazelnut coffee beans from the refrigerator. He'd always been a good cook. Preparing meals together had been such fun, negotiating for the cutting board, dodging each other, not always successfully . . .

She bit her lip, blocking the image that had been stirred by her father's letter. Sharing a kitchen amiably did not a marriage make.

As he measured beans into a grinder, he said, "Why not explore on your own? There's nothing off-limits."

Relieved to tour the house alone, she opened the door leading to what had been a dismal basement, despite her best efforts with paint and lighting. The area had been completely transformed, more than doubling in size when the wing was added. The south wall was now mostly windows that looked into the woods, and the expanded space had been divided into a spacious family room, a full bath, a large, well-organized workshop, and a sizable room containing exercise equipment. The home gym would be convenient if she came here. A big if.

She returned upstairs and checked out the small laundry room that had been tucked between the kitchen and the door to the garage. As a female architect, she approved; it was convenient to be able to keep an eye on the laundry while cooking.

Professional curiosity engaged, she crossed the entry hall and entered the old living room. Now it was a den and TV room. None of the casual furniture was familiar, for which she was grateful.

She lingered to study the bookshelves. An eclectic mix of fiction and nonfiction, including a copy of the *Blasters' Handbook*. And, damnation, here was the beautiful coffee table edition of the *Book of Kells* that she had given him

one Christmas. They'd both loved the ancient Celtic man-
uscript illuminations.

She turned away from the books, preferring to admire
the first-rate sound system. Donovan had probably wired
the house so that music would play into every room.

A new door opened from the den into the new living
room. Oscar Wilde was padding in that direction, so she
followed him down the three steps. Then she halted,
stunned. Dear God, it was *her house*! No wonder the other
areas had seemed so right.

Her gaze swept over the magnificent, cathedral-ceilinged
room, the fieldstone fireplace flanked by narrow stained-
glass panels. Sunshine poured in through skylights, and tall
windows afforded sweeping views of the surrounding
woodlands. It was all exactly as she had visualized when
drawing up the plans.

Hearing a footstep behind her, she whirled to find Donovan coming through the kitchen door, a mug of coffee in
each hand. Voice choked, she exclaimed, "You used the
plans I drew up when I was studying at Maryland!"

"It seemed silly to reinvent the wheel when your ideas
were so good," he said as he handed her a steaming mug.
"I made some minor changes, but basically it's the house
you designed as your first big residential project."

Her hand was shaking so badly that scalding coffee
slopped over her fingers. The original structure was so
small and nondescript that Kate had felt no compunction
about making major changes. She'd wanted to create a
home filled with sunlight, and incorporating some of the
wonderful architectural elements salvaged from PDI jobs,
like the carved oak mantelpiece and the stained-glass panels
beside the fireplace.

She'd drawn a blizzard of sketches, selling her ideas to
her husband as if he were a paying client. Discovering her
design brought to vivid life in wood and stone was more
upsetting than the original house would have been. She'd
put so much of herself and her dreams for the future into

her plans. Seeing her house was like—like finding out that she'd had a child she didn't know about.

She sipped at her coffee. Milk only, just the way she liked it. Damn Donovan!

Wrapping her hands around the mug for warmth, she paced the length of the room. As in the rest of the house, the furnishings were comfortable but sparse. The empty spaces cried out for pictures and plants, woven hangings and tapestry pillows—

She cut her spiraling imagination off. This was *not* her house. Not anymore. But there were haunting similarities to her home in San Francisco. She and Donovan had similar tastes in Persian rugs and softly neutral overstuffed furniture, creating ghostly echoes between her house and his.

Trying to take refuge in professional detachment, she said, "Very nice. When did you have this built?"

"I did most of the work myself. The living room was the last major project. I finished it a year or so ago."

His shuttered expression made her wonder what he had felt while working from the drawings and floor plans she'd labored over for months. Had he thought about her, or done his best not to? "You used your spare time for building as a counterbalance to wrecking things for a living?"

"Something like that."

Stopping by the glass doors, she gazed over the deck into the trees. One end of the deck was screened in, with a door that led into the kitchen. A great place to eat and hang out in the summer. Donovan's idea—her design hadn't included that.

Blocking out memories of the walks she and Donovan had taken through the woods—and the times they'd come back smudged with leaves or grass stains—she turned away from the window. "I've always wondered where you got the money to buy out my share of the house. I couldn't have afforded to go to Berkeley if you hadn't done that. Did Sam give you a loan?"

"Not Sam—Julia. Your father was so furious about the

divorce that he wasn't about to do anything that would make it easier for you to stay away. Julia was more practical. She said she didn't want her daughter to have to drop out of school and become a topless dancer or worse."

Kate smiled involuntarily. That sounded just like her mother. "I assumed that once the dust settled from the divorce, you'd sell this place."

"I was tempted. But this was my home. I didn't want to have to find another."

She should have known that. He'd loved this neighborhood as much as she had.

The thought produced a cascade of memories. It was her friend Rachel Hamilton who had mentioned that a neglected house near her parents' home would be going on the market soon. Kate and Rachel had checked it out together. The small rancher wasn't much, but the three-acre setting was spectacular. Part of an estate sale, the property could be had for a bargain price by someone willing to settle quickly and accept the house's run-down condition.

Without telling Donovan, Kate had asked her parents for the house as a wedding present. They'd agreed, and the contract had already been signed when Kate had brought Donovan to see the place a week before the wedding. She'd been bubbling with excitement, sure he'd be delighted to have a home of his own.

Instead he'd been enraged. Whirling around, he seized her shoulders with bruising force and shook her furiously as he shouted that he wasn't a damned pet, and the wedding was off. She'd gaped at him, stunned. Occasionally he'd shown flashes of temper, but they always passed quickly. Usually he was sweet and romantic and easygoing, her dream man.

The incident had been over in an instant, horrifying Donovan far more than her. He'd released her, his face white as he stammered an apology.

She hadn't been hurt, only shocked, and appalled at her own stupidity. Knowing that Donovan was uncomfortable with her family's prosperity and position, it had been idiotic of her to make such an important decision without consulting him.

Shaking, she went into his arms, saying she'd only wanted to please him and would never, never be so inconsiderate again. They would break the contract and live anywhere Donovan wanted. Talking at the same time, he said vehemently that he loved the house, that it was the most wonderful present anyone had ever given him, and he would be delighted to live here forever if only Kate could forgive his horrible temper.

Mutual remorse exploded into passion, and they'd made love on the bare oak floor with raging intensity. Afterward he'd been so tender, so gentle, that she'd been positively delighted with their first major disagreement because it had brought them even closer.

If she knew then what she'd learned later, would she have ended the engagement? Perhaps—but she couldn't be sure, even now. There had been good and bad in their marriage. For better and worse, she was what those three critical years of matrimony had made her.

Resting her gaze on an ice-encrusted shrub, she asked with careful neutrality, "Have you been seeing someone regularly?"

After a slight hesitation, he said, "Yes."

"Would you keep seeing her if I was living here?"

"Do I look nuts? Of course not. Life will be plenty complicated enough without that. What about you? Have you been dating someone in San Francisco?"

"Yes." She thought of her easy relationship with Alec. "Geography would put a swift halt to that."

As the silence stretched, he said, "It sounds as if you're considering staying."

She bit her lip. Apparently she *was* considering it. Before breakfast, she'd read and reread her father's letter, profoundly affected by his sincerity.

Equally significant had been her mother's observation

that the two of them were still being ruled by the past. That had struck uncomfortable chords when Kate thought about Alec and the other men she'd dated through the years. All had been bright, pleasant, attractive—but maybe not emotionally available?

Such choices weren't accidental. Though she'd vaguely assumed that someday she'd marry again, preferably before her biological clock struck midnight, she had made no real progress toward that state. Maybe the time had come to deal with what had been too painful to bear then. Yet the mere thought produced a twist of alarm.

Apparently reading her mind, Donovan said, "If you stay, I promise I won't ever touch you."

And he was a man of his word. Or perhaps it would be more accurate to say that his intentions were always good. "If . . . anything happened, I'd be out of here in a heartbeat."

"It won't come to that, Kate. I swear it."

She studied him, trying to be objective, as if they'd never met before. Donovan looked exactly like what he was—a strong, no-nonsense man who was equally skilled at business, engineering, and hard physical labor. His dark, silky hair was still on the long side, but it no longer brushed his shoulders. He'd had it cut when he began dealing with clients, though Sam hadn't asked him to. Donovan had worked hard, in small ways as well as large, to achieve the right to command.

But that was on the surface. The internal changes mattered more. Years of success in a tough, demanding business had made him steadier. More confident. The edginess that had fascinated and alarmed her when they'd first met seemed to be gone.

They were both adults. Perhaps . . . perhaps they could do this. "If you don't touch me and you stop dating, it would be a long year."

"They say that men reach their sexual peak at about nineteen, and it's all downhill after that. Someone of my advanced years should be able to manage twelve months of celibacy," he said dryly.

She sniffed; there was nothing over-the-hill about Donovan. "Are you sure about that?"

"Neither of us would want to go back to the way things were."

A stunning understatement. Frowning, she drifted across the room. He was absolutely right that their problems had been rooted in sex. So, no sex, no problems, right? Well, maybe. And if problems did surface, she could leave at any time.

The marriage was beyond salvation, but the business was a different matter. "I read the letter from my father last night. He explained why he wrote such a bizarre will, and conceded that he could no longer keep me from working for PDI. He seemed to think that I might want to step into Nick's job."

"Sam was stubborn, but he wasn't stupid. Since Nick left, we haven't had an account rep. You'd be great at that. As an architect, you already understand a lot of the technical end, and I'll bet you're first class at client work."

Yes, she was, but being an account rep was not the dream of PDI she'd had growing up. She wanted to blow up buildings, not spend most of her life on the telephone. This was the chance she'd always wanted. And if Donovan balked—well, she liked the idea that he'd have to make a hard decision, just as she did. "If I'm to put my life on hold for a year, there has to be something in it for me personally."

"That's only fair." His expression was wary.

Her hands clenched involuntarily as she prepared to go through the door that had opened in front of her. "I'll stay on one condition."

"Which is?"

"That I work for PDI in the field, handling explosives. Just like you."

9

"Hell, no!" Donovan exclaimed.

"Do you think I'm incapable of doing the work?"

Recognizing that he was on the verge of falling into very hot water, he said, "It's not a matter of capability, Kate. You're smart enough to do anything you set your mind to. But Sam was right—demolition is no job for a woman. Fieldwork is filthy and exhausting and potentially dangerous."

"Do you think I've forgotten that the business just killed my father? But everything has risks—teaching high school can be more hazardous than working with explosives. You know how much I've always wanted to work at PDI. Now is my chance. I certainly can't move here and spend the next year doing lunch and twiddling my thumbs."

"True. But honestly, you'd be more help in the office than in the field. A large part of being a foreman or project manager is very routine. Drilling holes and ordering around crews of highly politically incorrect construction workers."

Looking as if she was enjoying herself, she crossed her arms and leaned against the fireplace. "What do you think architects do, Donovan? I've stared down two-hundred-pound laborers and worn out as many hard hats as you have. Who would know better how to bring down buildings than someone trained to put them up?"

He imagined her giving orders to a hulking laborer, and didn't doubt that she could hold her own. But that was *con*struction, not *de*struction! "Call me a Neanderthal, but the thought of you working with dynamite gives me chills."

"Is it just me, or would you feel that way about any female with a yen for dynamite?"

He almost blurted out that Kate was the one who made him feel so chauvinist, that he couldn't bear to think of her being hurt, but managed to restrain himself. "It would be easier to hire a total stranger for this work than anyone I know. Remember my little cousin Lissie? Connie and Frank's granddaughter?"

"Of course. How is she? I haven't seen her since her first Communion. What a sweetheart she was."

"She is now two inches taller than you, tops in her class at Western High, and won't answer unless called Melissa. Her current ambition is to go through the same Loyola College engineering program I took, then come to work for PDI so she can blow things up."

Kate laughed. "You'll have to come to terms with your wimpiness sooner or later, so it might as well be now. You've always had a reactionary streak, but you're a generation younger than Sam. You're not incapable of accepting females as equals."

"Easier in theory than practice." Donovan remembered a casual coed softball game the first summer of their marriage. He had been pitching, while Kate, a darned good infielder, was playing second base. She'd just caught the ball to make an out when the runner, a big guy called Denny, got so carried away by the excitement of the game that he slid into her hard, trying to knock the ball from her glove. Kate was thrown a half-dozen feet and knocked breathless.

When Donovan saw her lying motionless on the ground, he went crazy. He raced off the pitcher's mound, shouting, "Kate! *Kate!*"

Gasping for breath, she managed to sit up and assure everyone that she wasn't seriously damaged. Fear allayed, Donovan spun around and slugged Denny with a force that nearly broke the other man's jaw. "You bastard, you know damned well there's no sliding in this kind of game!" He was swinging again when Kate and two other players pulled him away from the cowering, apologetic Denny.

He calmed down quickly, mostly because he hated to see the alarm in Kate's face, but he was left shaken by the intensity of his reaction. That day he had recognized how primitive and powerful was the desire to protect one's mate. The compulsion to defend his loved ones was as volatile and dangerous as nitroglycerin—and now Kate wanted to implode buildings. He supposed it was karmic justice coming home to roost.

His thoughts were interrupted by Kate saying, "It's your decision, Donovan. If you and I have to be under the same roof every night, that means business trips together, so I might as well make myself useful. Agree, and the firm will be yours. Refuse, and you'll have to choose between starting your own business, or becoming a hired hand for Bud Marchetti."

Torn between exasperation and reluctant admiration, he said, "You're Sam's daughter to the core. Pigheaded and hell-bent on getting your own way."

"Which means I should be darned good at demolition."

Kate was right, unfortunately. With proper precautions, working with explosives wasn't unduly hazardous. Hard to remember that when Sam had just died in a freak accident. "You've got yourself a deal, Kate. Just remember that I'm the boss, and I expect you to obey orders like everyone else in the firm. This business is too dangerous for you to go off half-cocked on the basis of your childhood memories."

"I'll be a model employee."

"I doubt it." But though his words were dry, inside he wanted to turn cartwheels. She was going to stay! Through the grace of God and Sam Corsi, he had the chance to redeem past sins—and sweat blood as Kate learned the fine points of explosive demolition.

• • •

On the drive back to the Corsi house, Donovan and Kate discussed practical details. She estimated that it would take her two weeks or so to sort out her affairs in California. Then she would return to Maryland. To his house. *Their* house.

In the meantime he could work on his willpower. Prepare himself to see a sexy, sleepy-eyed Kate over the coffee grinder every morning, and to hear that warm, seductive voice in the office and on job sites.

His mind continued to churn after he dropped her and Oscar off. He remembered all too clearly her expression when she'd learned that Sam had offered his future son-in-law a summer job at PDI—exactly what Kate had yearned for. She reacted as if she'd been slapped. Unable to bear her wounded eyes, he quickly said he'd turn Sam down.

Kate had swallowed hard, and said that wasn't necessary. Her father's refusal to hire her had nothing to do with Donovan. He wanted to work for PDI as much as she did, and the generous salary would be very welcome. Since they were getting married, they had to be practical.

He'd been delighted, and selfishly relieved, to have her permission to take the job that he desperately wanted. Not only had he been fascinated by explosive demolition, but he was panting to adopt Sam as a surrogate father. Kate, never a sulker, had buried her disappointment and found herself a summer internship at an architectural firm. On the surface, his work at PDI had never been an issue. But he'd always been uncomfortably aware of how much he'd benefited from Sam's chauvinism.

Trying not to think of all the accidents and near disasters he'd experienced at PDI, and which Kate would now face, he turned the Jeep toward the university neighborhood around Johns Hopkins. It was Saturday, so with luck he'd be able to do what had to be done right away. It wouldn't get any easier.

A few minutes later he pulled up in front of a neat rowhouse on a quiet side street. The owner's car was parked in front.

He let himself into the house with his key. The air was heavy with mouthwatering scents. As two cats materialized and began stropping his ankles, a light feminine voice called from the kitchen, "Is that you, Donovan?"

"Nope. It's your friendly neighborhood ax murderer."

Chuckling, Val Covington emerged from the kitchen, her red hair curling wildly and a bulky sweater falling to mid-thigh as a concession to the January freeze. "Perfect timing. A pot of fifteen-bean soup has been simmering all morning, and the honey-wheatberry loaf is about to come out of the bread machine." She stood on her toes and gave him a hug. "It seems like forever since we've seen each other. The funeral doesn't count. How are you doing? Losing Sam must be like losing your own father."

"Worse. Much, much worse." He hugged her back, thinking how easy it was to be with Val. She always reminded him of a wickedly intelligent leprechaun.

"How are Kate and Mrs. C doing?" she asked. "They looked numb yesterday."

"They're coping. I suppose that's the best that can be expected."

Val frowned. "I'll have to call Kate before she goes home. Maybe we can get together." Curls bouncing, she led him toward the kitchen.

"I'm afraid there have been some . . . unexpected developments." In the past he would have gone straight to the soup pot for a sample. Instead, he halted in the doorway. "I've come to return my key."

Val paled until her freckles stood out like copper haze. "Oh?"

Feeling like a heel, he said, "I'm sorry, I should have been more tactful."

"There is no tactful way to say good-bye. Why?"

He concentrated on removing Val's key from his ring. "Sam's will specified that Kate and Tom get most of his money and I get PDI, but only if Kate and I will live in my house for a year. She's decided to give it a try."

"I see." Val dropped onto a chair. "Well, it isn't as if our relationship was going anywhere, Donovan. It's basically been a mutual convenience. A healthy sleeping partner with no strings attached."

That hurt. "Don't cheapen what's been between us, Val. We've been good friends. I hope we still are."

"If we hadn't been sharing a bed, we'd never have seen each other. That's not my definition of friendship."

She was probably right. He'd first met Val as one of Kate's bridesmaids. They'd always liked each other, but since she was one of Kate's closest friends, they'd lost touch after the divorce. Then they ran into each other one Saturday in the local Borders bookstore, had a cup of coffee together, and drifted into a relationship. "There's no question that sex always adds interest, but we wouldn't have been sharing a bed if there wasn't more than sex."

"I suppose not." She toyed with a dangling bead earring. "But you're certainly right that we can't see each other when you're living with Kate. Too much like adultery."

"Kate and I are going to have a strictly platonic relationship."

"If you say so." Her hazel eyes were troubled. "Does Kate know that you and I have been . . . involved?"

"I just said that I'd been seeing someone. Not who."

"Good. Kate and I have been friends for a long time. I don't think she'd be thrilled to find out that I've been sleeping with her ex-husband. It's against the Good Girlfriends Code."

"Isn't there some kind of statute of limitations on that? After all, until this week Kate and I hadn't seen each other in almost ten years."

"It was okay while she was in California. Not when we're all in the same city."

He reached out and stroked her hair. It was red and springy and crackled with vitality, like Val. There had been no passionate highs and lows, but they'd been good company for each other. Especially in bed. "You'll have to wait to get together with Kate. She's returning to California tomorrow, and won't be back for at least a couple of weeks."

Val swiveled away from his caressing hand. "Don't tell me—the subliminal message here is one of those guy things. 'Let's have sex one last time.' No dice. I'm not into maudlin partings."

He winced. "Did it seem like that's what I was doing? Sorry."

He'd never made any attempt to learn what made Val tick, and he'd certainly never considered sharing his darkest secrets with her. Might there have been a deeper relationship possible between them? Maybe, maybe not.

But he would never know. It had been easier to stay on the surface. Safer. "I'm going to miss you, Val. More than I realized."

"Yeah. I'm going to miss you, too, big guy."

"You'll probably find someone better long before I'm free to date again."

"You say that like a joke, but it's not." Her voice was serious. "You're a catch, Donovan. Smart, funny, a hunk, pleasantly prosperous, and a nice guy. Yet you always act as if you can't believe anyone could care for you. Is that why you and Kate split up?"

Abruptly he remembered why he preferred staying on the surface. "If you want to know the whole story, ask Kate. Maybe she'll tell you."

"Not her. Kate has never said word one about why she left you. She's a poster child for ladylike discretion. Most females would have poured out the whole story so I could have made soothing noises, but not Kate."

The breadmaker dinged. Val slid off the stool and went to the stove. "The sex shop is closed, but the offer of soup is still open."

"Great. I'm going to miss your soups, too."

"I'll e-mail you some recipes," she said, voice cool.

As she went to a cupboard and took out two bowls, he wondered how many more ways his life was going to be disrupted by Kate's return.

10

A week had passed since Kate returned to San Francisco to organize her affairs, and Donovan had been missing her the whole time. As he ripped lettuce for a dinner salad, he speculated on how much longer it would be until she came back to Maryland. Another week, by her own estimate, but given her comments about the cold weather, he suspected that he might not see her before March.

Then the door from the garage opened, and Kate erupted into the kitchen. Purse in one hand and flight bag in the other, she wore an elegant coat that was way too light for the fifteen-degree temperature, and an expression that reminded him of a smoldering fuse. Obviously she'd used the garage door opener he'd given her before she left, but why on earth hadn't she called to say she'd be arriving earlier than expected?

To put him off balance, he realized. To score a point in the conflict that thrummed just under the surface. Trust was a long, long way off.

Well, he couldn't blame her for being uneasy; he was nervous as a cat himself. But glad—very glad—to see her, even though her fair hair was pulled starkly back, and she looked as slick and glittery as a glass angel. "So the official residency has begun. I didn't expect you for another week or so."

"Things fell into place quickly." She set her purse and flight bag down, then wrapped her arms around herself to control her shivering. "Unnervingly so, but at least that has the advantage that the sooner I start, the sooner it's over."

He wouldn't touch that with a ten-foot piece of rebar. "How was the flight?"

"Long. Tiring. I was insane to leave California in midwinter." As she hung up her coat in the closet, he wondered if she would be willing to borrow something of his until she could go shopping. At least her navy slacks and sweater looked warm.

He wiped his hands on a towel. "I'll bring up the rest of your luggage."

"I can do it," she said brusquely.

He crossed his arms and leaned back against the counter. "I know you can, Wonder Woman. But do you really want to?"

"Cut the gentlemanly stuff. We are not a couple. We are not friends. We are merely sharing the same house."

Identifying the source of her snappishness, he said tactfully, "You must be hungry. Take a seat and I'll find something to feed you."

She opened her mouth to protest, then stopped, realizing the truth in his statement. "You're right. A pity that airlines have practically stopped serving food these days."

As she circled the U-shaped counter and perched on a padded stool, Donovan poured olive oil onto a plate. After he sprinkled on Parmesan cheese and a grating of pepper, he unwrapped a flat loaf of fresh focaccia and sliced off several pieces. Bread and olive oil, just like his Italian grandmother used to give him when he was little. He pushed the bread toward her on the carving board. "Wine?"

"Please." She pulled off the band that held her hair back and shook her head. Blond waves fell forward around her face, making her look softer and more approachable.

He'd bought and refrigerated several bottles of the Chardonnay she'd always liked. Taking one out, he filled a stemmed glass and set it by her hand, then returned to his salad, more than doubling the quantity. Kate had always been able to tear through a bowl of greens with a zest that would shame a rabbit.

She ripped off a piece of focaccia and dipped it into the oil-and-cheese mixture. After swallowing the first bite, she gave a small sigh, the tension lines in her face easing. "Thanks, Donovan. One day you're going to make someone a fine wife."

Glad to see that her mood was improving, he took a bottle of ginger beer from the refrigerator and poured himself a glass. "Have some more focaccia. I figure another two pieces and you'll be civil."

"Civility is going to require a year of time, not olive oil," she said, the bite gone from her voice. "We shouldn't share food, Donovan. It's too . . . too intimate."

Keeping the width of the counter between them, he dunked a piece of bread in the olive oil. "Kate, living together isn't going to be easy, but I can't believe that artificially ignoring each other is the answer. There's lasagna baking in the oven. Wouldn't it be easier just to set two places at the table and eat together?"

"Sure it's easier in the short term, but we have three years of habit patterns waiting to reactivate. How long does it take to go from lasagna to feeling like we're a couple again? And if that happens, then what?"

"We're not kids anymore, Kate. We don't have to be ruled by the past. Wasn't that the point of this exercise?"

She tore a piece of the dense bread into minuscule crumbs. "I'm just . . . not handling this very well. In the abstract, trying to fulfill the will seemed like a reasonable idea, but in the last week, I've lost my business, my house, my cat, and maybe my moorings as well."

"You could have brought the cat."

"Ginger Bear is old, and will be much happier in familiar

surroundings. My friend Jenny will take good care of him. Just like she'll take good care of my house and my business." Kate closed her eyes, emphasizing the dark shadows under her eyes.

Deciding she needed time to pull herself together, he went to the garage to collect her luggage. After dropping off her bags in the bedroom wing, he returned to the kitchen and remarked, "You're driving Sam's Cadillac?"

"My car is being driven cross-country by a couple of graduate students on their way to Johns Hopkins. Julia said I could use Sam's car until mine arrives. The blasted thing is the size of a tank truck, but a lot fancier. Sam must have loved it."

"He did. None of those foreign luxury cars for him." Donovan began to set the kitchen table. "Technically the Caddy belongs to PDI, not your mother. That will have to be sorted out eventually."

"It's a company car? Since you already have a Jeep, a red vintage Corvette, and a huge Harley motorcycle, if I counted the boy toys correctly, I presume you don't want the Cadillac yourself. Maybe you should give it to another employee, like Luther. He's been at PDI longer than anyone."

"I'll ask if he wants it, but I suspect that he shares your opinion of the car's charms. Now that his kids are grown, he has a little sports number so he and his wife can zip around like teenagers." Donovan took a large dish of steaming lasagna from the oven and set it on a table mat, then tossed the salad with oil and vinegar. "If he doesn't want the tank car, I'll sell it. PDI could use the cash."

Kate moved the drinks and the focaccia to the table. "Really? I thought the company has been wildly profitable for the last couple of decades."

"It always has been, but Sam's death is having an effect. There are still only about six companies in the world that do explosive demolition, and PDI had the distinction of being the only one never to have caused a fatality. Well, except for Nick's company, which is too new to count. Now we've lost our aura of infallibility. Not only has that sent our insurance rates up, but when I've called firms that had contacted us about possible jobs, several said I needn't bother following up with a written estimate."

She served the lasagna. "It's a nuisance that business is off, but surely this is temporary."

"Your dear cousin has been doing his damnedest to take as many clients as he can to his new firm, Implosions, Inc."

"Only to be expected, I suppose. But unless he's improved on the technical end, Nick is no match for you."

"He's no sharpshooter, but his fieldwork is certainly competent, and he took a couple of good people with him. His big advantage is that he did so much of the account representative work that he knows the clients better. No sooner was Sam buried than Nick got on the phone to rustle up as much PDI business as he could. Not only is he underpricing us, but I hear that his sales pitch strongly implies that Sam died because Nick wasn't there to see that everything was done exactly right. Charming."

Kate frowned. "Is PDI in serious trouble?"

"Nothing terminal, but things have been better. Sam hadn't gotten around to replacing Nick or the foreman who went with him, and now Sam's death has shot morale to hell. We're shorthanded, and everyone is on edge. I've been going nuts trying to pick up all the loose threads. Sam had let some things slide lately." Donovan could feel the weight of the business on his shoulders. He'd carried a lot of the responsibility in recent years, but Sam had always been there as backup. "Then there's Concord Place."

"That's a public housing project in the city, isn't it?"

"Right, and its time has run out. Five mid-rise buildings, one of those urban renewal projects that seemed like a great idea forty years ago, but haven't worn well. We've dropped a number of similar projects across the country. The city wants to put town houses on the site. Safer, and more like a real neighborhood." Donovan took another piece of lasagna. He'd never been one to lose his appetite when stressed. "PDI won the contract for the demolition."

"There's a 'but' in your voice."

Donovan stabbed his salad with unnecessary force. "Nick had surveyed the buildings and drafted the proposal. Just before the contract was awarded, he left PDI. Then Sam died. So Nick went back to the city board of estimates and tried to convince them that the contract should be transferred to his company on the grounds that he'd done the work, and with Sam gone, PDI was in effect no longer the same company that had received the contract."

"Nick has always been one tough competitor. Did he persuade them to change?"

"Charles Hamilton is not the PDI lawyer for nothing. After he got through baring his teeth and explaining the legal ramifications to the board, Nick didn't have a chance." Donovan wound mozzarella strands with his fork. "It would be bad public relations to lose a job like this that's right on our doorstep. Though to be honest, if we didn't need the money, I'd be tempted to let Nick have it."

"Why?"

"Because it's turned into a political football. Despite the gang and drug problems, a lot of decent people live in those apartments, and they don't like losing their homes. Plus, a community organizer is using the demolition as a way to draw attention to the city's housing deficiencies. In short, a media circus, with PDI in the middle of it. I expect picketing when the weather gets warmer."

"I see why you have mixed feelings about the job."

He regarded her thoughtfully. "Having you at PDI may turn out to be a real plus."

"I'm just going to be an apprentice foreman."

"You're more than that. As Sam's daughter, you're also the keeper of the flame, whether you want that or not."

"If you say so. I was thinking of myself more as the prodigal daughter."

"That, too," he said. "I suppose it's time I gave you the

bad news. Tomorrow morning I have to go to Las Vegas for a few days, then on to San Francisco. I hadn't mentioned it because I thought I'd be finished before you returned to Baltimore. If you have the energy, I hope you'll come with me."

"Another cross-country flight? Tell me you're kidding!"

"Afraid not. If I can get you a seat, we'll have to be out of here by seven tomorrow to catch the plane." He rose and cleared away their plates, then poured two cups of coffee and set biscotti on the table between them. "PDI is taking down a major hotel casino, and the client's in a hurry because he loses a couple of hundred thousand dollars every week until his new place opens. I'll understand if you'd rather skip this trip, but it's the sort of high-profile job where having Sam's daughter would be a real asset."

That seemed to please her. "I'll go then, but I warn you, I'm going to have serious jet lag." She dunked a chocolate-topped biscotti in her coffee. "Though I might not have the nerve to reappear in San Francisco after all those wrenching good-byes."

"You can sneak in and out of town incognito. We'd only be there long enough to survey a building for a proposal. At least it will be warmer in Nevada than it is in Maryland."

She gave him the first genuine smile since she had stomped in the kitchen door. "How can I resist an offer like that?"

11

Over coffee and dessert, Donovan filled Kate in on PDI, the current employees, and upcoming projects. By the time the coffeepot was empty, she'd absorbed her first lesson in the business. Smothering a yawn, she rose and started to clear the table. That had always been their rule—if one person cooked, the other cleaned.

"I'll take care of this," Donovan said. "You must want to unpack and settle in."

"Thanks. I'll take you up on that." Before leaving, she spent a moment prowling around the kitchen, opening drawers and cabinets to familiarize herself with where things were kept. "Which room is mine?"

"The guest room is the old master bedroom."

She should have known—the other original bedrooms were tiny, and neither had a private bath. The old master bedroom it would have to be. "I'm going to call it a night after I unpack. See you in the morning."

She left the kitchen and made her way to her new bedroom, bracing herself. Even so, she wasn't ready for the impact of stepping inside. The room had been redecorated, and she thought she detected her mother's fine hand in the color scheme, bedspread, and draperies. But the furniture was painfully familiar. She and Donovan had refinished every piece themselves.

Lightly she touched the warm chestnut wood of the country-style dresser, remembering how it had been painted a violent red. Though she'd paid only fifteen dollars, Donovan had questioned her sanity even as he carried it into the house. But when the wood had been stripped and oiled, the dresser had been revealed as a beauty.

And the bed . . . she turned away quickly. Not only did it have its own story of acquisition and rehabilitation, but it must be saturated with the memories of a thousand nights of passion and closeness. Well, seven or eight hundred, anyhow. Toward the end, tension had replaced closeness. The last couple of months she'd been tiptoeing around Donovan like a mouse trying not to wake the cat.

Her gaze fell on a framed photo on the desk. *Hell.* It was a picture of her that Donovan had taken on their honeymoon, a close-up that was all blond hair and dreamy, satisfied smile. It hurt to remember how happy they'd been then. How confident that they would be in love forever. Dear God, but they'd been young. No wonder their marriage had failed. If she had a daughter who looked that young, she'd lock the girl in her bedroom and refuse to allow her to date.

She was surprised that Donovan hadn't destroyed the picture, or at least packed it away. Of course, he probably seldom entered this room. Not wanting to face her naive younger self, Kate placed the picture in the drawer of the bedside table.

At least the attached bathroom stirred no memories. Originally it had contained only a shower stall, but Donovan had managed to fit a short but deep bathtub into the available space when he remodeled, so she wouldn't have to borrow the master bathroom when she was in the mood for a soak.

She studied the decorative border of hand-painted tile. Donovan did beautiful work. On his mother's side he was descended from generations of Italian craftsmen, mostly stonemasons and cabinetmakers. His precision and care had made him a natural for explosive demolition, where there was no margin for carelessness.

But dear Lord, how was she going to sleep in this house?

In this bed? Would she ever be able to tune out the ghosts?

With a sigh, she began unpacking her bags. More belongings were being shipped, but she'd brought enough to mark the turf as her own. On the dresser, she put a picture of her main man, except that Ginger Bear was a cat, not a man. She'd like to think that he missed her, but knew that a furry opportunist like him was already sleeping with Jenny.

It took an hour to unpack and prepare for the next day's trip. When she was done, she locked the door, then changed into a warm robe and curled up in the old wing chair she had reupholstered with the help of a library book. She'd been quite a little nest builder in those days, using her spare time and creative talents to make the small house beautiful for herself and her husband. Once, she'd imagined their children racing through the house and playing in the woods . . .

She called Charles Hamilton's office. On his voice mail, she left a terse message saying that she had just moved into Brandy Lane, and he could start the meter running on her forced residence.

There was only one major task left—telling Alec Gregory that their yearlong affair was over. Their last conversation had occured when she'd called to say that her father had been killed and she was flying east. He had been heading out the door on a business trip to Asia, and they hadn't spoken since, though he'd sent her concerned e-mail from exotic places. She'd kept her replies neutral, not mentioning her move to Maryland. She was pretty sure that Miss Manners would not approve of breaking up with a man by e-mail.

She did a mental calculation. Alec was still abroad, but he should be back in San Francisco just about the time that she and Donovan would be breezing through. Which meant she really should try to see him face-to-face. Breaking up with a man over the phone might be acceptable when they were on opposite coasts, but not when they were in the same city, even if only briefly. She wasn't looking forward to it. True, theirs hadn't been a great love affair, but they'd always had fun together. Good companionship, good sex, no conflicts. That was almost as rare as love. Maybe rarer.

Her gaze strayed to the bed, and she suddenly wondered if her easy relationship with Alec was the real thing, and what had bound her and Donovan was not love, but obsession. Her mind spun irresistibly back to the night when their marriage had taken the dark turn that led to eventual ruin.

Yawning, Kate pulled her Mustang into the carport next to Donovan's old Chevy, glad that his study evening with other Loyola engineering students hadn't turned into an all-nighter. The spring semester was almost over, and long hours of preparation for final projects and exams meant that she and her husband had scarcely seen each other. Hoping that he was awake so they could spend some quality time together, she flipped the lights on as she entered the living room.

Her husband was sitting on the sofa with a can of beer in one hand and ice in his eyes. "Where the hell have you been?"

She dropped her handbag and portfolio by the door. "College Park, of course. My urban design team decided to work late. None of us were satisfied with what we'd done so far."

"It's after midnight. Do you expect me to believe that you and three men spent the whole night talking about some slum?"

"Yes, Donovan," she said patiently. "We sat around with pencils and sketch pads until we figured out how to make a run-down neighborhood into a nicer, more livable place. After we had a quick drink to celebrate coming up with some great solutions, I drove home, which takes close to an hour even this late at night."

"So you were out drinking with the guys. How many of them did you screw?"

Her jaw dropped. "Good grief! Where did that come from? Maybe you should stop drinking alone. You must be drunk to say something so . . . so *revolting*." She headed for the bedroom. Two years of marriage had taught her that her husband had a possessive streak and an occasionally ferocious temper, but this was outrageous.

He moved so swiftly that she didn't realize he'd come off the sofa until he grabbed her arm and swung her around. "Don't try to change the subject! If you're so innocent, why didn't you deny that you've been screwing around?"

"Why should I deny something so absurd?" She jerked her arm from his grasp. "Either you trust me or you don't. And if you don't, you're crazy."

With a shout of anger, he smashed his open hand across her cheek with a force that slammed her backward into a chair. The padded arm jabbed bruisingly into her hip as she tumbled to the floor. She lay there, stunned.

This wasn't possible. No one had ever struck her in her entire life. Yet she could feel the imprint of his hand on her cheek, every finger length etched in pain.

Shock was followed by fury. How *dare* he! She raised her gaze to her husband, and saw that his expression had changed from rage to stark horror. For a moment they simply stared at each other, both of them frozen by the ugly moment of violence.

"My God, Kate, are you all right?" White-faced, Donovan dropped to his knees beside her.

"I . . . I guess I am." She raised a trembling hand to her cheek. She'd seen Donovan explode before, but never at her. "How could you do such a thing?"

"I don't know! I was mad as hell, but I didn't mean to hit you. It just happened." He cradled her against her chest, his breathing harsh. "It sounds so stupid when I say it out loud, but I hate knowing you spend more time with your classmates than with me."

Tears of pain and distress spilled from her eyes. "You're

darned right it's stupid. You've met most of my classmates. They're like my brothers."

"You may think of them as brothers, but trust me, they notice how beautiful and sexy you are. It . . . it scares the hell out of me to think you might decide one of them is a better deal than me."

Her anger faded as she recognized that his bizarre fury had been triggered by fear. Though he never spoke of his childhood, she'd learned enough from his aunt Connie to know that it had been difficult, making it hard for him to accept that his wife truly loved him. She should have reassured him instead of losing her temper and snapping back. Her mother was right—anger created more problems than it solved.

Wanting to ease his wretchedness, she pulled away from him, saying earnestly, "I love you, Patrick. I've never been with another man, can't even imagine wanting to be. I'm your *wife*. Remember? We promised to forsake all others till death do us part." She shook her head, wincing as pain stabbed through her jaw. "But I know darned well that the marriage service didn't say anything about you being allowed to hit me."

"I deserve to be *shot*." He slammed his fist into the floor.

Kate caught his wrist before he could smash his hand into the wood again. "Patrick, don't! There's been enough craziness tonight."

She felt his muscles and tendons flex under her grip before he relaxed and lowered his arm. He stared at her, guilt and misery stark in his face. "More than enough for a lifetime. This will never happen again, I swear it."

"It better not!" Seeing his stricken expression, she said more quietly, "You have to learn to trust me, Patrick. There isn't anyone else. There never will be."

"What I've learned is that you're even more wonderful than I realized." He slid his arms under her and lifted her from the floor.

As he carried her to the bedroom, she realized that she'd

always loved his strength. It hadn't occurred to her to consider it a potential threat.

As he laid her on the bed, he asked, "Should I take you to the emergency room?"

"The last thing I need is to spend hours sitting in a hospital until some doctor has time to tell me there was no damage done." She touched her cheek, which was starting to throb. "Besides, I'd have to explain what happened, which I'd rather not."

"Christ, no." He disappeared for a minute, and returned with an ice pack. She held the ice to her face for a few minutes, until the ache subsided. Then she started to get up so she could take off her clothes.

"Lie back and relax. You were already tired when you got home, and you must feel like hell now. I'll take care of you."

She obeyed, sinking into the pillows and closing her eyes. The mattress sagged as he sat beside her and began undoing the buttons of her shirt. He eased the garment off, then went to work on her jeans. His touch was so gentle, so kind. This was the real Donovan, the man she loved. Already that moment of crazy violence seemed more dream than reality. It had been a ghastly aberration, never to be repeated.

The brush of his hands over her bare skin as he removed her garments was soothing. By the time all her clothes were off, she was half-asleep.

His lips touched her bruised cheek in the most delicate of caresses. "You're so generous, Kate."

He kissed the sensitive skin of her throat exactly the way she liked best. She exhaled with pleasure. Nice. Even nicer when his lips trailed along her collarbone toward her breast. When he tugged gently on her nipple, heat blazed through her. She reached up to draw him close.

He caught her hands and returned them to the sheets. "Don't do anything, *cara mia*. Just relax while I make up to you for what I did."

Usually they were both active partners when they made love, but she found a dreamy pleasure in passively accepting his caresses. His mouth moved lower, tender on her belly. He exhaled warm breath into the soft curls between her thighs. "I don't know what I'd do without you, Kate," he whispered.

She shivered as his tongue licked into her. Mild arousal turned into passion, driving out fatigue and pain with a physical and emotional intimacy that she could not imagine ever finding with another man. His hurt was hers, his remorse palpable.

He took his time, using his knowledge of her body to build her passion to a fever pitch until she could bear no more. Then she shattered, crying out from a scouring intensity that went on and on before finally leaving her limp and panting.

He stripped off his clothing and lay down beside her. "Forgive me, Kate. I don't deserve it, but . . . please forgive me anyhow."

"Of course I forgive you," she whispered. "I know you didn't mean to hurt me."

He was going to let her go to sleep, but she touched him in a wordless plea for greater intimacy. He entered her hesitantly, as if expecting rejection.

She felt his doubt and his need to erase what had happened as clearly as if they were her own emotions. Tears stung her eyes again. She had thought there was so much love and trust between them that nothing could ever tear them apart. But tonight a dark shadow had fallen across their marriage, if only for an instant, and the knowledge that it was possible frightened her.

"I love you, Kate, more than I thought it was possible to love anyone." He buried himself in her, then held still, his body throbbing, his cheek pressed to her temple. In the darkness she felt tears that weren't her own.

To the extent that she'd ever considered being struck by a man, she'd always thought of it as an unforgivable act.

Yet now that it had happened, she found that reality was much more complicated than theory. Marriage brought people so close that the worst was visible along with the best. So her husband wasn't perfect. Neither was she.

Her mother had said more than once that forgiveness was a vital component of love, and heaven knew that Kate loved her husband. "It's all right, Patrick," she whispered as her hips began rocking hips rhythmically against his. "Everything is all right now."

"Oh, God, Kate." His body convulsed and he enfolded her in a crushing grip as he repeated hoarsely, "I love you, love you, love you . . ."

They slept, exhausted, in each other's arms.

But it wasn't all right. Much later she recognized how much their relationship had changed that night. There was still love, fierce and consuming, but it was tainted by a faint undercurrent of wariness. She was more cautious around her husband, doing her best to avoid triggering his temper. A little spontaneity was lost. A little trust.

She had started along the road to ruin, and didn't know it.

12

That night Donovan lay on his bed and stared into the darkness as the arctic wind rattled bare branches against the house. He'd thought himself prepared to have his former wife under his roof again. Pretty stupid of him not to guess what a bitch the reality would be. From the moment she marched into his kitchen, he'd had an overwhelming desire to pull her onto his lap and hold her until she was warm and relaxed again.

Of course, if he'd laid a hand on her she would have walked out the door permanently, probably after bending a frying pan over his head. But at least she'd accepted some pampering. Clear proof that she was exhausted.

Was she upset at having to leave the boyfriend in San Francisco? He found himself wondering what the bastard was like, and immediately cut the thought off. It was none of his business who she'd been sleeping with.

And might sleep with again. He forced himself to face that fact. She'd said that geography would end the relationship, but the country was less than six hours across by jet. The other man might come to Maryland, or they might meet somewhere else. PDI field personnel traveled a lot.

His initial elation that Kate had agreed to Sam's deal began to subside into anxiety. She'd walked out on him once before, and she'd do it again in a New York minute if he gave her any excuse.

So he'd better not be jealous. Once he'd believed jealousy was proof of how much he loved her. Instead, it had contributed to messing up his mind until he'd struck her. Unforgivable.

How could he have hurt her as he did? How *could* he?

He cut off his circling, self-hating thoughts. Better to think of something useful, such as running the company that was now his, at least for the time being. Sam had been an idiosyncratic manager, and sorting things out was an uphill job.

Or he could think about Sam's death in an impossible accident.

Think about anything but Kate, and how much he still wanted her.

Kate awoke to the buzz of an unfamiliar alarm clock. It took a moment to remember where she was. Ah, yes, Mary-

land. Not yet six in the morning, with her tired body thinking she ought to be in California, sleeping peacefully. Say
what one would about the discomforts of crossing the continent in a wagon, at least the pioneers never had to worry
about jet lag.

Since she'd packed the night before, she could afford
another few minutes in bed. She dozed a little, missing
Ginger Bear's furry body next to her. A year without a cat
was in some ways worse than a year without a man.

A bad thought—it instantly triggered memories of sharing a bed with Donovan. It wasn't just the wonderful sex
she'd missed when they split up, but the affection. They'd
slept tangled like ivy, always touching even as positions
shifted in slumber. When they came to bed there would be
a brief period of settling in together—tucking a thigh between his knees, his head coming to rest on her shoulder.
They'd both give soft little exhalations of contentment as
they let go of the tensions of the day. She'd loved the
warm, solid feel of his body. The scent and saltiness of
him. The way his arm curved around to hold her close.
He'd been a world-class cuddler.

That had been true even at the end. Her grandmother
Corsi had died only a month before their marriage ended.
By that time the two of them had been lying side by side
like granite statues, not touching, each aching with alone-
ness.

She'd been awakened by a ringing phone at three in the
morning, the kind of call that never brought anything good.
Dopily she grabbed the receiver and propped it over her
ear without raising her head.

Julia's voice said without preamble, "Bad news, Kate.
Nonna Corsi had a stroke and died. It ... it was very
quick."

Kate swung her feet to the bare floor as her mother gave
her the name of the funeral home. The time and place for
what would be the first of several family gatherings. Yes,
your father is taking it hard, of course he is. But she had a

long, full life and went quickly. They could be grateful for that. Julia's voice cracked. She'd been closer to her mother-in-law than to her own mother.

Kate hung up, feeling as if her body temperature had dropped ten degrees. She began to shake. Widowed young, her Sicilian grandmother had cleaned houses to support her four children, encouraging them to get educations though she had never gone to high school herself. In the Highlandtown rowhouse Sam later bought her, she'd taken in foster children and bossed her family and made the best pasta fagiole in the world.

Donovan laid a warm hand on her spine. "What's happened, Kate?"

"Nonna's dead."

He swore under his breath. "Hell. I'm so sorry. She was special. Like my grandmother Russo." Gently he drew Kate into his arms and pulled her under the covers. Then he wrapped himself around her, using his body heat to dispel her trembling. "You're freezing, Kate. Do you want coffee or brandy or something?"

"No. Just . . . stay close." Then she wept. Donovan could be a crazy bastard sometimes, but she never forgot how he'd reached across their increasing estrangement to give her tenderness and comfort when she needed it.

Hard knuckles rapped on the door, jarring her back to the present. "Time to get up," Donovan called. "If you're decent, I'll bring in a cup of coffee."

Kate rolled from the bed and grabbed her long bathrobe. Tying her sash, she unlocked and opened the door.

Donovan, bright-eyed and fully dressed, held a mug of coffee in each hand. She accepted one, muttering, "Morning people. Ugh."

"Luckily I was able to get you a seat on my flight, but we'll have to leave in less than half an hour. Don't forget that wool can't be worn once we start loading explosives. A static charge could set off the whole shooting match." His gaze avoided her.

She flushed as she became aware of her state of undress. "Right. Go on. I'll be ready in twenty minutes."

Donovan had used to tease her about taking too much when they traveled. Not this time. She was traveling light, the perfect damned employee. She took a lightning-swift shower, then finished the coffee as she dressed.

Three minutes under her deadline, she headed out the door with the wheeled suitcase following her like a well-trained dog. Inwardly, she bubbled with excitement. It was finally time for a baptism of fire at Phoenix Demolition.

As the jet took off, Donovan said, "Time to find out how much you actually know about explosive demolition."

Kate came instantly alert. "Ask away."

"I'll start with something simple. What are the main construction types we deal with?"

"Reinforced concrete and structural steel," she said promptly.

"How do you prevent a structure from walking?"

"Walking? Right, that's what Sam called it when a building fell out full-length like a tree. By removing as many of the inner stiffeners, like elevator shafts and stairwells, as possible. That way, the building can be dropped straight down into its own footprint."

Speaking of footprints, her left shoe was touching his right foot. He moved his leg away. Even using his frequent flyer miles for first class didn't give enough space to keep a safe distance between them. Telling himself to concentrate on his quiz, he asked, "How do we control exactly how it falls?"

"By the timing of the charges." She started gesturing with her hands, Italian style. "Using different delays can kick the structure any way we want, if it's done right. Plus, having sequenced explosions spreads out the impact and reduces the chance of damaging nearby structures." One sweeping hand brushed his forearm. His skin tingled in response.

He made the questions harder, which had the benefit of keeping his mind more on the subject and less on her. By the time the jet was over West Virginia, he'd established that Kate understood the principles and the physics perfectly. Of course she didn't know the intricacies of engineering and implementation, but as an architect she already understood vectors and forces and transfer of loads. She was an ideal candidate to become a project manager.

He reminded himself that the explosives they used were mostly very stable and safe. Another part of his mind immediately pointed out that accidents happened, and buildings being prepped for demolition could be hazardous. *Very* hazardous.

Telling the multiple voices to shut up, he reached under the seat in front of him for his briefcase and pulled out a sheaf of papers. "Time to go from the general to the particular. This is the preliminary explosive plan for this project. It should be basically sound, but there's always fine tuning required before the shot."

She studied the drawings, which were simple elevations and plan views showing the shape of the building, structural supports, and proposed placements for explosive charges. "So we're going to take down the Nevada Palace."

"You've been there?"

"Not inside, but I've driven by." She smoothed a hand over the folds of the drawing that draped over her lap.

She'd always had lovely hands, not dainty and helpless, but well shaped and competent. He remembered watching those long fingers rubbing steel wool across a table she was refinishing. Chopping red peppers for a salad. Sliding down his body . . .

A wave of heat washed over him. He looked away, grateful that her attention was on the plans in front of her. "I've worked with Bill Berrigan, the developer, on a couple of other jobs, but this will be my first visit to this site because it was Sam's project. The hotel was built by a paranoid tycoon, and Sam mentioned that it's full of surprises. I'd hoped to visit earlier to check the place out, but I was too busy."

She was still frowning over the drawings. "So it isn't just my imagination that this is a very odd structure."

"I've thought the same thing. The final explosives plan may require more adjustments than usual." He considered telling her what else might happen in conjunction with this shot, then decided to wait until he knew for sure. Instead he began to explain the background and general approach to the project. Kate picked everything up so quickly that there was time for a nap before lunch.

But he couldn't sleep. Not with his ex-wife inches away—and untouchable.

Crossing the country two days in a row was a good way to become disoriented. Kate landed in Las Vegas with a devout hope that she wouldn't have to get on another airplane for at least a week.

Her sense of unreality increased when they entered the gigantic, high-ceilinged hall that contained the luggage carousels. Hundreds of people were milling about, which wasn't surprising in a busy airport. But she was startled to hear the magnificent chorus from the last movement of Beethoven's Ninth Symphony blaring over the loudspeakers. The effect was surreal, to say the least. And there was neon. Lots of neon, even though it was midday. "Viva Las Vegas."

"I've always thought of this city as Disneyland for adults."

Her gaze went to a towering aluminum palm tree. One of many. "There's no danger of Las Vegas expiring from an excess of good taste."

"All of those years in California, and you're still an Eastern snob at heart."

She smiled with lethal precision. "Did you ever get one of those Elvis-on-velvet paintings that you yearned for?"

"Careful, or I'll actually buy one and hang it in the breakfast nook."

She returned his smile before she realized the danger. Humor was one of the most seductive things about a man. Dangerous, because it was hard to be angry with a man who made you laugh.

Donovan had sworn not to touch her, but she suspected that he wouldn't mind charming her into touching him. The hell of it was, he might succeed. Less than twenty-four hours together, and already they were bantering. It was hard to remember the past when enjoying the present.

She pulled her suitcase from the carousel. "I can't believe that we're actually working together. My father was about as subtle as a freight train."

Donovan retrieved his own bag, then led the way through the crowd toward the exit. "Sam might have been a freight train, but in any showdowns between him and the steel magnolia, who always won?"

"Mother always did, in the most ladylike way imaginable."

"And you're a bud off the old magnolia. Neither man nor beast nor raging freight train will push you into anything you don't want. I learned that very early."

"Would it be better if I'd been a doormat and let you walk all over me?"

"No. Of course not." He hesitated before continuing. "But sometimes I've wondered if there might have been a middle path between total submission and total abandonment. Maybe if we'd worked on it. If we'd asked for help—"

"No!" She didn't like the way this conversation was going. "That wasn't an option."

She had to believe that, because the possibility that their marriage might have been saved was too painful to contemplate.

13

As Donovan turned the rental car into the vast parking lot of the Nevada Palace, Kate shaded her eyes against the pale winter sun and studied their target. An octagonal structure covered with glittering glass, the casino hotel stood on Las Vegas Boulevard, the broad street more familiarly known as the Strip. The building had been considered high style when it went up in the late nineteen-fifties.

Clustered around the Palace were cranes and lifts and other heavy equipment, along with giant construction Dumpsters to hold debris. Turning away from the activity, Donovan pulled up by a mobile site office in one corner of the parking lot.

Inside, an attractive, middle-aged woman with black hair and an imperturbable expression worked at the front desk while a gruff male voice could be heard barking orders into a phone behind a partition. The woman glanced up when the door opened. "Nice to see you again, Donovan. Bull is in his office."

"I can hear him bellowing," Donovan said. "Kate, meet Carmen Velasquez, the power behind the throne of Berrigan Enterprises."

"I heard that, you unreliable Irishman," the gruff voice roared. A moment later the speaker emerged from behind the partition, a smoking cigar in one hand. It was easy to see why Bill Berrigan had been nicknamed "Bull." A brawny man in his fifties, he looked exactly like what he was—someone who'd worked his way up from laborer to contractor to multimillionaire developer. "Brought your girlfriend along so you could have some Vegas fun in your spare time?"

"Hardly," Donovan said. "Meet my professional associate, Kate Corsi."

Bull's bushy brows rose. "Sam's daughter? Pleased to meet you, honey. I was real sorry about what happened to your dad. He was a helluva guy."

"That he was. We all miss him."

The developer's face brightened. "Didn't Sam say you were an architect?"

"Could be," she admitted, pleased her father had mentioned her.

"Then you'll want to see what's going up in place of the Palace. C'mon, I've got the model in here."

Kate and Donovan followed him around the partition. In one corner of the crowded office was an elaborate architectural model. Berrigan proudly gestured toward it. "I'm going to build a theme hotel called the Harem. Pretty, isn't it?"

Kate studied the model, which showed an array of domes and palmed courtyards and graceful arches. It made her think of the Alhambra on steroids and would make an architectural purist cringe, but what the heck, sometimes good taste was boring. "This will be a wonderful fantasy destination."

"Exactly. A family resort, too. See that back courtyard? The camel rides will be there." After a moment of fond regard, he turned away from the model. "But first we gotta get rid of that ugly glass box." He dropped into his swivel chair, waving for them to take seats. "Two people don't seem like enough to do the job. Thought you were going to be here with bells on as soon as I hollered."

"I assumed that you might holler before the prep work was quite finished," Donovan said. "Was I wrong?"

Bull chuckled, unabashed. "Nope. There are a couple of

days of work still to do on the lower floors, but you can get started on the upper levels now."

"After I've checked the place over and confirmed the schedule, I'll call in more men from Maryland."

Bull brandished his cigar. "Just got some good news. Hank Hawkins definitely wants to use this shot in his current movie, which will be good publicity for the Harem, as well as making us a few bucks. It won't affect your work, will it?"

Kate arched her brows at the reference to one of Hollywood's top action directors, but Donovan was unfazed. "Hardly at all. I talked to Hawkins several weeks ago. Basically, he just wants a nighttime explosion with lots of flames. Adding a few hundred gallons of aviation fuel to the shot will give him that. And maybe some commercial-grade fireworks, if he wants extra razzle-dazzle."

Kate felt a pulse of excitement. It wasn't uncommon for PDI shots to be incorporated into movies—in fact, film rights were a substantial source of income for the company—but it was pure luck to have that happen on her first job. Fun! Trying to sound businesslike, she said, "Sounds great, but will the movie people delay the demolition? Donovan said this project is on a rush schedule."

"They're going to do location shooting in Vegas anyhow, so it will work out real nice. Hawkins swears he'll have his film crew and actors here tomorrow or the next day." Bull grinned. "Carmen is swooning at the prospect of seeing Kenzie Scott, but Raine Marlowe is the one I want to meet. What a babe."

"I do not swoon," Carmen called over the partition. "Not even for the sexiest man alive, which *People* magazine assures us that Kenzie is."

"Rainey is going to be here?" Kate said.

"Yes," Donovan said. "I didn't want to tell you until the deal was confirmed."

"It will be great to see her again."

"You know Raine Marlowe?" Bull exclaimed.

"We went to school together. I haven't seen much of her in the last few years, but we keep in touch."

"Well, I'll be a son of a bitch," Bull said. "You hang out with Raine Marlowe."

Carmen's sleek dark head appeared around the partition, her eyes bright with interest. "Is Raine's hair really that red-blond color, or does she dye it?"

"It's natural," Kate assured. "The first time I saw her, I thought she had the prettiest hair in the world."

"She and Kenzie make a beautiful couple," Carmen said dreamily. "It was so romantic, the way they met making *The Scarlet Pimpernel*. People say it was the greatest on- and offscreen chemistry since Bogart met Bacall."

Not for the first time Kate gave thanks for the fact that her own life wasn't treated as public property. She often wondered how Rainey, an essentially private person, could stand it. The price of success.

Bull regarded Carmen with disgust. "A movie junkie. And here I thought you were a sensible woman."

Carmen gazed at him haughtily. "The hot air is building up in here. If you aren't careful, the state health department will close this trailer down." She walked to the window and tugged a pull chain to activate a vent fan, then left, her voluptuous figure swaying provocatively.

"Sometimes I wonder why I keep that woman around," Bull muttered.

"For the great sex," Carmen called.

When Bull blushed beet red, Donovan grinned at Kate. "I neglected to mention that these two are married."

"I thought it would be cheaper to marry her than keep paying an extortionate salary."

"Boy, was he wrong!" Carmen caroled over the partition.

"I'll take you over to the Palace." Bull plucked a down vest and a hard hat from a peg on the wall. "Since Carmen is already hassling me, you might as well, too." Despite his complaints, he gave his wife a thorough kiss on the way out.

Outside, Donovan stopped by the rental car and opened the trunk. After rummaging in his luggage, he pulled out two hard hats and tossed one to Kate. "Here."

"Thanks." The shiny white hard hat was screened with the PDI logo on the front and sides. After she put it on, he handed her a two-way radio, a match for the one he hooked to his belt. Donovan might wish that she'd stuck to needlework, but he was treating her like a real coworker.

They climbed into Bull's pickup truck and he drove them the short distance across the parking lot to the Palace. There was a bite to the wind, but the temperature was still a relief after the bitter cold of Baltimore.

With its shining, mirrored windows in place, the building looked normal enough for movie use. Then Bull drove around to the back. Debris generated by the soft-stripping process was removed from this side, so banks of windows were broken or missing.

All three of them climbed to the highest of the five shot floors, which were the levels where explosives would be placed. Inside the Palace, the illusion of normalcy vanished. The hotel was a shell of its former self, the interior echoing with the harsh sounds of the demolition work being done. The shot floors were being completely stripped of furniture, carpeting, and non-load-bearing walls, leaving bare concrete floors, concentric rings of support columns, and emptiness.

As Kate sniffed the distinctively acrid, dusty scent of a stripped building, she wondered about the human dramas that had been played out here—honeymoons and holidays, business trips and illicit rendezvous. In a matter of days these listening walls would be gone, taking their memories with them.

She glanced at Donovan. Backlit by the light that poured in the windows, he looked lithe and strong and completely at home, like a lion prowling the savanna. For a moment she was struck again by the sheer weirdness of the situation— how after years of separation, she and her ex-husband were now working and living together. It was stranger than anything she could have imagined.

Unaware of her thoughts, Donovan said to Berrigan, "Sam told me this place was pretty eccentric, but didn't give any details. What have you found?"

"For starters, no blueprints. Ray Farmer, the guy who built the palace as his personal playpen, was loony as a goose—as each floor was finished, he had the contractor burn the plans."

"Bizarre," Kate said.

"Gets even stranger." Bull gestured to a rectangular hole in the concrete floor. Looking through, identical holes could be seen in every floor below all the way down to the basement. "I thought this would be a utility well for plumbing and wiring. Turned out to be a secret staircase that ran all the way from Farmer's penthouse down to a hidden exit on the street. God only knows who snuck in and out that way."

"Starlets, if Farmer's reputation is to be believed." Donovan looked into the open space. "Time to start checking if your boys have done the prep work properly."

Berrigan groaned. "All the times I've worked with PDI, you still don't expect me to do the job right. You gonna make me walk through every square foot of every floor?"

"Not at all. Kate and I will do it. The inviolable law of explosive demolition—take nothing for granted."

That had been one of Sam's guiding principles, she remembered. A compulsive streak was essential for this kind of work.

"Have fun," Berrigan said. "I'll get back to the office." He touched his hard hat in an informal salute to Kate, then left them to their work.

When the developer was gone, Donovan said, "Now it's time to get acquainted with this building. Find out all her strengths and weaknesses and secrets. Then we can bring her down." He made a slow circle, his gaze going to every corner of the empty floor. "Usually a project manager has weeks or months to study a building. This time I'll have to learn it in three or four days."

"Then it's time we got to work," she said briskly. "What do you want me to do?"

He led her around, explaining what she should look for. Any stiffening elements that should have been removed but hadn't been. Oddities that might have been uncovered during the stripping process. Anything that might complicate the implosion of the building. His explanation helped pull her rather erratic knowledge of the business into a more unified whole.

On the next lower shot floor, he said, "This time you take the lead."

Kate was slower than Donovan, but by the time she finished the inspection, she was getting the hang of it. Doing this work that had been her father's life gave her an uncanny sense of connection with him. Suppressing the thought that Sam should have been the one to train her, not Donovan, she finished her survey of the floor.

When she was done, Donovan said, "Continue with the lower floors while I go to Bull's trailer and call the office. It may be a while until I come back—the administrative side of the business is pretty chaotic at the moment."

"I can see why, since you're doing both your job and Sam's."

"On top of that, a lot of time has been taken up with the accident investigation."

"The state fire marshal's office?"

"Plus the state police, and the state health and safety inspectors because there was a fatality. Everyone who worked on that job has been interviewed at least three times."

She guessed that such interviews had left Donovan beating up on himself mentally the whole time. "Accidents happen."

"Yes. But we need to find out why so it never happens again. The fire marshals are sifting through the building debris with mesh screens. I hope to God they find out what happened soon." The lines around his eyes deepened. "I'll see you later. If you notice anything you don't understand, make a note of it and talk to me later. Assume nothing. Ninety percent of what happens in an implosion is predictable, but there are always some surprises. It's our job to make sure that there are as few as possible."

He left, knowing he would have to check Kate's work later, but thinking that she needed a chance to work on her own. The sooner she was qualified to work independently, the better for the firm.

His call to the office ran longer than expected. Not only did Janie, the office manager, need to talk to him, but half the other employees as well. Janie ended with the ominous promise to fax paperwork to his hotel.

Getting away back to the Palace was a relief. Kate had inspected two more floors. He asked, "Any problems?"

Her gaze swept the vast space. "I don't think this building has any cross beams. The drawings you showed me on the plane assumed beams, but I think the floors are just slabs of concrete hung from the columns and the elevator core in the middle of the building."

He gave a soft whistle. "Damn, I think you're right. That explains why this structure has been giving me an itchy feeling. More eccentricity to lay at the builder's door. The explosives plan is going to require major revisions."

"Good. I can watch you do the calculations."

"The sooner you learn how, the sooner I'll make you do the work," he warned.

"You do that," Kate said with a spontaneous smile.

For the moment, at least, they were partners again.

14

It was dusk by the time Kate and Donovan finished surveying the hotel. After they climbed into opposite sides of the rental car, Kate asked, "Now that you've seen the place, how does the timetable look?"

"The soft stripping should be finished by the end of the day tomorrow. Having the movie crew come in gives us a couple of extra days beyond that—enough time to work up a new explosives plan and implement it before Bull starts tossing his horns." Donovan started the car and drove to the parking area exit, waiting for a gap to appear in the heavy traffic. "I called Luther and Jim. They'll arrive tomorrow."

Traffic thinned, and he pulled onto the Strip. Kate noticed lines of weariness around his eyes. Of course, he was on East Coast time, where it was well into the evening. Here, the gaudy lights of Las Vegas were coming on, turning the night to carnival. "Will four people be enough?"

"Luther's the most experienced man in the office, and Jim is head of engineering as well as a project manager." He braked for a red light. "We can have that building ready to go pretty quickly once the explosives plan is set. You'll earn your pay."

Pay? She hadn't thought about what salary she'd get. Eventually she'd have to negotiate a reasonable sharing of the household expenses, but she didn't have the energy to tackle Donovan about that yet. "I remember the first job you did on your own, that office building in St. Louis. All the charges went off, but it didn't come down."

"Don't remind me! I was scared to death when I went inside to figure out what had happened. Every column in the place was gone, but the building still stood. I expected it to fall on my head at any second. I almost wished it would—the whole thing was damned embarrassing."

Kate had been alarmed when Donovan phoned her that night and told her the story, though at the time he had treated the misfire as a hilarious joke on himself. That was the moment when she'd really recognized how dangerous explosive demolition was. As a child, she'd thought the process was a kind of magic, and that her father and his company were infallible. But they weren't. Even someone as smart and careful as Donovan could make a potentially lethal miscalculation. "As I recall, the whole structure was supported by a single beam that you'd underestimated. You never did that again."

"I sometimes wondered if Sam let me make that mistake just to teach me a lesson. If so, it worked. Every project I've done since has been calculated six ways from zero."

"No more buildings that fail to come down." Kate started to smile, then stopped when she realized that they had slid into another moment of intimacy. A shared past was a dangerous bond. "Where are we staying?"

"A suite at the Grand Maya."

Their destination was coming into view. One of the gaudier hotel casinos, it was shaped like a giant step pyramid, surrounded by lush jungle gardens, and bathed in colored spotlights. "I thought PDI was counting pennies."

"Berrigan is part owner of the Grand Maya, so he's comping us the suite."

They both fell silent as fatigue kicked in. It had been a very long day, and it wasn't over yet. Kate sighed. Demolition was easy; shacking up was hard.

To reach the front desk of the hotel, they had to pass a hall full of raucous, nightmarishly jangling slot machines. Assault by electronic muggers. After registering, they took a glass elevator up the central atrium to one of the top steps of the pyramid.

Kate groaned when they entered their suite. It was decorated in Love Nest Modern, the wide windows bracketed by flamboyant draperies, a chrome-paneled bar, and lots of white carpeting and mirrors. A blatant invitation to sin, Las Vegas style. "This place looks like a bordello."

"But a high-class one. Take your choice of the bedrooms."

She wheeled her suitcase into the nearer one and was unsurprised to see that the bed was set on a carpeted dais, with a mirror on the ceiling. The view of sparkling city lights outside was much more to her taste. "Suit yourself for dinner. I'm going to shower and call room service."

"That's exactly what I'm planning," Donovan said. "If our meals arrive together, would you object to our eating at the same table at the same time?"

"I suppose it would be pretty silly to take my food into the bedroom just to get away from you." It wasn't a very gracious acceptance, but Donovan smiled at her words.

Exasperated, she locked the door, then dug out her toiletries bag, peeled off her clothes, and headed for the bathroom. Sam had known it would be impossible for her to be stiff and formal with Donovan for a whole year. She hadn't even managed a full day.

On a superficial level, Donovan was easy to have around. Amusing. Considerate. Sinfully attractive. No wonder her diabolical father had assumed that regular contact might make her rethink why she had ended the marriage.

She turned on the shower and waited for the temperature to stabilize. It had been her choice to ask for a divorce without explaining why. From a murky mixture of guilt and compassion, she'd chosen to look like the villain of the breakup. If she'd revealed her reasons, Sam would have gone after Donovan with a horsewhip. It would have cost her husband his job with PDI, and a good deal more. She hadn't wanted that.

Had it been a mistake to conceal the truth? Maybe. There were those who argued that the truth, no matter how ugly, was always better than lies. Kate wasn't so sure. She'd chosen the path that seemed as if it would cause the least damage to Donovan and her family. Though it really hadn't been a choice—her shame and humiliation about the situation had left her unable to talk about what happened then, or now.

Belatedly noticing that the bathroom had filled with steam, she adjusted the water and climbed under the hot spray. Like cats and ice cream, showers were among life's simple, uncomplicated pleasures.

Donovan heard the phone ring on the suite fax machine while he was drying after his shower. Probably Janie following through on her promise to send any paperwork he needed to see. Oh, joy, he could work on that as well as the explosives plan.

But Kate would be around, which would be nice. Very nice. How many nights had he spent alone in hotel rooms over the last dozen years? Too damned many.

Though Kate was keeping her distance physically and emotionally, he felt a sense of comfort, of rightness, in her presence that was downright scary. Reconciliation after so many years, so much water over the dam, was not an option. Yet he still felt as if he'd known her for a dozen lifetimes, though someone like him, who'd been educated by Jesuits, wasn't supposed to think about reincarnation.

One of many things that had fascinated him about the Corsis was the way different religions had coexisted side by side within the same family. Early in their relationship, Kate had explained that Sam had wanted Julia enough to agree to marry in her church. Afterward, her parents had adopted a centuries-old way of dealing with religious differences—sons were raised in the father's religion, and daughters in the mother's. Luckily Sam and Julia had one of each, so Tom was a devout Catholic, Kate an Episcopalian who went to a Quaker school. In addition, Julia had encouraged her children in reading about and discussing other religions. Very different from the unquestioningly Catholic neighborhood he'd grown up in.

He dressed and went into the living room. Kate was standing by the fax machine, staring at a sheaf of papers. Her hair was damp, and she'd put on a long blue robe that managed to cover her entirely, yet look enticingly feminine.

"Reading my office mail?"

She looked up, eyes like flint. "I saw a letterhead from the state fire marshal's office, so I took a look. I thought it might be the report on Sam's death, but apparently it's more of a status update from the lead investigator, a Chief Stanski."

"Phil Stanski and I have gone over the floor plans of the Jefferson Arms, the wiring diagrams, the explosives manifest—anything that might provide a clue. Is he ready to write a final report?"

"Not yet. Read this."

He sat down and skimmed the letter, reading the last page twice. "Jesus. So Stanski thinks that some damned implosion junkie got into the building and tampered with a blasting cap, not realizing the possible consequences. Sam might have triggered the detonation of the cap by investigating. Because that job used a nonelectric initiation system, the blast propagated through the whole structure rather than being limited to a single charge."

"What's an implosion junkie?"

"PDI fascinates people." He set the faxed letter on the end table. "There's even a club. Fans travel all over to see implosions in person. That's harmless, but there are people out there who want to poke around job sites, not to mention the nutcases who want to steal some dynamite for their very own. That's why we post guards twenty-four hours a day once explosives are brought on-site."

"Could someone like that have gotten into the Jefferson Arms?"

"The weather was bitter cold. It wouldn't be surprising if a guard holed up in a corner and didn't do his job. Total security is a myth even under the best of conditions."

"So my father might have died because some kid got in and tampered with something he didn't understand," she said, her voice bitter.

Donovan faced the likelihood that Sam's death had been a result of vandalism rather than a real accident. *Shit.* "I'm afraid so."

"Since he was doing the walk-through, I assume you were at the other end of a two-way radio. Did he mention seeing anything unusual just . . . just before the explosion?"

"Actually, he did. When he went to check, the blast went off, so Stanski's probably right."

"What happens now?"

"Because there was a fatality, the investigation will stay open until they reach a firm conclusion." He wondered how long that would take. A conclusion would make it possible to start coming to terms with the raw wound of Sam's death.

"At least you can stop feeling guilty. He didn't die because of a mistake you made."

"Maybe not. But if someone tampered with one of the charges and left a sign that Sam saw, I should have seen it first."

"You're overdoing the guilt, Donovan. You weren't the only one working on that job. No one else noticed anything wrong, either."

He considered telling her that he lived with guilt, that it was his middle name. But she probably already knew that.

Over room-service seafood ravioli, Kate started to learn the art and science of designing an explosives plan. The food and drink were gone and the trays long since put outside when Donovan pushed back the pile of papers spread on the table between them. "You're picking this up faster than anyone I've ever taught."

"Maybe I'm drawing on buried memories of things I overheard in my years of hanging around the office." She rolled her neck to work out the kinks. "The information you're giving me about timing delays and kinds of explosives and controlling the blasts—is any of it codified anywhere? Is there a Big Book of Explosive Demolition I could study?"

He leaned back in his chair. The lamplight played over his face, emphasizing the angles. "Not really—a lot of our techniques were invented at PDI, and they're proprietary information. For the last couple of years, though, I've been putting together a database of variables and results on all kinds of PDI jobs. It'll never be a substitute for experience, but it gave me an excuse to pick the brains of the senior staff members about their most memorable projects."

"So some of Sam's expertise lives on." She was glad of that. "And of course you have all those fabulous videotapes of buildings being imploded."

"I turned one film clip of a falling bridge into a screen saver on my computer."

She laughed. Leave it to Donovan.

A warm stillness stretched between them. Then came tension. Sexual tension, as unmistakable as the ebony table between them.

After a moment of acute mutual awareness, Donovan said, "I'm beat. Guess it's time for bed."

Bed. A simple word, and a too-vivid euphemism for sex. With hallucinogenic clarity, she remembered the times when she came to bed late and he was already sleeping, his beautiful bare body sprawled under the covers. She would slide in next to him and wrap an arm around his waist. Even asleep, he'd respond, turning to draw her close.

Sometimes he'd wake and perhaps press his lips to her temple while his hand drifted to her breast. Or she might lazily explore to see what she might find. In those days they'd regarded each other's body as joint property. Even when she was dead tired, it was surprising how swiftly desire could rise and dissolve fatigue. Middle-of-the-night sex was soft and slow and tender, a bringer of pleasant dreams.

They'd lost so much, so damned much. Near panic, she jumped to her feet and headed to her bedroom. "Since we're going to be here for several days, I'll rent a car of my own. No reason for you to have to haul me around."

"You can run, Kate, but you can't hide," he said softly.

"Want to bet?" She bolted into her room and slammed the door behind her. After turning the lock, she leaned against the door, shaking.

The hell of it was, he was right. As much as she wanted to deny the attraction between them, as much as she would like to control it by sheer will, she couldn't.

You can run, Kate, but you can't hide.

15

It was almost too cold for the dogs. They did their business quickly, not even pausing to check if other canines had left messages at the bushes along the quiet lane. Charles Hamilton walked briskly, as anxious to get out of the bitter night as Tort, the golden retriever, and Retort, the anybody's-guess mutt.

Rather than walking up his long curving driveway, he cut across the moon-flooded lawn, the frozen grass snapping under his heavy shoes. Cold though the winter had been, at least there hadn't yet been much snow.

As he headed toward the back door, he saw a car turn into his driveway and climb to the house rather faster than vehicles usually approached. Who would be visiting at this hour?

The moonlight was bright enough to identify Julia Corsi's silver Mercedes. She had turned off the engine and lights, but was still sitting inside, a darker profile in the shadowed interior.

He tapped at the car window. "Julia?"

She climbed out, her face a pale oval and her ankle-length wool skirt sweeping gracefully over high black boots. The dogs twined around her. "I hadn't decided whether or not to come in. It's late."

He glanced at her jacket. It was far too light for the weather. "Not that late. Come on inside before you freeze to death." He took her arm and guided her toward the front door.

The warmth of the two-story-high entryway struck like a blow, albeit a welcome one. The dramatic hall, with its sweeping staircase descending across a huge leaded-glass window, was cherished by brides seeking memorable wedding pictures. His older daughter, Sandy, had looked wonderful there. He hoped that one day Rachel would pose there for a bridal portrait, but so far, no luck. Apparently doctors were too busy to date.

"How about some hot chocolate? It seems appropriate to the weather."

Slowly she removed her hat and jacket, revealing a beautiful sweater in shimmering peacock colors. "That sounds . . . nice."

After hanging their coats, he led the way into the kitchen and took milk from the refrigerator. Julia perched on the antique walnut bench, rubbing her arms for warmth. "You've taken up cooking."

"If I didn't have a housekeeper I'd starve, but I have picked up a few basics. I figure that a man with a law degree ought to be able to heat milk without burning it."

The powerful kitchen light showed lines in her face and silver threaded through her blond hair, but she was still a striking woman. Or would be, if she didn't look so drawn. He made mental calculations as he went to the cupboard for cocoa. "Good Lord, Julia, I just realized that we've known each other for over fifty years."

"I remember the day we met. You pulled my pigtails."

"I had to get your attention somehow." He leaned against the counter, keeping an eye on the saucepan of milk. "You were more interested in my sister's dolls than in me."

"The older I get, the more I realize how much life is an accumulation of details and textures. How much we depend on the comfort of the familiar. It never would have occurred to me on the day we met that you and I would end up knowing each other our whole lives."

"You probably wouldn't have liked the idea then. Isn't that why you broke our engagement all those years ago? I was *too* familiar."

"That was part of it." She fidgeted with the golden hoops of her engagement and wedding rings.

Had he ever seen her fidget before? Not that he could remember. "You look ready to jump out of your skin, Julia. Have you thought about getting away for a while?"

Tort nudged Julia's knee. She brushed his silky golden head. "Tom is urging me to visit him, but at the moment it seems like too much effort."

He didn't like the sound of that, but the milk was ready to boil so he took it off the burner and mixed in the cocoa. After pouring the steaming beverage into large mugs, he stirred a measure of hazelnut liqueur into each mug and added a healthy dollop of whipped topping from the refrigerator, along with a dusting of nutmeg. "Here you are. Guaranteed to overcome the coldest winter night."

She sipped, then licked off a whipped-cream mustache as delicately as a cat. "I'm impressed."

"I'm thinking about retiring from my law firm and becoming a bartender. It's time for a career change."

"You're joking, aren't you?"

"I am about becoming a bartender, but I am ready for

some changes. Probably I'll be offered the next seat that opens up on the circuit-court bench. I think it would be interesting. Less money, but maybe more useful."

"Congratulations. You'd make a wonderful judge."

"I hope so. The older I get, the more I understand how vital the law is to a healthy society." He led her into the large, casual family room next to the kitchen, turning the dimmer switch to bring the lights to a restful level. Then he picked up a remote and turned on the gas logs in the fireplace. "This fire doesn't crackle like wood, but it has the virtue of being easy."

Julia sank onto the wide sofa in front of the fire. In her subtly patterned skirt and hand-knit sweater, she looked like an illustration from an upscale country-living magazine. He sat beside her and stretched out his legs as a gust of bone-chilling February wind rattled the windows. It was a good night to be beside a fire. The dogs trotted in from the kitchen and flopped in front of the hearth. Like him, they weren't as young as they used to be, and enjoyed their comforts.

They drank in silence, until he said, "This spring I'm going to put the house on the market."

She gave him a startled glance. "Charles, no. This is such a wonderful place. So much you. I can't imagine you living anywhere else."

"So much me and Barbara, you mean. I took my time, like everyone advised, and didn't do anything rash after she died, but it's been two years now. This is far too much space for one person. By the time I get home, LaDonna has left for the day. I see her so seldom it's like having my housekeeping and cooking done by elves."

He finished his cocoa and set the mug on the end table. "It might be different if the girls were in and out of here, but Sandy and her family are in Chicago, and I seldom see Rachel even though she's only an hour away. I rattle around here with the dogs like a penny in a bass drum."

"I suppose you're right." She sighed. "So many changes,

Charles. Inside I don't feel that differently from when I was twenty. But now my life is effectively over, even though I might live another thirty years."

"You're hurting now, but your life isn't over. You've always been an active woman with endless friends and interests."

"That doesn't help!" Suddenly she hurled her empty mug at the fireplace. It smashed on the fieldstone mantel and fell onto the hearth. "They'll all be couples, like Noah's Ark, while I'm alone. So *alone*."

Shocked by her unexpected action and aching for her grief, he put his arms around her. "It will get better, Julia, I swear it."

Her fingers dug into his arms as if she was drowning and he was a life preserver. "I can believe that in my head, but not my heart."

He stroked her hair, as if she was one of his daughters when they were small. She smelled like nutmeg. "Take it one day at a time, Julia, and don't ever be afraid to ask your friends for help. Believe me, we all want to do whatever we can."

When the policeman had come to the house to give him the news of Barbara's death, he had been so numb that the officer hadn't wanted to leave him alone and had asked for the phone number of a friend. Fifteen minutes later Julia was beside him, using one hand to anchor him to sanity and the other to call the girls and other family members to break the horrible news. And now, damnably, she was facing her own ultimate grief, and he was nowhere near as good at comforting as she had been.

Lightly he pressed his lips to her temple, not with passion but deep affection, a wordless promise that he would always be there for her. She turned her face upward, her anguished gaze meeting his.

He wasn't sure which of them moved, but their lips came together. Soft and warm and responsive, her mouth was not that of a friend. For a timeless moment sensation blazed between them, the instinctive attraction of male and female. Then he jerked his head away. "Sorry. I . . . I don't know quite how that happened."

"It happened because . . . because I wanted it to happen." She touched his cheek with shaking fingers. "Make love to me, Charles. Please."

He wondered if he'd misheard. "I think that would come under the heading of doing something rash."

"I don't care! I feel numb to my bones." She gave a hiccup of laughter. "It isn't only missing Sam, though I do, terribly. Frankly, part of it is the fear that . . . that I'll never feel real intimacy again. That I'm too old and dry and unattractive. Used up and worthless. That probably shocks you. Do you know why I married Sam? Because with him I felt like the sexiest, most desirable woman on earth. When you and I were engaged, it was a passionless arrangement, something we decided on because we were fond of each other, not because we were crazy in love."

His common sense began to crack. "That was because you weren't attracted to me, Julia, not because I wasn't attracted to you. I fell in love with you when I was seven years old. I kept hoping you'd feel the same way, but when we finally got engaged, you were the original ice princess, far too ladylike for passion."

"I didn't know anything about passion then." Hesitantly she laid her hand on his arm, barely denting his heavy sweater. "I've . . . learned a lot since then."

Doing as she asked would be a mistake, he knew it.

To hell with good sense. Sliding his fingers into her frosted blond hair, he bent his head for a kiss, not the chaste salute of long friendship, but an exploration and a question. She tasted of hazelnut and cocoa and tears. Her cool fingers slid around his neck, but her mouth was hot with yearning.

He had also learned a great deal since the last time they'd kissed. How to express passion, how to create it in his partner. Even so, he was stunned by the intensity of her response. She was frantic to lose herself, to drown in sensation if only for a handful of moments. This was Julia, who'd held the chubby hands of his daughters, just as he had taught her children to sail. She was the friend who'd offered good advice in the sometimes stormy early days of his marriage, who had always been there in the anguished months after Barbara's death.

And she was a woman he'd always desired. Barbara had been the light of his life, finding hidden areas in his soul that he hadn't known existed, yet he'd never stopped caring for Julia. Now the embers of desire burst into flame, as mind hazing as if he were twenty instead of almost sixty. With his last shred of good sense, he said hoarsely, "This is a mistake."

"*I don't care.*" Her hand moved down his body.

They came together with fierce urgency, heavy folds of her skirt crushing between them. Passion took command, burningly alive, wholly satisfying, as they obliterated themselves and the wounds of living in each other.

Afterward, as they lay panting in each other's arms, he felt more at peace than at any time since Barbara's death. He tugged an afghan over them. Julia turned away from him, her back pressed against his chest.

He smoothed her tangled hair gently, then realized that she was crying. "Julia, what's wrong?"

Not looking at him, she whispered, "You were right, this was a mistake."

"Only if you let it be. We're both well past the age of consent, and not exactly at high risk for any terrible diseases. Most important, we're not betraying anyone. We have every right to be together if that's what we want."

"Sam hasn't even been dead a month!"

"He loved you, Julia. He wouldn't have denied you what comfort you could find with a friend." He hesitated. "The last time I saw him, he . . . he told me to look out for you."

"I doubt that this is what he had in mind." She stood and swiftly put her appearance to rights. "I'm sorry for dragging you into my misery, Charles. It wasn't fair of me."

"For God's sake, Julia, don't apologize!"

She stepped over the dogs and bolted for the kitchen, moving with the speed of a first-class tennis player.

"And don't run away!" He went after her, and promptly tripped over Retort. By the time he disentangled himself from the dog, the Mercedes was barreling down the long drive toward Ruxton Road, blending into the moonlight-silvered trees.

Swearing, he stood in the door and watched her go. The sound of her car faded away, leaving only the hard, icy rattle of twigs in the night wind and a distant hum of traffic on the Jones Falls Expressway. His hands dropped to the heads of the dogs, who had followed him to the door.

Julia was right, having sex had been a mistake. Before, one of them had been miserable.

Now they both were.

16

In Las Vegas, the twenty-four-hour city, Kate was able to call for a rental car at midnight and have it waiting after she breakfasted at the coffee shop the next morning. She had sneaked out of the suite early to avoid Donovan.

Though she reached the job site before eight, he was already there. He walked out of the Palace as she parked her car, carrying a chopped broom handle in one hand and a stick of dynamite in the other. "Time for your first lesson in the nuts and bolts of the business, Kate. We're going to do a test shot."

Donning her hard hat, she said, "Ready when you are."

Together they climbed to the lowest of the shot floors and walked to a support column at the back of the building. A large pneumatic drill lay on the floor beside the column, and safety equipment, including goggles and ear protection, was stacked nearby.

"Ever use a feed leg drill?" Donovan asked. "These suckers weigh eighty pounds, which is why the bore holes are done by two-men crews. One person guides, the other holds the drill and keeps the pressure behind. You won't have to do this often, but you need to know how if you're going to be the boss."

Drilling holes in concrete was an aspect of explosive demolition that hadn't figured in Kate's childhood dreams, but she wasn't going to say that to Donovan. If she wanted this job, she had to be willing to be a laborer as well as an engineer. "I haven't used this type of drill, but I've operated smaller ones. I'll manage."

He gave her a brisk lesson on technique before they both donned safety equipment. Then he scooped up the drill, making it look easy, and drilled a pilot hole in the floor about six feet from the column with a shattering burst of noise.

After bracing the leg of the drill in the pilot hole, he said, "I'll guide the business end. You control the drill itself. You'll probably hit rebar, and you'll know when that happens, but keep going. The drill bit is carbide and designed to cut through steel."

She took hold of the drill, and almost dropped the damned thing. Eighty pounds was *heavy,* even with the support of a leg brace. If Donovan was amused by her clumsiness, he had the grace not to show it.

Donovan helped her wrestle the drill into position and wrapped a gloved hand above the chuck. Cautiously she compressed the handle grip switch. The drill kicked like a mule and made enough racket to raise the dead, but to her pleasure, she could handle it.

Boring into the column took concentration and strength.

The vibrations jangled through her hands and arms while dust and pulverized concrete spat from the deepening hole. About nine inches into the column, she hit a piece of rebar, one of the steel rods that provided the reinforcement in "reinforced concrete." Donovan had been right that she'd know when that happened—the drill shrieked and bucked, but she held on tight and kept going.

Inch by inch, she bored into the heart of the pillar. There seemed to be a *lot* of rebar. She couldn't say that she'd like doing this all day, every day, but there was a heady satisfaction in attacking concrete and steel, and winning.

When she judged that the hole was a little more than halfway through the column, she withdrew the drill and released the grip switch. Blessed silence.

Donovan helped her lower the drill, then picked up his broom handle rod and slid it into the hole. "You got the depth right. Now it's time to load your first explosive." He presented her with the stick of dynamite.

She was finally getting to play with explosives! She took the stick.

He pulled a brass punch from a loop on his belt and the thin metallic tube of a blasting cap from a pocket. "Punch a hole in one end of the stick and slide the blasting cap in. Always use brass for this, not iron, to avoid sparking."

The blasting cap was a narrow cylinder with two wires, one green and one red, attached at the end. After uncoiling the wires, she inserted the cap into the hole she'd made, leaving the wires trailing out.

Donovan showed her how to tie the wires around the stick in a half hitch. Then she used the broom handle to push the explosive into the drilled hole. So far, so good. "Isn't a sandbag usually put in to keep the force concentrated within the column rather than blowing out the hole?"

"Your memory is good." He pulled a sandbag from a pocket and tossed it to her.

She tamped that against the stick of dynamite. "Now what?"

"Before we connect the charge, we wrap the column with chain-link fencing and geo-textile fabric to keep debris from flying in all directions." Donovan ran a hand down the roughly textured column. "The fencing holds in the large chunks of concrete. The geo-textile is for the smaller pieces."

On the other side of the column were two long rolls of precut material, one a dark, synthetic-looking fabric and the other chain-link fencing. Donovan had been very thorough in preparing this lesson for her.

Working together, they wrapped the column in the fencing, then covered it with the coarse fabric. Donovan's tall body was only inches from hers, near enough so she could feel his warmth in the cool morning air as he secured the coverings with heavy steel wire. He looked unnervingly attractive in practical work clothes that emphasized his strength and fitness. She moved away as soon as her grip was no longer needed.

"Now connect wire from that spool to the detonator and run it outside," Donovan said. "I'll meet you there."

How many times had her father done this? Or Donovan? Now it was her turn.

By the time she'd brought the wire outdoors, Donovan was waiting with the well-worn blasting machine. "This is only a test shot, but the principles are the same as for bringing down a whole structure. The only difference is scale."

She knelt by the blasting machine to connect her wires, but he stopped her with a gesture. "Attaching the blast wires to the machine is the last—the very last—step. First we make sure the area has been cleared."

He unhooked his walkie-talkie and pressed the transmit switch. "Bull, Donovan here. We're ready to do the test shot. Your people all clear?"

"I think so." Berrigan's deep voice crackled from the radio. "But give me a couple of minutes to make sure."

After Berrigan called through the all clear, Donovan said, "Okay, hotshot. Wire up and fire when ready."

Her heart jumped. It might not be much of an explosion, but it was going to be her very own. Carefully she twisted the connecting wires to those of the blasting machine, then hesitated as she studied the two buttons.

"Warm up the machine by holding down the green button," Donovan said. "When the red light on the 'fire' button comes on, you're ready to go. That's when the countdown starts, going from 'ten' to 'fire.' Then push the second button. Both of them have to be depressed to set off the explosion. Got it?"

She pressed the first button. "Should I do a countdown?"

"Yep. This is the real thing, even if it is small scale."

After the red light came on, she began to count down. ". . . Ten, nine, eight . . ."

Fire! With a surge of pure excitement, she pressed the second button, completing the electrical connection. Above them, a boom rolled through the empty building, rattling windows and spitting dust into the clear desert air. Kate gave a whoop of triumph. She'd done it. *She'd done it!*

"Way to go, Kate!"

She laughed, a little embarrassed by her exhilaration. "It's a very childlike kind of kick, isn't it? Like a toddler knocking down a pile of blocks."

He grinned. "Right. No matter how much we talk about how this is a business and a necessary part of the construction cycle, at heart we do it for the pure kid fun of making loud noises and breaking things."

"That's the real reason it's not considered a job for women, isn't it? Blowing stuff up is such a guy thing."

"Yes, but you've just been admitted to the club."

The treacherous intimacy that lurked beneath all their conversations was present in full force. She wrenched her gaze away. "Time to examine the results."

"Here." He pulled a pair of dust masks from one of his pockets. She was no longer surprised at what he might produce from somewhere around his person.

She slid the elastic over her head so that the dust mask

covered her nose and mouth, then entered the building to investigate her first explosion. The dust was beginning to settle when they reached the test area, and she was disappointed to see that the column hadn't been severed. Though the concrete had shattered, the steel bones of rebar were almost all intact. "Did I do something wrong?"

Donovan's shrewd gaze studied the damaged column. "Nope, it's just that there's one hell of a lot of rebar here—far more than usual. No way to know in advance since we didn't have blueprints. That's why we do tests—to ensure that we know what's going to happen. I'll have some more test holes drilled to check that this level of reinforcement is standard throughout the building. Then we'll do another test shot. At a guess, these columns will take a stick and a half of dynamite."

We. Whatever Donovan's personal reservations about having her work in PDI, Kate was now part of the team.

17

The excitement of Kate's first blast was followed by mundane office work as Donovan set her to making phone calls. She was philosophical. Even as a small child, she'd known that for every grand bang, there were weeks and months of routine work.

She had just talked to the local explosives supplier when Hollywood invaded. Kate and Carmen were alone in the office when the other woman said excitedly, "There's a huge limousine pulling up outside. Do you think it's Kenzie and Raine?"

Kate looked up from her list. "I wouldn't think that movie stars would drop by to look at a location, but I suppose it's possible. Shall we find out?"

Carmen headed purposefully to the door. "If it's them, I want an introduction."

They stepped from the trailer in time to see Raine Marlowe, one of Hollywood's most bankable women, slide from the limo like an otter. She wore mirrored sunglasses and a teal-blue silk jumpsuit that did justice to every inch of her perfect figure, along with a flowing Isadora Duncan scarf and bitch-goddess boots with four-inch spike heels.

Kate thought back to the first time they'd met, when Rainey had been a frightened, angry child with haunted eyes. The illegitimate daughter of a famous female rock star and an unidentified lover, she'd been orphaned at the age of six by her mother's drug overdose. Clementine—just Clementine, no last name required—had been found wearing a T-shirt that said, *Live Fast, Die Young, and Leave a Beautiful Corpse.* Clementine had done all three. Somewhere in the Valhalla of dead rock stars, she was probably rejoicing in the knowledge that she had become a legend.

But while premature death was a good path to fame, it was a lousy thing to inflict on a little girl. Kate vividly remembered the day when Rainey—at that time still bearing the name Rainbow that her mother had bestowed on her—had showed up for classes at the Friends School. She'd looked dazed, both by the loss of her mother and the culture shock of being jerked from Los Angeles to the conservative Maryland home of her grandparents. The elder Marlowes had never approved of Clementine, but by God, they'd do their duty by her daughter.

From the depths of her own security, Kate had sympathetically set out to befriend the new girl. She'd been the one to start calling her Rainey. The nickname had stuck.

Of the five girls who eventually dubbed themselves the Circle of Friends, Rainey had been the zaniest. She grew up with apricot hair, a small-boned, perfectly proportioned body, and a passion for outrage. In the middle of her freshman year at Goucher College, she'd taken off for California and never looked back. Like Kate, she didn't return to Maryland after she'd made her escape. Her disgusted grandparents washed their hands of her, just as they'd done with Clementine.

Rainey had plunged into the world of moviemaking, studying acting, going to auditions, and even taking college courses purely for the fun of it. She'd enjoyed modest success right from the beginning, laying the groundwork for when she became an "overnight sensation" in her late twenties.

Through it all Rainey had kept in touch with her old friends. Living on the West Coast, Kate had seen the most of her. Every year or so they would take a long weekend together at some interesting spot. The last such getaway had been in Carmel over three years earlier, shortly before Rainey had met Kenzie Scott. Ever since, Rainey had been too busy for weekends with girlfriends.

Though there had been occasional phone calls, the conversations never went very deep. Rainey's professional and personal life were great, and how was Kate? The calls left Kate disturbed. Though her friend's career was soaring, the movie business took a heavy toll on its successes, and under Rainey's tough surface was vulnerability. But they had always respected each other's privacy, so Kate couldn't probe for more than her friend wanted to volunteer.

As she climbed from the limousine, Rainey's gaze found Kate. "There you are!" She threw herself forward into a hug.

Kate returned the embrace. For years she'd wondered if the day would come when Rainey would think of her as a distant and not very interesting part of the past, but it hadn't happened yet. "Damn, Rainey, you certainly have the scary-movie-star look down perfectly. How did you find me here?"

"We've been on location, and I just heard about your father's death. I'm so sorry, Kate. He was the best. But at least he went out with style."

"That he did. I just wish he'd done it thirty years from now."

"There's never a good time to lose a parent." Rainey pulled off her sunglasses, revealing changeable blue-gray eyes that looked much older than her flawlessly made-up face. "Anyhow, when I called your office to offer condolences, Liz told me you're working in the family firm for the next year. Since I knew PDI was doing this shot for the movie, I made the limo come by here before we went to the hotel, just in case. I'm glad that you finally made it into the business."

"I sure did. Want to see my hard hat?"

Her friend laughed. "I have a picture of you wearing one when you were in second grade. It looked right even then." Two men had emerged from the limousine after her, and were now surveying the shining shell of the casino. Rainey beckoned to the taller man. "You've never met my husband, have you? Kate, Kenzie Scott. Kenzie, this is Kate Corsi, my oldest friend."

It was said that actors usually looked diminished in person, but not Kenzie Scott. He was *big*—tall and broad-shouldered and beautifully fit, with charisma to burn and green eyes to die for. Kate barely managed to prevent her jaw from dropping.

"She doesn't look old to me," Kenzie said in a deep voice. "Quite the contrary." Though he could speak perfect American for a screen role, his natural accent was irresistibly British.

Kate offered her hand, then blushed when he gallantly bent to kiss it. She'd seen Kenzie Scott on the big screen, where he projected the action-hero excitement of Harrison Ford combined with the urbane charm of Cary Grant. And here he was, kissing her hand. "I feel some cognitive dissonance here. I've always thought you were twenty feet tall."

The tanned skin around his eyes crinkled as he smiled. "It's a common misconception. But here I am, alas, in the too, too humble flesh."

Kate saw Carmen lurking by the trailer. "I'd like you both to meet Carmen Velasquez, who, I am reliably informed, is the power behind the throne of the development company that is taking down the Palace and putting up something better. Carmen, meet Raine Marlowe and Kenzie Scott."

Wide-eyed, Carmen came forward. As Rainey and Kenzie greeted her, the other man who'd arrived in the limo, a rangy fellow that Kate recognized as Hank Hawkins, the movie's director, called, "Hey, Kenzie, over here."

With a word of apology, Kenzie joined the director. Carmen said shyly, "I've loved your films, Miss Marlowe. Every one of them."

Rainey laughed. "Even my first starring role, *Biker Babes from Hell*?"

"*Especially* that one. Not only did it give me courage to dump my jerk of a first husband, but I went out and bought me a Yamaha. Which had a lot to do with catching my present husband, actually. You wouldn't believe how that bike of mine turns him on."

"I'd believe it," Kate said, thinking of the motorcycle Donovan had owned when they were married. "Bikes are sexy."

"I'm glad that turkey of a movie had some good effects," Rainey said. "Even while I was making it, I knew that someday I'd be embarrassed to have it on my résumé."

"If Steve McQueen could do *The Blob,* honey, you have no reason to apologize for *Biker Babes from Hell*," Carmen said. "Excuse me for chattering, I know you two must want to talk. It was a pleasure to meet you, Miss Marlowe."

"Call me Rainey. I'm sure we'll be seeing each other again over the next few days, Ms. Velasquez." After a warm smile and a handshake, Rainey said to Kate, "Let's take a closer look at this building you're going to blow up."

"Technically, we're not going to blow it up. We're going to blow it down." They strolled across the broad parking lot toward the Palace, which glittered like a greenhouse in the mild winter sun. Realizing how little Rainey had ever said about her husband, Kate asked, "What's it like to live with an icon?"

"Icon status disappears pretty damned fast when His Highness leaves the toothpaste uncapped."

From the day of their hasty marriage, the tabloids had been predicting a divorce between Raine and Kenzie. Kate wanted to think such predictions were merely the usual rumors, but perhaps not. "I suppose it would."

Seeing Kate's expression, Rainey said, "The amazing thing about Kenzie is that under that totally unbelievable exterior, he's a really nice guy. A damned fine actor, too."

"Then you're very well suited, since you're a damned fine actress," Kate said. "The way you played the dying girl in *Home Free* had me dissolving in buckets on the theater floor."

"A good role. It's always great fun to chew up the scenery in a death scene."

"Your peers who nominated you for an Oscar certainly seemed to think you chewed it well. I still think you should have won."

"So did I," Rainey said with a grin. "But the nomination put me on the Hollywood A-list, so I did all right." Dismissing the subject, she asked, "Tell me about the old gang. Any exciting news?"

"Well, Laurel has been promoted to art director," Kate began. "And Val is swearing that she is sick to death of lawyering, and will flip burgers if that's what it takes to make a career change."

"Val is always saying that."

They stopped a little short of the casino. Rainey shaded

her eyes with her hand and studied the structure. "Except for the heavy equipment and construction workers wandering around outside, the building looks pretty much the same as always. I thought PDI had to rip the guts and windows out before demolition."

"Only the shot floors, where explosives are loaded, are stripped to bare concrete. The crews were ordered to leave the windows intact in case this movie job came through. Speaking of which, what's the movie about?"

"*Lethal Force* is your basic high-testosterone thriller. Kenzie takes on a bunch of paramilitary groups, naturally emerging triumphant. The climax has him bursting out of the hotel in a tank just before it's blown to kingdom come."

"A tank." Kate blinked. "In a hotel?"

"The paramilitary types are having a convention, and the exhibits include a tank. Try not to think too deeply about this—it will make your head ache. Since the hotel is full of bad guys, it doesn't matter that the body count is astronomical. I'm The Girl, and sort of a reward for Kenzie's superhuman heroism."

"Doesn't sound like you're enjoying it much."

"Actually, the script isn't half-bad." Rainey slid her sunglasses back on. "Kenzie and I wanted to do another picture together, and this one seemed like a good career move. I've persuaded Hank to give my character some intelligence and a little more to do. I even get to rescue Kenzie a time or two. This flick will never be remembered for character development, but it should make a good guilty pleasure."

"There's nothing wrong with entertainment. But how're you holding up to life in the fast lane? You seem a little stressed." More than a little, in fact.

"There's always another fence to jump, Kate. It's a strange life for an introvert."

Quietly Kate said, "You don't sound very happy."

"Happy. Who expects happy?" Rainey glanced over her shoulder at her husband, who was watching intently as

Hank Hawkins made sweeping gestures. "At least my life is interesting."

There was a long moment of silence before she burst out, "Sometimes I just want to jump off the carousel, Kate. Run away to a ranch or a desert island with Kenzie and raise cats and babies."

"You could if you wanted to. The two of you must have enough money for several lifetimes of luxury living."

"I could never leave the business. It's what I am." Rainey regarded her husband without expression. "And God knows that Kenzie would never walk away. But I'd love to be able to eat whatever I want and never wear any damned makeup again."

"There are other jobs in Hollywood besides acting."

"Interesting you should mention that. My secret wish is to direct. Allow myself to become fat and mean and get my jollies by terrorizing hapless actors."

"You'll never be fat, and I doubt that you'd enjoy terrorizing the weak. You always preferred going after the rich and powerful."

"You're right," Rainey admitted. "Even if I don't bully anyone, I still want to direct. That's where it's possible to really tell the story you want to tell. Create a whole vision instead of just being a tool expressing someone else's vision, which is what an actor does."

"In today's Hollywood, it's not impossible for women to be directors."

"No. But it's still damned difficult."

As they neared the Palace, Donovan, who had been conferring with the job foreman, saw them approaching. He wound up his conversation and turned to amble in their direction, his long, easy strides a treat for the eyes. Rainey gave a low whistle. "Who's the hunk in the hard hat?"

"My ex-husband and current boss. The infamous Donovan."

"Good grief. He's as gorgeous as Kenzie." She glanced at Kate. "The one time I almost broke my vow never to return to Maryland was for your wedding. If I hadn't been in the middle of my first film role, I'd have done it."

"No matter. The first wedding didn't take, so maybe someday you'll get an invitation to a second one."

"I'll be there, I promise," Rainey said. "What is it like working for your ex-husband? You've never said much about why you left him. Has enough water gone under the bridge that this doesn't bother you?"

"It's worse than just having him as a boss—we're house-mates." Kate outlined Sam's will as Rainey stared in disbelief.

"That's *diabolical.* How are you managing?"

Kate wondered how to answer that, and settled for, "So far, so good. But it's only been a couple of days since I started working with him."

"So tell me about how you're going to bring this building down. You were always the all-American girl when you were a kid. Who'd have believed you were a terrorist at heart?"

"Not a terrorist." Kate hesitated. "Destruction is an essential part of the cycle of life. Shiva the Destroyer, the god of annihilation and regeneration. The phoenix, perishing in flame and rising from its own ashes. The moribund swept away to make room for new life."

As Rainey nodded, understanding, Donovan arrived within easy speaking distance. "Were you able to set a time for the main explosives delivery, Kate?" he asked.

"Day after tomorrow. The security guards will start at eight that morning. Mr. Kimmel was just going out to make a delivery, so he said he'll drop off the dynamite and caps for our next test shot within the hour."

"Good." Having settled that, Donovan turned to Rainey. "I'm glad this job is giving you and Kate a chance to see each other again, Ms. Marlowe."

"So am I." Rainey turned her mirrored gaze to him. "You know who I am. And you, of course, are the SOB who broke Kate's heart."

"Rainey!" Kate exclaimed. "Behave yourself."

Ignoring Kate, Donovan said, "Perhaps I did. For what it's worth, it's the last thing on earth I would have wanted."

"That's not worth much," Rainey said, her flexible actress voice dripping icicles. "The road to hell is paved with good intentions."

"Believe me, I know that. Did Kate ever tell you why she left me?"

"No. She's too discreet and loyal to dish dirt on anyone, no matter how much they deserve it."

Kate said, "Will you two stop talking about me as if I weren't here?"

The atmosphere eased. Solemnly Donovan said, "No question that I'm the villain of the piece. Flogging at nine. Film at eleven."

"Don't make me laugh," Rainey said. "Makes it hard to maintain a good snarl."

"I have a pretty good line in lightbulb jokes," Donovan said. "Would that undermine your snarl any?"

She broke down and laughed, glancing at Kate. "I should have known you had some good reason for marrying him."

"If you two are *quite* finished, can we talk about something else?" Kate said acidly. "The weather, for example."

Behind her, a deep voice said, "The weather is always a suitable topic, Ms. Corsi. So much nicer than ancient emotional history. Can I make you an honorary Englishwoman, since you have such a fine grasp of British conversational style?"

Kate turned with relief to Kenzie Scott. "WASPs do rather well with such things, too, Mr. Scott. I got straight A's in meaningless small talk when I was in school."

"My kind of woman."

His gaze went to Donovan, and he put his hand on the small of Rainey's back in a gesture that clearly said *Mine.* Kate supposed that a man married to one of the most desired and desirable women in the world got a lot of practice in marking his turf.

The two men eyed each other measuringly as they shook hands. The assessment must have gone well, because Kenzie gave Donovan an easy smile. "I've been fascinated by the work your company does ever since I saw a film of PDI bringing down that huge hotel in Miami Beach. Magnificent. Wagnerian, in fact. I kept imagining the building collapsing in slow motion with a chorus of Valkyries wailing on the sound track."

"If you're interested, we have a videotape that shows a number of different shots. Not just buildings, but bridges and damaged oil platforms and other oddball structures. I'd be happy to send you a copy."

"Thank you. I'd enjoy that."

"I hear that Hawkins wants to have a tank blast out of the hotel?"

"Yes, that's why he needed a building faced with glass. Think of the magnificent mess that will make. Very satisfying in the international market, since 'boom, smash, tinkle' needs no translation. A lot can be done by the special-effects lab, but Hank wants film of the tank crashing through a glass wall. We can use an angle that won't be visible during the main filming." Kenzie turned to Rainey. "I think I've convinced Hank to let me fulfill a boyhood ambition by driving the tank myself."

"Can I come, too? Even highly insured superstars aren't likely to come to harm in a tank."

Kate felt a sense of relief. This conversation was a lot safer than talking about her, and more interesting than the weather. As the talk shifted to the movie, she said little, more interested in observing than talking.

Kenzie was an intriguing puzzle. Despite his charm, he had an emotional armor that made it hard to get a sense of the real man beneath the elegant facade. Perhaps that was inevitable for someone who would be recognized in any country of the world. No wonder it was common for stars to marry each other—both understood the pressures.

For Rainey's sake, Kate found herself hoping very hard

that Kenzie Scott was able to take off the armor when he was with his wife. Otherwise, what kind of marriage could it be? In the early days of her own marriage, when everything was working, Kate and Donovan had shared everything. It was only later that she had started to wall herself off from her husband.

And once she started to withdraw, she'd never learned how to stop.

18

Rainey and her husband's visit was short, merely a quick stop between the airport and the hotel they would use while shooting in Las Vegas. With a wave and Rainey's wistful hope that they could get together within the next few days, the limousine left.

Donovan turned and cast a meaningful glance over the job site. Sheepishly the workers who'd stopped to stare at the stars returned to their jobs. "Now that your friends have left," he told Kate, "we can do another test shot."

Kate collected her hard hat and the test dynamite, which had just arrived—trust Donovan to notice the arrival of the special explosive transport truck even in the middle of a conversation with two major movie stars—and they started climbing steps to the highest of the shot floors. Then the radios crackled to life as Berrigan's foreman said, "Donovan, could you come to the first floor now? We've got a question here."

"I'll be right there," Donovan replied into his radio. "You go ahead and start setting up the shot. Bull's men should have drilled a hole in a column by the elevator shaft. I'll be up in a few minutes."

She was carrying the explosives and blasting cap in her right hand, so she used her left to sketch a mock salute. "Aye, aye, sir."

Whistling, she climbed to the shot floor. She'd done her first little shot, seen an old friend, met the Sexiest Man Alive, and was now trusted enough to set up another test. Today columns, tomorrow skyscrapers!

With a grin, she uttered a mental prayer that she would never have to explain publicly why the work of Phoenix Demolition delighted her so much. Her enjoyment of destruction was surely a sign of low character.

The shot floor was tranquil, the afternoon light glowing through the mirrored windows and illuminating floating motes of dust. She quickly located the drilled column, which stood beside the empty space that had contained a bank of elevators. A thin yellow plastic safety tape outlined the shaft. She peered over the edge at the ten-floor drop. The harsh clamor of a generator in the basement floated up to her, not much more than a hundred feet away, but seeming much farther.

Stepping back from the shaft, she carefully prepared her charge. Puncture the end of the first stick with the brass punch, insert blasting cap. Straighten wires and half-hitch them around the dynamite, then slide into bored hole.

Suddenly routine went awry. Instead of coming to a stop, the wires continued to slither into the hole. Barely in time Kate realized that something was amiss. Swearing, she grabbed the wires just before they vanished. Apparently the hole had been drilled all the way through the column.

Assume nothing. She'd assumed that the hole was the right depth, and been wrong. Donovan would not have made such a mistake.

She tugged on the wires, but they didn't move. The explosive must be hanging out the back, directly over the elevator shaft. If she pulled too hard, she could break the wires, allowing the dynamite to drop straight down the elevator shaft.

She swore again, beginning to understand why demolition workers had a reputation for bad language. Probably the explosive was stable enough to drop ten stories without going off, but she certainly couldn't bet anyone else's life on that.

Even if there was no danger, she'd feel like a damned fool. Everyone on the site would know that Kate Corsi couldn't be trusted not to drop a stick of dynamite down an elevator shaft. She'd have to retrieve the explosive and get her job done before Donovan appeared.

First, secure the wires so she could let go of them. She wedged the tip of the brass punch into a small crack in the lip of the drilled hole. Then she twisted the wires around the shank of her improvised anchor.

Cautiously she leaned out over the elevator shaft. The dynamite was dangling precariously from the hole, supported only by the thin wire leads. She should be able to reach the back of the column to retrieve the explosive without a problem.

Though she'd never been particularly afraid of heights, she was very aware of the yawning chasm below her as she tried to get a good grip on the column with her left hand. Wishing it were square instead of cylindrical, she stepped to the edge of the shaft and reached around with her right arm. Easy.

Except that what looked like solid floor crumbled under her weight, plunging her left leg downward. *"What . . . ?"*

As she cried out, her body pitched forward into the shaft, snapping the thin safety tape. Her grip on the column broke and for a horrifying instant she was falling out of control. Lashing out frantically, she caught the corner where the column intersected the floor.

Before she could even scream, she swung around, her head slamming into the concrete, her left arm and leg yanked as if being pulled from their sockets. It took her a dazed moment to realize that crumbling of the floor slab had created the treacherous hole. Paradoxically, the hole had also been her salvation by trapping her leg long enough to stop her lethal fall.

Still jammed knee-deep in the hole, her leg was bent into an awkward hook that supported most of her weight, with some help from the handhold. Amazingly, her hard hat had stayed in place and protected her head from major damage. Though her position was precarious, with head lower than hips, at least she wasn't lying in broken pieces ten stories below.

She forced herself to take a deep breath and *think*. Should she yell for help? No, she'd never be heard over the roar of the generator banging away at the ground level. Someone might glance up the shaft and see her clinging there, but that wasn't particularly likely. She couldn't count on Donovan; he might be tied up downstairs anywhere from a few minutes to hours.

Was her leg wedged in so tightly that she would stay in place even if her hand grip failed and left her hanging upside down like a bat? No. The strain on her leg and knee was ferocious. Soon the limb would be too numb to maintain the tension that was holding her in position. When that happened, her weight would pull her loose and she would drop like a stone. Certainly her handhold alone wouldn't support her.

She hoped that she had the strength and leverage to pull herself up onto the floor again, because that looked like her best hope. Maybe she could find some kind of hold for her right hand on the column. She skimmed her palm over the rough surface. Ah, there was a rough depression about the same level as her shoulder.

Setting the heel of her hand in the depression, she warily transferred some of her weight to the hold. It felt secure, so she started levering herself upward, at the same time sliding her left hand along the floor to find another grip. Damn, but she should have gone in for gymnastics rather than softball and field hockey in her younger days—this was going to require a contortionist.

Painstakingly she raised her torso until her right arm was straight, but she found nothing to hold with her left hand. Her whole body shook with the effort of holding her position. With growing fear, she recognized that she might really die here.

"Kate!" Donovan's voice echoed around the bare glass walls.

An instant later he was kneeling above her. Bracing his left hand on the column, he wrapped his right arm around her waist and heaved upward. She whipped through the air and tumbled over him, her leg pulling free of the hole and her hard hat flying off. They rolled away from the shaft, ending with Donovan half on top of her.

Near hysteria, Kate's first surge of relief was followed by a panicky reaction to the weight of his body. Touching her. Trapping her.

"Christ, Kate! How could you do something so stupid?"

The terror flooding her veins connected to an older, deeper horror. She shoved him away and grabbed a ragged chunk of concrete. "Stay away from me!"

Donovan pushed himself to a sitting position while she raised her improvised weapon, ready to strike if he moved toward her. He stared at the concrete in her upraised hand. "Planning to bash my skull in, Kate?"

She dropped the concrete and wrapped her arms around herself, on the verge of nausea. "Oh, God, I'm sorry, Patrick. You save my life, and I react as if you're a mugger. I'm . . . sorry."

She rocked back and forth. *This* was why she had stayed a continent away from her former husband, because of this pain, this fear—this searing rage—that had never gone away, only been buried by time and her passionate desire to forget. Yet it had taken only an instant for the old scar to rip into an open, bleeding wound.

The worst he'd ever hurt her had been an accident, really.

He'd become furious for a reason she couldn't even remember. Some jealousy thing. She'd been putting together a peach pie when he came raging into the kitchen. He'd grabbed her wrist and pulled her toward him, his expression ferocious. She cried out.

Struggling to control himself, he pushed away from her and swung around to smash his fist into the refrigerator. His shove knocked her off balance and she fell, her head striking the corner of the counter. She'd blacked out for an instant, and come to with blood pouring from a laceration in her scalp as Donovan frantically tried to stanch the flow.

That time they did end up in the emergency room. The young doctor sent Donovan away while she cleaned the wound and stitched Kate up. Quietly she asked what had happened, adding that Kate could tell the truth, her husband wasn't there.

Shocked that the doctor suspected she was an abused wife, Kate swore that she'd tripped and fallen against the counter. It was almost true, after all. Donovan had been angry, but he certainly hadn't meant to injure her.

The doctor pressed her lips together, but said no more.

Later Kate recognized how much her fear had increased after that incident, which had demonstrated that her husband could hurt her seriously without meaning to. At the time, though, her most fervent desire had been to pretend it had never happened, and she had become world-class at denial.

The doctor had wanted her to stay overnight for observation, but Kate had been desperate to return to normality. Donovan drove her home and put her straight to bed. Hazy from a painkiller, wanting to show that she didn't blame him for the accident, she'd seduced him. Rather easily—he'd been as eager as she to repair the damage to their relationship. He made love to her with tender care, then held her as she slept.

Kate returned to the present to find herself compulsively tracing the ragged scar hidden by her hair. Her hand dropped, and she made an effort to collect herself. "Please excuse my temporary insanity. It was a side effect of practically getting myself killed."

"Kate, don't brush this aside. It's normal to be scared by an accident that could have killed you, but there's nothing normal about reacting like a cornered animal."

"I don't want to talk about it." She retrieved her hard hat. "Time to get back to work."

"No, dammit." He took off his hard hat, so that his eyes were no longer shadowed. "You've refused to talk for too long. After you left Baltimore, did you ever go to a therapist? Get counseling?"

"What could a therapist tell me? That I was an abused wife who had spent far too long denying and rationalizing? I already knew that."

He didn't back off. "A good counselor could have helped you come to terms with what happened, so it wouldn't hurt as much now."

"Which would let you off the hook for what you did? I didn't go into therapy, but I did a lot of reading. One thing I learned is that abusive men are nowhere near as out of control as they claim. They know who they can get away with hitting. Not the boss, not their friends, that would cause trouble. But wives and kids, that's okay. They're property. Perfectly all right to knock them around."

"It was never right, and even at my worst, I never thought it was," he said quietly. "I'd give anything to change the past, but I can't. The best I can do is try to make amends. That's why Julia supported the idea of us being forced into each other's company—so that we could get out of our emotional ruts."

She turned her hard hat restlessly in her hands. A scrape on one side marked where she'd bashed into the concrete column. "I kind of like my emotional rut."

"Oh? I think you can't forgive yourself for having gotten tangled up in such a sleazy situation, or for staying in it so long," he said. "Things always came to you easily, maybe too easily. You were attractive, intelligent, charming, doted on by everyone who met you. Yet you weren't spoiled. I always loved how nice you were to everyone, the geeks as well as the A crowd."

Thinking her youthful self sounded obnoxious, she asked, "So where did I go wrong?"

"You never really had to deal with the hard stuff. Until you met me, there *wasn't* any hard stuff. So when the first problems showed up in our marriage, you went into denial for a long time. Then, during the"—for the first time his voice faltered—"the last incident, something snapped and you got out of Dodge as fast as you could. You were right to leave. The situation was going to hell fast. I hate to admit it, but as long as you put up with me, I didn't have reason to change."

"Have you changed now?"

"I hope so." His eyes darkened. "God knows that I've tried my damnedest."

"Have you ever abused any other women?"

"No."

Her voice became edged. "How did I get to be the lucky one? Was I bitchier than your girlfriends?"

"Never that." His gaze slid away. "I . . . I was violent with you because I cared more, Kate. And I don't need to be told that's a lousy, sick reason."

"The East Baltimore guy I married never would have talked like this. Did you actually get counseling?"

"After you left, I couldn't hide from the fact that I was a rotten bastard. Basically it was a matter of change, or shoot myself. So I joined a group for abusive men sponsored by a women's shelter. The worst part was admitting to myself how much I had in common with the other men." He looked away. "After all, I loved you—I had never wanted to hurt you. Then I found that most of the other men said they loved their women, too. Obviously love wasn't enough."

She'd learned that, too, and it had been the saddest discovery of her life.

"I learned more practical stuff, too," he said. "Such as the fact that I had lousy impulse control. That the times I hit the wall instead of you might not have inflicted physical damage, but they were still emotionally brutal. That there's nothing romantic about irrational jealousy. I stayed with the group until I had a good handle on where I went wrong."

"So now you're all repaired."

"I don't really know. Frankly, I've avoided the kind of relationship that would put me to the test."

"You seem to have everything figured out. So tell me where I crashed and burned."

"I suspect that you swept everything under the carpet after you left," he said. "Not surprising, given the hell I put you through, but not a good long-term solution. Now the edge of the carpet has been flipped back, and you're finding that the pain and anger are alive and well."

Maybe there was some truth to what he said. She'd always prided herself on being able to control her anger. It was terrifying to learn how easily it could sizzle into ugly life. It had erupted with appalling force in the explosive end of her marriage, and it simmered inside her now.

She fingered the scrape on her hard hat. "Any suggestions, Mr. Enlightenment?"

"Forgive yourself for the fact that you were young, Kate. If you'd been older and wiser, you would have caught on sooner. But you were barely nineteen when we married, and my fatal weaknesses were heavily camouflaged by a lot of love. That was very real, and I'll never believe otherwise."

She felt the sting of tears. Yes, the love had been real. But as Patrick had said, it hadn't been enough.

"You used to be pretty good at expressing your feelings," he said. "It's time to get back in the habit. If you get mad at me, yell instead of being so damned civilized. You're half-Italian—you should be able to yell."

She had her "Italian moments," and when she did, she was apt to do a lot worse than just yell. That's why she tried so hard to control her temper. "This is a really strange conversation to have while sitting on the floor of a building under demolition."

"It would be a pretty strange conversation anywhere and anytime."

"But maybe overdue." She got to her feet, and almost fell as pain shot through her knee. Muscles weren't designed to be yanked the way hers had been.

"Your leg is bleeding."

"Scraped it on some rebar, I guess. When I loaded the charge, it went all the way through the column and out the other side. I was trying to retrieve it when I stepped into a concealed hole and lost my balance."

"Carmen has a first-aid kit in the office, so she should be able to patch you up. If your tetanus shots aren't up-to-date, you get one pronto. That's an order." Donovan crossed to the elevator shaft. Testing the security of his footing and avoiding the crumbling area where Kate had come to grief, he leaned out and retrieved the stick of explosive with a sharp jerk that undid the wires around Kate's anchor. Being over six feet tall gave him an unfair advantage.

He turned back to her, the stick of explosive held casually in his hand. "This wouldn't have gone off even if it had fallen down the shaft."

"I thought it probably wouldn't, but I didn't want to find out the hard way."

"Can't fault you for being careful." He tucked the dynamite into a vest pocket. "We'll have to get another hole drilled. Since this one goes all the way through, it might alter the distribution of force too much for a test shot."

"I appreciate the fact that you haven't turned this into a lecture on the dangers of demolition."

Humor glinted in his eyes. "Not saying 'I told you so' has been a real strain. Do you understand better why Sam didn't want you working under these conditions?"

She considered what it would be like to have a child of hers in danger of falling down an elevator shaft. "I concede the point—working demolition is dangerous. I've certainly learned a lesson in caution that I'll never forget. But if you're hoping I've decided this is not a career I want to pursue, forget it."

"The information doesn't surprise me." Because he knew her well—surprisingly well, given the number of years they had been apart.

And she didn't know him as well as she'd thought.

19

The day after Kate's near-fatal slip, activity at the Nevada Palace kicked into high gear. Movie set designers started grooming the surrounding area to restore the illusion of normalcy, while safety lines were strung around the outer reaches of the parking lot to keep onlookers at a safe distance.

Donovan had finalized the explosives plan, so it was time to start preparing the columns for loading. He put Kate in charge of the covering crew, which would wrap the designated columns with chain-link fencing and geo-textile fabric.

The local laborers who made up her six-man group regarded Kate with surprise when she walked up and introduced herself, then explained what they would be doing. As she asked each of their names, a cocky young devil named Luis studied her hair in fascination. It was long enough to make a short braid, and it hung from the back of her hard hat, blond and hopelessly frivolous. Expression innocent, he said in Spanish, "Think I'll ask little blondie to go dancing, then show her what a man's stick of dynamite is for."

Glad for her experience with California construction crews, she said in Spanish, "A stick of dynamite? More like a wet firecracker, chico."

Luis turned scarlet to his ears as the rest of the crew broke into roars of laughter. One of the older men clapped Luis on the back. "Never mess with a boss lady, hombre."

After that, the men accepted Kate with good-natured respect and gave her no trouble. Lugging the rolls of fencing and black fabric up to the shot floors was heavy work, as was wrapping and wiring the coverings in place. After nine hours of laboring with only a brief lunch break, Kate was more than ready to call it a day. She'd thought she was in pretty good shape, but whole new muscle groups were complaining loudly.

Back at the Grand Maya, she showered and emerged into the suite living room with damp hair as the phone rang. It was Luther Hairston and Jim Frazer, the other PDI men, who had just arrived from Maryland and checked into the hotel.

The four of them spent the evening working over room-service food in the conference area of Kate and Donovan's suite. Besides going over the explosives plan, the men discussed the problems that might be caused by the extra-heavy reinforcement. Kate followed the conversation silently, absorbing every word toward the day when she could participate as an equal.

As the main meeting broke up, Donovan and Jim started discussing some engineering fine points. Kate took the opportunity to visit with Luther, who had been Sam's first employee. The two men had met in the army corps of engineers, and learned explosives side by side. When Sam started PDI, he'd hired Luther at a time when it was a good deal less common for white and black to work side by side as equals.

Though Luther had been a pallbearer at the funeral, Kate hadn't had a chance to speak with him then. His hair was white now, which made his skin seem even darker, but his smile was the same one she'd loved as long as she could remember. "I'm glad you're on this job, Luther. You can keep me out of trouble."

"That husband of yours can do that, Katydid."

"Ex-husband, if you please. Sam deserves a few years in purgatory for drawing up such a will."

"Your daddy was high-handed, no denying it, but he was also no fool," Luther said. "You should take this time to think hard about your marriage."

"It takes two people to make a marriage. Neither of us wants to go back."

"Maybe not back, but that doesn't mean you couldn't go forward. I haven't forgotten how you and Donovan were together. There was something pretty fine there once. Maybe there could be again. I've worked with him for a dozen years now. He's got a temper on him, but he's a good man, Kate. Smart. Fair. Responsible. A sense of humor. You could do worse." Luther grinned. "After all, you aren't getting any younger. Time you got married again. At least with Donovan, you already know his bad points."

Too true. "The world is full of divorced people. Why does everyone have to have an opinion about me and Donovan?"

"Because we care about you, honey. But I won't belabor the point, or you'll dig your heels in just like your daddy would."

"They're already solidly planted."

"Then I won't say any more on the subject." Luther covered a yawn with one hand. "Time for bed. It's way past midnight East Coast time."

She was glad to see him go. The last thing she needed was more good advice.

• • •

Luther's departure triggered Jim's, leaving Donovan alone with Kate. He glanced up from his seat at the conference table to see that she was stacking dishes on the service cart left by the waiter. "You don't have to do kitchen duty. Leave everything for the maid. It's one of the great advantages of staying in a hotel."

"I fantasize that huge hordes of cockroaches will invade if we leave dirty dishes here all night." Kate piled silverware on the top plate. "I'd rather roll everything into the corridor and hope the cockroaches give us a miss."

"Since you put it that way . . ." Actually, if she hadn't started cleaning up, he probably would have. They were both pretty neat. In that area, as in so many others, they'd always gotten along well.

There was a clink of glassware as she collected the empty tumblers and wheeled the service cart outside. Stepping back into the room, she said, "Looking at the glassware made me realize that you didn't have anything but soft drinks, even though everyone else ended the evening with a beer. Then it struck me that I haven't seen you touch any alcohol since I came back to Maryland, not even when we were eating lasagna. Are you a recovering alcoholic?"

Jesus! He set his notes in his briefcase and snapped the lid closed. "No. But I could be. So I stopped drinking."

She dropped into an upholstered chair. "An interesting statement. Care to elaborate?"

Reluctantly he said, "After you left, I realized that every time I did something god-awful, I'd had something to drink. Maybe only a beer or a glass of wine, but there was always something."

"I don't remember you ever getting really drunk. You did the same kind of drinking everyone else did. Maybe you'd get a little high at a party or after playing softball with your buddies, but you always held your liquor well."

"The fact that I wasn't stumbling or slurring words or wearing lamp shades didn't mean I wasn't affected." He squared his briefcase on the table with great precision. "One thing I learned in the therapy group was that for some people, even a little alcohol is all the excuse they need to lash out if they're angry about something. Turns out that's what happened to me. Most of the time my reaction to drinking was normal, but if I was mad or jealous, a couple of beers were all it took to blow my impulse control to hell."

"I'll take your word for it that alcohol sometimes affected you badly. But is that the same as being a potential alcoholic?"

"Maybe not for everyone."

Her eyes narrowed. "If you're different, why?"

"Dammit, Kate!" He propelled himself from the chair and began to pace the room. "I don't want to talk about this!"

She flinched. "Is this the same man who said yesterday that I'd avoided talking for too long?"

"Hoist by my own petard." He stopped at the window and gazed at the desert night. "Did you know that phrase refers to a grenadier who was blown up by his own bomb?"

"I knew. Anything to do with explosives has always interested me. Don't try to change the subject, Patrick. What are you not talking about?"

His hands clenched. "I had to take my drinking seriously because . . . because my father was a raging alcoholic, and that's often hereditary."

There was a long moment of silence before she said in an edged voice, "Your father was a raging alcoholic. How very odd that you never happened to mention that."

"I couldn't, Kate. I just . . . couldn't."

"You told me your parents died in a car accident. Had your father been drinking?"

"His blood alcohol was more than twice the legal limit. He and my mother were killed instantly." He grasped the windowsill, fingers tightening until the knuckles showed white. "My little sister didn't die for almost a week." Mary

Beth had been so young. Only eleven years old. "The longest week of my life."

"I'm so sorry. I didn't realize that. I thought she'd died in the crash, like your parents."

"How could you know?" His voice was harsh. "I could never stand to talk about the accident, and I asked my relatives not to upset you with such depressing old news."

"A couple of times I asked Aunt Connie about your family, and she would just shake her head and sigh and say how sad it was," Kate said. "I thought she meant the accident itself. I didn't realize there was more."

"I don't know if she knew about my father's drinking. It was the Donovan family secret," he said bitterly. "That's another thing I learned in therapy. Families of alcoholics often have a tacit agreement to hide what's going on from outsiders. Even now it's hard, damned hard, to talk about my father's drinking."

"Rather like me and my inability to talk about being an abused wife."

There was enormous relief in knowing that she understood. "Exactly like that. A deep, irrational belief that to talk about the family secrets will destroy you."

"Was your father a mean drunk?"

Knowing that it was time—past time—to tell the whole truth, he turned to face her. "Sober, my father had the charm of the Irish, but when he drank he was a vicious bastard. Once he broke my collarbone, another time he cracked a couple of my ribs." He rolled back his left sleeve, revealing a thin scar on the inside of his arm. "I think I told you this came from tripping while I carried a glass?"

Kate nodded mutely.

"I lied. It happened when my old man knocked me into a window. An artery was cut. There was an amazing amount of blood. Good thing I was a Boy Scout and knew enough first aid to keep myself from bleeding to death."

"How old were you when that happened?"

"Twelve. The hell of it was that when my father was

sober, he could be a great guy. He coached my Little League team, took Mary Beth and me crabbing, did the usual good-dad things. But as I got older, he was sober less and less often. By the end . . ."

"Yes?" Kate's low voice was encouraging.

"My mother baked a cake for my sixteenth birthday. My father didn't show up for dinner, and we all knew what that meant—he was out drinking with his buddies. Eventually we went ahead and ate, trying to pretend we were having a good time while waiting for the ax to fall.

"He came home drunk, and exploded when he saw we'd eaten without him. He grabbed my mother to hit her. I went crazy. I was as tall as he was by then, and a hell of a lot more fit, so I slammed him against the wall and said if he ever laid a finger on Mom or Mary Beth or me again, I'd kill him."

He'd meant it, too. If he lived to be a hundred, he would never forget the sour scent of whiskey on his father's breath, or the play of emotions in the blue eyes that were so like his own. Shock. Rage. And then fear. When he was sixteen there had been triumph in seeing that fear. Now, on bad nights, his father's eyes haunted him.

"Did standing up to him help?"

"For a while." He'd been so proud of himself, thinking he'd been heroic. Perhaps he had. Yet though he didn't recognize the fact until years later, his actions had turned him into a bully like his father, using the threat of violence to achieve his aim. He'd gone over to the dark side. "The accident was only a couple of months later." And he would always wonder if his defiance, which had shifted the balance of power in the Donovan family, might have played a part in his father's last lethal drive.

"Why didn't your mother leave and take you and your sister away?"

"Where I grew up, people mated for life. A woman was expected to put up with her husband's little vices, as long as he was a good provider. My father was a steelworker at

Sparrow's Point, so by local standards, he was a good husband. And to be fair, she loved him. Or at least, she loved the man he was sometimes."

His fingers drummed the windowsill in a tense tattoo. He tried not to think of his family very often, especially not Mary Beth. His feelings about his mother were more complex. He'd loved her, and she'd done everything she could for her children—except protect them. "It . . . it half killed me when you left, Kate—but I was glad that you had the courage to leave before I hurt you really badly."

"That wasn't courage, but cowardice."

"No. You had the strength to break a downward spiral before both of us were destroyed." He had always been grateful that she'd had that strength. If she hadn't—it didn't bear thinking of.

"Why are you finally telling me this?"

"Speaking is hard, but silence is poison. Besides, I can hardly needle you to face the past when I've hidden so much myself." He studied her expression. "Would it have made a difference if you'd known I came from a textbook dysfunctional family, Kate?"

She hesitated. "I . . . I don't know. Probably."

Hell. So if he'd been brave enough to be honest about his childhood, their marriage might have survived. Kate had had endless compassion for wounded souls, and enough common sense to haul them both off to a family counselor if she'd had a better understanding of what was going on inside him. But he hadn't wanted to be a wounded soul— he'd wanted to be her hero.

And in his heart had been the conviction that if she knew the truth, she could never love anyone as tarnished and unworthy as he.

Though she was exhausted by the long day and the discussion with Donovan, Kate had trouble getting to sleep. Once she'd believed that she and her husband had shared everything. Instead, there had been this pain-racked side of him that she'd known nothing about. No, not a side, his very roots. Discovering that his father had been an abusive drunk explained so much. Driven to violence in defense of his family and himself, Patrick had learned a lesson that was not easily put aside. The edge that intrigued and alarmed her from their first meeting had come from his pain and anger.

She'd thought marriage consisted of a man and a woman, and someday, God willing, children. Instead, she'd been sharing her husband with demons of the past.

And she'd never even known.

20

The next days were full of furious activity as the Palace was readied to meet its doom. Luther and Jim were utterly reliable, and Kate was a trooper; Donovan was amused to hear how she had established her authority over the covering crew.

But the job was still exhausting, because he needed it to be perfect. A good thing he didn't require a lot of sleep, because he didn't get much.

After forty-eight hours of almost nonstop work, he fell asleep at the desk in his bedroom while double-checking that the required permits were in order. A demolition permit from the county so they could take down the Palace, and a blasting permit from the fire department to use explosives in the process. A street occupancy permit from the state to close down the Strip for a couple of hours, an air-quality permit as a pledge that they weren't going to wreck the city's air. Paperwork had been walked through fourteen different government offices.

He slouched back in his chair to rest his eyes before checking the special-events permit required because PDI would be causing a public disturbance. The next thing he knew, his eyes opened and it was almost six in the morning. Time to get up. He groaned and got to his feet, cramped muscles aching from the uncomfortable position. He felt three days dead and buried.

Deciding he needed a shower even though he was running late, he unbuttoned his shirt. Before he could take it off, the suite doorbell rang. He emerged from his room to see Kate signing for a room-service cart with two covered breakfasts on it. *Hell.* Somehow his groggy mind had misplaced the fact that they were sharing quarters.

Before he could retreat, Kate closed the door on the bellman and turned. Her brows arched when she saw Donovan's bare chest. Hardly for the first time, of course, but these conditions made him feel very . . . naked.

Kate poured a cup of coffee, added a dollop of milk, and handed it over. "I suggest you get dressed before breakfast. I'm not sure I can stand so much excitement this early in the day."

Blushing for the first time in more years than he could remember, Donovan beat a hasty retreat. He really could not afford to act brain-dead while living with Kate.

After gulping down the coffee, he took a hasty shower, which improved him to feeling only one day dead. He dressed and entered the living area to find a plate of bacon, eggs, and hash browns waiting under a silver cover.

Amused but mercifully silent, Kate poured him more coffee while he ate. Eggs over easy, just the way he liked them.

When he was done, Kate asked, "Have you decided to grow a beard?"

Lord, he'd forgotten to shave. He rubbed his chin, which bristled like an aspiring porcupine. "Actually, I'm trying the terrorist look. I've always envied how those guys manage to maintain a perfect three-day stubble."

"There are special razors that adjust to keep stubble at different heights. Sort of like lawn mowers for the chin. Though I would have thought that was a little too affected for your tastes, and that you've just forgotten to shave."

A pity that she didn't have the decency to forget how to read his mind. "Time is short. Shaving is a luxury."

Not fooled, she asked, "After all these years and implosions, are you still so uptight on every project? Or is there something about this one you're not telling me?"

His first reaction was to evade the issue, but he was practicing candor these days. "This is a high-profile job, and it has to be perfect. Having a bunch of dynamite jocks blowing up buildings in your community is a pretty scary thing. Our business wouldn't exist without trust. PDI has always been the best, the safest, the explosives crew you wouldn't mind having as next-door neighbors. Sam always emphasized the family connections in interviews. His nephew, his son-in-law."

"*Ex*-son-in-law."

"Sam glossed over that part. The old fox knew that the one-big-happy-family image helped establish confidence. That, and our record."

"But now the record is tarnished, Sam is dead, his nephew is gone, and you have to show the world that PDI is as good as ever."

"That's it in a nutshell." He spread jam on a muffin. "Not only would the Palace be a tricky project under any circumstances, but dear Cousin Nick is telling the world that he's the genuine Corsi, the shield bearer of the PDI tradition. If this job goes awry, everyone in the demolition industry will know about it five minutes later. That wouldn't be good for business."

"But Nick is only Sam's nephew. PDI has me, Sam's one and only daughter."

If Donovan hadn't been still dopey, he would have

thought of that himself. "You're right. TV and print journalists will be clamoring for interviews, and you'll be a terrific public-relations asset. Smart, a family member, and highly photogenic."

"And blond. Mustn't forget blond."

"As I said, photogenic. You'd look great on the cover of *Demolition Age*. They'd photograph you in your hard hat, perhaps nibbling suggestively on the end of a stick of dynamite."

"If you say so, Svengali. In the meantime we concentrate on making this job perfect. Right?"

"You make it sound easy."

"Perfect is never easy. But if perfection is what we need, we'll by God do it perfectly." She left the room to wash up.

Kate was a damned useful woman to have on his side.

By the end of the afternoon, the area around the Palace was in a state of controlled frenzy as construction and movie workers buzzed about their business. Donovan began to relax a little. His people would have to work late and put in long hours tomorrow, but they would be ready by two o'clock the following morning, the scheduled shot time.

Then Hank Hawkins, the movie director, rushed up to Donovan and Bull Berrigan, who were conferring outside the building. "Clear out!" the director ordered. "We're about to shoot the tank scene and you're in the way."

Berrigan said, "I thought you were going to do that after dark so you could match the footage with the night background of the implosion."

Hawkins snapped his fingers. "Right, I almost forgot. Donovan, the implosion will have to moved up to sunset tomorrow."

"Come again?" Donovan said.

The director waved his arm at the heavens. "Did you ever see such a sky? Shooting the tank scene to take advantage of it means the implosion footage will have to be filmed with similar lighting. Some minor inconsistencies can be fixed in the lab, but it would be hard to turn night into day."

Donovan saw that a sullen sunset had transformed the mirrored windows of the Palace into a molten gold that was startling against the dark clouds towering behind. It was a striking sight.

But Christ, they couldn't move the implosion forward! They would be working right up to the deadline as it was. "We can't do the shot tomorrow evening. It will have to be the next evening."

"Impossible! I have to be back in Los Angeles that day. I can't waste time sitting around here."

Fueled by fatigue, Donovan's temper went into melt-down. He opened his mouth to suggest that Hawkins, a notorious control freak, could either let an assistant oversee filming of the implosion, or Donovan would personally present him with a stick of dynamite in a place where the sun didn't shine.

Then Kate materialized beside him. "You're quite right, Mr. Hawkins. A sky like this is too good to waste. But we can't change the time of the shot unless the permits can be adjusted properly."

Hawkins waved one hand. "No problem—I'll get one of my people to help. This is Vegas, they'll listen to Holly-wood. But we've got to do the tank scene *now*—this light won't last more than a few minutes." He raced off to take position with his lead cameraman as crewmen chased peo-ple out of visual range.

"I'll get Carmen," Berrigan said. "She'll murder me if she doesn't see this."

Kate said, "Come on, Donovan, if we stand over there, we should have a great view."

"Dammit, we can't finish loading and wiring by sunset tomorrow!"

"Sure we can. If necessary, we call the office and get another couple of people here, by private jet if we have to, but I think the job is doable. Whatever it takes, we have to give Hawkins what he wants. Remember? We're in the business of rebuilding faith in PDI. We have to make per- fection look easy."

His temper ebbed. She was right. PDI would do what had to be done, and it wasn't good business for him to act like a rabid raccoon. "Actually, we shouldn't have to bring anyone in from Maryland. The contractor who supplied the dynamite is a licensed blaster. I believe he might be willing to pitch in if the price is right. And one of PDI's foremen, Randy Bates, is supervising a job down in Phoenix. He's ahead of schedule, so I can pull him up here for a day or so."

"Good thinking." She turned to the Palace. "I can't wait to see this. It's so absurd! This big scary war machine bash- ing its way out of a casino. Need I say that this is going to be a summer movie?"

"The news does not surprise me."

As the last extraneous people were cleared away, a stage- hand drove a shiny white Cadillac into the scene. After parking the car, he darted out of camera range. A hush fell over the site. The glass-sheathed hotel, the name "Arroyo" emblazoned across the facade, glowed with hellish red-gold splendor against the thunderous sky. The effect was surreal, both beautiful and ominous.

To the right, Hawkins, who'd apparently been waiting for the best moment, raised his hand, then chopped it down in a signal to begin. "Action!"

A mechanical rumbling came from inside the Palace, its pitch rapidly rising to a whine. Then a black tank smashed out of the building at full speed, the artillery barrel and broad treads demonic in the strange light. Windows shat- tered and sunset-tinged glass glittered as the tank crushed the gleaming Cadillac into scrap metal.

Donovan caught his breath as the massive vehicle roared toward the main camera. Hawkins stood his ground, un- concerned by the possibility that he might end up as roadkill. At the last moment the tank screamed to a stop in front of the camera.

There was absolute silence. Then the turret opened and Kenzie Scott emerged, his face covered with fake bruises. The actor looked powerful and dangerous in battered army fatigues.

A slim hand reached out of the turret to grasp his. Effortlessly he pulled Raine Marlowe up, her apricot hair cascading over her shoulders. She wore an artfully ripped showgirl costume. Donovan grinned. If her spangled and feathered outfit tore any farther, it would change the movie's rating.

The couple kissed, their entwined bodies silhouetted against the bloodred facade of the hotel. "I can see that wildly romantic kiss as a bedroom poster for half the young women in America," Kate murmured. "Kenzie Scott is definitely an answer to a maiden's prayer."

He suspected that she was baiting him to test his jealousy level. "Looks like it will be a fun movie," he said. "Mindless, but fun."

"That's pretty much what Rainey said, and she's a terrific judge of stories." Kate turned back to the hotel, where the light was fading from red orange to indigo. "Can you imagine how that scene will look on the big screen, shot from a low angle and maybe with a little slow motion?"

"Your imagination is better than mine. I'm just an engineer."

"Not 'just.' The best damned explosives engineer in the world. If you want to rebuild confidence in your company, you have to think big."

Her hard hat was smudged and grime was ground into her clothing, but her smile was that of the radiant girl who'd owned his heart from their first meeting. A wave of emotion flooded through him. On the night of Sam's funeral, he'd told himself that he wanted to help Kate get over the past. That he wanted what was best for her, and the best wasn't him. All very noble and objective.

Now any semblance of detachment dissolved as he recognized that he loved Kate in the same way he always had. He wanted her as his wife, forever and ever, amen. He had always loved her like that, even when he'd tried to deny it because there was no point to loving her anymore.

Was a real future possible?

Kate had taken off her hard hat, and her expression was relaxed as she watched the movie crew swarming around the tank. Their first falling in love had been so easy, so natural. She had accepted him with open arms. But her innocent trust and acceptance were long gone. He'd already seen proof that just beneath her pleasant, businesslike surface were anger and profound, visceral fear. She despised his violence—as he did himself.

Yet they were still connected by a shared past, and Sam's outrageous legacy was giving them a chance to rebuild their relationship. Donovan had changed from what he was at nineteen, and he was capable of changing more. Kate was the best possible incentive for him to deal with his dark side. Already he had told her the whole truth about his family, which he'd never done with anyone but his therapist.

Could he change enough to win her trust?

When rebuilding confidence, you have to think big.

21

Kate checked her watch. Half an hour until demolition time. The air pulsed with anticipation as thousands of people waited behind barricades around the site. In the distance she heard the bark of a bullhorn as a policeman ordered some onlookers back behind the barriers. Over a hundred officers were here for traffic and crowd control. Las Vegas loved a good show, and finally she was part of it.

Under Donovan's direction, they'd worked endless hours to get to this point, slitting the column coverings so the dynamite could be loaded. A stick and a half per column, more than three hundred pounds in all. The charges had been connected with detonating cord, which contained an explosive that burned with incredible speed. If "det cord" could be run from coast to coast, it would burn from New York to Los Angeles in a quarter of an hour.

The delays had been installed and triple-checked, because the timing sequence was critical to bringing the building down in a controlled fashion rather than with dangerous randomness. Earlier Donovan had spent an hour alone in the building, communing with it as he descended from top to bottom in a sort of meditation to ensure that he understood the structure well enough to give it the *coup de grâce*.

Kate had to admire his calm. With so much riding on this shot, he must be strung tight as a drum, but it didn't show. He was in charge, in control, and aware of every detail.

Her walkie-talkie crackled into life. "We're getting close," Donovan said. "Kate, check the gardens behind the Palace—it's the one place where some idiot who snuck by the police lines to get a better view might be able to hide."

"Right, boss." She swung around to the back of the building. Weeks of heavy equipment in the area had been hard on the gardens, but there were still shrubs large enough to conceal a thrill seeker. Though the area had been searched already, double checking was part of the PDI assume-nothing philosophy.

The sky wasn't quite as dramatic as the night before, but it was still a good sunset. The menacing throb of rotor blades intensified as she neared the point where a television-station helicopter hovered, preparing to broadcast the implosion live. Between television, the movie crew, and

PDI's own videotaping, every angle of the shot would be covered.

Kate moved through the gardens, checking everything. The shrubs were uninhabited, the fountain dry and filled with grit, and there were only a few small trees.

In the last tree she discovered a young man perched in the foliage, a cut branch in each hand. He tried to cover himself with the greenery when she spotted him.

"Down!" she ordered. "Now!"

"Aw, please, lady, I really want to see this from close up, not back in that crowd."

"You're only twenty yards from the building, and that's way too close. You want to look like chopped liver? I don't think so. Now *move*."

With a long-suffering sigh, he clambered down. He couldn't be more than sixteen. "I thought you dudes could bring down a building that's touching another one and not cause any damage."

"We can, but that's not how this shot is set up. Now move it. Your death would raise our insurance rates, and we wouldn't want that."

Trying to maintain his air of cool, the youth trudged toward the barricade. Kate waited until he was safely under the eye of a policeman, then went back to work, shaking her head at the dangerous allure of explosives. Not that she had a right to criticize the kid, when she was just as bad.

After finishing her sweep of the gardens, she reported, "I found one fool anxious to be turned into hamburger, but the garden is clear now."

"Human nature never ceases to amaze," Donovan said. "Return to the command post, Kate."

When she entered Berrigan's trailer, the tension was thick enough to taste. The broad window that faced the Palace was partially open, admitting wires, sounds, and cool evening air. Clustered in front were Donovan, Bull and Carmen, and Jim Frazer, the PDI engineer. Jim was carefully connecting the wires to the blasting machine, which sat on the table in front of the window looking innocuous.

Tensely Berrigan said, "Tell me again how it's going to come down, Donovan."

"It should twist on its axis about fifteen degrees to the left, shearing all that steel reinforcing and tearing loose from the outside staircase, then drop almost straight down." Donovan sounded as if he'd answered that question more than once. After checking his watch, he said, "Carmen, it's almost time. Do you want to do the honors?"

"No way! This is better than a Super Bowl game, but I'll throw up if I have to push the button. Kate, you do it."

"Kate it is." Donovan glanced at her. "You know the drill."

Fighting the urge to hyperventilate, she wiped damp palms on her jeans and moved to stand by her former husband. As a child, she'd innocently yearned to push the button, not understanding the implications. Now she felt the weight of the symbolism and the gritty consequences far more vividly.

As she pressed the first button to warm up the blasting machine, Donovan spoke into his walkie-talkie. "Okay, people, let's have a nice, safe job here. Luther, what's the electrical resistance?"

"Just where it should be, nine-point-five. We're ready for liftoff!"

Donovan switched to loudspeaker mode to begin the countdown. His voice boomed across the vast site, distorted by echoes. "Ten . . . nine . . . eight . . ."

The movement in the crowd ceased as everyone waited, many counting along with Donovan in a massive chorus. As the seconds trickled away, Kate lightly touched the firing button. The little red light came on.

Three . . . two . . . one.

Fire! She depressed the second button. So swiftly that it seemed instantaneous, flashes of light pierced the mirrored windows of the shot floors, followed a moment later by flat, crackling sounds like giant firecrackers as the detonators went off.

Then . . . nothing. The seconds seemed to stretch forever. A soft, collective groan of disappointment came from the onlookers. Kate gave Donovan an agonized glance.

Gaze riveted to the structure, he murmured, "Come on now, old girl. Show the world you know how to go out with style."

A second series of detonations thundered through the structure, generating a bone-shaking boom that rocked the trailer and hammered ear drums. The mirrored surface of the Palace shimmied like a monstrous snake, the hot colors of sunset sliding over the glass. With slow, breathtaking grace, the building twisted on its axis to the left and debris sprayed outward.

The hotel and its memories began to fold like an accordion. What had seemed eerily slow became too swift for the eye to follow as twenty-five thousand tons of steel and concrete collapsed, emptying the sky with shocking suddenness. Flames from the aviation fuel added for the sake of the filmmakers blazed spectacularly, accompanied by billows of suffocating dust that rolled out and up, turning the sunset into premature night.

Screams of excitement ripped the air as the crowd went wild. Triggered by shock waves, car alarms blared a surreal chorus. Berrigan wrapped an arm around Carmen, who was bouncing with elation, and pulled her into a jubilant kiss. "Harem, here we come!"

Pure adrenaline shot through Kate at the glorious release from tension, the catharsis of violence without consequences. She turned to Donovan, who exuberantly swept her from her feet, shouting, *"Yes!"*

For a crazed moment she gloried in the strength of his embrace, the familiar, beloved body hard against her. Then the euphoria of the shot vanished, leaving only him, and the blood beating through her veins. *Oh, God, Patrick, Patrick . . .*

She felt his awareness also shift as camaraderie transmuted into man and woman. The sheer rightness of his touch made her want, for an instant, nothing more than to stay forever in his arms.

Fear followed in the space of a heartbeat. Not the panic generated by her accident in the elevator shaft; more of a bone-deep anxiety that made her feel . . . unsafe. A need to be elsewhere before she lost her remaining wits.

Determined not to humiliate herself by losing control this time, she detached from his embrace as if it had been only a casual hug. "You did it, Donovan, a perfect shot. It came down exactly the way you said it would. You've proved PDI is as good as ever."

For an instant his eyes mirrored the disorientation that she had felt. Then a young woman stuck her head in the trailer. "Mr. Donovan, would you come outside for an interview?"

"Sure," he said. "Come on, Kate, you should be part of this, too."

Before she could protest, Donovan had her outside with the wreckage of the Palace behind them and lights and microphones in their faces. A reporter barked, "What does it feel like to destroy a piece of Las Vegas history?"

"Very humbling," Donovan said.

A female reporter asked, "How much dynamite was used?"

This time Kate replied. "Three hundred and thirty-one pounds."

"So little to cause so much destruction," the newscaster said.

"Eighty-five percent of a building is air," Donovan explained. "Our job was to convince the other fifteen percent that it no longer wanted to stand upright. Kind of like kicking a football player's legs out from under him."

He glanced at Kate. Taking his cue, she said solemnly, "Gravity. Not just a good idea—it's the *law*."

The reporters chuckled. Then one said, "Phoenix Demolition used to be considered the best in the world at explosive demolition, yet the company founder was just killed in one of your own blasts. How will that affect your business?"

Kate felt as if she'd been sucker-punched, but she spoke up. "When the great aerialist families of the circus world have suffered tragic accidents, they continued with their work. My father would have wanted the same."

The reporters hadn't made the connection that she was Sam's daughter. After an awkward pause the female reporter asked, "Ms. Corsi, what's it like to a woman in the tough world of demolition?"

"Not much different than when I did construction as an architect. But with demolition, I get paid for the privilege of knocking things down with a big bang."

There was more laughter, and the press conference broke up. After the cameras and reporters had left, Kate released her breath. "Does that happen after every shot?"

Donovan nodded. "Pretty often. Frankly, I prefer taking down oil-drilling platforms, alone on the sea."

"That might be your preference, but you're pretty smooth with the media."

"Goes with the territory. Speaking of which, you did well. Very well. Join me for a closer look at the wreckage?"

Kate nodded, and they headed across the site. Dust was still settling in a thick layer, and there was activity everywhere as spectators scavenged souvenirs from the wreckage and the movie crew began packing to leave. The production designer called out, "Great job! It's going to look fa-a-a-bulous," before returning to his work.

The rubble had fallen into a huge mound of glass, concrete, and broken steel, but much of the roof was intact. The outside stairwell lay across like it like a violin bow. Kate said, "You're good, Donovan."

"Damn good," he agreed. "We all are."

After circling the site, they returned to the trailer, which was filling up with people for a postshot party. Donovan was immediately cornered by Bull, while Kate literally ran into Jock Van Meeren, the seismologist who had been taking air-blast and vibration readings at PDI shots since Kate was a girl. "Hi, Jock, how's the seismograph? Are you all prepared if someone sues us for damaging their fish tank?"

"I half wish someone would sue. I have all this great data showing how little disturbance PDI causes, and I never get a chance to testify about it."

"Forgive me if I don't share your taste for litigation."

After a few minutes of catching up on news, she worked her way through the crowd to Carmen's desk, which had been turned into an impromptu bar. Kate was pouring herself a glass of wine when Berrigan boomed, "Come on back here, Kate. Got something to show you."

In the developer's office Donovan was loading a videotape into the VCR so they could watch the implosion. Berrigan clicked his remote, and the Palace crumbled once again.

What had seemed like an endless wait was much swifter now, a catching of breath between the detonators going off and the pulverizing explosions that shattered the support columns. They viewed tapes shot at different angles, both in real time and slow motion, as Donovan and Berrigan analyzed the patterns of the drop.

"A great job, Donovan," Berrigan said. "You can blow up my buildings anytime you want." He winked at Kate. "And be sure to bring along Miss Corsi. A dynamite moll is almost as sexy as a biker babe."

Carmen, who had drifted in, said, "Just don't forget that word 'almost.' "

Her husband put an arm around her waist. "*Nothing* is as sexy as a biker babe."

Carmen glanced at Kate, and winked.

22

Charles Hamilton had always thought of himself as having more than his share of willpower. He was a lawyer, a profession noted for calculation and detachment, and he'd managed to stay away from Julia for days. He hadn't even phoned.

But his willpower snapped the evening he drove through Roland Park. A winter storm had struck in late afternoon, so he stayed at his office through rush hour to avoid the bumper-car traffic. Though conditions improved later, the Jones Falls Expressway was closed due to icing, so he took slower surface roads home. The route took him within two blocks of the Corsi house.

Without conscious decision, he detoured, skidding a little on the narrow side street when he pulled up to the curb. The downstairs windows were golden with light. Julia was home.

He sat with his hands on the steering wheel, knowing he should leave. She'd been distraught when she'd fled his house, and he understood why. But surely a friendship that had lasted for half a century couldn't have ended forever because of a few minutes of mutual madness. Since she was probably too embarrassed to break the ice between them, it was up to him to make the first move.

He climbed from his Lincoln and went up the slippery walk to ring the bell. Then he held his breath, feeling as if he were sixteen again.

The door swung open. Julia was there, wearing tailored

navy slacks, a cool blue sweater, and a wary expression. "Charles. How . . . unexpected."

Since she didn't slam the door in his face, he stepped inside. "I've been worried about you. I wanted to see how you were doing."

"I'm fine."

Oscar trotted up and pressed Charles's ankle. He ruffled the sheltie's fur. "How are you doing, watchdog?"

"He is definitely a lead-the-burglar-to-the-family-silver dog," Julia said as she went into the living room. "Would you like a drink?"

"Please." He hesitated, wondering how to speak his piece without making a total ass of himself.

He'd been an ass before and survived. "Julia, you were understandably upset by what happened between us, but maybe you need to think more about where you are in your life at the moment. What . . . what will help you through the worst of times."

She turned from the drinks cabinet. "I don't quite follow you."

"You're vulnerable and hurting. You need some human warmth to help you endure. Where better to find it than with an old friend?"

Startled, she asked, "Are you saying that I should sleep with you for medicinal purposes?"

Damn, he was making a hash of this! "I was talking about friendship, not sex. Though I'd be a liar if I pretended that I haven't been thinking about what happened that night."

"I've been thinking, too." She set down the bottle of Scotch she'd taken out. "I've also been reading the books about widowhood and loss and grief that friends have given me. Apparently it's not uncommon for someone who has recently lost a spouse to . . . to seek comfort elsewhere, and to keep very quiet about it, for fear of what other people might say. Knowing that makes me feel less of a monster."

"Never that, Julia."

"After Barbara died—did you find another woman to help you through some of the bad spells?"

"No, but that's probably because there were no women I cared about who were single and willing. There were times when I felt I was dying from the lack of human touch." He took one of her hands, warming it between both of his. "Let's be friends again, Julia. I'm not asking you for love or commitment or to be disloyal to Sam. Simply companionship. The sharing of doubts and fears. Shelter from the storm, for both of us."

"You're so right about the hunger for touch." She leaned into him, her forehead resting on his shoulder. "More than anything, I miss being held."

"After Barbara's death, I invited both dogs onto the bed to help me make it through the nights." He put his arms around her without passion or demand. Simply friendship, because if he told her how he really felt, he'd scare her to death. Life had knocked out a lot of his pride. He'd settle for what bits of affection he could get. "Think of me as a larger version of Oscar, always available for a hug."

She laughed a little. "But I think you'd want to do something that Oscar, poor darling, hasn't been equipped to do for years."

"I won't deny that. But I don't want anything you don't want to give."

"What bothers me is that I . . . would want what you want."

"We can work things out as we go along, Julia. Fill up some of the empty places in each other's lives. It doesn't have to be a sexual relationship or nothing." He stroked her back and she relaxed, absorbing his embrace like a flower thirsting for water. There were undertones of desire between them, but for now that wasn't important. What mattered was that they were in harmony again. "Just don't shut me out."

She tilted her head back, and he saw that there were

unshed tears in her eyes. "Forget the law, Charles. You should have been a used-car salesman."

Recognizing that he'd won his case, he relaxed into a smile. "Maybe I should. It would be a step up in status from being a lawyer."

She gave the first real laugh he'd heard from her since Sam's death. They were friends again.

Maybe, God willing, someday they would be something more.

Kate enjoyed the postshot celebration, but after an hour of chatting and grazing the sandwich buffet, fatigue hit hard. She drove back to the Grand Maya and took a long, leisurely bath. Then she put on her lounging robe, dug a small, overpriced bottle of wine from the mini-bar, and sprawled on the sofa. The vague dreams she'd harbored all her life had been turned into reality, and the results had been beyond her expectations.

She was lazily trying to decide if she was ready to go to bed and sleep for ten hours when Donovan returned. "You didn't last long," he said.

"When I started yearning to curl up underneath Carmen's desk for a nap, I knew it was time to call it a night." She smothered a yawn. "Can't wait to get back to Maryland and have a few days of peace and quiet."

"Not until day after tomorrow. Remember, we have to go to San Francisco to look over some old bank building."

"I'd forgotten." Or rather, she hadn't wanted to remember. Her conscience might not let her take the easy way out when breaking up with Alec, but that didn't mean she would enjoy doing it the hard way.

Donovan straddled a chair and folded his arms across the back. "If he has the time—maybe we can have dinner with Tom?"

She came instantly alert. "Why—so you can call him a faggot to his face?"

"No. So that I can apologize for being a jerk."

Donovan hadn't been the only jerk—Sam had been far worse. Even for Kate, the most doting of little sisters, Tom's coming out had been a shock.

It had been a Saturday in spring—the last spring of her marriage—and she'd been planting flowers along her front walk when her brother dropped by for a visit.

Tall and dark-haired and handsome, he ambled across the new grass, his eyes less relaxed than his posture. "Got another trowel, or is this a one-person garden party?"

"Heck, no, if Donovan was home, I'd have roped him into planting petunias."

Tom went for a trowel, then dropped to his knees on the other side of the slate walk and began to dig. Kate found it soothing to have him there, especially since things had been very tense between her and Donovan lately.

Would talking to Tom help? He was the best sounding board she knew. But if she revealed that Donovan was sometimes a little . . . a little too angry, her brother would not be objective. Worse, it seemed a dreadful betrayal of her husband to discuss their marriage with an outsider.

"Kate, there's something I want to tell you." He looked up, regarding her with the blue eyes that were so much like their mother's.

She sat back on her heels and wiped her forehead. "Are you and Rachel getting married? You two have been hanging out forever. Now that you're out of school and making pots of money as a programmer—"

"No! Nothing . . . nothing like that."

"What, then?"

"I'm not going to be marrying anyone. Ever." He placed a geranium in a hole and patted the dark soil around it. When he could delay no longer, he took a deep breath and raised his gaze to his sister. "I'm gay, Kate."

She blinked at him, at first not processing the words. Then she recognized what he meant, and the blood drained from her face.

Tom said tightly, "Say something, Katie. Please."

She reached across the stone path and took his hand. Though she was numbed by the news, this was still Tom, her brother. His fingers locked around hers.

"Sorry. I . . . I have to readjust my assumptions here." How could Tom be gay? He liked women, enjoyed their company. But as she looked back, she realized that his behavior toward her friends had been that of a brother.

Lord, what had it been like for Tom, having to hide something so basic about himself? "I . . . I've always looked forward to you having kids so I could be an aunt. I'm going to miss that. But I'll get used to it."

"Probably quicker than I will."

"How . . . how long have you known?"

"All my life, I think. Some of my earliest memories are of knowing that I was different, and that I mustn't talk about it. I've spent years trying to deny what I am, but I can't live a lie any longer."

She thought of Rachel Hamilton, who'd been dating Tom since high school. "Does Rachel know?"

"She figured it out a while back."

"How did she react?"

"Rachel's going to make a great doctor—she was totally calm. In fact, she's the one who raised the subject a couple of weeks ago, saying it was time I sorted myself out. I almost passed out from shock, but once I recovered, it was an incredible relief to be able to discuss what I am openly. She encouraged me to tell the family. I figured that I'd start with you, because you're the most likely to . . . accept me." His voice wavered.

"Oh, Tom, how could I not?" She knee-walked over the flagstones and hugged him. "You're the best brother in the world, and I love you. I always will."

He embraced her so hard her ribs hurt. They clung together for a long time as tears stung Kate's eyes. He was the kindest and most compassionate man she'd ever known, but many would judge him on his sexuality without learning anything else about him. "This must have been so hard for you to carry alone."

"It . . . hasn't been easy." He released her and sat back on his heels. "At least you haven't told me to never darken your door again. It's a start. But I'm worried about telling Mom and Dad."

"They love you, Tom. You're no different today than you were yesterday. They aren't going to toss you out for being who you are."

"I think Mom will react like you—shocked, but able to handle it. But Dad . . ." He scooped a handful of soil and crumbled it in his hand. "This will break his heart. It was bad enough when I refused to follow him into PDI, but this is far worse. His only son, a fag. Queer. He's going to be devastated, and it's going to come out as rage."

Tom was probably right. Their father was stubborn and an unrepentant traditionalist. The man who wouldn't allow his daughter to work in the family business would be horrified to learn that his only son was homosexual. "He'll be upset, but he'll get over it. He always does."

"This is different, Kate. Very different." Tom turned his trowel restlessly in his hands. "Donovan is going to have trouble, too."

"He'll be startled, but he's always really liked you. Also, he's got less invested—it's easier to accept a gay brother-in-law than a gay son."

"True. But would you mind not telling him until I'm ready to tell Mom and Dad? This coming-out business is a real energy drain."

"Not to be rushed," she agreed. "Now get to work, or I won't feed you lunch."

Her brother laughed, and they went back to planting flowers. In later years Kate had occasional moments of wishing that her brother had been given an easier lot in life, but his sexuality had never once been an issue between them. He and his friends had been a godsend when she ran away to San Francisco, bruised in spirit and body. Their support had carried her through the worst time of her life. She wouldn't have changed her brother even if she could, because she loved him so much exactly the way he was.

But others had not been so tolerant.

Kate realized that she was holding her stemmed wineglass like a weapon. Donovan had noticed, too. "You look like a mother cat ready to defend her kittens to the death," he said.

"Sorry. Tom doesn't need me to defend him."

"I've wondered . . . since Tom has lived in San Francisco for so many years. Is he . . . ?"

"HIV positive? No, Tom's fine. But Mick, his 'longtime companion,' as the obituaries say, died three years ago." In the final terrible days, she had taken her turn at nursing, and had wept for days after the funeral. After the initial devastation, Tom had sublimated his grief by hospice work, offering his strength and compassion to others who were dying. "Mick was a great guy."

"I'm sorry," Donovan said. "For what it's worth, having to figure out how I felt about Tom helped later, when a friend of mine came out. Instead of freaking, I was able to say, 'Big deal, let's go to the ball game.' He appreciated that."

"A pity you weren't so enlightened about Tom."

"I was a total idiot. Plus . . . there were other complications then, too."

That was true. "After mature consideration, how *do* you feel about Tom?"

"That he's a terrific guy who happens to prefer men to women," Donovan said. "I'd like to make amends to him for past behavior. Grovel a little, sackcloth and ashes, whatever."

"A good grovel will probably work. Tom isn't the sort to hold a grudge. I'll call and see if he's free. I'll call my partner as well. I really miss having Liz around."

She withdrew to her room, thinking that Donovan had changed over the last ten years. For the better.

23

"Welcome to Sa-a-an Fra-a-an-*cis*-co, Baghdad by the Bay!" Kate caroled, the wind whipping her hair as she accelerated the rental car onto the Bayshore Freeway. To her surprise, Donovan had tossed the car keys to her, saying this was her turf, so she could chauffeur him around. In the old days, he'd automatically taken the wheel when they were together, and she'd found a certain retro pleasure in letting him drive.

Her elation at being home again surprised her, considering that she hadn't been gone that long. As she drove north into the city, she decided it was because, as Donovan had said, she was on her turf. Not living in his house, not a neophyte learning the business from her ex-husband. In San Francisco, she was strong and in control.

"What are you grinning about?" Donovan asked.

"The fact that humans are as territorial as wolves, and this is my territory."

"Does this mean you get all hairy at the full moon?"

"Maybe." Realizing that she was almost flirting, she kept her attention on the freeway. It was one of the perfect days that sometimes came to the Bay Area in winter, when rains had washed the sky, and the air was so brilliantly clear that it was possible to pick out individual buildings on the East Bay. A day to walk along Fisherman's Wharf like any tourist, and eat crab soup with hot sourdough bread.

Instead, they were going to the offices of PDI's prospective client to discuss a job. But after work—playtime, and a night in Kate's own house, courtesy of Jenny Gordon, who would stay with her parents for the night. Apart from the short visit she intended to pay Alec Gregory in the evening, it should be a fun day.

Donovan, who'd been gazing out over the bay, said, "It would be dead easy to bring down the Bay Bridge. Two hundred pounds of explosives, tops."

A little startled, she asked, "Do you always look at structures in terms of how you'd demolish them?"

"Always."

It wouldn't be long until she did the same.

As Kate pulled away from the El Dorado Bank, Donovan loosened his tie. The site visit he and Kate and the bank's real-estate manager had made to the structure slated for demolition had been straightforward, though at the meeting back at corporate headquarters they'd been unexpectedly joined by the company president. "I wonder why the CEO showed up for something so routine."

"He was drawn by the glamour of PDI, of course," Kate said. "You impressed him. You're going to get the job of taking down his old office tower."

"I hope you're right. It's hard to tell with corporate barracudas."

She pulled up at a light. On the street corner, a mime was entertaining a small group of entranced, or possibly baffled, tourists. "Trust me, the barracuda liked you."

His gaze dropped to the glimpse of knee visible where her long skirt fell open from a series of buttons that ran from hem to waist. She'd unfastened buttons to just above the knee to show off her elegantly booted legs. Remarkable how much more provocative that was than a mere short skirt. "You're the one who did the impressing. If you'd unfastened one more of those buttons, he'd have fallen into your lap."

"When dealing with barracudas, a woman's got to use

every weapon she has. Why do you think I wore this skirt? It's gotten results before."

"You're shameless. Here I thought that you conducted all your business meetings in a spirit of professionalism and low-key intelligence."

"Damn. I was hoping you wouldn't figure that out."

Relaxed by the bantering, he gazed out at the city. Kate had been a real asset at the meeting, even though Randolph had first assumed that she was Donovan's secretary or girl-friend, if not both. Her brains impressed the CEO almost as much as her hemline. If PDI got the job, Kate deserved a good share of the credit. Nick Corsi had made a pitch for the project, but even if he'd brought his wife to the meeting, Angie was no Kate.

Donovan wasn't fond of having to face people he'd in-sulted, and Tom Corsi didn't make it particularly easy for him. His former brother-in-law was already seated at the Khyber Pass, the Afghan restaurant in Kate's old neigh-borhood where they'd arranged to meet for dinner. He got to his feet when Kate and Donovan came to the table. Tall and lean, he had his father's dark hair and his mother's blue eyes. His face showed the decade had passed, and perhaps a few years more.

Tom had always been easygoing, but today his eyes were like flint. After hugging Kate, he said to Donovan, "It's been a long time."

"Too long. For years I've wanted to apologize. When I should have been trying to help, I made things worse." Donovan offered his hand.

After a brief pause, Tom accepted the handshake. "Apol-ogy accepted."

It was a start. They sat down, Kate covering any awk-wardness by launching into a colorful description of the Las Vegas shot.

A few minutes later Liz Chen came tearing in with apol-ogies for being late. Petite and graceful with a mane of black hair, she was a true San Franciscan. "So you're the infamous Donovan," Liz said. Her hand was small, but her shake no-nonsense.

"I don't think I want to know what that means." This was indeed Kate's turf; he had the distinct impression that pretty little Liz would rip his throat out if she thought he was giving Kate a hard time.

"Actually, what makes you infamous is that Kate said so little about you." Liz gave Tom an affectionate kiss, then took the seat opposite Donovan. "California is full of ex-spouses, and usually one hears entirely too much about them. Kate was so discreet that I was able to speculate endlessly."

"And Liz has a great imagination," Kate said.

Before Liz could voice any of her speculations, the waiter came to ask for drink orders, and the conversation moved on. Though Tom said nothing to Donovan, Kate and Liz's easy chatter prevented that from being obvious.

Ease ended with the meal. As the waiter cleared the dishes, Tom said to Kate, "I know you and Liz are dying to talk shop, so I'll take Donovan for a walk. We can meet at your house in an hour or so for dessert and coffee."

Kate gave her brother a narrow-eyed glance. "Fine. I'll take back some Khyber Pass elephant ears. I warn you, though, if you spend too long exploring, there might not be any left when you get to my place."

After a brief tussle over the check, which Liz won by explaining that she'd learned so much about demolition that the meal was clearly deductible, Tom led Donovan outside. It was dark, and February in San Francisco was damp and bitingly chilly.

They walked a block in silence, cresting a hill. A splendor of lights gilded the undulating highs and lows of the city. Wondering if he should speak, Donovan glanced at Tom, whose profile was cool and reserved. No, leave the first move to Tom, who'd wanted this encounter.

At the bottom of the long hill, they passed a shabby

Mission-style church, pale fog ribboning the bell tower. Tom asked, "Do you still go to mass?"

It was not what Donovan expected. "Not lately."

Tom turned toward the church's front door. "Then come in for a visit. Good for the body on a cold night. Benefit for the soul is optional."

"Is this your church?"

"No, I live a couple of miles away in another parish, but I drop in here regularly." Tom genuflected, then ambled up the left aisle. "I like churches. Any flavor will do. My idea of a vacation is going on retreat to a monastery in New Mexico."

In the dim light Donovan saw the Stations of the Cross painted in traditional Spanish style. Though different from the churches of his boyhood, he would have known it was Catholic with his eyes closed. Decades of incense and piety had saturated the wood and stucco. "How do you reconcile the Church's official attitude toward gays with your faith?"

"The Church is more than bricks and mortar and decrees. I accept its failings even if it won't accept me. Luckily, San Francisco has a number of parishes that welcome gays. One of many reasons for moving out here." He halted at the rack of votive candles, where only a single, nearly exhausted candle burned. After clunking a few coins into the metal box, he took a fresh candle and lighted it from the one that was guttering to its end. "For my father," he said softly. "With his rock-hard head and generous heart."

It had been years since Donovan had lit a candle for anyone, and now he was struck by the power of the symbolism. The triumph of light over darkness. Perhaps a purification by fire of complicated feelings. He pulled a ten-dollar bill from his wallet and folded it small enough to fit into the box. Then he took a short white candle and lit it from Tom's. "For Sam, who was maybe a better father to me than he was to you."

He lighted another candle for Mary Beth, his sweet little sister who had never had a chance to grow up. Another for his mother, whose deep religious faith had been unwavering despite the hardships she had endured. Then a candle for his own father, who had done bad things but had not always been a bad man.

Enough flames were burning to create perceptible warmth. On impulse, Donovan ignited one more. "For Mick."

Tom gave him a sharp look.

"Kate told me. I know how hard it is to lose a love, for whatever reason," Donovan said. "For what it's worth—I was never as upset by your . . . your orientation as I was by the effect it had on your father. Ever since you came out, I've regretted that my desire to support Sam seemed like an attack on you. I've regretted it a lot."

"I figured that out, eventually. I was even glad that Sam had you, since he blew his relationships with me and Kate so badly." Tom lit another candle, placing it on the top row of the rack. "What do you want of Kate?"

They had reached the crux of this discussion. "What makes you think I want something?"

"No games, Donovan."

"Kate told you why she left me?"

Tom nodded. "As far as I know, she only ever told two people."

"I want her to get over the damage I did to her. Then . . . I want her to fall in love with me again."

Tom showed no reaction. "Do you want *her,* or that crazy-in-love feeling of being nineteen?"

"It's Kate herself I want. God knows I don't deserve her, but she moves me like no one else ever has. I . . . I would do anything for her."

"If you say so. What would she get out of a renewed relationship?"

A good question. "For what it's worth, I doubt that any other man will ever love her as much as I do."

"Is that why you hit her?"

The cool words were like a slap in the face. "The terrible

truth is that the love and the violence were undoubtedly connected."

"Recognition is a step in the right direction, but sex and violence are a scary mix. Sometimes fatal." His troubled gaze moved over Donovan. "You should know that."

"I haven't forgotten for a single damned moment." He wondered if it made sense to light a candle for a dead marriage. Worth a try. As he touched the wick to a flame, he asked, "Are you going to tell Kate what I've said?"

"Not unless she asks. She needs to work things out in her own way."

"Good." Donovan wasn't ready to bare his heart to her just yet, not when she would probably stomp on it.

Tom turned away from the candle rack, stopping to genuflect again. This time Donovan did the same. There was comfort in old rituals.

As they left the church, Tom said, "Time to go back to Kate's. I'm ready for coffee and elephant ears."

"I can go for the coffee, but I'm going to require some explanations before I eat any elephant ears."

"They're sheets of puff pastry about the size of a dinner plate, flavored with powdered sugar and cardamom."

"Ah. The Afghan version of fried dough. That I can manage."

After several blocks, Tom asked, "My father. Did he ever talk about me?"

"He hadn't in years, but just before his walk-through at the Jefferson Arms, he said that maybe he should give you a call one of these days."

"My God. Really?"

"Really."

"He must have been thinking about that for a while to put me in his will. A pity he didn't get around to actually making that call."

"The will was his way of apologizing. He wasn't good at making the first move, so he started by making the last one."

"Sometimes I've wondered if I should have flown back to Baltimore and just walked unannounced into the house. What do you think he'd have done?"

"I honestly don't know. He might have exploded, but there's a chance he would have given you a glass of red wine and showed a videotape of the latest demolition."

"Maybe I should have taken my chances and gone back for a visit, but . . . I was afraid. My life was working, I was happy. I had a terrible fear that if I went back to Baltimore and saw Sam, I would . . . would lose myself," Tom said. "It sounds absurd when I put it into words."

Donovan thought of the times he'd considered flying to San Francisco to visit Kate, then decided against it. "Rejection hurts. It hurts like hell. Don't be too hard on yourself for not wanting to risk Sam's bigotry again."

Tom said quietly, "Thanks, Donovan."

"You're welcome. Now that you've had your chance to point out my despicable behavior, it's my turn. Why haven't you come east to see your mother? Julia needs you, but she won't ask you to come."

"I've been trying to persuade her to visit me here."

"That's not good enough. She needs to know that you care enough to disrupt your life and do something you'd rather avoid. You and Julia aren't as close as you once were, but she's still your mother. She did her best in an impossible situation. Don't let your problems with Sam get in the way of doing the right thing."

The fog was thickening, cool and mysterious. When they reached the top of the hill, Tom said, "I hate it when someone tells me I'm being a jerk, and he's right."

"You're not a jerk, but you have your share of Corsi stubbornness and pride."

"What a horrible thought. But . . . you're right."

Given the havoc that pride had wreaked on all their lives, Donovan understood why it was considered a deadly sin.

24

Kate's house was pure San Francisco, a small Victorian with bay windows and woodwork painted to highlight the elaborate trim. Inside, Kate and Liz were curled up on the right-angled sofas, talking and drinking cappuccinos while a marmalade tomcat purred possessively on Kate's lap. Even if Kate hadn't been present, Donovan would have known the house was hers as soon as he entered. It glowed with her personality.

He glanced around, noting how she'd opened up the space without sacrificing a funky period flavor. One would expect an architect to have a great house, but Kate's went beyond impressive into the more challenging territory of welcoming. Warmth was in the lovingly refinished furniture and moldings, and the textured fabrics that begged to be touched. In the eclectic little objects tucked into open spots in the bookcases, and the clustered photographs of family and friends artfully arranged on one wall.

His own remodeling had been done with dedication and painstaking care, but he was an engineer to the bone. The special touches that made a home memorable were not in his vocabulary. "It's a lovely house, Kate."

"Thanks. After dealing with eccentric clients, it's a pleasure to come back home and do exactly what I want." Kate uncoiled from the sofa. "Cappuccino?"

"Please."

Donovan gave his coat to Tom, then studied the photo

collection. Kate and her four oldest friends were photographed together on a California beach, probably at the reunion they'd had ten years after graduating from Friends School. Val had mentioned the meeting to him once. Next to it was a picture of Tom and a red-bearded man who was too thin, but had a wonderful smile. Mick, presumably. As Kate had said, he looked like a great guy. There were plenty of other pictures of family and friends, including a number he didn't recognize. None of Kate's ex-husband, which was no surprise.

Interspersed with the photos were several framed certificates from community groups. Apparently Kate donated her time and skills to projects such as playground design. Friends School would be proud of her. Taken together, the pictures and certificates were the portrait of a life. She had prospered here in San Francisco.

Kate appeared and handed him a glass mug topped with whipped cream. "I gather you and Tom managed to bury the hatchet somewhere other than between each other's shoulder blades?"

"Yes. It was good to clear the air."

They joined Liz and Tom. The coffee and dessert session was more relaxed than dinner had been, and the elephant ears tasted better than their name. The best part was the powdered-sugar mustache Kate briefly wore, and the delicate lap of her tongue when she licked it off.

The party broke up about nine-thirty, with Tom and Liz leaving together so he could walk her to her car before continuing to his own apartment. After bidding them goodbye, Kate lingered on the small porch, her gaze going over the city. "I can't imagine San Francisco without hills. When I first came out here, I kept wondering how people managed when these steep streets iced up."

"I had the same reaction. I assume the answer is that they never ice up."

"Right." She turned to him, her earlier levity vanished. "I'm going out for a while. There's someone I have to see."

He tensed. "Your boyfriend."

"Right." She took her coat from the Victorian bentwood rack. "I shouldn't be out too late."

Donovan managed to hold on to his control as she went down the steps. He closed the door, then turned blindly into the living room.

She was going to another man.

Christ! Once he would have slammed his fist into the wall, or maybe kicked a chair to pieces, but one thing he'd learned was that expressing anger violently usually just made the anger worse. He dropped onto the sofa, planted his elbows on his knees, and buried his head in his hands, blood pounding.

Get over it. Their marriage was ancient history. Whatever his secret hopes, he had no legal or moral claims on her now. Kate had every right to take any lovers she wanted. It wasn't as if he'd lived a celibate life himself.

He forced himself to imagine her in bed with another man. Laughing, sweating, sharing lovers' intimacies. Large male hands and body on her; Kate responding rapturously, her dark eyes soft with pleasure, as he remembered so well.

At first the images almost made him ill. Gradually his anger faded to a more manageable level. He supposed he should be pleased that he'd managed to master his temper without lashing out. But he wondered if the day would ever come when the anger wouldn't be lurking inside him, waiting for a chance to boil over.

Probably not.

Lights were on in Alec's house. Kate lingered in her car, thinking of the year she'd known him. She had met Alec Gregory when he hired Chen and Corsi to remodel his kitchen. He'd liked her work, and her. The feeling had been mutual, and they slid into a relationship effortlessly.

A call to Alec's office earlier in the day had confirmed that he was returning from his Asian trip in late afternoon, so she'd left a message on his answering machine that she would stop by his house. She knew his routine. He'd spend the evening at home, going through the mail and doing laundry. In the past, he would invite her to join him later if she was free.

Girding herself, Kate climbed from the car and went up the steps to ring the bell. He opened the door quickly, greeting her with a smile. In his mid-thirties, Alec Gregory had wavy brown hair, a square jaw that would do justice to an FBI recruiting poster, and expensive taste in clothes. At the moment that meant a gray cashmere sweater that did lovely things for his light gray eyes.

Liz, who prickled like an irritated cat around Alec, said he was a yuppie workaholic who'd never let anything but designer clothing touch his well-maintained body in his whole life. Maybe that was true, but he was a *nice* yuppie.

"Kate, great timing. I was about to call you. I just got back from Singapore and I'm jet-lagged like crazy, but my stomach seems pretty sure that it's hungry. Shall we find some food?"

Before he could kiss her, she walked past him. The exquisite Japanese tansu chest that he used as a hall table was one she had found and persuaded him to buy. "Sorry, I can't stay. I only stopped by because I have to talk to you."

He followed her into the living room, where piles of mail overflowed a chair. "Better a few minutes than nothing. How is your mother doing?"

He had met Julia when her mother had visited in San Francisco, and the two had liked each other. "She's as well as can be expected for a woman who just lost the man she was married to for over thirty-five years."

"You're right, dumb question," he said wryly. "Give her my best wishes."

"The flowers you sent were lovely." Enough small talk. "My father left a crazy will that's going to keep me in Maryland for the next year. I've already moved and this is just a flying visit back. I . . . I wanted to say good-bye in person."

"So that's why your messages have been so cryptic. Oh, well, we can manage for a year. I get to the East Coast pretty regularly, and you can come out here now and then. It won't be so bad." He smiled. "Absence makes the heart grow fonder, and it affects other body parts as well."

"Alec, no. That won't work. Under the terms of my father's will, I have to share a house with my ex-husband. There's nothing romantic about the arrangement, but I can't imagine carrying on a long-distance affair at the same time."

He stared at her. "You're kidding, right? No will can force you to do something so . . . so medieval."

"I'm not being forced."

"Then why are you doing it? What is so important that you're willing to put your life on hold for a year?"

She took a fresh look at her motives. "I'm moving back partly to work in the family business, but also because this is a chance to deal with a lot of emotional baggage that I've ignored for too many years."

"In other words, you'll be so busy sorting baggage with your ex-husband that there's no room for me in your life."

"I . . . I didn't think you'd want to try to keep the relationship going when I was three thousand miles away."

The skin drew tightly over the bones of his face, and he looked ten years older. "No? I've been hoping that eventually we'd get to the point where the next logical step would be marriage. I guess I was kidding myself."

If he'd asked, would she have accepted? Maybe. She liked him better than anyone else she'd met since her divorce. Perhaps the desire to be settled, to start a family, would have made marrying Alec seem like the right thing to do.

But getting along well wasn't love. Love meant craving another person with every fiber of being. Feeling complete only in his presence. She hadn't known that depth of emotion for years, had half forgotten it existed. Having met Patrick again, she remembered what it was like to love, and having remembered, she could no longer settle for less. "I'm sorry. I . . . I didn't realize you felt that way."

"You didn't want to know."

Silence, heavy and uncomfortable, lay between them. "You're right. I haven't wanted to know a lot of things. That's why I need to stay in Maryland—to figure out where I went off the track and how to get back on it. I'm sorry, Alec. I never wanted you to be hurt."

"I know that, Kate. Just . . . don't throw away my phone number. I'm not going to sit at home and wait, but if you come back, maybe I'll still be on the market."

"I'll be back. But for now—good-bye, and God bless."

"Take care, Kate." He pulled her into a last embrace. The bleakness in his voice made her want to weep, but it was his whispered, "I love you," that sent her into the night with tears running down her cheeks.

Going to bed was impossible, so Donovan simply sprawled on one of the sofas, his mind circling uselessly. The sound of the key in the lock snapped him back to attention.

Kate entered, wisps of blond hair curling wantonly around her face as if caressed by an intimate hand. He held very still, not allowing himself to react.

"Just for the record," she said, "the man I've been sleeping with for the last year or so is named Alec."

"I didn't need to know that."

"He's a terrific lover. Surprisingly playful for a financial wizard. We would rip each other's clothes off. Give names to favorite body parts."

She stopped beside Donovan, so close they were almost touching. "Sunday mornings were best. Food and sex and the *Chronicle*. The sex was even better than the Belgian waffles. Alec was really good with syrup. He used to—"

"Stop it!" Donovan sprang up, catching her upper arms to save her being knocked over by his sudden movement. "What are you trying to do, Kate? Provoke me into proving I'm as bad as you remember?"

"Maybe that *is* what I want. Then . . . then I'd have an excuse to fight. To yell and scream and be furious." Her voice sounded shaky.

"That is *crazy*. Damned if I'll help you prove how worthless I am." He let her arms go and took a step backward.

Her anger crumbled into stark misery. "He said he loved me, Patrick. He never told me before because he knew I didn't want to hear it. There could have been so much more between us, but I wouldn't allow it. Couldn't even *see* it! What's wrong with me that I can't love, or let a man love me?"

He pulled her onto the deep sofa, holding her as she sobbed. "You're capable of love, *cara*." He smoothed back her silky hair. "Endless, selfless, generous love. Maybe the ability is in deep freeze for now, but it can't have disappeared. It's part of you."

He thought about Val, and how he'd been blind to any possibilities in that relationship. For two allegedly smart people, he and Kate had made a mess of their lives.

As Kate's agitation faded, he became uncomfortably aware of how much he wanted to continue holding her. The curve of her body against his was as familiar as his own heartbeat. He rubbed her back, feeling the tension ease.

Sensual awareness flared into life, taut and unmistakable. His pulse quickened, sending hot blood through his veins. He held very still, wondering what would happen if he gave her a gentle kiss, or if his stroking hand moved to one of her well-remembered curves. She was lonely, craving comfort . . .

A flickering spark of sense held him in check. Even if she was willing, he'd be a damned fool to act. And, of course, he'd promised not to touch her, though it was hard to remember that when she had come weeping into his arms.

He held still a moment longer, feeling the siren call of her body. The prospect of burying himself in her, of mating with the woman who had imprinted his soul, was almost unbearable. Perhaps intimacy would bridge the chasm that had separated them for so long.

No. During their marriage, sex had been the icing on the cake and the Band-Aid that covered the cracks, but it had never solved an underlying problem. It wouldn't now. If they were to have a future, their minds must meet before their bodies did.

Besides, he didn't want to be the villain again, which he would be if he took advantage of her distraught state, and she regretted it later. Exhaling roughly, he disentangled himself and moved to the far end of the sofa. Trying to keep his voice even, as if they were involved in a continuing conversation, he said, "First love is easy, Kate. Mostly instinct. But you were badly burned, and need to learn how to love again. As your mother said, we both have to come to terms with the past, and move on."

She straightened up, her nose endearingly pink. "I'm open to suggestions on how to do that. Do you have any?"

"We started this spend-a-year-together business locked in old boxes. You didn't want to be touched, bent, folded, spindled, or mutilated. And I . . ." He shook his head, unsure how to explain.

"And your box was . . . ?"

"Hating myself, and tired of it."

"That doesn't sound very pleasant for either of us. What do you suggest as an alternative?"

"Demolish the boxes. Allow the future to be full of possibilities, not dead ends and emotional land mines."

"Possibilities," she repeated, her voice soft.

For a moment he considered telling her that he still loved her, but instinct warned him that it was too soon. Any fragile understanding they might achieve tonight would be crushed by the weight of a declaration.

Instead, he laid his left arm along the back of the sofa so that his hand rested on the middle cushion. For a long moment nothing happened. Then, jerkily, Kate reached out and placed her hand over his, her slim fingers cool.

He laced his fingers through hers undemandingly.

Possibilities.

25

Being home in her own bed should have given Kate a good night's sleep, but it didn't. She lay awake in the dark, feeling like an onion whose outer layers were being peeled away one by one. Alec's whispered declaration of love had been deeply unsettling. Clearly he had hoped for a response, but she couldn't reciprocate.

She'd misjudged their relationship, and misjudged him. Just as Donovan had said later, she'd been locked in a box.

In the darkness, her face burned at the realization of how close she had come to hurling herself at her former husband. When he held her, she'd felt like she had come home. If she had signaled that she was willing, the odds were high that he would have taken her up on her offer.

They would have had a brief, passionate interlude that drowned her misery—and gone from the frying pan to the fire. While Alec could scramble her emotions, Donovan was capable of annihilating her. She had known that any degree of physical contact between them would be lethal, and she'd been right. Those aching minutes of closeness had brought every sensual, intoxicating memory of their marriage to life. Now she must deal with a renewed physical attraction that could not be buried again while Donovan was so much a part of her life.

Her gaze moved over the shadowy shapes of her bedroom furniture, each with a story of discovery and rehabilitation. Her home had been her project and sanctuary. And as carefully as she had remodeled her home, she had constructed a calm, comfortable life in San Francisco that was pretty as a dollhouse, and about as real. For years she had been drifting, avoiding emotional risks, her deepest feelings reserved for her brother and the easy, nurturing bonds shared with her female friends. Safe.

Once she had been afraid of nothing. A sign of youth and inexperience. Then she had learned about fear, and retreated from life. Become a victim, God help her.

Even though Donovan had also avoided making a new commitment, at least he had faced hard truths about himself. He was behaving more like an adult than she.

It was another dismal thought. Behaving with calm maturity was a very important part of her self-image. She didn't like having to acknowledge that she had been more numb than mature. But at least she *could* acknowledge it.

Sighing, she felt for Ginger Bear's warm shape against her side. He made a small feline chirruping sound as she stroked his back. No wonder people had pets. All you had to do with a dog or cat was give it food and uncomplicated affection. So much simpler than maintaining relationships with people. She'd unconsciously put Alec in the same category with Ginger Bear—a pleasant companion, good to sleep with as long as it was mutually convenient. But while Ginger, faithless feline, was perfectly content to bed down with the house's new tenant, humans did not recover so quickly.

She rolled onto her side, her body curving around the cat. Why the devil did growth have to be so blasted uncomfortable?

• • •

After the temperate winter of Nevada and San Francisco, Maryland was cold enough to freeze vital body parts off a brass monkey. On the way back from the airport, Kate and Donovan stopped by her mother's house to say hello, and so that Kate could commandeer a winter coat.

Julia was glad for the visit, hugging them both warmly. Despite the shadows under her eyes, she invited them for dinner and produced a large container of coq au vin from her well-stocked freezer. Probably she'd been cooking up a storm as a hedge against grief. Kate had a second serving, along with the mental note that Julia's coq au vin was one heck of a good coping mechanism.

By the time they pulled into the garage on Brandy Lane, Kate was yawning. "All this traveling has kept me in a continuous state of jet lag for over a week."

"There aren't any trips scheduled for the next month. Today Luther started prepping Concord Place. You can work there under his supervision whenever you haven't got office work."

He pulled both suitcases from the back of the vehicle and carried them into the house. She didn't object. The previous night's discussion had brought them to a new level of ease. Besides, it was no longer possible for her to play Ms. Self-Sufficient when she'd broken down in front of him. The memory of that sent several kinds of heat beating through her.

She took off the hooded black wool coat she'd borrowed from her mother and went to her room to unpack her suitcase. As she gathered her laundry, the phone rang. It was immediately picked up by Donovan.

Several minutes later he appeared in the doorway of her room. "That was Chief Stanski, the investigator from the fire marshal's office. Still no conclusions about Sam's accident. Stanski wants to question me again tomorrow about some of the things that don't add up."

"I suppose they might never find a definitive answer." She picked up her laundry basket. "Do you have anything to be washed? I'm going to do a couple of loads now."

"That would be really nice. I'll get my stuff and bring it along in a minute."

She carried her clothes to the laundry room, which lay between the garage and the kitchen. The oak kitchen cabinets and state-of-the-art washer and dryer were a great improvement over the dismal basement area she'd used a dozen years earlier. It was hard to be enthusiastic about laundry when dodging spiders.

Balancing her dirty clothes with one arm, she opened the door and felt for the light switch. Before she could find it, a furry missile rocketed from the darkness, brushing by her arm. An instant later howling creatures raced past her ankles. Caught by surprise, she yelped and jumped backward, dropping her laundry.

Hearing her cry, Donovan came to the rescue in seconds. "Kate?" He wrapped an arm around her.

Shaking from shock, she hid her face against his shoulder. Warm. Solid. Alarmingly desirable.

"Was there someone out there?" He glanced through the darkened laundry room at the window, which faced into the woods.

Telling herself to get a grip, she stepped away from him. "No. I . . . I just opened the door and animals roared out. At least two clipped me. No damage, but I was so startled I almost jumped out of my skin."

"What kind of animals? Bats?"

"It happened so fast I didn't see. Squirrels, maybe, or large rats."

"I came from the bedrooms and didn't see anything, so they must have gone into the kitchen."

They checked out the kitchen and dining room. Nothing was amiss. Donovan flipped on the living-room lights, revealing three feral cats. A tabby cowered in the corner while a calico and a skinny black-and-white cat darted away from the intruders.

Donovan closed the kitchen door behind them. "These

guys just want to get out. You stay here while I open the sliders."

Opening the door admitted a blast of bone-chilling air, but the cats figured out the strategy as soon as Donovan moved away. One by one they tore outside, across the deck, and down the steps into the night.

He asked, "Is that the lot?"

"I think so. I feel silly for panicking over three cats, but at the time I felt like I was being assaulted by rabid weasels, or worse."

"Who would expect raiders in the laundry room?" He closed and locked the door.

"It gives me a lot of sympathy for our hunter ancestors. What if those cats had been saber-tooths? I'd have been dinner. Speaking of which, those poor kitties are skinny as rails. It's been so cold. Do you have any cat food?"

"My supply of canned tuna should take them through the night. Tomorrow I'll pick up a couple of bags of dry cat food."

Kate had always fed hungry strays. Ginger Bear had been a scrawny street cat when she adopted him. While Donovan set off to find how the cats had broken in, she opened two cans of tuna and set the fish outside in shallow bowls, hoping the cats found the meal before it froze.

Then she returned to the laundry room, on the way collecting the basket Donovan had dropped when she screamed. She was just setting it down when he emerged through the basement door, opposite the laundry.

"They're ingenious beasts," he reported. "They managed to get into the furnace room by taking out an outside vent. Then they ripped up some insulation and got into a nice warm duct." He gestured across the laundry room. "This vent was a little loose, so they knocked it out and moved into the laundry room. They've probably been coming and going for days."

"Cozy." She glanced around. A set of folded towels on top of the washing machine showed a basketball-sized dent.

Obviously someone had been sleeping there. That must have been the cat who'd brushed her arm as it leaped for safety.

She was about to start sorting laundry when she heard a tiny, high-pitched cry reminiscent of a bat squeak. It seemed to be coming from the narrow gap between the washer and dryer. She knelt to investigate, and saw two bright green eyes and a tiny triangular face. "Someone got left behind."

She laid her hand palm upward on the floor between the appliances. The kitten hissed and skittered backward. Kate made a quick grab and scooped it up with both hands. After a moment of wild thrashing, it settled down to watch her warily.

Making soothing sounds, Kate got to her feet. The kitten was gray with tan patches and a couple of spots of white, and weighed almost nothing. She felt her heart melt as it gazed up at her. "Oh, Patrick, she has such pretty green eyes."

He regarded the creature dubiously. "I know that voice, but how can we keep a kitten when we're going to be traveling regularly?"

"We could leave her with my mother when we're out of town. Julia likes cats." Kate began to pet the kitten. "I can't just put her out. She's probably only a couple of months old. It's amazing that she's survived such a cold winter."

"She? Are you sure?"

"She's a blue cream, one of the variations of tricolored cats, all of which are female." The kitten suddenly scrabbled up Kate's arm and clung to her shoulder, the tiny claws like needles. "There's the calico, the tortoiseshell, and the blue cream, which is sort of a faded tortoiseshell, only gray and tan instead of black and orange, and a little bit of white."

"To think that I reached my present advanced years without knowing that."

Kate unhooked the kitten from her sweater, then handed

the small creature to Donovan. "You take her, tough guy."

He raised the kitten to eye level. They stared at each other. "You're right. She has pretty eyes."

His tone struck Kate with a force that tumbled her back a dozen years. On the night they met, he'd had the same expression with his little cousin Lissie. She'd known then he'd make a wonderful father. Later she sometimes daydreamed about the children they'd have after they became established in their careers. Strong, mischievous children with their father's warmth and laughter, and she'd love them so much that they'd never know the pain she sometimes saw in his eyes. The dreams had ended when she left her husband, but now she ached with regret for their lost children. "That kitten has your number."

"Don't look so smug. Have you picked a name yet?"

"She's got plenty of energy. How about Dynamite? Dinah for short."

"Let me guess. The next step is a dog named Detonator."

Trying to match his light tone, she replied, "If we find a homeless puppy in the heating ducts, definitely."

He scratched Dinah's minuscule chin with one fingertip. "Did you save any tuna?"

"There's one more can, plus the milk we picked up on the way home." As she went to the kitchen, she thought of how a house was more a home if there was a baby. Even if it was a cat baby.

26

For the rest of the evening, Dinah explored her new home with high energy and no fear. She cottoned instantly to the concept of a litter box, which Kate improvised from an old microwave brownie pan.

When bedtime came, Kate left her door open a few inches. Sure enough, soon after the lights went out, she felt a faint jar in the bed as the kitten launched herself at the hanging quilt, dug in her claws, then swarmed onto the bed like a rock climber.

With an audible thump, Dinah threw her small body down onto the mattress and curled into a furry ball a few inches from Kate's shoulder. Kate woke the next morning to find Dinah still sleeping soundly rather than doing aerobics on Kate's face. This was definitely one special cat. Kate prepared for her first day at the office with a smile.

Phoenix Demolition was housed in an eighteenth-century mill on a country road that twined through the rolling Maryland hills about twenty minutes north of Ruxton. Kate followed Donovan to work in Sam's car, parking next to him in the lot behind the office. It was early, and only one other vehicle was in the lot.

Kate had always loved the weathered stone mill. At the age of thirteen, she'd researched Colonial architecture when her father decided to do some remodeling, so the job would be done right. She'd had a great time inflicting her design ideas on her father and the contractor.

Janie Marino, the office manager, was sitting at the receptionist's desk in the front hall, under a long bulletin board detailing the status of all PDI projects. A comfortable-looking woman with silver streaks in her dark hair, she'd been the second employee, hired after Luther Hairston. "Hi, Kate, good to see you," she said. "Nice shot in Vegas, Donovan. Yesterday we looked at the videos Luther brought back." She kissed her fingertips with a flourish. "Magnifico."

"It went well. Has Ted checked in from Brazil yet? He left a message yesterday that he wants to talk to me about that hotel job he's prepping."

"Hasn't called yet. There should be time for coffee and a quick tour, if Kate needs one."

"I'd like that," she said. "There must have been some changes."

"Not many," Donovan said. "Everyone here is always too busy to change things without a good reason."

Kate poured herself a mug of coffee, then wandered down the hall to her father's office. She was unprepared for the upwelling of grief at the sight of the familiar, sunny room, with the clock made of dummy dynamite sticks and a lingering scent of her father's cigars. *Papa. Oh, Papa.*

Behind her Janie said, "I can't get used to the fact that Sam isn't coming back. I see him in every corner of this place."

"If he's hanging around, he's a friendly ghost," Kate said.

"Friendly, hell. He'd be roaring at me to do three things at once, and in half the time." Janie pivoted and headed for her office.

Donovan leaned against the door frame. "I haven't figured out what to do with this room. No one wants to move in. God knows I couldn't."

The spacious room had a working fireplace and a view of the woods and stream. In the summer, ducks would be paddling around in the old millpond. "The building isn't crowded, is it?"

"No, we've only got fifteen employees, so we still have room to spare. Why? It would be kind of sick to keep Sam's office as a shrine."

"Turn it into an employee lounge and lunchroom. With the sunshine and the view, it's one of the nicest rooms in the building," she said. "A counter and sink would have to be installed, but otherwise, it would just be a little redecorating. Fresh paint, a couple of sofas and chairs and dinette tables. Easy. Once people start microwaving their burritos in here, they'll get over their discomfort."

"Great idea! You have your first independent project. Draw up a plan and a budget for me. If you can keep the cost down, it can be done right away."

"Okay. But I still get to do fieldwork, right?"

"Right. Come on up to my office. I like the second floor because it's quieter. Sam preferred being in the middle of things."

Upstairs, engineering and accounting had expanded, but as Donovan had said, it wasn't too different from how she remembered. They ended in his office, which was directly above Sam's. One wall was all oak shelves, books intermixed with souvenirs of different projects. At the opposite end was a drafting board. Next to his magna cum laude engineering degree hung a Loyola MBA diploma. Useful for running a business, but earning it must have kept his evenings and weekends busy for a few years.

She gestured at the elaborately carved mahogany mantelpiece. "It's not the right period for the building, but that's a great mantel. Where did it come from?"

"I salvaged it from a hotel job in Boston." He set his coffee mug on his impressively neat desk. "I thought you could take the office across the hall. It's been empty since Nick left."

Before Kate could respond, a female voice came through the intercom on the desk. "Donovan, Ted's on line two from Rio de Janeiro."

He reached for the phone. "Because I've been away, it's

going to be a crazy day. I'm not going to have much time to work with you. Try to stay out of trouble."

Her new office was the same size as Donovan's, with an equally nice view. She gazed out into the woods. A single male cardinal provided a scarlet accent against the subtle winter grays and tans. Once she'd dreamed of working here, she and Donovan full partners in life and in business. Such a long time ago.

For the next hour she wandered through the building. PDI had always had a very low turnover rate, so she knew more than half the employees. The others she introduced herself to. Everyone welcomed her warmly, partly on general principles, partly, she suspected, because she was Sam's daughter, which supplied a comforting sense of continuity. She was glad to be back.

It would be hard to leave again.

Donovan was halfway through his mail when the intercom buzzed to life. "You'd better get down here," the receptionist said. "We've got picketers."

Swearing, he raced downstairs, and found Kate and the receptionist at the front window. Outside, people of all ages from toddler to senior citizen were pouring out of cars, many of them clutching handmade signs saying things like THE SECOND BATTLE OF CONCORD and HELL, NO, WE WON'T GO.

"You did predict that better weather would bring out demonstrators," Kate said.

A television transmission truck parked on the lawn. "Luther called from Concord Place a few minutes ago," he said. "There are protesters all around the job site, but I sure as hell didn't think they'd picket us out here."

Grabbing his parka, he went outside, Kate following two steps behind him. The demonstrators were marching back and forth in ragged lines. He guessed that most were Concord Place residents. Only two of the five project buildings were completely clear of tenants. The others still housed people who hadn't yet found new homes, and were under notice to leave within the month.

Donovan sympathized with their plight, but having them wear holes in the lawn was a damned nuisance. Not the kind of publicity he liked for PDI.

A burly man wearing an army fatigue jacket that Donovan guessed had been earned the hard way stormed up. "You bastards are driving my mama from her home!"

"The decision to demolish Concord Place was made by the city, not us. From what I've heard, current residents will be at the top of the list for the new town houses that will be built."

"Hell of a lot of good that does anyone now!"

A camera zoomed in on the confrontation. Donovan balanced on the balls of his feet, knowing that the head of PDI really shouldn't get into a fight. But if the other guy threw the first punch . . .

Kate stepped between the two men. "It's terrible that people are being evicted, but the townhouse community will be safer and more attractive."

"If it's ever built!" the protester said. "What matters now is that my mama's losing her home and friends after thirty years. Me and my brothers grew up there."

"That's awful. Housing is one of the most important urban issues we face in America today." Kate launched into an eloquent—and endless—discussion of urban policy. The television crews hadn't come to learn about the intricacies of housing law. With no angry brawls to film, they packed up their cameras and left.

As the demonstration started to break up, an aging hippie with grizzled beard and ponytail ambled up. Donovan said, "I should have known you'd be behind this, Steve."

"Made a great photo opportunity, didn't it? The downtown demonstration wouldn't rate much time on the evening news. But this—distraught people losing their homes, driven by desperation to venture into the posh green hills of Baltimore County—*this* is newsworthy."

"Spare me," Donovan said.

"You know this character?" Kate asked.

"Meet Steve Burke, head of the St. Francis Housing Center. He does some very good things, and some very dumb ones."

"Donovan helps on our fix-up weekends, when we repair run-down houses for the elderly," Burke explained. "One of my most valuable volunteers."

"And this is how you repay him."

"I'll do any damned thing I can to make smug suburbanites like you think about what's going on in the city. Sure, someday there will be town houses on the Concord Place site, but there will only be about half as many units as there are now, and where the hell do the displaced people live until then?"

"Those are serious questions, Mr. Burke. But you might as well picket the hammer that drives the nail as come after PDI for a decision that has already been made by the city housing authority."

The fatigue-clad protester said, "Nazis always say that— 'I was just following orders.' But you bastards are doing the dirty work."

"Joe and I have tried fighting city hall over this with no success," Burke said. "So here we are, scrounging for publicity. With luck, we can shame the city into finding new housing for some of the people being evicted."

Donovan retorted, "I have no problem with your goals, but I damned well don't like PDI being made your scapegoat."

Before the discussion could deteriorate further, Kate said, "Good day, gentlemen. I can't say that it's been a pleasure meeting you, but it has been interesting." She took firm hold of Donovan's elbow and marched him back to the mill house.

"Thanks for driving off the camera crews," he said as they went inside. "Nothing like substance to panic the news media."

Kate smiled. "This is a great place, Donovan. Never a dull moment."

After raiding the stationery closet, Kate returned to her new office and tried to settle down. Though the demonstration had ended peacefully, both Burke and his sidekick, Joe, had struck her as men who could be dangerous opponents. She'd never really thought about the political dimensions of PDI's work. So much to learn.

She sketched some thumbnail layouts for the proposed employees' lounge, then set down her pencil and reached for the phone. Since she didn't have a lot to do today, it would be a good time to visit with her mother. Julia picked up on the first ring.

"Hi, Mom," Kate said. "Can I take you to lunch?"

"That would be lovely. I can't believe I'm seeing you twice in two days, when for years it wasn't even twice a year."

Kate arranged to meet at a restaurant halfway between the office and Julia's house. As she hung up, she thought how strange it was to be able to see her mother so easily. Strange, and really, really nice.

27

Kate was already waiting when Julia reached the Valley Inn, a long-established local institution. "It's soothing to see how little this place has changed," Kate said. "Not like California, where things often change simply for the sake of change."

"No one has ever accused Baltimore of that." Julia kissed her daughter's cheek. For years she'd told herself that it was a child's right to fly long and far from the nest, but at heart, she had a secret, reactionary desire to have Kate and Tom living five minutes away. So much was missed when living on opposite coasts. Not the great dramas of life, but the little moments like this, the talking and laughing and discussing the weather that were the warp and weft of a relationship.

They'd finished dessert and were on coffee refills when Julia asked, "When you were in San Francisco, did you see your friend Alec?"

"He was just back from the Far East, so I was able to say good-bye in person."

So Kate had ended the relationship. Julia wasn't sure if she was glad or sorry. "He was an intriguing young man, but three thousand miles is too far."

"That's what I thought." Kate set down her coffee cup. "I don't know if you've heard, but the state fire marshal's office is still investigating Sam's death. They can't seem to get a handle on the cause of the accident, but they think it might have been tampering by an implosion junkie who sneaked onto the site and messed around with things he didn't understand."

Julia sucked in her breath. "Lord, I forgot all about the accident investigation."

"They're doing their best, though they may never have the full answer."

Julia had intended to tell her children the whole truth, but hadn't felt ready. Perhaps she would never have been ready. "There's something I have to tell you, and the in- vestigators, too. A month before he died, Sam was diag- nosed with pancreatic cancer."

Her daughter paled. "Good God."

Julia had felt equal shock and horror when the doctor announced that her husband had one of the fastest and most lethal of cancers. How could someone as vital as Sam harbor such a swift, remorseless killer inside his powerful body? But the truth of the diagnosis had been swiftly evident. "They said he had maybe three or four months. The disease was advancing rapidly by the time he died. He couldn't have carried on a normal life much longer."

"Why didn't you tell me sooner? Knowing that he didn't lose decades of life, only weeks or months, makes his death a little easier to accept."

"I was still coming to terms with it myself. I've suspected all along that Sam's death wasn't an accident. I . . . I'm pretty sure that he set off that blast himself."

"I . . . see," Kate said after a shaken silence. "I've read that people don't fear death anywhere near as much as they fear dying. Sam must have hated knowing what lay ahead. What better way to go than in the heart of an implosion, at a time and place of his choosing?"

"The accident was right after he'd finished tying up all the legal and financial loose ends. I can't believe that's a coincidence. I'd made arrangements so that when the time came, he could have hospice care at home instead of dying full of tubes and needles in some ghastly hospital. I was even ready to start hoarding pain pills just . . . just in case."

Her fingers tightened around her coffee cup. "But in the end, Sam made sure that I didn't have to do anything difficult. He always insisted on taking care of me, whether I needed it or not. He would have said he didn't want to burden me. But he . . . he robbed me of the chance to show that I was more than just a fair-weather wife. To care for him. To do what any woman will do for the man she loves."

"Oh, Mom, how ghastly for you! And how *typical* of Sam to decide to spare you without considering if it was what you wanted."

For a long moment they were simply two women who had loved the same stubborn man. Julia sensed their relationship shifting, becoming not only closer but more equal, one adult to another. "I sound horribly selfish, don't I? As if he should have died in agony just so I could prove my loyalty. Of course I didn't want that. But when he died so suddenly, I felt . . . cheated."

"And angry. I'm angry with him, too," Kate said.

"I'm not angry with your father, dear." Julia halted. "No, that's not true. I *am* angry. In fact, I'm *furious*. That pig-headed, know-it-all Italian husband of mine stole what time we had left. I wasn't ready to let him go yet."

Her suppressed rage erupted, fierce and cleansing. So this was what one of Sam's Italian moments felt like. Maybe on the occasions he'd yelled at her, she should have yelled back.

Kate took her hand until the anger ebbed. "He didn't give me a chance to say good-bye," Julia said quietly. "To say how much I loved him."

Her daughter regarded her with eyes that were painfully like Sam's. "If there is one thing I'm absolutely sure of, it's that Sam knew how much you loved him. You were the great wonder and joy of his life. Even more than dynamite."

"Surely I didn't rate quite *that* highly."

"I gather Sam didn't tell anyone else about his illness?"

"Just me and Charles Hamilton." Julia withdrew her hand from Kate's as she thought uneasily of what she and Charles were doing. "Charles had to know to help Sam wind up his affairs properly. Haven't you wondered about the bizarre way his will threw you and Patrick together?"

"The crazy conditions make a lot more sense now that I know what a short horizon he was looking at. It wasn't the will of a man who expected to live another thirty years. He knew that Donovan and I were still single, so his ham-handed matchmaking had at least a faint chance of working."

"Does it?"

Kate flushed. "Of course not. I think Donovan and I can manage to survive a year under the same roof. We're even beginning to make peace with the past. But that doesn't change what separated us."

"What did separate you? People change a lot in ten years. If Patrick did something foolish back then—well, it doesn't mean that he's incapable of making a good husband. He was very young. People make mistakes."

Kate bit her lip, clearly teetering on the brink of confession. The moment passed. "Donovan and I both made our share of mistakes."

As an answer it was probably true, but it certainly didn't explain much.

Donovan was questioned again by Chief Stanski and a state police detective, Lieutenant Miller, a middle-aged black man with a misleadingly bland face and shrewd eyes. By the time they left PDI, everyone else had gone home.

Everyone except Kate. After Donovan escorted the two investigators to the front door, he made a circuit of the building to check that all the doors were locked, then wearily returned to his office to get his coat and car keys. Kate was perched on the corner of his desk. The sight was energizing.

"What are you doing here still?" he asked. "The place is so deserted that I presume more snow is predicted."

"Sleet, actually. Janie asked if people could leave a little early, so I said yes."

"Generous of you."

"Hey, I can't help it if she thinks I have authority even though I'm just a humble trainee."

"You have the natural authority that comes from being a WASP princess. Or at least, a semi-WASP princess."

"I thought the investigators would never leave. What took so long?"

"They're leaning toward the implosion-junkie theory, with Sam's death an accident. But it's possible that whoever messed with the explosives was crazy enough to actually be trying to kill someone." He hesitated, then decided to tell her the rest. "They asked if I could identify some scraps of smashed electronics they found in the rubble of the building. It wasn't a piece of PDI equipment. I couldn't be sure, but it might have been the remains of a radio-controlled detonation device."

Kate gasped. "You mean that someone planted a remote and set it off from a safe distance?"

"It's possible. If their lab decides that's what happened, this will turn into a murder investigation."

"It wasn't murder, Donovan. I had lunch with Julia, and she told me that Sam had pancreatic cancer and only a couple of months to live."

"Cancer?" His shock was quickly replaced by relief. "You know, I'm not really surprised. Sam had been looking pretty tired, and he'd lost some weight. He let the office work slide, too, and that wasn't like him. I thought he was just overworked and upset that Nick had left, and that he'd get over it soon. Maybe it's a blessing that an implosion junkie chose that time to go nuts."

Kate's expression tightened. "Julia believes Sam set that blast off himself."

"Sam didn't kill himself," Donovan said flatly.

"No? I should think it's pretty clear that he decided to go out with one dramatic, larger-than-life gesture. Just his style. No one but him was hurt, and he made headlines in a grand farewell."

"You and Julia are Protestants, so you weren't raised with the Catholic doctrine that suicide is a mortal sin. A ticket straight to hell. As a devout Catholic, Sam wouldn't have killed himself. I'm sure of it."

"Are you saying no Catholic would hasten the end if he was dying miserably?" Kate asked.

"Maybe when the end is near and the pain unbearable," he admitted. "But Sam wasn't that far gone, not by a long shot. Hell, Sam was a fighter. He wouldn't throw in the towel when he had weeks, maybe months, of life ahead of him. If the doctors told him everyone with pancreatic cancer died in three months, he'd have been convinced that he'd be the first known exception."

"I hear what you're saying, but imminent death might change things. It's hard to know what another person will do in extreme circumstances."

"True, but his death was too sudden. He would have wanted to see you one last time, even if he didn't tell you why. Plus, just before the accident he said that maybe he should call Tom. I'm sure he would have tried for a reconciliation before he died."

"You think so?"

"Positive. I told Tom that in San Francisco. Knowing he was terminally ill, Sam must have decided it was time to put his stubborn pride aside."

"I hope you're right. But I'm still not convinced that Sam didn't blow up that building himself."

"Then I'll give you a good reason that doesn't call for speculating about what was in Sam's mind that night. He would never have done anything to hurt the business. He was proud of the fact that PDI had never caused a fatality. He wouldn't ruin that record by killing himself on a job. He'd have made a mistake blowing up a stump on his own time, or something like that. He sure wouldn't have used a detonator in the Jefferson Arms."

"That makes sense," Kate said, expression troubled. "But Sam's illness raises a different possibility. Maybe it wasn't an implosion junkie that blew the Jefferson Arms prematurely. Could someone close to him have learned about his illness, and decided to give Sam a mercifully quick death so he wouldn't have to commit the sin of suicide?"

"Jesus." Donovan thought about it, then shook his head. "I really doubt that. Even if someone at PDI knew he was ill, no one here would have the arrogance to play God with Sam's life. I certainly didn't. I hope you believe that."

"If you say you didn't, I believe you."

Their gazes locked. He knew he should move away, and couldn't. The erotic current that always pulsed between them was rising to flood tide. It would be so easy to bend forward, to press his lips to hers. And this time she wasn't distraught about another man. If she responded to him, it would be from choice, not desperation . . .

"If sleet is coming, we should go home," she said.

He clenched his hand, resisting the desire to touch her. "Do you want a ride? The Jeep will be better if the roads are bad."

She peered outside. "Nothing falling yet. I'll take Sam's car. Better to put it in the garage than leave it here and have to chip ice off tomorrow."

She left his office while he stared blindly out the window, and wished the ice was in his veins.

Julia had attended a committee meeting after her lunch with Kate, but she had to go home eventually. She'd never minded walking into an empty house when her husband was alive, because it would only be a matter of time before Sam would return, filling the quiet rooms with his booming voice and expansive personality. Now he'd never come home again, and there was a black core of grief at the center of her being. She found it curious that she could respond to Charles's kindness and passion, yet always be so aware of Sam's death. Charles, bless him, understood and didn't resent that.

She was wondering if she had the appetite to heat up some food when she noticed a light coming from the family room. She went to investigate, and was startled to see a tall, dark-haired man kneeling by the fireplace with his back to her. Donovan had a key to the house, but this wasn't him. It was . . .

"Tom!"

He stood and turned to her. "Sorry to surprise you, Mother, but I came on impulse. When I called from the airport, all I got was the answering machine. A good thing you haven't changed the locks since I lived here."

"Darling, how wonderful!" Julia hugged him, delight burning away her depression. While there had been no formal breach, she could count the number of times she'd seen him in the last decade, and have fingers left over. "After the way I failed you, I never thought I'd see you in this house again. I'm so sorry, Tom. For everything."

He held her tightly, rocking them both a little. "I'm the one who should apologize. There was a small, childish part of me that wished you'd acted differently, but my head and heart never wanted that. You stood up for me when it counted. Anything more would have broken your marriage, and that would have devastated Sam and you both."

"I can't believe you didn't feel at least some resentment."

"Only a little, and that's gone now." Tom knelt by the fireplace again, where he'd already laid pieces of split wood on the grate. "I should have been here sooner. When I said I couldn't come to Sam's funeral because of a dying friend, it was the truth, but not the whole truth. Frankly, I was scared to death about returning. Afraid of the bad memories, I guess. Then Donovan read me the riot act when I saw him in San Francisco. Enough to make me recognize how badly I was behaving."

"You're too hard on yourself. I suppose you get it from me. Even after all of these years, I keep brooding about how I could have handled the situation better."

"What happened after I left?"

"I told Sam that he might have disowned you, but I hadn't, and that if he objected to me keeping in touch with you, I'd file for a divorce."

Tom struck a wooden match and lit the fire starter. "I gather that he backed down."

"I think he was glad that I didn't agree with him. It . . . it was a way of keeping track of you at second hand. He couldn't free himself of his prejudices, but he loved you too much to lose you entirely. He never tried to take your pictures down."

Tom gazed at the first flickering flames as they licked around the wood. "How convoluted and Sam-like."

"Is being in Baltimore as bad as you expected?"

He stood, his slow gaze going around the family room

to the sofa where he and Kate and their friends would
sprawl, the comfortable wing chairs that she and Sam had
preferred, the corner that had always held the Christmas
tree. "No. There are a lot more happy memories than bad
ones." He smiled a little. In San Francisco, he'd found himself. In Maryland, his presence was healing a decade-old
family schism.

"I'm so glad." She linked her arm through his. "Would
you like some coq au vin for dinner?"

It was amazing how her appetite had come back.

The next morning, Kate studied the photo of the Concord
Place demonstration on the front page of the local news
section of the *Sun*. As Burke predicted, the protesters in
front of PDI's historic mill house was newsworthy. The
photo identified Burke and his friend Joe Beekman. She
was glad that neither she nor Donovan had been included.
On impulse, she picked up the phone and called Val Covington at her office.

"Hi, Kate," Val said. "I was about to call you. Are you
up for lunch two weeks from this Saturday? Rachel will be
back from her fellowship in Australia, and I thought it
would be nice to get together at Morgan Millard."

"Great idea." After settling on a time, Kate said, "You're
a lawyer and must know all about research. Could you run
down the backgrounds of a couple of men?"

"I could try," Val said cautiously. "Are they local?"

"They're protesters of the Concord Place demolition.
Probably they're just raising their voices, but I thought it
might be handy to know if they might be likely to commit
vandalism at the job site."

"Worth looking at. Give me the names, and I'll check
'em out."

Kate spelled the names and thanked Val. Probably neither of the men had anything to do with Sam's death—but
it wouldn't hurt to know more about them.

28

From the door to the garage, Donovan called, "See you tonight."

Kate glanced up from her newspaper, where an earthquake story was enlivening her breakfast. "Have fun. Say hi to Connie and Frank for me."

"Will do." The door closed, and Donovan went off to spend Saturday helping his uncle Frank remodel a bathroom in one of those male-bonding projects men loved.

Connie, smart woman, encouraged such projects. Her house certainly had benefited. The weekend before, she'd invited Kate and Donovan to dinner. It had been good to see the Russos again, though Kate knew darned well that she was being examined and judged for the sin of leaving Donovan. By the end of the evening, the Russos seemed to have accepted her again.

Newspaper finished, Kate rose and washed her mug. She'd lived on Brandy Lane for three weeks now, and except for that first eventful day at PDI, life had been peaceful. Donovan had muttered several times about an unusually high rate of quirky accidents at scattered job sites, but otherwise, the company was running smoothly.

She'd fallen into a routine where office work alternated with field training under Luther at Concord Place. As the demolition prep proceeded, the protests had ended, mostly because Steve Burke's demonstrations had embarrassed the city into finding housing for the remaining tenants.

In the woods, the first cautious sprigs of green were raising their heads. The day before, Friday, she'd officially christened the new employees' lounge with a catered buffet luncheon. By the time people had eaten the apple kuchen, any uneasiness about the fact that the room had been Sam's office was gone for good.

Time to get moving. Today was the luncheon with Val and Rachel. A pity Tom had returned to California, or he could have joined them. It had been wonderful having him around for a few days. Julia had glowed, and the aunts and uncles had greeted him with open arms and mounds of pasta. If any of them cared that he was gay, there'd been no sign of it.

Before meeting her friends, Kate had an appointment at the vet for kitten shots. "Dinah, come to Mama."

Dynamite the Blue Cream Cat had been snoozing, but when Kate called, the kitten decided it was playtime. Dinah had only two speeds—full-tilt boogie and coma. At the moment she was in her active phase. Fat little tail straight up, except for the right-angle bend at the tip, she darted into the master bedroom and under the king-size bed.

Kate halted in the doorway. Donovan's room. It seemed like an invasion of his privacy to enter, but the kitten needed catching.

"Dinah, sweetheart, you little demon, where are you?" Kate flattened herself on the carpet and peered under the bed. Dinah was under the headboard, and wanted to play. She skittered along the wall, eluding Kate's outstretched hand. When she retreated to the corner formed by the wall and the bed leg, Kate made a grab. Dinah squirted off, and Kate's middle finger stabbed into something sharp.

A woman's earring had become wedged between the leg and the wall. Carefully Kate pulled the earring loose. Long and dangly, it was a distinctive creation of beads and amber. Lost by one of Donovan's girlfriends, a woman with a dramatic sense of style. Kate wanted to smash the earring into the floor.

Instead, mouth tight, she got to her feet. Why was actual

evidence of other women so much more upsetting than abstract knowledge?

As if by magic, Dinah materialized beside her, bumping her little head against Kate's shin as if she knew her adopted mother needed consolation. Kate scooped up the kitten and nuzzled the soft fur. No wonder single women traditionally kept cats. Much more reliable than men.

As soon as Kate entered the restaurant, the hostess said with a smile, "Your friends are already seated."

Morgan Millard was the neighborhood eatery of Roland Park, where Kate had grown up, and she loved the comfortable atmosphere, the golden wood, and patterned navy wallpaper. Good food, too. As she approached the booth, Val Covington got up to welcome her. Petite and vibrantly redheaded, Val bounced forward with a hug. "You look great, Kate. Being in Maryland agrees with you."

"The same can be said for you, Val. Your love life must be blossoming."

"In a manner of speaking. I'm doing celibacy now. Very empowering, just like all the feminist theoreticians say."

"Celibacy? It will never last." Kate turned to the booth to greet Rachel, and saw another old friend. "Laurel, how wonderful!"

Laurel Clark slid from the booth, looking very New York in black knits and a thick braid of cinnamon hair falling down her back. It was hard to imagine her in a fluffy white debutante dress. "Val persuaded me to come down for the day to surprise you."

Kate embraced her with delight. The five members of the Circle of Friends had once been as close as sisters. They'd gone off in different directions after graduation, yet even after all these years, if one of them needed a sympathetic ear, she knew that another member was only a phone call away.

When any of them met in person, the months and years dropped away and there was an instant sense of connection.

Kate suspected that if they'd first met as adults, they probably would never have come to know each other well enough to become friends. Yet the shared past, and very real trust and affection, had forged enduring bonds.

Kate turned to Rachel. Dark-haired and formidably composed, Rachel looked like the kind of doctor anyone would trust. Rachel had always known she wanted to go into medicine, and had pursued her goal with a single-mindedness that had awed Kate. "How was Australia?"

"Busy. Hot. I should have stayed another few weeks, until spring made more progress in this hemisphere." She lowered her voice. "I'm so sorry about your father."

"I got the note you sent. Thank you." Besides offering condolences, Rachel had written movingly of the shock she'd felt at the sudden loss of her own mother, showing an understanding that had made Kate cry. Sam's death had been a loss for Rachel, just as Kate had mourned the passing of Barbara Hamilton.

Though each of the other women had visited Kate in San Francisco, having a Baltimore reunion made her think back nostalgically to high-school days. Feeling young and giddy, she lifted her water glass. "To Rainey, who isn't here this time. May she join us when next we meet!"

"Hear, hear." With a solemn clinking of glasses, they made the toast.

Val said, "Okay, guys, it's show time! Who has news? Any pictures?"

"I've got a shot of Sandy and her family." Rachel laid a photograph on the table.

"You lucky aunt. What darlings the kids are," Laurel said.

Rachel agreed, then started to tell about her months in Australia. It was interesting, but Kate couldn't help thinking that for a group of reasonably well-adjusted women, they hadn't done very well in terms of settling down and starting families. Rachel had dated Tom for years, and the two were still good friends, but that's all it was—a friendship.

Val adored men, and with her redheaded zest and enthu-siasm, they adored her back. But she had a record of pick-ing losers. Under her New York polish Laurel was a little shy, so maybe she just hadn't found the right man yet. Well, at least there was Rainey. Kenzie seemed like a nice guy, even if he was a superstar, and they certainly seemed very much in love. Maybe there was hope for all of them.

At the first lull, Kate asked, "What are you doing now, Laurel? Tell all."

"Nothing too dramatic. The publisher I work for has moved into the Decatur Building, an early skyscraper. You'll have to come visit, Kate—I think it would be pretty interesting to an architect."

"I studied that building in school," Kate said. "I'd love to see it. Maybe I can take a day trip to New York later in the spring. Any exciting men in your life?"

"In New York City? Not likely. From a dating point of view, it's like a really large rummage sale—lots of strange items, but darned little that you'd want to take home. I'm holding out for a man with a voice like Sean Connery."

"Sean Connery," Val repeated with a rapturous sigh. "If you find a man like that and decide not to keep him, I want an introduction."

"I thought you were into celibacy," Laurel said. "That it was empowering."

"If a man with Sean Connery's voice shows up, I'll show you how empowered I can be. He won't stand a chance!"

Then it was Kate's turn to tell them about Kenzie Scott, who actually did have a voice rather like Sean Connery now that she thought about it.

When Rachel and Laurel went off to the rest room, Val pulled a sheaf of papers from her voluminous purse. "Here are the results of the search you asked for. Sorry it took so long. If you ask me, either of these clowns could rationalize vandalism if he felt provoked enough."

Kate read the papers, frowning. Burke had been a po-litical activist since his college days in the late sixties. In fact, he'd been a member of a student protest group linked to bombing a university laboratory, although he hadn't been charged in the case.

Joe Beekman was a decorated Vietnam combat veteran who knew something about explosives and weapons and had learned to kill for his country. Now he ran a community drug rehabilitation program. A valuable man—but might his anger over his mother's eviction make him hark back to the violence of his younger days?

Probably the investigators on Sam's case had already considered the protesters, but it wouldn't hurt to pass the information on. "Thanks, Val. Things have calmed down at Concord Place, but if there's more trouble, we'll know where to start looking."

"Anytime."

Kate noticed Val's colorful, gypsylike jewelry. "I like the three gold ear hoops. Are you doing body piercing in any less visible spots?"

"I've considered it," Val admitted, "but thinking about what might happen if a navel ring got caught in a zipper always freaks me out."

Kate's gaze fell on a pendant hanging among Val's multiple necklaces. Dangly beads with amber, and very familiar.

"Pretty, isn't it?" Val said. "Actually, it was one of a pair of earrings but the other got lost, so I put this on a chain."

A woman with a dramatic sense of style. Donovan and Val, together in that bed. Kate felt as if she'd been kicked. She wanted to cry, But you were my friend first! Instead, she counted to ten, then said, "This is your lucky day. I found the lost earring this morning. Under Donovan's bed."

Val's face went rigid. "I . . . I don't suppose there is any yarn I could spin that would convince you of anything other than the obvious explanation."

"You don't have to. I mean, it's none of my business who either of you were sleeping with."

"Maybe not, but you're human. Heck, we're all far, far

too human. I broke the Good Girlfriends' Code by sleeping with your ex-husband."

"Hardly. I hadn't laid eyes on the man for almost ten years. He was up for grabs." Then, hating herself for wanting to know: "How long did you go out together?"

"About a year and a half. We ran into each other one day and got to talking, and, well, you know." Val shrugged uncomfortably.

"Recently?"

Val ran her fingers through her curly mop, looking like Little Orphan Annie on a bad hair day. "Yeah. He came to say good-bye after finding out about Sam's will."

Wondering if that had been the same day he'd taken her out to Brandy Lane and persuaded her to stay in Baltimore, Kate moistened her dry lips. "He must have wanted PDI a lot to break up with you to get it."

"We didn't have a big serious thing going, Kate. It was just fun. Company. Donovan is a hell of a nice guy, and he treated me so well that I couldn't remember why I've put up with what I did from so many jerks over the years. But it was no grand passion on either side."

Telling herself that maturity was definitely in order here, Kate said, "I'm sorry my coming back messed things up for you. But I'll be gone again in a year. Less now."

"Your return didn't make that much difference." Val began twining red curls around her forefinger. "I'll admit I wouldn't have minded if things had developed further, but Donovan didn't want more, and if there's one thing I've learned to spot in my checkered career, it's a man who isn't interested in a deeper relationship. If anyone has the key to his heart, it's you."

"If I ever did, I've lost it." Kate tried to look composed since Laurel and Rachel were returning. "And frankly, I don't want to find it again."

"If that's true, you're a damned fool, Kate. Take it from an expert—good men are hard to find," Val said. "Are we still friends? I couldn't forgive myself if I've wrecked that."

Her friend's stricken face put the situation into perspective. This was Val, with whom she'd shared years of her life. She'd had every right to go out with Donovan. Kate leaned over and hugged her. "Of course we're still friends. You have nothing to apologize for. Remember our old school motto?"

They recited, "Men come and go, but friends are forever." They'd invented the motto in junior high, and it still had merit.

The others sat down and started talking dessert, but Kate didn't participate in the rounds of "I will if you will." Her mind was stuck on Donovan. Everyone had thought she was crazy to leave.

Everyone except the two who knew the whole story: Tom, and Rachel Hamilton.

29

The shattering of Kate's family had begun at a perfectly ordinary gathering. Most Sunday evenings, Kate and Donovan joined her parents for dinner, often with Tom, and sometimes Rachel as well. Today only Tom, just back from visiting friends in San Francisco, was a guest.

It was a pasta night, which Kate usually enjoyed, but this time she was not in the best of moods. Though she'd managed to finish her spring course work without disgracing herself, the last few months had been very rough, because her marriage was going to hell in a handbasket.

Donovan was sitting on her right. He wore a navy blazer and looked very grave as he finished the gin and tonic he'd started before dinner. She knew he was as worried as she was, but he reacted by becoming increasingly possessive, asking where she'd been if she was even ten minutes later than expected. She was becoming cut off from her friends, because he didn't like her visiting or even calling them. She understood why—with her schedule, she hardly had any time for him during the school year, and he was feeling neglected.

But she missed her friends, especially since her marriage was deteriorating. There had been several incidents when he'd shaken her violently, or pinned her to the wall as he vented his temper. He always cooled off quickly and apologized, and he'd never really hurt her. Still, it was profoundly unnerving not to know what might set him off.

Donovan caught her looking at him and gave her a private smile. Yes, they were going through a bad patch, but they would survive. They loved each other too much not to work out the problems.

Her father's voice cut through her preoccupation. "Where's Rachel, Tom? Haven't seen her in weeks."

"She's studying. Final exams this week. Future doctors don't know how to relax."

"Time for you to marry her. She can go to medical school later. Babies are best to have when you're young and full of energy."

Kate had heard the baby rap often herself. Three years of marriage and not pregnant yet? Maybe she hadn't finished college yet, but Donovan had. He could support a family. She handled such comments patiently, promising the various aunts, uncles, and cousins that babies would come in good time.

But Tom's situation was different. His gaze went to Kate, and she saw torment in his eyes. "Dad, Mother. I have something to say."

Julia put down her fork, her expression unreadable. "Yes, dear?"

"Rachel is my best friend in the world, but we'll never

get married." A muscle jumped in his cheek. "I . . . I've come to realize that I'm gay."

"No!" Face gray, Sam lurched to his feet, throwing down his napkin. "You're joking, right? Christ, it's a lousy joke."

"It's not a joke, Dad. Believe me, if I could be different, I would be. But God made me this way, and I can't change."

"No!" Sam shouted again. "Don't bring God into this. You're sick, screwed up. We'll get you to a doctor, someone who can cure you."

Donovan scowled as if his brother-in-law had just turned into a cockroach, and a spasm of pain contorted Julia's face. "This . . . this isn't what I would have wished for you, Tom. But you're my son. Nothing will ever change that."

Sam stared at her, almost as shocked as he had been at Tom's announcement. "How can you act as if this disgusting idea of his is . . . is normal?"

"Tom isn't sick, Sam," she said. "I've wondered for a long time, but hoped I was wrong."

"Because you can't stand the idea of having a gay son?" Tom asked, voice edged.

"No. Because I know that life is harder for those who are different, and what mother could want such difficulty for her child?" Julia reached across the table and laid her hand on his for a moment. "But sometimes a hard path is the only one there is."

Tom looked terribly alone on the opposite side of the table. Kate went to stand by her brother, resting her hand on his shoulder. "I know this is a shock, Dad. It was for me when I found out. But Tom hasn't changed. Everything that has made you proud of him is still there."

"Dammit, Kate, don't encourage him!" her father snapped.

Donovan said, tight-lipped, "You knew about this and didn't tell me?"

"It wasn't my place to speak before Tom was ready."

Tom said, "I think it's best if I leave. I've been offered

a job in San Francisco. The Bay Area is the place to be for anyone interested in small computer development."

Sam swore. "It's also America's capital for perversion. Are you going there so you . . . you can . . ." His mouth worked, unable to speak of what he loathed.

"I'm moving for a number of reasons," Tom said quietly. "One of them is to have more freedom to be myself in a place where my . . . my preferences won't embarrass you."

"Stay here, Tom, I'll get you into treatment," Sam begged. "I don't care how much it costs or how long it takes, just so long as you try to get over these . . . these sick ideas."

"I won't go to a therapist. A good one would say I am what I am. A bad one will give you false hope and try to make me think I'm a revolting pervert, which I'm not. I'm just . . . different in one way."

"Tom, maybe if you just tried, until Dad adjusts to the idea," Kate said under her breath.

"He won't, Kate. And if I surrender now, I may lose myself forever."

Voice shaking with anguish, Sam said, "If you refuse to change, then get out of my house *now*. Don't ever come back."

"It's my house, too," Julia said sharply. "My children will always be welcome."

With a roar of fury, Sam swept his arm across the table, knocking wineglasses to smash on the rug in bloodred stains. "Goddammit, Julia, if you allow that . . . that degenerate into my house again, I swear to God I'll leave for good."

"For good? I don't think so, Sam. For bigotry and pride, maybe, but not for good." Julia's words were emphatic, but her face was ashen.

Dear God, would her mother be forced to choose between her husband and her son? Kate pressed a hand to the pain in her stomach, sick with the knowledge that her family would never be the same again.

Tom intervened, "It's all right, Mother. You belong here. I'll manage." To his father, he said, "You needn't worry about me polluting your precious house. I promise never to set foot here again."

Then he turned to Kate and hugged her hard. "Thanks, Katie. You don't know how much your support means," he said quietly. "I'll be leaving for San Francisco within the week."

He'd been planning this for some time, Kate realized. She couldn't blame him for wanting to escape.

"To hell or San Francisco, it's all the same to me." Sam's chest heaved as he struggled for breath. "You are no longer my son."

He stalked from the room. Julia watched him leave, her expression devastated.

"I'm sorry you had to sit through a Corsi family fight, Donovan," Tom said. "Not a pretty sight."

"How could you do that to Sam?" Donovan asked furiously. "He's given you everything, and instead of being grateful, you break his heart." He shoved his chair back and stood. "You stay the hell away from Kate."

"Don't you dare talk to Tom like that! You have no right to tell me I can't see my own brother."

"I have every right!" He grabbed Kate's wrist. "Sorry to walk out in the middle of dinner, Julia, but I think it's best to leave."

Seeing Tom's frown, Kate gave a small shake of her head to tell him she was all right and mouthed the words, "I'll call."

She had to jog to keep up with her husband's angry strides as he took her outdoors. After shoving her into his car, he slammed the door and went to his side of the vehicle, his expression thunderous.

Kate said coldly, "You hurt my wrist."

He started the car, then gunned it up the quiet tree-lined street. "You're lucky that's all I hurt!"

She wanted to snap back, but she'd learned to be more

cautious. When Donovan was in this mood, there was no telling what he might do. It was wiser, and safer, to wait until he'd cooled down.

Neither of them spoke again until they reached their carport. She climbed out without waiting for him and headed into the house. Donovan caught up with her as she was digging in her purse for keys.

"I'll do that." He opened the door, then stood aside for her.

She brushed past him and into the kitchen, where she pulled a block of cheese from the refrigerator and took a slicing knife from the silverware drawer. She hadn't eaten since breakfast, and knew from experience that if she didn't get her blood sugar up right away, her temper would snap. God only knew what might happen then.

Donovan followed her into the kitchen. "Sam won't have anything to do with Tom, and I want your promise that you won't, either. Your father has enough to upset him without having your disloyalty thrown in his face."

"Disloyalty!" Kate slapped the knife on the counter. "Sam is the one that's disloyal. How can he disown his own son over something that isn't Tom's fault?"

"If Tom can't help himself, he should have had the decency to stay in the closet! I sure as hell was happier not knowing what turned him on."

"No one should have to live that kind of lie." Kate took a deep breath, trying to slow her hammering pulse. "I'm not going to turn my back on Tom, and my mother won't, either. Frankly, I expected Sam to take the news badly, but I thought better of you. How could you be so rotten?"

Canisters jumped as Donovan banged his fist onto the counter. "You're no one to talk about behavior! Christ, Kate, how could you lie to me? What else have you been hiding?"

"There's a big difference between a lie and keeping someone else's secret! I couldn't tell you about Tom when he'd specifically asked me not to. He knew better than I what a jerk you'd be."

Donovan exploded across the kitchen, tall and broad and furious. "Don't you talk to me that way! You're my wife, and I won't allow you to hurt Sam, or hang out with a bunch of queers."

"Why? Do you think that homosexuality is contagious?" she screamed, searching for words that would hurt him as much as he'd hurt her. "Are you secretly afraid you're really a Patsy, not a Patrick?"

His fist smashed into her jaw, flinging her backward, slamming into the edge of the counter. Head spinning, she clung to the cabinet, dazed and hurting but too furious to feel fear.

After an appalled instant Donovan said, "Jesus, Kate, you shouldn't make me do things like that."

His words struck her harder than his fist had. "You bastard! Don't you *dare* try to make this my fault! I've bent over backward to be understanding about your rotten temper, to make allowances, but I've had enough! The problem is *you,* not me, and I'm not going to stay here to get hit again."

Donovan stared at her in horror. "No. Kate, you can't leave me."

She touched her numbed jaw, and knew with absolute certainty that if she didn't leave now, their marriage was doomed to a downward spiral of violence and fear. Gradually he had undermined her confidence, cut her off from her friends, isolated her more and more. If she stayed any longer, it would be as a broken woman.

"I have to leave," she said unsteadily. "Maybe counseling will help, but I'm not staying in this house while we find out."

She reached for her purse, but before she could get it, Donovan grabbed her. "You can't go! You're the best thing that ever happened to me. I swear to God I'll never hurt you again!"

Jerking her arm from his grip, she said bitterly, "You've said that before. And you know what? I don't believe you anymore."

"We have so much! Don't throw it away in a moment of anger." He caught her shoulders, pleading, "I . . . I can't live without you."

She could see his desperate fear of losing her, but this time she was desperate, too. "Let me go!"

Lost in his own private hell, he didn't hear her entreaty. Knotting his hand in her hair, he pulled her head back and locked his arm around her waist to hold her close as he kissed her with suffocating intensity.

They had come together in passion and love a thousand times before. More than once, conflict had been healed by intimacy. But this time she felt revulsion, and rising panic. God help her, she was at his mercy, helpless against his size and strength. Near hysteria, she wept, "Don't do this! Oh, God, please don't do this."

As easily as if she were a child, he pushed her back against the counter. "You're mine, Kate, mine. I love you so much. I can't let anyone else have you."

His hands trapping her in a bruising grip, he kissed her again. Her frantic hand swept across the counter, seeking a weapon. Found a familiar long, narrow shape. Clutched. Raised.

Stabbed.

He cried out and let her go, staggering back against the refrigerator as blood spilled from a slash that ran from his left shoulder to his elbow. With shaking fingers he touched the wound, then stared at the crimson stains.

She almost vomited at the sight of his blood. Dear God in heaven, she might have killed him!

He raised his gaze, and the expression on his face would haunt her forever. For an eternal moment they stared at each other as the fabric of their marriage, the last threads of intimacy and commitment and trust, ripped asunder.

Trying to deny the shattering truth, Donovan said in a

voice of eerie calm, "Don't worry, Kate, it's not deep. I've been hurt worse working on my car. I'll be fine. Let's just . . . sit down and give ourselves a chance to unwind."

Numbly she looked at the stained knife still in her hand. "It's too late, Patrick," she whispered.

"No! It can't be too late."

She shook her head wordlessly. Wishing she were dead.

A terrible resignation came over him, like a man who had been mortally wounded and knew that further struggle for life would be futile. He sagged back against the refrigerator and slowly slid to the floor. "It's all my fault. I'm sorry, Kate. So . . . damned . . . sorry."

She gazed at him for one last time, the handsome face that she loved, the strong body that had given her such joy.

The blood that seeped between his fingers.

This was the man she had thought would be beside her as long as they both should live. How could she bear to leave him?

In a voice laced with anguish, he whispered, "If you're going to go, do it quickly, Kate. For both our sakes."

Saturated with pain beyond anything she had ever imagined, she carefully laid the stained knife on the counter. Then she lifted her purse and walked out of the house that had known her greatest happiness and her blackest sorrow.

She didn't see the man she had married for ten long years.

30

"Kate, you still with us?" Val's voice broke Kate's reverie. Pulling herself back to the present, she said, "Trying to decide between peach cobbler and Death of a Thousand Chocolates cake is serious business and requires concentration."

"Get the peach cobbler," Laurel advised. "I'm doing the chocolate cake. We can share. That way, we'll both survive."

When they finally ended their three-hour lunch, Laurel said, "Kate, Rachel, do you want to come with Val and me to the crafts expo?"

"I was there yesterday, buying the place out," Kate answered. "There won't be anything left for you today."

"Would you like to go for a walk, Kate?" Rachel said. "I could use some fresh air."

Kate knew that more than a walk was being offered. "That would be nice. We can look for crocuses."

"Croci," Val said. "Remember your Latin declensions, girls."

On a wave of laughter and hugs, they settled the bill with a tip that would double the waitress's income for the day, then went into the pale spring sunshine. Laurel climbed into Val's old Toyota, and the two of them headed for downtown.

As Kate and Rachel crossed the small lot to the street, Kate said idly, "A silver Honda just like mine is parked next to my car."

"The burgundy one is yours? The silver car is mine."

"We always did have similar tastes. When my Honda arrived in Baltimore, courtesy of a couple of East-bound grad students, Donovan told me I was a lemming with no automotive imagination."

"Men. What did you say?"

"That if it's lemminglike to appreciate a reliable, well-designed car, then lead me to the nearest cliff. Donovan, naturally, prefers vehicles with attitude, like his Harley and classic Corvette."

Rachel turned left along Roland Avenue, the tree-lined residential boulevard that ran through Roland Park. "You were off in never-never land there for a while."

"If only it had been never-never land. I went somewhere very real."

"I thought as much. Were you thinking of the day you left Donovan?"

Kate had driven around in a daze, ending at Rachel's apartment. Her shocked friend had put aside her textbooks and tended Kate's hurts. She wanted to see Donovan arrested and thrown into jail immediately, but Kate had flatly refused to allow Rachel to call anyone but Tom. Instinctively she'd known it was essential to think through what had happened before setting into motion events beyond her control.

"Yes. I still think silence was best. My father was devastated at Tom's coming out, and my insistence on divorce was almost as bad. Donovan was the son he'd always wanted, the most satisfactory of his children. It would have broken Sam's heart to know that Donovan was abusing me. Besides, maybe the police would have arrested *me*. Donovan was the one who got knifed."

"If you'd told your father the whole story, he might have lost Donovan, but he'd still have had you. And you were the apple of his eye."

"I needed to leave Maryland, so he'd have lost me anyhow. This way, he still had Donovan, and I think they were each other's salvation." Kate believed that to her very marrow. Tom had rushed to Kate after Rachel called him. Unable to persuade Kate to call the police, he suggested she join him in California. There, safe from Donovan, she could start a new life. She had seized on the idea. More than anything else, it was her brother's kindness and understanding that had pulled her through.

The next morning, Kate had called her parents and announced she was filing for divorce. All hell broke loose. Sam had become enraged all over again. The only thing he might have accepted as legitimate grounds for divorce was the truth, and Kate would not reveal it. Julia had attempted to mediate, but Kate wouldn't talk to her, either. Within twenty-four hours of leaving her husband, she was estranged from her father in a breach that was never fully healed. Later Kate realized that Sam had blamed Tom for the divorce, widening the family schism still further.

Rachel broke into her thoughts. "Does Donovan know how lucky he was that you let him off the hook?"

"He knows. Frankly, he might have been happier if I'd crucified him. But what good would it have done to destroy his life?" Kate kicked a pebble along the sidewalk. "Incidentally, Donovan recently told me that his father was an abusive alcoholic. In earlier days he couldn't bear to talk about it."

"That explains a lot—abusers were often abused themselves when they were children. Donovan's family may have been caught in a cycle of violence for generations," Rachel said. "But I gather you two are getting along well now."

"Surprisingly so. As housemates, we're quite compatible. We stay out of each other's way."

"Not a bad recipe for marriage, actually."

"This is nothing like marriage." The thought made the chocolate cake Kate had eaten coagulate in her stomach like lead.

"Sounds as if the scars are still tender."

Kate sighed. "Why do men batter their wives, Doc?"

"Some men like inflicting pain, but usually abuse is a way of establishing control, showing who's boss. Some abusers must control everything. Others are losers who can control very little in their lives except their own household, so they keep the wife and kids in line with anger and ridicule and violence. Then there are motives such as fear of losing the partner. Control your wife, don't let her have normal relationships with others, keep her dependent so she won't slip her leash."

Donovan had always been horrified by his own violence. And, while he was precise and well organized in his work and personal life, he wasn't a full-spectrum control freak. Apparently he was the sort who had battered and controlled from fear of losing his wife. Kate quoted, "Each man kills the thing he loves best."

"Not always, but too damned often. If you doubt it, spend Saturday night in an emergency room sometime. With a family history of alcoholism, drinking was probably the trigger that set Donovan off."

"He told me that himself. I never caught on, because most of the time his drinking didn't seem to affect him," Kate said. "Lord, but I was stupid. I thought that love was enough, but it isn't. Do batterers ever change?"

"Sometimes, if they're motivated enough," Rachel said. "But more often they just find another woman to abuse. Maybe that's what Donovan has been doing."

"He told me that I'm the only woman he's ever struck. A singular honor, don't you think?"

"Assuming he's telling the truth."

"I think so. For one thing, he's given up all alcohol, which is bound to help." Kate watched two squirrels chasing each other amorously along a branch. "Until I came back, he and Val had a thing going. Since Val just told me what a great guy he is, I assume he never slammed her against any walls."

"Val?" Rachel made a face. "How messy."

"Not really. She and I were both terribly civilized and more or less apologized to each other for the situation."

"Thank God for friendship. It's more reliable than passion."

They walked through streets they had known their whole lives. Kate felt herself relaxing, partly from the familiar scenes, partly from the calming influence of her friend. Rachel had the kind of composure that could look into a volcano and ask the lava if it was having a nice day.

At length, Kate said, "But sometimes abusers do change."

"Sometimes. If they're very young, as Donovan was, the odds for change are better, especially since he's smart enough to have stopped drinking. But most abusers *don't* change." Rachel faced her. "Are you seriously thinking about getting back together with him, or is this just a mental exercise?"

"Of course I'm not thinking of getting together with him again! Even if I wanted that, there's no guarantee he would. But . . . I'm confused, to put it mildly. He's grown in good ways during the last ten years. Mostly he's easy to have around. But he still has a hell of a temper, even though he seems to be better at controlling it now."

Rachel shook her head, the perfectly cut dark hair falling into place effortlessly. "What frightens you most—the fear of actual bodily harm, of being injured, possibly even killed? Or the fear of emotional damage?"

The words rocked Kate. When she'd arrived at Rachel's on that long-ago night, she'd been bruised and stained with her husband's blood, but her injuries had been nothing compared with her psychic devastation. "The emotional fears are far worse."

"All right. Now that you know what you're most afraid of—deal with it."

"You're tough, Hamilton."

"Damned right I am. If there's even a remote chance that

you're going to jump back into the fire with Donovan, you'd better know what you're risking."

"I need to think about this. I act weird around him. Attracted, but twitchy. I don't approve of my behavior."

"No one's perfect, Kate. Not even you."

"What is that supposed to mean?"

"When we were growing up, I always thought you were the most together person I knew. A sunny-tempered extrovert, at ease under all conditions. I was glad you'd decided we were friends before you went to school and realized that I was a geeky kind of kid, not an asset to your reputation."

Kate was appalled. How was it possible to be friends with someone for a lifetime and know so little? "Geeky? That's as absurd as the idea that I was some kind of Wonder Girl."

"I was shy and nearsighted and smart in an obnoxious sort of way," Rachel explained. "You were just as bright, but not offensively so. I learned a lot from you."

"This conversation is getting very strange. If I was so great, how did I manage to end up a battered wife and general coward about relationships?"

"For the first part of your life you were running on autopilot, everything working without much effort on your part," Rachel said slowly. "Then Donovan broke your sense of inner safety, and you didn't have very good coping skills. You survived pretty well, but at the price of avoiding genuine intimacy. Until you recover from the damage he did, you're not going to be able to put yourself at risk again. And recovering means that you have to look not only at the fact that you were abused, but also at how you were affected by committing an act of violence yourself."

While Kate was trying to sort out her friend's meanings, Rachel glanced at the street-corner sign above them. "We're almost at your mom's house. Think she'd mind if I stopped in to say hi?"

"She'd love it, and Oscar Wilde would go mad with joy."

As they turned the corner to walk the short block to the

Corsi house, Kate tried to decide what she wanted from Donovan. Punishment? Closure? The opportunity to work in PDI?

Or something different, and far more dangerous?

31

At home, Donovan was surveying the inside of the refrigerator speculatively when Dinah materialized and began batting his ankles. He scooped her up. The blue cream was the happiest little cat he'd ever seen. Everything in the world delighted her. She didn't walk like normal felines. Instead, she had a buoyant trot, almost like dancing.

Bracing her paws on his chest, she threw her head back and vibrated with pleasure as he scratched her chin with one finger. Her earnest, total enjoyment touched a chord of memory. Good grief, the kitten was like Kate at eighteen—full of anticipation, sure that the world was a place of miracles. No wonder he adored this handful of patchy gray fluff. A pity that humans who lost their trustful innocence could never really regain it.

Loss of innocence . . .

His gaze went involuntarily to the place where that last harrowing struggle had taken place. In the years since, the kitchen had been completely remodeled, enlarged, refloored—but like Lady Macbeth and her ceaseless attempts to cleanse her hands, the psychic stain remained. His mind wanted to veer away. Instead, he forced himself to remember, for the past was the key to the future.

He'd been tense when they went to dinner at the Corsis

that last night, knowing that things were going badly wrong with Kate, yet unsure how to change. He made his predinner gin and tonic himself, more than doubling the amount of gin in the hope it would help him relax.

Then Tom had dropped his bombshell, and everything went to hell. Donovan had been shocked and unsettled at the news, but it was the sight of Sam's pain that drove him to fury. Why couldn't Tom have kept his tastes to himself? Doing this to Sam was unforgivable.

Worse, the image of Kate standing with Tom against her family had chilled him to the bone. How long until she stood against her husband like that?

The next hour was hazy in his mind, the details blurred in a mist of gin, anger, and anxiety. He had taken Kate home, the terror that he was losing her like a stake through his heart. Then they reached the house, and his worst fears came true: after a searing quarrel, she announced that she was leaving him.

He freaked out, grabbing her in a frantic attempt to prove how much he loved her. Intimacy would draw them together, make the damage of the day fade away. He scarcely noticed she was struggling, until the knife sliced into him.

The pain and shock had jolted him back to reason, and the wrenching knowledge that a line had been irrevocably crossed. He did his best to downplay the disaster, to change her mind, but it was too late. Too damned late. Kate left, and he had known she was right to go.

He was shaken from the past when Dinah's sharp little ears suddenly went up. She scrambled from Donovan's arms and raced to the garage door just in time to greet Kate. Feline Early Warning System.

"Hi." He shook off the cold, black past. "How was the old gang?"

"Fine." Kate closed the door while Dinah did a scamper dance around her. As happened at least once a day, Donovan found himself staring at Kate to appease the hunger of so many years of missing her. Her golden hair falling forward, obscuring her expression. The graceful figure that was the exact, perfect balance of slimness and curves.

Hanging her tailored jacket in the coat closet, she added, "And such good luck. This morning I chased Dinah under your bed and managed to find one of Val's lost earrings. A favorite of hers, too."

Shit. "I'm sure she was delighted."

"More guilty than glad."

He felt a surprising stab of nostalgia for the relationship he'd had with Val. Simple, mutually enjoyable, with no pain or guilt. Why couldn't he have settled for that? Why did he long for the hurtful complexities of his relationship with Kate?

As soon as his mind formulated the question, he knew the answer. In order to reach the highest peaks, it was necessary to risk the deepest lows. Only with Kate had he known joy. Only with her had he known wholeness.

"Maybe we should introduce Val to your friend Alec."

Amusement lit Kate's face. "They'd probably like each other. A pity there's a continent between them." She bent to scoop up Dinah. "Unfortunately, I got to thinking about . . . the day I left you."

"I wish to God that the memory could be razed from both of our minds."

"Impossible. That was one of the defining moments of my life. Take it away, and nothing that happened afterward makes any sense."

"That's a little too metaphysical for me. I'd settle for oblivion." Yet there were things that should be said. "When we had that final argument, you asked if I was afraid that I was a Patsy, not a Patrick. My father yelled things like that when he was drunk. I wasn't tough enough for him. He thought any male who wasn't macho must be queer. He used to call me Patsy and threaten to make me wear my sister's clothes."

Kate winced. "And because I wanted to hurt you like

you were hurting me, I pushed the worst possible button at the worst possible time."

"It doesn't matter how furious we both were, *nothing* justifies my behavior. Christ, Kate, how can you bear to be in the same room with me?"

"I should be asking you that. Especially here in the kitchen, with so many knives within reach." Her tone was wry, but her eyes were serious.

He'd kept the knife she stabbed him with for years. Finally, knowing what a really sick memento of their marriage it was, he'd dropped it into the Chesapeake Bay. "You're no killer, Kate. What you did was in reaction to my violence."

"Joseph Campbell said that love is the burning point— the stronger the love, the greater the pain. If he's right, maybe we're better off without it."

"Never! Love comes in all varieties, Kate. Don't let the fact that my feelings for you shaded off into craziness put you off love altogether."

She regarded him with intense, unreadable eyes. He was relieved when the phone rang. The man on the other end of the line rattled off a series of terse sentences that made his expression turn grim as his attention was drawn away from personal issues.

The call ended, and he hung up the phone. "That was the State Department. I hope you've got a valid passport, because we're going to Mexico."

"Mexico?" Kate's startled tone caused Dinah's head to pop up.

"Did you read about the earthquake in Mexico City?"

"Yes, but I thought it wasn't too serious."

"Not compared to the big Mexico City quake a few years ago. That was a bad, bad time." Sometimes he dreamed of the people searching the ruins frantically for their loved ones. "We took down twenty-six damaged buildings then. This quake was nowhere near as bad, but the epicenter was right under a mid-rise housing project that turns out to have been built on a site that had been badly filled. The ground moved like jelly."

"Those are the damaged buildings shown in today's paper?"

"Right." He found a notepad and started a list. "Almost all of the casualties were there, in La Casa Miranda. The Mexican government wants the buildings down ASAP, before more people are injured."

"I see. And because PDI worked with them before, they want you."

"Naturally. So the Mexican government asked the U.S. government, and presto, half of PDI is on the way to the airport."

"High level. I'm impressed."

"What's even more impressive is the government citations for classified work we can't talk about."

"Dinah, you're going to have to stay with your grandma and your uncle Oscar again. When do we leave, Donovan?"

"Tomorrow if possible. If not, then Monday morning. Your Spanish will come in handy."

"And this time I know enough to be useful on the job."

"Kate, I don't want you working in those buildings. Earthquakes make structures incredibly unstable—all bets are off in terms of predicting how they'll come down. Sam had an instinct for knowing how damaged buildings would behave. Without him, the work will be even more dangerous than the other times we've done this kind of job."

"Let's see if I've got this right," Kate said. "You're saying that I'm so incompetent that I might accidentally bring down a structure if I'm allowed inside?"

"Kate . . ."

Her eyes widened. "Oh, it's the women and children and lifeboats. In other words, my life is more valuable than yours, or Luther's—what would his wife and kids say about that?—or Jim's, or Ted's—"

"Sarcasm will get you nowhere. This kind of job is a bitch, and I don't want you in a place that might collapse at any minute. Believe me, you'll earn your pay. There will be plenty of work for you without actually loading explosives."

"Can you honestly say that you'd tell me to stay out of quake-damaged buildings if I were a man? Surely not."

But she wasn't. She was Kate. Fudging, he said, "If the man was a novice at this work, I might."

"I really, really doubt that. Protectiveness is normal and it goes both ways, but I can't accept it on the job," she said soberly. "It's not that I'm panting to have a building fall on my head, Patrick. But if I'm going to do this work, I have to do *all* of it—the routine, the boring, the fun, and the scary. Otherwise, I might as well go back to San Francisco."

Once he would have done his damnedest to lay down the law. She'd almost fallen down an elevator shaft in Las Vegas, for God's sake, and that had been as safe as a demolition job could get. But if he was to have any kind of future with Kate, it must be built on new foundations. He would have to accept her as an equal, no matter how much he hated the thought of her in danger. "All right, Kate, you win—you work under the same conditions as everyone else. Just don't take any foolish risks, macho woman."

"No, *sir*."

Her smile was almost worth the knowledge that she would be risking her neck.

Almost.

A major aftershock hit. The structure shifted, groaning, and Kate lost her footing in the treacherous rubble. Terror spiked through her as she hit the floor, chunks of plaster banging her hard hat and bruising her ribs and shoulders. God in heaven, the building was coming down on her! Was this how Sam had felt in the instant before he died?

Kate came awake with a jolt. For an instant she was disoriented. Then the angle of the morning sunshine told her that she was home in Maryland, safe, after an intense

week of work in Mexico. During the quake's terrifying af-
tershocks, she'd had trouble remembering why she'd been
so hell-bent on proving herself equal to anything. Only a
damned fool would volunteer to go into the crumbling
death traps of La Casa Miranda.

But the work had to be done. She'd spent much of her
time sweating and making mental deals with God. After
grueling sixteen-hour days, she was fit only to stumble back
to the hotel, shower, and fall into bed.

And yet, Kate wouldn't have missed that job for anything, for she'd mastered her fears, and the payoff had been
sweet. Maybe the rush of exhilaration produced by surviv-
ing danger was the reason policemen and firemen and sol-
diers did what they did. By the end of the week she'd felt
an intense camaraderie with her coworkers that must be
rather like the experience of sharing foxholes together.

She'd turned out to have her father's gift for predicting
how damaged structures would come down. Donovan had
been impressed. She'd also learned that there was a healing
sense of catharsis in demolishing structures that had seen
great sorrow.

But now she was home on a sunny Saturday with a pile
of laundry to do. Whistling softly, she swung from the bed
and headed for the bathroom.

After a long shower, she dressed and ambled into the
kitchen. Wearing jeans and a blue shirt, Donovan was
grinding beans to make coffee.

She halted in the doorway, struck by the sight of his taut
back and neck. Once she had known that splendid body
intimately—the hard jut of shoulder blades, the taper from
broad shoulders to narrow waist, the salt taste of warm,
smooth skin. For a moment she wondered what it would
be like to cross the room and slide her arms around his
waist the way she had done in the days of their marriage.
Damn her father! He'd known that living together was very
different from working together.

Then Donovan glanced over his shoulder. "When I went

out to get the paper, I found that spring arrived while we were in Mexico. Forsythia bushes are going crazy all over Ruxton, and daffodils will be opening any second now."

"Maryland has such wonderful springs. I missed the dramatic seasonal changes in California." She headed toward the refrigerator. "The Mexican job was really interesting, but the more business travel I do, the more I appreciate being home."

"Savor this weekend, then. On Tuesday, we go to Atlanta for three days or so."

She groaned theatrically as she opened the refrigerator. "How about some eggs scrambled with sausage and one rather depressed-looking green pepper that has survived from last week, but only just?"

"Sounds good. Then, *cara mia*, we're going to play hooky."

"Come again?"

He held the coffeepot under the faucet and turned on the cold water. "It's going to be one of those gorgeous early spring days where the temperature will shoot up to eighty, everyone will throw their sweaters away, and the local journalists will swarm down to the Inner Harbor to get pictures of pretty young things in tank tops."

"Does that still happen?"

"It's a journalistic rite of spring. Then in a day or two the temperature will turn cold again, and people will dig out their sweaters, complaining bitterly that it isn't really summer yet."

"It's reassuring to know that local rituals persist. But spring will have to get along without me today. I've got a ton of things to do."

"The laundry can wait. In the past week you've put in eighty to a hundred hours of work. For the sake of your mental health, you need some playtime, and this is too lovely a day to waste."

"Since you put it that way . . ." She began cracking eggs. "Did you have something in mind?"

"I'll get out the bike, and we can go down to Annapolis."

Kate knew darned well what that meant: roaring through the hills with bodies touching, the sexy vibration of the Harley pulsing through them. He'd always had a motorcycle, and in the good days of their marriage they'd loved riding on it together. Invariably a bike trip had led to lovemaking. She hesitated, doubt in her face.

"The state legislature finally passed a mandatory helmet law. Remember how we used to think they never would?"

"You sure know how to bait a hook, boss. Okay, we'll take advantage of premature spring by surrendering to an attack of adolescent fantasy." The Mexico City job had taught her that taking risks could be worthwhile. Maybe it was time to take a few in her personal life.

32

It was a day made in heaven. Kate threw her head back and laughed with pure delight as they roared along a back road in Anne Arundel County, a few miles outside of Annapolis. A week ago nothing could have gotten her onto a motorcycle with Donovan, but now it seemed exactly the right thing to do.

In some ways, so little had changed. The hard waist she clasped, for example. Or the sexy intimacy of the two of them alone in the wind. Definitely an adolescent fantasy, and a damned good one. She could almost imagine that they were newlyweds still, with not a cloud in their personal sky.

They drove into the historic district, the three-century-old heart of colonial Annapolis, and left the Harley in a parking garage. For Kate, the sight of the narrow streets and old buildings was another homecoming. The capital of Maryland, Annapolis was a funky mix of tourists and navy personnel and politicians. She drew in a lungful of delectable spring air. "This was a great idea, Donovan. I love Annapolis."

"What's not to love? It's pretty, educational, and full of great shops and restaurants. Something for everyone."

"But small." They entered State Circle, a loop of street with the statehouse in the middle. "It's a scale-model state capital."

"A triumph of quality over quantity. No one else has a statehouse where George Washington resigned as commander-in-chief of the Continental Army."

"Spoken like a true Marylander," she said, smiling.

The scary part was how much she felt like a Marylander herself. When she moved to California, she'd assumed it was a permanent transplant. Now, older and wiser, she recognized how deeply her roots were sunk in this small corner of the world. Her mother's family had been in Maryland for centuries; her father's parents had come impoverished from Italy, and embraced their new home and its opportunities with passionate gratitude. Both family histories were part of her.

A pair of midshipmen from the academy, bandbox neat in their crisp navy-blue uniforms, passed them walking in the other direction. Under her breath, Kate said, "They look so *young*. A sure sign that I'm not."

"Speaking of young, do you know the first time I ever visited Annapolis?"

"I don't think you ever told me. I imagine that your parents brought you down when you were a tyke. Or was it a school trip?"

"It was with you."

She stopped and stared, causing a group of tourists behind her to swerve abruptly. She remembered that occasion very well. A couple of months before their marriage, they'd come down on the bike, wandered around, had lunch. Just like the plan for today. "You never visited the state capital, an hour from your home, until you were nineteen?"

"Strange but true." Lightly he touched her elbow and got her moving down Main Street toward the waterfront. "Annapolis is a rich man's town. Look at what it's known for—politics, sailing, the naval academy, historic preservation. Upper class interests, except maybe for politics. It just wasn't on my parents' mental map. We'd drive right by on our way to Ocean City."

"When we were married, I thought I knew you as well as myself. Now I'm continually learning how little I knew. On our first visit, it never occurred to me that you were a stranger to Annapolis. It certainly didn't show."

"I spent the evening after you suggested a visit studying a map of the town and talking to a friend who'd lived a less insular life. I was afraid you'd decide you were marrying beneath yourself and change your mind. That was part of the reason I worked so hard to look and talk like someone with a more educated background."

"Occasionally I was surprised by things you didn't know, but then, there was plenty that you knew and I didn't. I guess social barriers look a lot less important to someone like me who never had to worry about them," she said. "You seem to have gotten over that particular shoulder chip. How?"

"It was gradual. I owe a lot to Sam, of course. With him I never felt as if I had to pretend to be more than I was. At work, I became more confident as I gained experience. After five or six years I got to the point where talking to Pentagon generals and company presidents didn't put me into a flat panic anymore."

"Competence is a great creator of confidence. And you've picked up a lot of polish over the years. You don't sound like blue-collar Baltimore now." Not that she'd ever minded when he did. In fact, she kind of missed the Hell's

Angel, but she understood Donovan's need to fit into the world he married into. She'd been lucky; growing up as both Carroll and Corsi had made her feel at ease everywhere.

"In the small world of explosive demolition, I'm an expert. Very good for my working-class ego. In most ways I'm comfortable with myself. Except where you're concerned."

"Is that because of class, or guilt?"

"Guilt, definitely. Class isn't an issue anymore."

"If there was a market for selling guilt, we'd all be rich. But everyone is a seller, no one wants to buy."

"What do you feel guilty about, Kate?"

"For being a coward. For running away from the hard things."

"I've never known you to take the easy way out. You're the one who walked over to say hello at Sam's funeral, not me. You insisted on going into buildings that could have collapsed at any time."

"In both cases, I was scared out of mind."

"Which made your actions brave. You're avoiding the question, I think. I wish I knew what really bothered you about yourself."

"You get points for being willing to reveal some of your darker layers, Donovan. I admire that—but I have neither the desire nor the intention of doing the same."

"That's nothing if not honest," he said, his voice dry.

Honesty was one of the few virtues she could claim. Conversation lapsed as they reached the market at the foot of Main Street. At Donovan's suggestion, they lunched at a second-story restaurant that overlooked the City Dock. Kate's good mood returned as they laughed and talked and watched the yachts and the throngs of people enjoying the day. Donovan really was first-rate company. Smart, funny, well informed.

Perhaps it was the glass of wine she had with her meal, but she began to wonder how she'd react to Donovan if they'd met for the first time when she started work at PDI. Take away their complicated, tortured past, think of him as a new acquaintance who was teaching her a demanding, exciting new job.

God help her, she'd be halfway in love with him. The realization made her stomach knot. He was still—again— the most attractive man she'd ever known. There was nothing sexier than a man who laughed at her jokes, the way Donovan did. If they really had just met, she would be calling her friends, describing the mental, physical, and emotional chemistry, and speculating endlessly on whether she'd found the love of her life. How appalling to realize that she was still a raving romantic at heart.

She flipped a coin with him for the privilege of paying the check. She won, and he didn't even try to change her mind. The caveman had become positively liberated.

In the sunshine again, they walked to the visitors' gate that led onto the campus of the naval academy, the same route they'd always taken when rambling through Annapolis. The academy was surrounded by water on three sides, so the next step was to walk around the perimeter. Kate shaded her eyes to look at the distant sails of pleasure boats on the bay, glad that the city and the waterways that gave it life hadn't changed since her last visit.

They reached the end of the bay side of the campus and turned left to follow the edge bounded by the Severn River. Despite the other strollers, Kate felt as if they were in a bubble of privacy, isolated with the cool wind and the poignant cries of the gulls. She could almost imagine that they were eighteen and nineteen again.

Donovan interrupted her reverie. "Do you ever think about the future, Kate?"

She looked up at a gull wheeling through the sky. "Not really."

"What, no goals?"

Odd to realize how few goals she'd had over the years. She'd wanted to qualify as an architect and eventually have her own practice, but those had seemed like normal milestones of life rather than true goals. Working at PDI had been a dream, not a goal, and she'd accomplished that by chance, not will. Feeling vaguely slothful, she said, "My chief goal at the moment is to survive this year."

"That's the sum of your ambitions? Mere survival?"

Images of the children she'd wanted to have with Donovan flitted across her mind. She could almost feel the soft weight of an infant in her arms, hear a wordless gurgle of delight. Ruthlessly she suppressed her imagination. The goal of building a life and a business with the man she loved had been left dead in the ruins of their marriage. "Don't underestimate survival. Sometimes it's the most one can manage."

He took one of her hands between both of his, stroking with his palm. "I promised that I wouldn't touch you. I haven't entirely kept to that."

She felt as if she were fourteen, and for the first time in her life a boy she liked had taken her hand. She was acutely aware of textures, the faint roughness of calluses, the hollow of his palm as it glided over her sensitive skin.

Part of her wanted to jerk away. A larger, yearning part wanted to slide into his arms. "The first time you broke your word I was on the verge of falling down an elevator shaft, so I can forgive that pretty easily."

"The other times haven't been life or death. Slowly, the walls between us have been coming down." He continued to caress her hand. It was a G-rated seduction in broad daylight. Her blood bubbled through her veins with excitement and alarm.

Then his hands stilled. "I give you fair warning, Kate. The past has left us with a lot of heavy baggage, but maybe we can still build a future together. There's never been anyone for me but you. I can't let you go again without at least trying to change your mind."

Kate was trapped by his gaze, his intensity. Pure panic boiled through her at the thought of allowing him into her life, her body, her soul, again. Yet she didn't run. For that, perhaps, she deserved some credit. "Warning noted. But, Patrick—we've both changed. Are you really interested in me, or in memories of the golden past?"

His clasp tightened. "In *you*, Kate. You've acquired a lot of edges, not all of which are comfortable, but at heart you're still the girl I fell crazy in love with when I was nineteen. I can survive without you—but I'd rather not."

Earlier she'd speculated on how she might react to him if they had just met as strangers. But that could never happen—the past and its shadows would always be with them. Between them. "Don't . . . don't rush me. I don't know if I can give back what you want."

"But you're not saying absolutely never. God, Kate, if there's a chance . . . any chance at all . . ." He raised her hand and kissed her fingertips with a tenderness that made her want to weep.

"I don't know if there is a chance, Patrick! Maybe it will never be possible to get rid of that baggage."

He laced the fingers of one hand through hers, raising his other hand to skim her cheek. "Trees can grow from tiny cracks in stony cliffs, Kate. This may be a very small crack indeed—but it's a beginning."

33

The doorbell fluted its two-note chime as Julia set the baking dish of lemon chicken into the oven. She closed the oven and headed to the front hall, wondering who might be calling late on a Saturday afternoon. Was it Girl Scout cookie season already?

Not yet. Charles Hamilton was standing on her front steps with a bouquet of variegated carnations and two dogs. "You're an hour early, Charles. Dinner just went into the oven, and I haven't taken a shower yet."

"I know this is a rotten trick. But I'd finished the Saturday yard work, so I decided to be selfish and disguise it under the pretext of promoting spontaneity."

She buried her smile in the spicy carnations. "What excuse do the dogs have?"

"They wanted to visit Oscar."

"Naturally. All right, Tort and Retort, come on in."

They trotted inside with impeccable manners. Oscar Wilde advanced, and a round of ritual sniffing began. The dogs were longtime friends. Julia was always amused by the fact that little Oscar was leader of the pack.

She led the dogs to the back door so they could chase each other around the fenced yard. When she returned to the kitchen, Charles raised her chin and gave her a thorough kiss. "I thought that after I've messed up your schedule, I can walk the dogs while you shower."

"A good plan. Let me get these into water." She put the carnations in a vase, thinking how quickly she and Charles had drifted into a comfortable pattern. They had dinner together several nights a week, sometimes at her house, sometimes at his. While not eliminating the primal sorrow over Sam's death, the relationship did help her get through the days, and the nights. Especially the nights.

After placing the flowers on the dinner table, she said, "Maybe I'll join you on that dog walk. There's plenty of time before dinner will be ready."

He led her into the living room and drew her down to the sofa beside him. "I have a better plan. Let's neck."

She emerged from his embrace laughing. "Charles, this is absurd at our age!"

"Why should kids have all the fun?"

"A good point, but I think necking was abolished sometime during the sexual revolution."

"It's a fine old custom, worthy of being reinstated." He began to toy with the top button of her shirt. "So is petting. Remember the incredible excitement that a single button could inspire in the long-ago days of our youth?"

Actually, she could remember. A little breathlessly, she said, "Were you always this playful and I just didn't notice?"

"No, it was Barbara who washed the starch out of my stuffed shirt. It was impossible to live with her and be stuffy," he said. "Does it bother you when I mention her?"

"I can accept our relationship as a kind of private retreat that exists apart from the normal world, but talking about Barbara, or Sam, or our children, pulls me back to reality. When Tom was staying here, and when Rachel and Kate dropped by unexpectedly, I felt as if I had a scarlet 'A' on my forehead."

"Then let's go back to necking and pretending we're adolescents." He scooped her up and lowered her to the carpet, then kissed her again. "If we were sixteen, I can imagine us getting so excited we'd fall off the sofa and hardly notice."

"These days, of course, we have to be careful not to do anything disastrous to our aging joints." Her arms went around him. "I must say that not all of you seems to have aged."

He waggled his thick eyebrows. "I'm not as good as I once was, but I'm as good once as I ever was."

She groaned. "That's an old one."

"Old is good—that's the whole point." He returned to her shirt buttons. "I wonder if I can manage to get to second base before dinner?"

She'd always liked Charles's sense of humor, but this private, sweetly silly side of him was new to her. It was nice that someone she'd known almost her whole life could still surprise her. In a quavering, adolescent voice, she said, "I'm a nice girl. My mama says that if I let a man touch me like that, he won't respect me in the morning."

Charles waggled his eyebrows again. "Trust me, little girl, the more I touch you tonight, the more I'll respect you tomorrow."

She was giggling and he was unfastening the last of her buttons when the front door opened, and Kate and Donovan walked in, windblown in jeans and carrying motorcycle helmets. Paralysis was universal. Kate's jaw dropped, Donovan looked thunderstruck, and Julia wished that she were dead.

Charles recovered first. He swiftly redid a couple of Julia's buttons, enough to make her decent, then got to his feet and helped her from the floor. "There is no point in pretending this is anything different than what it appears to be."

Julia stammered, "Kate, I'm so sorry that . . . that . . ."

"No, we're the ones who should apologize," Kate said, her face pale. "We were just coming back from Annapolis and thought we'd stop by and see if you wanted to join us for dinner. We shouldn't have . . . I mean, it never occurred to me that . . ."

"That an adult child with a key can't walk unannounced into the house she grew up in," Charles supplied. "An understandable attitude. Any errors in judgment here were mine."

A white-lipped Donovan was about to speak when Kate grabbed his arm and hauled him away. "Good night. I . . . I hope you both have a nice evening."

When the door closed, Julia sank onto the sofa and buried her face in her hands. Charles sat down and put an arm around her shoulders. "I'm sorry, Julia. Getting caught by one's children is worse than getting caught by one's parents, I think. And it's all my fault."

She couldn't go on like this any longer. "It was as much my fault as yours. I could have said no. So I . . . I'll say no now. Better late than never."

He became very still. "Are you ending things between us?"

"It's not that I haven't enjoyed our time together, but I . . . I . . ."

"You're ashamed to be seen with me."

In a sense that was true. Being caught with him by Kate and Donovan seemed like a negation of the marriage that had occupied the center of her life for almost forty years. "I'm sorry, Charles. The simple truth is that at the moment, I'm too . . . too mixed up to be any good for anyone."

Charles's earlier playfulness vanished and he looked every minute of his age. "I thought that being together would be good for both of us. I know it was good for me. But I've had a couple of years to adjust to being alone, and to want something more." He got to his feet. "You haven't, and from your point of view, the most significant thing about me is that I'm not Sam. I can't change that, and wouldn't if I could."

A word from her would prevent him from leaving, but it was a word she couldn't say. She had an identity, and it was defined by sorrow. That giggling teenager was a stranger. "Thank you for trying to help. I . . . I wish I could accept that better."

"People heal in their own time and fashion. I think it's best if we don't see each other at all. Good-bye, Julia."

As he headed to the backyard to collect his dogs, she dropped onto the sofa again, knotting up in the corner with misery. Would she ever get over her current craziness, the mood swings and desperate loneliness that would exasperate a saint? Someday, perhaps.

But at the moment she couldn't believe that would ever happen.

Donovan was at the explosion point by the time Kate got him outside. "Christ, Kate, how could she?" He yanked on his helmet. "How could Charles? I never thought he was the kind of guy who hit on grieving widows."

He swung onto the Harley and tilted it upright, then turned the key in the ignition. "Get on." The engine roared to life with his furious stamp on the kick-start pedal.

Kate had an eerie memory of the day Tom had come out. On that occasion Donovan was the one who'd pulled her outside, not vice versa, but the rage was familiar.

He's mad as hell, and I'm not going to take it anymore. She reached forward and turned off the ignition, then yanked away the key ring. "We're not going anywhere until you calm down, Donovan," she said in the sudden silence. "In your present state, you'll kill us both before we're half-way to Ruxton."

"Give me the keys!"

"Why are you flipping out? I'm the one who just found my mother about to get naked with the family lawyer. Is this some weird Oedipal reaction you're having?"

He slammed his hand down on the bike's handlebars. "Goddammit, Kate, don't psychoanalyze me!"

She flinched. The terrified uncertainty of what might happen next was far worse than any physical injury had ever been. It was time to change the script. "Patrick, earlier today you said you wanted a future with me. That's never going to happen unless you get a better grip on your temper. Anger is normal, but bullying and intimidation are *not acceptable.*"

His face whitened, and for a scary moment she had no idea what he'd do.

"Jesus." He lowered his head and pulled off his helmet, his fingers trembling as he ran his hand through his hair. "You sure know how to hit a body blow, Kate."

"This isn't a fight. It's more like the journey of a thousand leagues that begins with a single step. And if you want to make this journey with me, you'll damned well have to prove that you've changed."

A pulse hammered in his jaw, but slowly the tension eased from his rigid body. "I'm sorry, Kate. I keep thinking I've made progress on keeping my temper under control." He exhaled roughly. "Then something like this happens."

"Cases involving sex and your womenfolk seem to set off weird primitive reactions."

"Primitive isn't the half of it. My feelings about Julia aren't Oedipal. More filial, I guess. Since Sam isn't around to protect his woman, I feel like I should. Dumb, right?"

"Right. Not that I blame you for being shocked. I am, too. I mean, she's my mother, we all grow up thinking our parents found us under cabbage leaves and that sex didn't exist before our personal coming-of-age. But Julia's love life is basically her business, not ours. It's not as if Charles is an ogre or a sexual predator. They've been friends for-ever. Charles is a really nice man, and a thoroughly eligible widower. I can understand why they've been drawn closer."

"But Sam has only been dead for a couple of months!"

"People react to grief in many different ways. What right do I have to criticize my mother, who was always there for me?" Kate realized that she had always taken her mother's quiet love and support for granted. Her father, who was so often away on business, was the parent whose approval she had yearned for. Only now, in the wake of death, was she beginning to learn Julia's heart. The least she could do was accept her mother's choices.

"After you left me—how long was it until you got in-volved with another man?"

"Do you really need to know this?"

He looked away. "Probably not."

"It was over two years before I went out on a date. More than four until I found someone I wanted to sleep with. Does it make you feel better to know that I didn't rebound into another relationship right away?"

"Not really. It's a measure of how much I'd hurt you."

She poked him in the ribs. "All right, Romeo, your turn to say how long it took for you to get back into circulation."

"More than a year. Less than four. A damned good thing I didn't know where to find you. I might have slipped over the edge into really dangerous craziness if you'd been nearby. For months I was so sure that if I could just see you face-to-face, talk to you, I could persuade you to come home again."

"That's why I did the divorce long-distance. I was afraid that if we were in the same room, even a lawyer's office, it would feel so natural, so right, to be with you, that I'd have jumped right back into the fire. And if that had happened—I don't know if I would have had the strength to escape again."

His fingers locked on the handgrips of the motorcycle. "I can't bear the thought that under any circumstance, no matter how angry I was, that I might have . . . Christ, I can't even say it."

She had a swift, nightmare vision of the knife in her hand, the razor edge crimson with blood. "I don't know if it was luck or wisdom but the worst didn't happen." She buttoned up her jacket. "Are you safe? I'm getting cold and hungry."

"Yeah, I'm safe." He held out his hand again. When she hesitated, he said quietly, "As God is my witness, I swear that I will never touch you in anger again. I don't expect you to believe that right away, but I hope that you will someday."

She dropped the keys onto his palm and swung into the saddle behind him. Tonight, thank God, they hadn't even come close to the kind of explosion that had ended their marriage. She'd spoken up instead of denying and avoiding the issue, and he'd mastered his temper in a tough emotional situation. Progress had definitely been made.

As she wrapped her arms around his waist, it was impossible to suppress a faint tingle of hope.

34

Another day, another city. Atlanta in this case. Donovan finished his sandwich and threw the wrappings into the trash. Eating at his desk on a job site was seriously uncivilized. Though when he looked across the cramped office and saw Kate polishing off a portion of pasta salad, he had to admit that she looked civilized.

The phone rang, and he picked it up to find Brian, a PDI foreman working on a job in Honolulu. After hearing why Brian had called, he swore under his breath. "Go ahead and hire new equipment, even if the price is exorbitant. We can't afford to get any further behind on that job. And . . . be careful."

"More trouble?" Kate asked as he hung up.

"Arson on the Honolulu job site. A Bobcat and a loader were destroyed. I've never seen such a run of bad luck at so many job sites. Arson, accidents, labor problems—you name it, we've had it."

"Anyone hurt?"

"No, thank God."

Kate folded a pasta dish, plasticware, and napkins into the brown bag from whence they'd come, then dropped everything into the wastebasket by the table where she'd been organizing the necessary demolition permits. "That's good. Bad luck tends to come in clusters. Pretty soon the luck will change."

"I hope so." In his more superstitious moments, Donovan wondered if God was telling him he shouldn't be in charge of PDI. Then he'd remind himself of other accidents the company had experienced over the years. The only difference now was that a number of things were going wrong at once. Pure coincidence.

Kate continued, "I've gone through your list. Do you have any more office work for me, or can I swagger over to the site and play construction boss this afternoon?"

"You do that. I'd go with you, but the client, Bob Glazer, will be here in half an hour or so."

Reaching for her hard hat, she got to her feet. "See you later."

An elderly gentleman in a sober suit and old-fashioned hat opened the door. "Excuse me," he said in a soft Southern accent. "Are you the folks from Phoenix Demolition?"

"Yes, we are," Kate said. "Come on in."

He entered, followed by a sweet-faced older woman wearing a flowered dress and carrying a tote bag. "I have a question you all are going to think is very foolish," he said.

"I doubt it," Donovan said. "I like off-the-wall questions."

"My name is Wilfred Bowen, and this is my wife, Essie. It was fifty years ago this weekend that we got married right here in the Hotel St. Cyr."

"Yes?" Kate said encouragingly.

"Wilfred is indulging me, honey," Mrs. Bowen said. "When I heard that you were fixing to knock the hotel down, I asked him to bring me by for a last visit."

"I'm sorry, Mrs. Bowen, but the soft-stripping process has already started," Donovan said. "It won't look the way you remember."

"Nothing ever does, honey. Has the ballroom been ripped up?"

"Actually, I think that's one area that's still pretty much intact," Kate said. "I could take you over there, but you'll have to wear hard hats."

"A hard hat! Oh, my, wouldn't that be fun," Mrs. Bowen said happily. "Can we go right now?"

Donovan glanced at his watch. He had time before Glazer arrived. "Now would be good. The crew is on lunch break and the building is quiet. Once they get back to work, it will be too noisy to think."

After introducing herself and Donovan, Kate pulled visitor hard hats from a box and gave them to the Bowens. Wilfred wore his hat with grave dignity, while Essie looked so cute she could have been a model in a commercial.

Kate led the way outside and across the small plaza to the Hotel St. Cyr. After picking their way through rubble-strewn halls, the group reached their destination to find that it was dusty and shabby, but intact.

Essie circled slowly, her gaze fixed on the molded plaster ceiling high above. "Do you remember our wedding reception, honey?"

"Oh, yes, Essie Mae. I remember."

Essie pulled a large object from her tote bag. "My youngest grandson lent me this gizmo of his, a boom box, he called it, and my daughter gave me a music tape. Would you mind terribly if we had one last dance?"

"Of course not," Kate said.

"Wilfred, honey, could you make this go?"

Her husband frowned over the small buttons for a moment, then hit play. The lilting strains of big-band dance music filled the room.

Essie handed a small camera to Kate. "Could you take some pictures, please? So we can show the family at our anniversary party this weekend."

She began shooting as Essie and her husband danced with the expertise born of decades of moving through life together. In the dim light of the ballroom, it was easy to imagine how they had looked on their wedding day.

Donovan tried to imagine what Kate would look like in forty or fifty years. She'd have silvery hair, fragile skin stretched over lovely bones, and that smile. She'd be beautiful.

When she finished shooting, Kate set the camera down by the boom box. Donovan said, "Miss Corsi, is this dance taken?"

She blinked. "Sir, have we been properly introduced?"

"No. I'm the bad-boy gatecrasher."

"Wonderful. I have a secret weakness for bad boys."

He clasped her right hand with his left, his other hand going to rest on her supple waist, just above her heavy belt. In hard hat, denim work shirt over T-shirt, and jeans, Kate was as graceful as the debutante she had once been. Donovan envied those young men who had danced with her that night when they'd met. But she'd ended the evening with him, so he'd been the lucky one.

Silently they spun through the room. If this were a real date, he'd pull her close so that her head could rest on his shoulder and he could feel the rhythmic sway of her body against his. The mere thought made his breathing change. Damnation, she'd been wise to insist on no touching in the beginning, because the more they touched, the more he wanted to make love to her. In passion, perhaps, he could truly make amends for the past. Say what couldn't be said in words. A pity this was only an unusual break in the middle of a workday, not a date or a seduction.

The music stopped. Kate lowered her arms, but she didn't move away. For the space of a dozen heartbeats they stared at each other.

The roar of a Bobcat coming to life on the floor above broke the mood. Kate turned to the Bowens. "You timed that exactly right."

"Thank you for letting us have our romantic moment." Essie smiled as she packed away the camera and boom box. "Don't you and your young man ever forget to take time for romance. It helps keep you going through the hard times."

While Kate blushed, Wilfred said sincerely, "Essie, with

you there were never any hard times. You were always the sweetest thing in Dixie."

"You see why I've kept him all these years?" Essie said with a smile.

Donovan said, "I'll take you back to the site office now. I have to meet our client there in a few minutes."

"Time to get back to work," Kate agreed.

As Donovan ushered the elderly couple outside, he thought of Essie Bowen's comment about taking time for romance. He liked that idea a lot.

Another city, another building to implode. Kate would never get bored by PDI's work, but already she'd passed through the excited novice stage into matter-of-factness. Born to be wild, or at least to bring buildings down. Despite her parents' best efforts to civilize her, she felt more alive, more herself, on a job site than she had at that cotillion.

The Hotel St. Cyr had been solidly built, and a lot of careful calculations and prep work would be required to bring it down cleanly in the middle of a mess of skyscrapers. The project had originally been handled by Sam, so Donovan had to make his own survey of the structure before finalizing the explosives plan. When he'd learned what he needed to know, they'd return to Baltimore, and a PDI foreman would fly in to supervise the rest of the prep work.

Taking Dinah to Julia's house before this trip had given her a chance to get past the awkwardness of the scene Saturday when she and Donovan had chosen the wrong time to drop by. In a triumph of WASP communication, neither of them speaking about the subject openly, Kate had indicated that she had no intention of passing judgment on her mother, while Julia had made it clear that the affair with Charles was over.

Kate wasn't quite sure how she felt about that. A selfish part of her had been relieved by the news—yet how could a daughter be glad to know that her mother had lost a source of comfort at one of life's most difficult times?

When Kate got back to Baltimore, she'd have to talk with her mother.

She made her way down to the basement, where a front-end loader was making enough noise to raise the dead while ripping away great chunks of nonloadbearing walls. Kate spent several minutes with Gil Brown, the local foreman, going over what needed to be done before demolition. Luckily, Brown was quick, and he'd worked on a PDI job before. So far, this project was going very smoothly.

Brown left to go upstairs, leaving Kate in the basement with the front-end loader. Kate did a circuit of the area, which she hadn't seen before. Originally the basement had been divided into a warren of storage and service rooms. The loader had already ripped away more than half the partitions with a violence that cracked the plaster even on the opposite side of the basement from where the machine was operating.

A flick of her flashlight into one of the storage rooms turned into a closer examination when a crack in the ceiling caught her eye. There seemed to be an extra-wide beam up there. Exactly the kind of deviation that could affect the explosives plan.

A heavy old wooden crate sat by one wall, so she dragged it under the crack and climbed up for a closer look. Using a screwdriver from her tool belt, she chipped at the plaster to get a better view of the beam.

The front-end loader struck one of the massive support columns so hard that Kate felt vibrations through the wooden crate. She frowned. The equipment operator was a blank-faced redhead who seemed to think he could demolish the building all by himself. She'd have to have a little talk with him before going upstairs again.

The loader bashed into another column. This time the ceiling above her shivered. More than shivered, Christ, it was moving toward her . . .

There wasn't even time to scream before the ceiling collapsed, smashing her into oblivion.

•　•　•

Groggily, Kate became aware that she was trapped in crushing darkness. She tried to move, and couldn't. Was she paralyzed? No, trapped under a weight so heavy she could barely breathe. Instinctively she tried to inhale to call for help. The constriction instantly worsened. Oh, God, there was such a weight on her chest, she couldn't breathe, she couldn't *breathe.*

She clamped down on her panicky reaction. She couldn't move her head, which was turned to the left and trapped in place, but her face was clear and she could draw in air if she didn't inhale too deeply.

After regaining a measure of control, she evaluated her position. She'd fallen backward and was lying on the cold concrete floor, pinned by a smooth mass of material. Flattened like a specimen on a laboratory slide.

Though she was bruised and badly shaken, she felt no real pain. Starting with her toes, she cautiously flexed muscles in successive parts of her body. Everything seemed to work. The harsh mechanical clamor of the front-end loader sounded about the same as it had when the ceiling fell, so probably little time had elapsed. She'd been dazed by shock rather than knocked out by a head injury.

The slab of material pinning her to the floor slanted from right to left. Her left side and rib cage were compressed to the point where numbness would soon result. On the plus side, she could move her hands and lower arms a little, especially on the right side. And the darkness was not absolute. Dim light seeped around the edges of the slab, which was much better than being trapped in tomblike darkness. Lord only knew where her flashlight had ended up.

Was there any chance of getting out of here under her own power? Experimentally she pushed against the slab. A few fragments of debris rattled around the edges of her prison, and a dusting of particles fell across her face, but she had no success in moving the weight. She sensed that even if she had more leverage, the material would be far too heavy for her to shift.

Gingerly she explored with her right hand. Her questing fingers touched splintered wood. The crate she'd been standing on was supporting the slab. If not for the narrow wedge of space created, she would have been crushed. She uttered a prayer of thanks for solid old crates.

The loader was getting closer. With sudden horror, Kate realized that when it reached this room, the operator would simply sweep this pile of rubble away in the loader's steel bucket—and cut Kate in half in the process.

She considered screaming, but even if she'd been able to fill her lungs enough for a good shout, nothing could be heard over the noise of the loader. So she couldn't move, couldn't yell. Would anyone miss her before that damned loader got to this corner of the basement? Probably not.

The floor vibrated as the loader struck another support column. The slab settled a fraction lower, reducing her ability to breathe even more. Panic surged as she recognized that death was minutes away. She'd never been so terrified in her life, not even when she'd been clinging to the edge of the elevator shaft in Las Vegas.

Facing death stripped her life down to stark simplicity. There weren't too many things she regretted, and all of them had to do with people. She should have worked harder to bridge the estrangement with her father, and to maintain her relationship with her mother during the California years.

And she should have risked herself with Donovan while she had the chance. The fears and doubts she'd experienced since coming east had been legitimate, but Rachel had been right—Kate had been avoiding intimacy. Only by braving the smoldering fires of her broken marriage might she have become free. Now, perhaps, it was too late. If only she could call Patrick, apologize for her cowardly evasions . . .

Call him! Cursing herself for not remembering the walkie-talkie sooner, she scrabbled around with her right hand until she located the radio on her belt. It seemed un-damaged.

She swore again when she realized that she couldn't raise it to her face to speak. For a moment she wanted to weep with despair, or rage. Unless the loader operator took a break and turned off his engine before reaching this room, she was dead. *Papa, was this what you feared—that I'd die the way you did?*

A curious sense of calm came over her, almost as if Sam were present, tucking her in at bedtime as he had when she was very small. If she died here today, she'd find out if there really was a tunnel of light with the spirits of people she loved waiting at the other end. If so, Sam would be there for sure.

But she wasn't ready to die, dammit! She made another fierce attempt to move the slab. This time the crate creaked ominously and the mass settled painfully lower. Cold sweat formed on her face as she realized that her efforts might bring on the collapse of the crate, with lethal results.

Her hand touched the radio again. So near, yet so far.

Then she realized that the transmit switch was under her thumb. She couldn't raise the device to her mouth, but she could depress the switch. That would produce a click on the other radios on the circuit. People working inside the building probably wouldn't notice because of the demolition noise, but the sound should be audible at the base station radio in the site office. With luck, Donovan was still there.

Grimly she started pressing the switch in and out, using the only Morse code message she knew.

Please God, let someone hear.

35

After saying good-bye to the Bowens, Donovan just had time to make a fresh pot of coffee and review his notes before Bob Glazer showed up for their meeting. A shrewd, affable man, Glazer was a major Southern developer. If he liked working with PDI, it would mean more business down the road.

Naturally, Glazer needed the building down as soon as possible so he could start work on the office tower that would replace it. Now that Donovan had evaluated the structure, he could project with fair accuracy how long each demolition phase would take. They were discussing the schedule when he realized that the radio had been making odd little clicks. He made a mental note to look at it later.

The meeting was almost over when the clicks again caught his attention. "Excuse me. Do you hear that clicking sound?"

"Yes. What about it?" Glazer listened. "Three quick clicks. Three slow. Three more quick ones."

Their gazes locked. "SOS." Donovan swore, then picked up the handset of the base radio. "Attention, radio check! Please sound off by number and location."

A few seconds later Gil Brown said, "Unit one here, fourth floor."

Another voice, one of the two crew chiefs, said, "Unit two, third floor," followed by, "Unit three here, on the first floor," from the other crew chief.

Unit four was Kate, and he himself was unit five when

he was on-site. But after the third response, there was only silence. *Kate, where the hell are you?* Speaking into the handset, Donovan said, "Unit four, report *now*."

The receiver clicked rapidly in reply. "Kate, is your radio malfunctioning?"

The radio responded with another burst of clicks. During the intervals when the transmitter switch was open, he heard construction noise in the background. So her handset was working properly. Why wasn't she talking?

Because she *couldn't*. "One click for yes, two for no. Are you in trouble?"

One click.

"I read you." Donovan glanced at his client. "I'm going over to the hotel. My associate seems to be having problems."

"Of course. First things first. Anything I can do to help?"

"If you have any prayers, toss a couple at the St. Cyr." On the run, Donovan keyed his walkie-talkie again and barked, "Does anyone know where Kate is?"

The three voices came in together, each saying that she wasn't on his floor. Donovan snapped, "Has anyone seen her since lunch?"

"She and I talked down in the basement," Gil Brown replied. "She was still there when I came upstairs."

Donovan entered the hotel. "Are you in the basement, Kate?"

One click.

Christ, the front-end loader was busy ripping out walls down there! He raced down the stairs, heart hammering with fear.

More than half the basement was now an open, rubble-strewn space. To his left, the loader was crunching partitions with its steel maw. Donovan leaped into the operator's line of vision, both arms waving. The redheaded driver almost ran over him before noticing and halting the loader. Donovan barked, "Turn this thing off!"

The operator obeyed. Voice loud in the sudden silence, Donovan asked, "Is Kate down here?"

"I saw her earlier, but not lately. I guess she went up-stairs."

"Take a break," Donovan ordered. He keyed the radio again for a general announcement. "We've got a missing worker. Stop all pieces of heavy equipment."

One of the Bobcats upstairs cut off, followed a moment later by the other. The hotel fell abruptly quiet. Ominously so. Slowly, Donovan turned, scanning the basement. There were piles of rubble from the loader all over the place. God, he hoped Kate wasn't under one. If she'd been run over ... "Kate, are you in the section of the basement that hasn't been cleared yet?"

One click.

"Northwest corner?

A pause, then two clicks.

He spun and headed to the southwest corner of the base-ment. Not using the radio, he shouted, "Can you hear my voice?"

One click.

Moving at a trot, he headed down the corridor that con-nected the rooms remaining at this end. "Am I getting louder?" he yelled.

One click.

He saw odds and ends left behind when the hotel was closed, but nothing large enough to conceal a person until he passed a storage room where half the ceiling had come down in a single massive piece. Sweet Jesus, could some-one be alive under that? "Are you in here, Kate?"

This time it was her strained voice that answered. "I'm here, and more or less okay. It's not as bad as it looks. A crate is supporting most of the weight."

Too wired to rationally analyze the best way to free her, he flattened his hands underneath the edge of the slab and heaved. Straining legs and back and arms, he raised the fallen piece and shoved backward, using the edge that rested on the floor as a pivot.

Kate's cramped body was revealed. As the slab crunched into the wall and cracked into irregular chunks of plaster and wood, he dropped beside her. "Kate?"

She doubled up in a paroxysm of coughing as her first frantic gulps of air drew dust into her lungs. He supported her as she struggled for breath.

Shivering violently with cold from lying on the damp concrete floor, she pushed herself stiffly to a sitting position. "Thanks."

His relief changed to fury. Why did she insist on doing such hazardous work? He wanted to shake her until her teeth rattled . . .

He cut off the thought, appalled at himself, and drew her closer as a childhood memory scorched through his mind. He'd climbed on the roof to get a neighbor's cat, then slipped and fell to the ground. As he lay there, stunned, his parents had rushed from the house. His mother sobbed with relief when she saw he was all right, but his father had exploded with rage. Shaking Donovan viciously, he threatened that if his son ever did anything so stupid again, he'd be beaten within an inch of his life.

That was the male model Donovan had been raised with: a man could show anger, but not softer feelings. Despite his mother's influence and his own vows to be different, the grim truth was that he was much like his father. Christ, he was a fool! When his emotions threatened to spiral out of control, which happened with Kate regularly, he too often responded with fury, which was far more masculine and acceptable than tears or fears. The connection was so damned obvious now that he thought about it.

From the doorway, someone said, "Son of a bitch, did you see him move that?'

"It musta weighed seven, eight hundred pounds," another voice said.

Donovan realized that an audience had collected—the

men who carried radios, along with the driver of the front-end loader, and several laborers from the first floor. Even Bob Glazer had come, complete with hard hat.

His gaze shifted to the debris he'd moved. Good grief, no wonder people were amazed. Score one for adrenaline.

To help Kate, he'd have moved Mt. Everest. "How do you feel?"

Her hair was a dusty mess and her face streaked with filth, but she managed a crooked smile. "I'm fine. Really. I was lucky. A little numb on my left side, but that's passing now that the blood is flowing again."

He helped her to her feet. "Real luck would have been to avoid being flattened like a bug on a windshield in the first place."

She stumbled a little when she put weight on her left leg, but moved without apparent pain. Maintaining his grip on her arm, he said, "You're a magnet for trouble."

"Some of us are just talented. I've always believed in getting into my work."

The remark produced a rumble of relieved laughter. These were men who knew how close disaster could be on any job.

Donovan said to Kate, "I know you eat rebar for breakfast, but I'm still taking you to the hospital for a checkup."

"Not necessary. Besides, you haven't the time. The schedule on this project is too tight."

Chuckling, Glazer stepped into the room. "A woman after my own heart. But just to make me and my insurance company happy, let me take you to a walk-in clinic near here for a quick examination. Then I'll drop you by your hotel. Anyone who has been buried alive deserves the rest of the afternoon off."

Kate exhaled roughly. "I must admit that I'm ready to call it a day."

Donovan would rather have taken her himself, but this made more sense. "All right, but call right away if there are any complications."

"There won't be. By the way, I was checking that beam when the ceiling fell. It's double width, which will affect your calculations."

He shined his flashlight on the chasm in the ceiling and saw that she was right. "I'll look for others." He had to smile. Kate was Sam's daughter to the core.

Gil Brown lingered after Kate and the others left. "She your girlfriend, Donovan?"

"Ex-wife."

"Maybe you should do something about the 'ex' part of that."

Donovan pulled off his hard hat and ran tense fingers through his matted hair. "Yeah. Maybe I should."

Glazer called later on his car phone to say that Kate's clinical examination had revealed no serious injury. When he'd dropped her off at their hotel, she had declared her intention to have a bath and a nap, not necessarily in that order. There was no reason for Donovan to continue worrying about her.

Nonetheless, he wrapped up his work as early as possible. Atlanta was packed to the gills with a homebuilders' convention, so they had ended up in a small luxury hotel in a bridal suite that was so expensive he was picking up half the cost personally rather than billing it to PDI. As a bridal suite, it didn't even have two bedrooms, but the sofa in the living room opened into a bed. He'd slept there the previous night while Kate took the bedroom.

What the suite did have was lots of lace and mirrors. When they'd checked in the day before, they had both laughed about the candy-box decorations. Tonight Donovan stalked through the elaborate living room like a twitchy tiger. No sign of Kate, so he quietly opened the bedroom door, expecting to find her sleeping.

The lace-canopied bed was rumpled but empty. Frowning, he glanced around. The bathroom door was closed, and a low rumble emanated from inside. He tapped on the door. "I'm back. You're taking advantage of the whirlpool?"

The rumbling stopped. "You bet. Feels very good on sore muscles. Could you do me a favor?"

"Sure. What do you need?"

"There's a split of red wine in the mini-bar. Would you open the bottle and bring it in, please?"

Before his imagination could get too wild, she added, "I'm decent. Relatively so, anyhow."

Wondering what the devil that meant, he went to the mini-bar. Apparently there had been two splits of wine, because an empty bottle of Chardonnay sat on the bar. He took the little bottle of Zinfandel from the refrigerator, twisted off the cap, and opened the door to the spacious bathroom.

He was met by a cloud of warm, fragrant air, but that wasn't what stopped him dead in his tracks. "Relatively" decent meant Kate was lying back in the pink tub, hair clipped on top of her head and immersed in bubbles. Technically she was visible only from the tops of her shoulders up—but knowing she was naked under a shimmering layer of foam made his mouth go dry.

There were shadows under her eyes, but she still looked delectable. "I hadn't realized quite how quickly a whirlpool generates foam if bubble bath is added," she said. "I can't run the jets for more than a couple of minutes at a time."

He inhaled rose-scented air. Intoxicatingly feminine and romantic. "This hotel definitely gives honeymooners their money's worth."

"I suspect that most of the guests are parents who hire a baby-sitter for the night and come here for a romantic getaway."

He poured the wine, concentrating on her glass. Studying the amount of creamy flesh revealed by the bubbles would have been an exercise in pure masochism.

He was about to retreat when he noticed an abrasion on her right cheek. "I thought you weren't hurt."

"Only a brush burn. That and some bruises are the sum total of my injuries. Pretty amazing." She reached for the wineglass, iridescent foam trailing from her arm.

He tried not to notice the way the movement exposed half her right breast. "Did the clinic give you a sedative? If so, you probably shouldn't be drinking."

"They said to take ibuprofen. Very low-tech."

"Well—don't fall asleep in here."

His hand was on the doorknob when she said hesitantly, "How about getting yourself a drink and joining me?"

She just wanted to talk out her nerves after the accident. He could handle that. "I'll get a soda."

When he was safely outside the bathroom, he unbuttoned his shirt and used it to wipe perspiration from his face. He felt as if he'd just spent a night in the tropics.

He unlaced his boots and kicked them aside, sending his socks after them. After filling a glass with ice from the bucket she'd left on the bar, he poured himself a ginger ale and returned to the bathroom.

She took a sip of her wine. "Any idea why that chunk of ceiling fell on me? It really shouldn't have."

He sat on the floor with his back against the door, one knee drawn up. "I took a look after you left. Old termite damage had badly weakened the rafters. The shock waves from the loader were the last straw. Sheer bad luck that you were underneath when gravity won."

"Any accident you can walk away from doesn't count as bad luck."

"You've had more than your share of accidents in your short history with PDI. I should ban you from all job sites."

Instead of flaring up at him, she said, "You've had plenty accidents and near misses, haven't you? I remember a couple from when we were married, and even then I suspected you weren't telling me everything because you didn't want me to worry."

"I should have known I wasn't fooling you."

"What was your most dangerous accident?"

The bubbles had declined to just above the level of her

nipples. He looked away. "Turn the whirlpool on to raise the suds level, and I'll tell you about it."

Coloring, she hit the button that activated the jets. He practiced multiplication tables to distract himself until she turned the whooshing waters off again. Since a cautious glance showed bubbles up to her clavicle, he let his gaze rest on her again. "The worst was a fluke, not really a normal accident. I was spreading out leftover dynamite after a shoot so we could burn it off when a lunatic walked up, whipped out a pistol, and fired into the explosives."

"My God! What happened?"

"One hell of an explosion. Because I was kneeling, most of the blast went over me. Not entirely—there was enough force to throw me seventy or eighty feet. A couple of ribs were cracked, I lost some hearing in one ear, and my college ring was wrenched off. Not that I'm complaining. I got off lightly."

"What happened to the man who set off the explosion?"

"Dead. A frustrated implosion junkie." He pressed the icy glass against his forehead, remembering. It had been Phoenix in August, and hotter than the hinges of hell. "Apparently he wanted to kill someone from PDI because our security guards had prevented him from stealing any explosives from the site. He didn't mind blowing himself to smithereens in the process."

"And you tell me *I'm* trouble-prone! I just fall down elevator shafts and get bopped by ceilings. You've had someone actively try to blow you up."

"You've got a point."

Kate crossed her arms on the edge of the tub. "When you've come close to death like that, have you ever had your life pass in front of your eyes? Thought about unfinished business?"

"To be honest, no. The incident has always been over before I had time to think about such things. Did you have those kinds of thoughts today?"

"Yes." Her wineglass was empty, so she set it against

the wall. "You must be ready to wash the day's sweat and dust off. Why not join me? This tub is big enough for two."

He stared. "Jesus, Kate! How much have you had to drink?"

"Only two glasses of wine. Not enough to get drunk." She took a deep breath. "Just enough to give me the nerve to . . . to proposition you."

Her words triggered a rush of heat that dizzied him. "Don't start something you won't want to finish."

"I don't intend to." Her eyes closed for an instant. "When I was lying under that slab, wondering if I was going to suffocate or get crushed by the loader, I realized that my biggest regret was being too afraid to . . . to be with you. I'm still scared, and Lord only knows if anything worthwhile can come of it—but I know now that this is one risk I'll have to take, or I'll never forgive myself."

"You're sure about this?"

"I'm sure."

He stripped off his T-shirt and tossed it to one side. "Then let us hope, *cara mia,* that there is enough water in that tub to wash away a dozen years' worth of very heavy baggage."

36

Despite the warmth of the water, Kate shivered as she watched Donovan peel off his T-shirt. Years of construction work had layered hard muscle on his chest and arms, as well as adding a scar or two.

She couldn't quite believe that after weeks of doggedly

repressing her attraction, she'd finally had the courage—or craziness—to confront her fears head-on.

He unsnapped the waistband of his jeans. Before undressing further, he bent over the tub to tenderly touch his lips to the abrasion on her cheek. "You look ready to jump out of your skin. It's not too late to change your mind. But it will be soon."

She slid her hand around his neck and turned her face, bringing their mouths together. *Patrick, Patrick.* She'd have known his lips, his kiss, anywhere in the world. Warm, firm, familiar. They'd shared so many kisses once. Some of passion, others of affection, sometimes as a casual token that they were bonded.

This was a slow, gentle kiss of welcome and exploration. She could feel the desire in him. Her fear was replaced by tension of a different sort. "I won't change my mind. I promise," she whispered.

She made herself look at the thin, almost invisible scar that ran from his left shoulder down his upper arm to almost his elbow. The sight made her stomach knot. She traced the faint line with her fingertip. "What about you, Patrick? Are you sure you want to get so close to someone who stabbed you?"

He caught her hand and held it against his heart for a moment. "The only harm you ever did was what I drove you to, Kate."

He'd learned a thing or two about patience in the intervening years. Rather than following up the first kiss with another, after undressing he slid into the far end of the tub. The water level rose as his powerfully muscled legs bracketed hers. Both of them had to bend their knees to fit comfortably into the tub.

"I think this is a project worthy of some serious anticipation." He stroked the side of her hip with the arch of his foot. Sensuous. Sexy.

"This tub seems much smaller than it did with just one

person in it." She laid her hand on his ankle, then slowly skimmed upward over his shin and calf.

"Togetherness is the whole point. Speaking of which, I haven't been celibate for the last ten years, but I had a blood test with a physical not long ago, and I don't have any horrible viruses."

"Same here. And the contraception part is okay, too." She blushed a little. A modern woman was never supposed to trust what a man might say when he was under the influence of raging hormones, but this was Patrick. Though he'd wounded her more deeply than anyone else in her life, at the same time she knew he could be trusted absolutely to protect her health. As he could trust her.

He captured the washcloth floating around the tub and did a little scrubbing. Thinking he might like the water jets, she restarted the whirlpool action.

He leaned back in the tub as the currents swirled around him. "That feels good. I should use the whirlpool at home more often. Usually I just shower." His hand drifted up her leg, sliding from outside to inside on the way to her knee. Lazily he caressed her inner thigh with his knuckles.

Sensation blazed through her. It took so little for him to kindle her. "Showers are good for washing hair. Baths are for serious recreation."

"I'm willing to recreate."

"It's odd that the first time we were together—and not even on a real date!—sex was so easy and natural. Now I'm tied in knots."

"Not so odd." His palm skimmed down her calf in the same relaxed tempo as his voice. "That night, we were both operating on instinct—a higher kind, not the purely hormonal. We knew that we should be together. But so much has happened since then. Hardly surprising that your mind has serious doubts."

"I think too much. You used to tell me that, and you were right."

"Like anything else, thinking can be good or bad." He

sighed. "I can't blame you for thinking I'm trouble. I took a relationship that was a gift from God, and destroyed it."

While she had lain trapped and frightened in the old hotel, she'd faced not only her cowardice where he was concerned, but other hard realizations as well. "There's enough fault to go around, Patrick. I handled the situation badly from the beginning. I made excuses for you, blamed myself for not being understanding enough, swore I'd try harder. And . . . and maybe I didn't take the problem seriously enough, because making up was always fantastic." In other words, from a mixture of motives, some good and some bad, she had to some extent colluded in her own abuse.

"Great sex has a way of masking underlying problems. To me, the fact that we were still so passionate with each other meant there wasn't anything *really* wrong," he said. "It was also an excuse for me not to look at my own behavior. Since I was satisfying my woman, I must be a real man."

She'd shared that unspoken belief that passion meant their relationship was solid. "When things got really bad, I fell apart. If I'd been braver and smarter, I would have stayed in Maryland and at least tried to fix our marriage rather than running as far and fast as I could. I only understood yes and no. Yes, this marriage works, or no, it's hopeless. 'Maybe' wasn't in my vocabulary."

"Don't second-guess yourself, Kate. Maybe things couldn't have been fixed then. Maybe we needed years of growing and learning before it was the right time. I'd like to think that."

She scooped up a double handful of suds and watched them flow from her cupped palms down her wrists. So many perfect little bubbles, exquisitely iridescent. Could he be right, that there was a pattern and order to why things happened as they did? "I'd like to believe that, too."

"Kate, I don't want anything about tonight to remind you of . . . the last time. So it's up to you to initiate, to do what you want, when you want it. You're in charge."

With a shock of understanding, she recognized that he'd put his finger on her underlying anxiety. Their marriage had shattered in a conflict rooted in desperation and possession and power, not love. She'd been able to live and work with Donovan by denying everything she'd felt that day, but it would be impossible tonight. So he was doing his best to put the power in her hands. "In charge. I like that idea."

After turning off the water jets, she glided to the other end of the tub. She settled on top of him, breasts brushing his chest, her body lightly resting over his. "Much nicer than being a victim."

She nuzzled against him, licking his throat, running her hands over his broad shoulders and the darkly patterned hair of his chest. Pressing her lips to the ragged upper end of the knife scar. Under the dizzying fragrance of roses, she identified his personal scent. Unique, exhilarating. "Remember that night on the beach in Antigua, on our honeymoon?"

"Of course. Moonlight and madness." His body came alive under hers, his hands planing down her back and hips with silken smoothness.

She slid over him, buoyant in the water. She tasted and touched as every square inch of heated flesh imprinted the present, and recalled the past. "I tried to forget, but I couldn't."

His erection was a velvety pressure against her belly, taut and unmistakable. She rubbed against it, teasing herself as much as him. He caught her hips, holding her close. "Ah, *cara mia*. I swear memories of what you do to me are engraved on my DNA."

She'd wanted power, and she had it. Not the power of physical force but of shared passion, desire that was a fever in the blood. She flowed around and over him, kissing and rubbing and caressing, scarcely able to believe that they really were together again after so many years. This must be the most vivid dream of her life. Yet he was too real, too *present*, to deny.

When she could bear to wait no longer, she raised her hips, then impaled herself on him. Satin heat, wicked promises. He groaned and arched upward, his whole frame rigid as he buried himself more deeply.

It felt so good, so right, to have him inside her. She tangled one hand in his hair and wrapped her other arm around his waist as her body led his in a primal dance of thrust and retreat. She didn't know where she ended and he began, only that together they were one, united in passion and searing pleasure. Time was arrested, superseded by a higher harmony as he matched her rhythm exactly. No one had ever suited her so well, no one, no one . . .

Time returned shatteringly when she convulsed, grinding against him as she lost all control. He surged inside her, his arms locking around her like iron as he gave a long-drawn-out groan of raw urgency. Culmination, and completion, as she had not been complete in almost ten years.

Dizzy with release, she wilted on his chest. "Lord, Patrick, I've missed you so much. So damned much."

"*Cara.*" He kissed her temple, her cheek, her ear. "*Carissima.*"

Dearest one. He'd always saved the endearment for their most intimate moments. For the space of a dozen heartbeats she basked in the sense of rightness.

Euphoria faded swiftly. She'd learned that the passion was powerful as ever. No surprise there, given the sexual tension that had been thrumming between them.

But she'd also learned, again, that desire wasn't enough. Secretly she'd hoped that if she had the courage to make herself vulnerable, her fears would magically fall away and they could deal with each other as they were now, unshadowed by the past. Instead, fear had crystallized into a terrible conviction that she was teetering on the brink of an abyss. That loving him would come at the price of her soul.

Where could they go from here? The genie of passion had escaped from the bottle and would not go back inside. She could not imagine them continuing to live under the same roof without being lovers, yet neither could she en-vision the shadows dissolving and her daring to make a forever commitment.

She reminded herself that he wasn't asking for that. He wanted to test what was between them, but great sex didn't mean he was interested in remarriage. They'd always been physically compatible. It hadn't been enough then, so maybe he'd decide that it wasn't enough now.

It was a remarkably liberating thought.

Dreamily, Donovan stroked Kate, hoping she'd never move. Hard to believe how many years had passed since they'd made love. How had he lived without her?

Very badly.

The phone on the vanity rang, destroying the mood. He groaned when she sat up and climbed from the tub. "Don't go," he protested. "Whoever it is can leave a message on the voice mail."

"We can't stay in a tub forever. We'd wrinkle like prunes."

"On you it would look good."

Dripping, she picked up the phone on the third ring. "Hello? Oh, hi, Mr. Glazer. It was nice of you to call. I'm fine." She rolled her eyes at Donovan. "I just had a nice relaxing bath. Tomorrow I'll be as good as new."

Since there wasn't much point in staying in the tub alone, he climbed out and wrapped a towel around his hips. Then he took another towel and began drying the elegant curves of Kate's back. He always enjoyed seeing her shining hair loose over her shoulders, but he had to admit that he also liked how the delicate line of her nape was exposed when her hair was pinned on top of her head.

She caught her breath when he circled her thigh with the towel and slowly patted downward, absorbing droplets of water. "Yes, Donovan stopped by to see how I was doing. He's very . . . conscientious."

He examined her body in leisurely detail. Her figure was

a little fuller. Sexier than ever. But he frowned at the ugly bruises she'd acquired earlier in the day. There was an enormous purple patch on one hip where she'd hit the floor, and smaller ones in a dozen other places. He kissed each mark with gossamer lightness, wishing he could make them vanish.

Then, because he was in the neighborhood, he touched one of her nipples with his tongue, lapping it to tautness. Kate's breathing quickened. Hastily she said good-bye and hung up. "That's a rotten trick, Donovan."

"Is it?" He transferred his attention to her other breast.

"Darned right. You said that tonight I got to call the shots."

"Me and my big mouth." He exhaled, his warm breath sliding over her skin.

"Well—I don't entirely object to your mouth. But it's my turn to dry you off."

"I can live with that." He removed the clips that held her hair in place, enjoying the cascade of glossy tresses. She ducked away before he could play anymore, and got a towel of her own. Very thorough, Kate was. By the time she'd finished drying him, taking special care not to neglect any vital body parts, he was ready to adjourn to the bedroom.

She was reaching for the doorknob when he drew her into a kiss. After a moment she pulled away. "You're in a very oral mood, and you know what that means."

"More wild sex?" he asked hopefully.

She tossed him the other terry robe. "Time to call room service and get some food up here."

And what could be better than a quiet evening together, secure in the knowledge of the waiting bed?

Later he couldn't remember what they talked about over their meal; he only knew that he was more content than he'd ever been in his life. Or perhaps when they were married he'd been content, but he hadn't recognized the feeling until it was gone.

Gradually he realized that Kate didn't fully share his

mood. While she was pleasant and didn't avoid his frequent touches, she spoke little and there was a shadow in her dark eyes that he couldn't read. He caught her hand, lacing his fingers through hers and drawing her close. "Is it still lady's choice?"

She skimmed his face with her fingertips. "Your turn to take charge, I think."

He untied her sash with a tug. "You know what I want to initiate."

"In some ways, you haven't changed at all." A roll of her shoulders dislodged the robe. One whole wall was mirrored, creating two Kates, a multiplication of riches.

Desire flared with unbearable heat. He felt as if he'd been dying in the desert for almost ten years, and his thirst for her could never be slaked. Cupping her face between his hands, he kissed her again and again, drinking in her essence until fever heat blazed through them both.

Then he swept her into his arms and carried her into the bedroom, laying her on the lace-draped bed. In the candlelit darkness, he used skill and patience and intimate knowledge to keep her on the edge of culmination until she wept with urgency.

They came together like wild creatures, rolling and writhing, losing and finding themselves together until all strength was drained and they lay panting in each other's arms. Yet though his body was sated, inside was an ache that wouldn't go away.

He rolled to his side and cradled her spoon style. It was so good to hold her that he was tempted to keep silent, to deny what his instincts were telling him. But there could be no future in avoiding the truth. Softly he said, "You're not quite all here, are you?"

"Maybe . . . I'm as here as I can be. Some pieces seem to be permanently missing."

The piece called love? He nestled his face against her silky hair, inhaling a lingering scent of roses. "Are you still afraid of me?"

"I . . . I'm not afraid of you, exactly. More like . . . un-nerved."

Despite her tactful reply, she clearly still felt some fear. He *hated* that she was afraid of him, yet he couldn't blame her. "I'd like to be able to swear I've outgrown dangerous anger. But I don't think I can. All I can promise is that I won't strike out. But physical blows aren't always the worst, are they?"

"Too true. Trust is such a fragile thing. Easy to break, impossible, perhaps, to ever mend."

Her quiet words struck like nails being hammered into a coffin. For a few hours he'd felt that the past had been resolved, that all that remained was working out the details of fitting their lives together again.

That hope collapsed. He tightened his arm around her waist. "I love you, Kate. That's never going to change."

She turned her face into the pillow, and he realized she was crying. Gently he rubbed her midriff with a slow, cir-cling motion, wanting to dissolve the tension he felt in her. "Are things that bad, *cara*? Surely not."

"I'm a coward still, Patrick. You're so much a part of me. When you're cut, I bleed. But if I were to stay with you, it would destroy me. I can't imagine spending the rest of this year living together as lovers, then walking away. Yet now that we've slept together, how can we live under the same roof and not do it again? I . . . I think I should go back to California now, before things get any worse."

He couldn't lose her now. Not again.

He turned her so that she was facing him, drawing her close and rocking her a little. "Don't act in haste, Kate. We've come so far in two months. Further, I think, than either of us dreamed possible. Give us time."

She didn't reply, but she didn't turn away. As he held her to his heart, he took comfort in that thought.

She didn't turn away.

37

Kate lay sheltered by a warm, solid body when the phone jolted her from sleep. It took her a moment to remember where she was, and to recognize that this wasn't a dream.

Brrring! She grabbed at the phone. "Hello?"

Luther Hairston's voice asked, "Is Donovan there, Katie?"

The clock said it wasn't yet five A.M., and she and Luther were in the same time zone. Something must be badly wrong. "Yes, but if this is business, I'm interested, too."

"It's business. There's been a gas explosion at Concord Place."

"Damn! I'll get Donovan right away."

She flipped on the bedside lamp. Holding the receiver against a pillow, she said, "It's Luther. Gas explosion at Concord Place. I'll get on the extension."

She scooped up a fallen terry robe on her way to the living room, yanking it on without stopping. Behind her, Donovan swore under his breath, then lifted the receiver. "Anyone hurt, Luther?"

On the desk phone, Kate heard, "No, praise be. Building Four was messed up pretty bad, though. About a third of the structure collapsed, and the part still standing is unstable as a house of cards. It'll have to come down right away."

"Was the explosion accidental?" Donovan asked.

"The fire marshal's office has only just started to investigate, so who knows? Gas lines do blow now and then."

"But given the problems on that project, you think otherwise."

"Does seem like an almighty coincidence. The gas company turned off service to the building when the tenants left, but it wouldn't have been that hard to turn back on."

Could this be related to the other problems PDI had experienced? Since the protesters had wanted to save Concord Place, Kate couldn't imagine why one of them would try to blow the place up. But an anonymous explosives junkie who had brought down the Jefferson Arms and killed Sam might be itching to do more damage.

Kate asked, "When can we get inside Building Four and start to work?"

"Probably not until tomorrow. But I've already heard from the mayor's office. They're going to want that building down about ten minutes later, if not before," Luther said. "The mayor wanted this project to be a public relations plus, not a black eye."

"By the end of today, I should be done with the explosives plan for the Hotel St. Cyr, so I can fly home this evening," Donovan said. "Kate can stay in Atlanta and supervise the prep work tomorrow. If I recall the master schedule correctly, Ted will finish his job in Chicago tomorrow afternoon. He can fly here afterward and take over at the hotel so Kate can come home."

"Musical chairs." Kate made notes on a pad. Luckily, Sam's will had allowed Charles to make allowances for temporary separations like this one. "I'll call Janie's voice mail so she can get to work on the plane tickets when the office opens."

After a few more minutes of shop talk, Luther hung up. From the bedroom, Donovan said, "I suppose before setting schedules, I should have asked if you're even going to be on the eastern seaboard."

She sat on the bed next to him. "I once read that the flight-or-fight response is hardwired into us, and a person doesn't know if she's a runner or a fighter until danger threatens. Based on the evidence, I have a flight response that would do a jackrabbit proud. Whenever I panic, the urge to head for the far horizon is almost irresistible. But I can't run away with everything unresolved. Not again."

"Thank God for that." His hand dropped over hers in a warm clasp.

"My staying doesn't mean everything is all right, Patrick. I . . . I really don't think it will ever be all right."

"Are you saying that you can't ever love me again?"

Her gaze dropped to their joined hands. His was large and callused, several shades darker than hers. A very capable hand. One that had hurt a lot when it struck.

Yet he had learned to deal with the demons that had driven him to abuse. Though he'd lost his temper several times in the last weeks, he'd always calmed down quickly without doing anything physical. But . . .

"I don't know if I'm capable of letting go enough to fall in love," she said. "The mere thought of 'falling' makes me think of hitting bottom. Hard."

"Love doesn't always hit bottom. Sometimes it soars forever."

"More often it doesn't."

He didn't pursue her statement any further, for which she was grateful. Saying she was afraid of an abyss in the center of her soul would sound even sillier than her previous comments.

He put an arm around her shoulders, drawing her close. "Breakfast is coming at five-thirty, so we have almost half an hour." Then he kissed her, untying her sash, bringing his naked flesh to hers.

No point in wasting half an hour.

Kate's shoulders were tense when she entered the St. Cyr again, but within an hour her accident of the previous day was a distant memory, of no relevance. The night she'd spent with Donovan was far more vivid and distracting.

Fortunately, he spent much of the day in the office on

the phone or his computer, so she didn't see him more than a couple of times. When their paths did cross, though, the looks he gave her threatened to melt her bones.

At the end of the day, after the laborers had left, he called her and Gil Brown into the site office and went over the explosives plan. When the meeting was over, Brown left but Kate stayed to say good-bye to Donovan.

He pulled Kate into an embrace. "I'm beginning to find a light dusting of construction debris downright sexy. I wish to hell that you were coming back to Baltimore with me tonight."

She rubbed her cheek against his shoulder, much the way Dinah did. "Remember, any missed days during the year get added on at the end."

"I don't want to think about endings."

His taxi arrived before she had to answer. He gave her a swift kiss, then raced out, duffel bag in one hand and laptop computer in the other. A fine example of *Homo modernsis,* male variety.

After Sam had barred Kate from the family business, she'd decided to finish college, then simply hang out around PDI until her father got used to having her there. Now Donovan, the sneaky devil, was following the same strategy, behaving as if they were a couple in the hope that eventually she'd simply accept it. They needed a day off from each other, to slow this alarming slide into that old married feeling.

Even though Kate knew that separation was good, the hotel suite felt very empty that night. She lay awake in the lace-canopied bed, her body burning with memories of the previous night. Even before they'd become lovers again, she'd become accustomed to having him close.

Simply breathing the same air had become vital to her.

Kate dozed all the way back from Atlanta, and regretted that the flight wasn't longer. Though her day at the Hotel St. Cyr had been tiring, she had enjoyed being the boss.

Her years as an architect had taught her that giving orders was much nicer than following them.

Her mother was waiting at the gate. "Mom, what a treat." She gave Julia a one-armed hug. "I'd been planning on taking a taxi home."

"When Donovan called about your cat, he mentioned that you were flying in tonight, so I volunteered to pick you up. We can go through the city and collect Dinah on the way to your house." Deftly Julia took Kate's computer case and slung it over her shoulder. "I learned with Sam that you have to create your own quality time."

"I don't know if the quality will be that high. I changed my clothes in a rest room in the Atlanta airport, but I suspect that I smell like a goat that's been rolled in crushed plaster."

"Ladies don't perspire, they glow, and they definitely don't smell like goats," her mother said with a smile.

They entered the main terminal from a concourse Kate hadn't used before. Their path took them by a pedestal holding a giant stained-glass sculpture of a Chesapeake Bay blue crab. Kate regarded it with fascination. "How marvelously Maryland."

"They say airports are all alike, but it's not true. Every one has its own regional character. When Sam and I traveled—" Julia's words cut off.

"How are you doing?" Kate asked.

"Ups and downs."

Kate wanted to ask more, but Julia's stoic mask was in place. The code of the WASP. They walked the rest of the way to Julia's car without speaking.

After dumping her luggage in the trunk, Kate sank into the passenger seat. Her mind drifted as they left the parking garage and pulled onto the airport access road. The code of the WASP. Stiff upper lip. Strong emotion is vulgar, weak. Don't let it show. *Anger is unbecoming, dear.* The lessons of her childhood.

The code had its points, which included strength and dignity and integrity. But sometimes repressing emotion was a mistake, and maybe this was one of those times. Kate and her mother were sitting side by side, both of them troubled. Maybe a little openness would benefit them both. Lord knew that Kate could use some wise maternal advice. But where to start?

As they turned north to I-95, Kate said, "Donovan and I are sleeping together again."

After a startled moment her mother said, "How . . . how nice for you both. Does this have long-term implications?"

"Probably not." Kate fingered her seat belt as she struggled to find the words to reveal herself. Yet if she couldn't speak honestly to her own mother, she was in bad shape. "You must have wondered why I divorced Donovan."

"Of course. Obviously it had to be something that hurt you very, very deeply. I thought perhaps he'd had a fling with an old girlfriend, or a one-night stand on a business trip—something of that nature."

"Patrick, unfaithful?" That was one thing she'd never worried about. For better and worse, he'd always made her feel that she was the only woman in his world. A pity that obsessive jealousy had gone along with that.

It wasn't too late to back out of this conversation. But being a jackrabbit was getting her nowhere. "I left him because he was . . . violent. Not much at first, but getting progressively worse. At the end, it was . . . bad. Very bad."

"Dear God!" Julia gasped. "I . . . I have trouble believing that Patrick would ever hurt you."

"Believe it. Until finally I hurt him back, then ran like hell."

"How could Sam and I have missed such a thing?" Julia exclaimed. "I know that Patrick had some rough edges when you first married, but he always seemed so devoted to you. He was—is—such a kind, considerate young man."

"All true. A good heart, unfortunately paired with lousy impulse control. Meaning that sometimes he went a little crazy and hit me."

Julia bit her lip. "Hence California, and never coming home. And because you didn't want to talk about such a horrible situation, you wouldn't tell us why you left."

"Silence seemed best for Donovan, for Sam, for everyone. Me most of all. I . . . I couldn't bear to publicly admit that I had gotten myself into such a sordid mess. Nice, upper-middle-class girls don't get battered. It was easier to run."

"If Sam had realized why you left, he never would have written his will the way he did. Now that I know, I'm amazed that you agreed to try to fulfill the conditions. What persuaded you?"

"At heart I welcomed the chance to come back and join the company. Plus there was your very sensible point about dealing with the past. I was wary of Donovan, especially at first, but I knew that I could leave if there was even a hint of trouble."

"*Has* there been trouble?" her mother asked.

"So far, so good. His father was an abusive drunk, so it's not surprising that Donovan had a capacity for violence. After we split up, he came to realize that he was affected by even small amounts of alcohol, so he quit drinking altogether. The wonder isn't that he was occasionally violent, but that he turned out to be such a decent guy most of the time."

"So avoiding alcohol might be all that's needed to prevent future violence. Does knowing that he's stopped drinking make you feel safe?"

"Not really. I still can't bring myself to fully trust him."

"Which would certainly get in the way of a permanent reconciliation. Does either of you want that?"

"Donovan might, but I don't know if I'll ever be able to make such a leap of faith. There's a big complicated knot tied in my psyche. And I can't quite get over watching for a fist whenever he raises his voice."

"The mere thought of him striking you makes me ill. You're my daughter, and he's almost like a son. How could such a horrible thing happen?" Julia bit her lip. "That's another reason why you never told me, isn't it? Because you didn't want to have to deal with my emotions as well as your own."

"Well put."

They came to the end of the interstate spur that led into the city and descended onto Martin Luther King, Jr. Boulevard. "That knot in your psyche. Is it fear? Anger? Or both?" Julia asked.

"I'm not sure. Both, maybe."

"Perhaps forgiveness is the key. It takes a lot of forgiveness on both sides to keep a marriage working. Sam and I might have separated after Tom revealed his orientation, but we managed to accept our differences even then, though it was terribly difficult." A light rain was starting to fall, so Julia turned on the windshield wipers. "If you can forgive Patrick his trespasses, it might banish the anger. Perhaps the fear would follow."

"He never intentionally hurt me. Whenever anything bad happened, he was as appalled as I was. He's still drenched with guilt."

The wipers slid across the windshield with a slow, hypnotic rhythm. "You may understand why he behaved as he did, but that comes from the head," Julia said. "Forgiveness is more than understanding, and it's more than just letting go. True forgiveness comes from the heart and is ultimately spiritual, I think. The mundane version of grace. It's worth forgiving Patrick for what he did not only for his sake, but for your own. To untie that knot in your spirit."

"I thought Tom was in charge of theology for the Corsi family."

"This is pragmatic stuff, Kate, not just theory. I learned the hard way that anger corrodes the soul. I suggest you think about it."

"Did you learn because of problems you and Dad had?" Though the fact that her mother had assumed infidelity had come between Kate and Donovan probably wasn't random.

If so, Kate didn't really want to know more.

"Our marriage almost ended while I was carrying Tom. But Sam's mother gave me some good advice—pretty much what I'm telling you," Julia said. "Do you know the other fact that saved our marriage? My stubborn pride. I didn't want to have to admit to my family and friends that they'd been right about Sam. It gave me extra incentive to accept and forgive. Our marriage survived, and became stronger than I would have dreamed possible when I was on the verge of ending it."

How strange to think that she herself might never have been born if her parents hadn't overcome what had almost divided them. As evidence that it really was possible to rebuild a fractured marriage, her mother's testimony was impressive.

But was Kate capable of doing the same? She looked inside herself, to the bruised place in her soul that hid her most painful secrets, and recognized that Julia was right: there was still anger over Donovan's abuse. Intellectually she'd come to understand, even feel compassion, for what he had suffered. But buried deep in her gut was a molten core of anger. She hadn't forgiven from the heart, because her heart was still bleeding.

The rain-slicked urban streets were almost empty at this hour. As bricks and concrete gave way to leafy residential neighborhoods, Kate thought about what her mother had said, turning it over six ways from zero. Forgiveness made sense—if she could manage it. That part would be hard. But it offered at least a chance for the future.

Only now did she recognize, with bone-biting intensity, how much she wanted for there to be a chance.

38

After they pulled up at the Roland Park house, Kate leaned over and gave her mother a quick hug. "Thanks, Mom. I needed that."

"Glad to be of use. I'm way behind in the maternal advice department." As they went into the house to collect Dinah, she asked, "Did you get any dinner? I have some chili in the Crock-Pot."

Kate scooped up her cat, who was dancing around her ankles, and popped her into the carrier. "Thanks, but I'd rather get home. I did some cholesterol loading at the Atlanta airport while waiting for my plane." She saw disappointment in her mother's eyes as she bent to ruffle Oscar Wilde's ears.

In the car again, Kate asked, "How are things between you and Charles Hamilton?"

"That's really none of your concern, my dear."

"Yes and no. You're both adults. But I'm also your daughter and concerned about you." Since Dinah was the rare feline that traveled well, Kate opened the carrier and released the little cat onto her lap. "The last time I saw you, before going to Atlanta, you implied rather strongly that you'd ended things with Charles. Is that the case?"

"If you must know, I realized how very unbecoming it was to be dallying with another man when your father is hardly cold in his coffin. I knew already, of course, but had managed to avoid thinking about it. Until I saw what I was doing reflected in your eyes."

"I was startled. Stunned, in fact. But that didn't mean I thought you should stop seeing Charles. It's not like he's some worthless Casanova. Last night I gave Tom a call and mentioned this. He didn't have a problem."

"You told your brother?" Julia exclaimed.

"Tom sort of blinked, if one can do that on the phone, but said immediately that it sounded like a great idea. He and Charles have always gotten on well. If being with Charles makes you hurt less, we're both in favor. After all, if you'd been the one to die, would you have wanted Sam to spend the rest of his life alone?"

"Of course not. Sam needed a keeper, and he wasn't cut out for celibacy. The sooner he remarried, the better."

Kate let the words hang in the air for a long moment before she said with sudden laughter, "Heavens, if you and Charles got married, Rachel and Sandy would be stepsisters to Tom and me. That would be great!"

"Don't be absurd! There is no marriage in the offing. We're . . . we're not even speaking to each other."

"Why not?"

Julia sighed. "Guilt got in the way, I'm afraid."

"Val says that all women are born guilty, but anyone who knew you and Sam also knew how much you loved each other. It's the people who were happy in their first marriage who are most likely to find another partner quickly. Being willing to accept a new relationship is a compliment to Sam."

"Very eloquent, but you're assuming Charles is seriously interested. In my confusion, I flip-flopped several times, hurting him and his pride. I can't imagine him wanting to face that again. I think he was just being kind, and was repaid rather poorly for his efforts."

To Kate, her mother sounded like a woman who wanted to be with a particular man, but didn't know quite how to go about it. A distinguished, prosperous, and attractive widower had no shortage of potential partners. Yet according to Rachel, Charles had resisted his daughters' suggestions that he consider starting to date. Julia had changed that. They had appeared to be getting along very well indeed on the disastrous occasion when Kate and Donovan had dropped in. Friendship was the foundation of a good relationship, and Julia and Charles had been friends their whole lives.

Julia was not likely to make a move toward Charles, and from what she'd said, by this time he might be too wary to make a move toward her. What they needed was an old-fashioned go-between.

What the hell. Kate picked up her mother's car phone, turned on the power, and punched in a number she'd known since she was four.

Julia asked, "Who are you calling?"

"Charles, of course." The phone began to ring at the other end.

"Katherine Carroll Corsi, don't you *dare!*"Julia yelped.

Kate whisked the phone out of reach. "Mom, look out for that parked car!"

The warning pushed Julia's attention back to the road. After straightening the wheel, she said, "Hang up that phone *right now.*"

"Too late, he's picking up." Kate held the receiver to her right ear and answered the familiar hello with a cheerful, "Hi, Charles, it's Kate Corsi."

"Good evening. How are you doing?"

"Actually, I'm calling to ask if your intentions toward my mother are honorable."

As Julia shrieked, "Kate!" Charles said in a choked voice, "Good God, you don't pull your punches, do you?"

"I'm concerned for my mother. I don't want her taken advantage of by aging swingers cutting notches on their bedposts. So—what are your intentions?"

"You're not too big to ground, young lady." He drew a deep breath. "But since you ask—if what you mean by 'honorable intentions' is whether I'd like a lasting relationship, the answer is yes. The question is academic, though.

Julia gave me my walking papers after you wrecked everything by dropping in unannounced."

"I'm sorry about that, and busily trying to make amends. If you heard a shriek a moment ago, it was Julia. I'm calling from her car phone, and we're about a mile from your house. Would you like to see her after she drops me off?"

"I'd like nothing better. But you can't force her do something she doesn't want to do."

"I don't think wanting is the problem." Kate considered handing the phone to her mother, then decided that would cause an accident for sure. "For what it's worth, I wouldn't mind having you for a stepfather."

"Which would definitely give me grounding privileges. Kate, if this works, thank you. And if it doesn't—well, thanks for trying." He hung up.

Kate clicked off the power and set the phone down. "Pretend for a moment that guilt and socially approved ideas about mourning periods didn't exist. If that were the case, would you want to be with Charles?"

There was a long silence while Julia turned onto Bellona Avenue. "Yes, I'd want to be with him."

"Then maybe you should forgive yourself for not being quite proper. Some of the best things in life happen at inconvenient times. You and Charles have a very special friendship. Don't throw that away for the wrong reasons."

"Sometimes I've thought you're like me, and other times that you're very like your father," Julia said. "But you've just made it clear that under your ladylike exterior, it's your Sicilian grandmother's blood that burns hottest in your veins."

Preferring not to know if that was an insult or a compliment, Kate maintained silence and concentrated on coaxing Dinah into her carrier while they pulled up in front of the house on Brandy Lane. "I know what I did was pretty outrageous. But . . . I did it because I love you."

"Love, the most dangerous of blessings. I know you meant well, dear."

After waving good-bye, Kate went up the sidewalk, cat carrier in one hand and pulling her wheeled luggage with the other. She was searching for her keys when the door swung open, revealing Donovan, his blue eyes both eager and cautious. The usual tangled emotions of pleasure and wariness—and yes, anger—skipped through her at the sight of him. His youthful violence, the secrecy about his difficult childhood, had brought their marriage down in a smoldering ruin of pain and fury. Yet he had suffered at least as much as she.

"Kate. I've missed you." He opened his arms and she walked straight in.

Home. She rested her head on his shoulder, and felt an old, deeply buried knot of anger slowly begin to dissolve. *Forgive.*

Forgive him, forgive herself. And then, *live.*

Emotions flapping like sheets in a gale, Julia halted at the stop sign at the foot of Brandy Lane. God help her, should she turn right and go home? Or left, to Charles's house? As her hands clenched the wheel, she gave a mental cry that was nearly a prayer. *Sam, what should I do?*

A strange calm came over her, and she felt almost as if he were sitting next to her in the car. Sam, christened Sansone, her husband, lover, friend, father of her children. She could almost feel the touch of his hand on her cheek. *It's okay,* cara, *you can love someone else, too. I know you're not going to forget me.*

If there really were ghosts, Sam's was giving his blessing. Did that make things better, or worse?

A horn honked behind her and a set of headlights appeared in her rearview mirror. With an apologetic wave that probably couldn't be seen in the dark, she put on her blinker, and turned. Left.

Three minutes later she parked in front of Charles's house. The lights were on. Not stopping to think, she climbed from the car. A push of the doorbell. Inside, the first few bars of Beethoven's Fifth played. The doorbell had been a lighthearted gift she'd given Charles and Barbara ten years earlier.

The door swung open and Tort and Retort bolted out, panting happily and whapping her with wagging tails. Behind them was Charles, his hair silvery in the cool light.

They stared at each other until he broke the silence. "I didn't think you'd come."

"I almost didn't." She stepped into the front hall, thinking that Kate must have inherited her jackrabbit tendencies from her mother, because the urge to run was almost overpowering. "Can you forgive my to-ing and fro-ing?"

"Julia, I could forgive you anything. But I must admit that the to-ing and fro-ing, as you put it, has been pretty hard on my aging nerves."

"I'd better say my piece before I lose my nerve entirely. To begin with, it's a given that losing a spouse makes one crazy, and I've certainly been half-crazed. Crazed, and guilty."

"I can't imagine that you have any reason to feel guilt, except the general guilt of the fact that you're alive and Sam isn't. I get regular attacks of that. Why Barbara and not me? Life and death are equally unfair."

"This . . . goes beyond that. I loved Sam from the day that I met him, in good times and bad. Some of the best years were when I was working in the PDI office and he was building the business. My whole life was centered around him. But, Charles . . ." She hesitated. "Sometimes it was as if he took up all the oxygen, and there wasn't enough left for me. Being with you is so . . . so restful— and I hate myself for being so happy with you when I'm also missing Sam so desperately. What kind of woman am I, to feel this way?"

Charles came up behind and put his hands on her shoulders, kneading the rigid muscles gently. "Sometimes I felt the same way about Barbara, you know. She was probably the most honorable, dynamic, principled person I've ever known. I give thanks daily that she was my wife, and that we had as many years together as we did. But restful? Not very."

She reached up and rested her right hand over his. "I've wondered sometimes. If you and I were the ones who died, do you think Sam and Barbara might have gotten together?"

"I think it's quite possible. They adored each other. But if that had happened, it's a safe bet it would have been a much noisier relationship than what is between you and me."

Knowing she must reveal the whole truth, she said, "I've always loved you as a friend, Charles. What frightened me witless was realizing that . . . that I'm in love with you, too. Not the same way I loved Sam, of course, because you're very different. But—close enough."

His hands tightened on her shoulders. "Loving me doesn't take anything away from Sam. He was one of the most generous men I've ever known. Do you think he'd have wanted you to be any more miserable than was absolutely necessary?"

"No, he wouldn't." She turned to meet Charles's gaze. "Kate said some of the best things in life happen at inconvenient times, and that something so special shouldn't be thrown away for the wrong reasons."

His long face broke into a smile. "God bless the child." And then he kissed her.

39

The alarm clock gave a shrill, migraine-inducing buzz, and a floor lamp blazed on, six hundred watts' worth. Finally, Kate was waking up to the cathedral ceiling she'd designed so many years earlier. Though her imagination hadn't involved rising at god-awful hours before the sun came up.

Donovan batted the clock and the buzzer cut off. "I rigged the lamp to come on with the alarm because it's easier to get up when the room is light. After a couple of snooze cycles, I'm generally ready to face the day." He kissed her temple with sleepy affection.

A shifting weight on Kate's chest proved to be Dinah, who opened her tiny mouth and yawned. Donovan, a cat, and a warm bed. Bliss unbounded.

The worrying part of her mind started to wonder how long such happiness could last. She'd come home to a message from the detective investigating Sam's death. He'd been interested in the information she'd sent on Steve Burke and Joe Beekman. Maybe he'd learned more while she was away. "What's on the agenda? When I came in last night, you mentioned a rush project, but before you could explain, we got . . . sidetracked."

"And how! Today we're going to make a full-fledged assault on the damaged Concord Place building. This project has been jinxed from the get-go, and that gas explosion has made Building Four very, very unstable. If it falls on its own, it could wreck the church across the street, so we need to bring Building Four down in a controlled way as quickly as possible."

"The concrete in that project is such poor quality that it crumbles when you look at it cross-eyed. Would conventional demolition with a wrecking ball be better for taking down at least the damaged section?"

"That would be safer, but too slow. The city wants that building down now. Destroying neighborhood churches is real bad public relations."

"What did you mean by full-fledged assault?"

"Just what it sounds like. Every available PDI field person is going to be in there today, along with Nick and Joe Flynn, the foreman he swiped from us."

"Nick's being helpful?"

"Don't be shocked, it's not altruism. He's getting paid very well as a PDI subcontractor. Since he and Joe worked on Concord Place before Nick started his own shop, they know the structure, which is handy. If all goes well, we could bring this building down tonight or tomorrow morning."

"So soon? You're kidding!"

"The soft stripping was just about done before the gas explosion, so if we can design an explosives plan today while the prep crews are drilling and loading the solid part of the structure, a shot is doable. Your talent for unstable structures is going to be damned useful. The place is a mess. You and I will have to go over every inch of the damaged section before we can finalize the timing sequences."

"This is a historic moment. You're actually saying that you want me in a dangerous structure instead of huffing and puffing about how I should stay outside where it's safe."

"Don't worry, I'm thinking that, but you were right on the money predicting how the buildings in Mexico City would drop. I can't afford not to take advantage of your special talents."

The alarm started buzzing again. This time it was Kate who turned off the sound, her movement sending Dinah off in an indignant huff. "The second snooze interval will have to wait for another morning. It's time we were up and about."

She swung her legs over the side of the bed, but Donovan caught her before she could escape and pulled her into a kiss. It was not primarily an embrace of passion, though desire was always present between them. Instead, he said huskily, "In case I haven't mentioned it lately, I love you, Kate."

He *had* mentioned it, several times, the night before. As then, Kate's response was an uneasy blend of pleasure and anxiety. But maybe this morning the anxiety was a little less than the night before. If the day ever came when she could freely, without doubt, trust him enough to put her heart in his hands . . .

That time hadn't come. She gave him a quick kiss on the nose, then slid from the bed. One day at a time.

It was going to be a pleasure to flatten Building Four, assuming it didn't flatten him first. Donovan swore and jumped back when his attempt to examine a damaged column caused a sizable slab of concrete to topple toward him. Luckily his caution saved him from harm, but pebbles rattled off his hard hat like hail.

The undamaged sections of the structure had been shoddily built—he hoped the city sued the original contractor—but at least those areas were reasonably stable. The devastated west wing was another matter. Donovan was reminded of photos he'd seen of bomb damage in Beirut and Bosnia. Partially demolished walls, concrete crumbled like sand, and rubble everywhere. The nearer he came to the end of the building, the more charred and treacherous the structure became.

Kate appeared with clipboard in hand and an interesting variety of soot smudges. Through the course of a long day, she'd been making notes and calculations as if this hellhole was a normal workplace. "Shall we compare notes?"

"Yes, but not here." Together they moved back to the more solid part of the building. After fifteen minutes of intensive study and discussion, Donovan said, "I think this is about as good as it's going to get. I'm almost ready to sign off on the explosives plan. How about you?"

Kate gnawed at her lip as she stared at her copy of the floor plan. "I want to take another look at the reinforcement on the eighth floor, but basically, I'm ready. I doubt we're going to get any better data than we have now."

"You check the eighth while I finish going over the fifth." He looked outside at the plywood that had been nailed across the stained-glass windows of the nearest structure. "Even if our calculations are a little off, I'm sure that we won't damage the church, which is the biggest concern. Nothing else is close enough to the west end to be endangered."

Kate checked her watch. "I heard Luther telling you that the loading is just about done in the undamaged part of the building. How long will it take to load this end?"

"Maybe six hours, mostly because we have to be careful moving through here. Then we can blow this beast into gravel, and good riddance."

"Emergencies can be kind of fun," she said.

"To a point, but don't spend too much time on the eighth floor or I'll send out a search party." Building Four was as hazardous as any earthquake-damaged structure; he'd ordered people to work in pairs when possible.

"This will only take a few minutes." She turned and picked her way through what had once been a living room. Now cold winds blew grimy plaster dust through what had once been someone's home.

His own clipboard in hand, Donovan worked his way cautiously westward. Jagged spikes of rusty rebar protruded from scorched columns like shattered bones. Not much dynamite would be needed to bring them down. Hell, a good kick might be enough. The trick was to cut the steel reinforcing bars in a controlled way that would work as part of the overall shot.

But he felt good about the plan they'd worked out. Jim Frazer, PDI's chief engineer, had already given his approval, subject to Kate and Donovan's final tuning.

He stepped around a pile of broken plasterboard, grimly noting old bullet holes. In its later years this had not been a happy place. A mistake not to watch his footing, though. The flooring sagged under his weight, and he almost fell.

Swearing, he caught his balance and retreated a few steps. The concrete floors were reinforced by a horizontal grid of rebar, but the gas blast and fire had caused massive damage. Slabs of ceiling concrete had fallen to the floor, and the steel had actually melted in some places.

He saw a flash of movement ahead. There shouldn't be anyone in this area, so he cautiously circled a sagging wall, stopping in surprise when he saw a familiar figure by one of the columns. "Nick? What the hell are you doing here?"

Nick Corsi spun around, a short crowbar in one hand. "Just . . . just checking things out." He kept his body between Donovan and the column.

It wasn't enough to block the view of what he'd been doing. Donovan said incredulously, "Are you putting plastic explosive in there? That's all wrong."

"Shit!" Nick snarled. "I was hoping I wouldn't have to do this." Dropping the crowbar, he reached inside his down vest to pull out a dark object that resembled a television remote. "Your timing is rotten, Donovan." He rammed the object into Donovan's solar plexus, and the world went away.

Dazed, Donovan found himself lying on his back on a rough surface. Where was he? And what the hell had happened?

Cracked concrete above, the smells of demolition: a job site. Glad to have figured that out, he tried to focus on the figure looming above him. Nick Corsi, leaning down, arm extended.

Instinctively, Donovan tried to evade the other man, but his muscles wouldn't respond. Christ, had he been paralyzed in an accident?

"If a second did that, five seconds should put you down long enough for me to finish the job." Nick pressed a dark object below Donovan's rib cage.

Donovan felt a wave of shock so intense that he had no name for it. Time and place and reason vanished, and he spun helplessly into hell's own limbo.

Kate returned whistling from her brief expedition. The visit to the eighth floor had confirmed her original conclusions. If Donovan was ready to sign off, they were in business.

This building would be no loss, either. Kate had regretted the grand old Hotel St. Cyr, but Concord Place had outlived its time. Particularly when she was alone, she felt traces of the lives lived within these battered walls. There had been happiness and laughter and warm family love, but there had also been anger and despair. Time to blow it all to kingdom come, and build a healthy new community.

There was so much construction noise in the building that she didn't bother to yell for Donovan, just headed down a dilapidated hall toward where she'd seen him last. Seeing her cousin picking his way through the rubble, she called, "Hi, Nick, Looking for Donovan? So am I."

"I should have known you'd be along soon." Nick beckoned her. "Donovan's back this way." He led her into an open area strewn with rubble that lay beyond the corridor.

Before Kate could figure out her cousin's odd behavior, she saw Donovan lying on his side by one of the fissured columns, his body curled limply and his hard hat several feet away. "My God, Nick, what happened? Have you radioed for help?"

She dropped to her knees beside him. No fallen concrete, no blood or bruises, yet he seemed unconscious. Surely not a heart attack, not at his age! Half-suffocated with fear, she checked his throat for a pulse. To her relief, at her touch his lids flickered open to reveal dazed eyes.

Since Nick apparently hadn't called for help, she unhooked her walkie-talkie from her belt. "Patrick, what happened?"

Her voice seemed to focus his attention. "Kate, look out," he whispered. "N . . . Nick . . ."

She whipped up her head to see that Nick was coming at her. "Your turn, Katie," he said with regret.

Donovan gasped, "Go!"

She scrambled up, but by the time she was on her feet, Nick had wrenched the radio from her grasp and was shoving a small black instrument toward her abdomen.

Donovan flailed out and caught Nick's ankle. "R . . . run, Kate!"

Cursing, Nick yanked free of Donovan's grip easily, but the brief interruption gave Kate time to put a dozen feet between herself and her cousin. "Nick, what the hell are you doing?"

"Correcting Sam's will. Your ex is recovering surprisingly fast. Must be his protective instincts. This should slow him down again." He jammed the device into Donovan's belly, holding it there for a dozen heartbeats. Donovan made a ghastly sound and went completely limp again.

Nick straightened, expression grim. "Don't bother trying to run, cousin. This is one game of hide-and-seek you're not going to win."

He tossed her radio aside. "A pity you and Donovan wandered in before I could finish loading that column, but the fault is really Sam's. He shouldn't have left PDI to someone who wasn't family. Christ, Donovan hadn't even been his son-in-law for ten years!"

Kate backed away, horror-struck. Dear God, it was *Nick* who had been harassing PDI! He had the skills and the opportunities to create trouble, and if she understood him correctly, he also felt he had a motive. Why hadn't she suspected him earlier?

Because it was hard—almost impossible—to believe that someone she'd known her whole life could be so wicked. "Did you cause the blast that killed Sam?"

"He was going to be dead in a couple of months anyhow. I figured I was doing him a favor by taking him out before it got really painful."

Any faint hope that this was some weird misunderstanding died with his admission. "You bastard! You stole those months from my mother and everyone else who loved my father."

"It wouldn't have happened if Sam had done the right thing in the first place. Personally, I think the cancer had affected his brain. I was really hurt when Angie told me about the will. I couldn't believe Sam would pass over his own nephew to leave PDI to your stupid Irish ex-husband. Hell, I could have understood if he'd left it to you or even your faggot brother, but Donovan? That was a damned insult." He moved another step closer.

Angie? That's right, Nick's wife worked for Charles Hamilton's firm. In fact, that was where Nick had met her. She must monitor files relating to her husband's family and the business. She'd probably seen Sam come in, and checked Charles's notes later to learn why. Nick had obviously taken the news of the new will very, very badly.

"Convenient for you to have a spy in Charles's office." Her cousin was between her and the undamaged part of the building, herding her into more hazardous territory.

"Angie is a nice old-fashioned girl who always does exactly what I tell her. She hasn't talked back or disobeyed since the second year of our marriage."

Bastard. "I'm family, too, Nick. Our fathers were brothers. We carry the same name. Does family kill family?"

"You should have stayed in California. But no, you had to work at PDI. If you hadn't, you wouldn't be here today. I just wanted to bring this end of the building down messily so the church got damaged, and PDI's reputation along with it. Not my fault that you and Donovan blundered in, so I have to get rid of you both."

He took another step forward. Kate retreated the same distance, the flooring creaking ominously beneath her. "What are you going to do—push us over the edge?"

"Has to look like an accident," Nick said. "That's why I brought the stun gun. When the explosives go off, you and Donovan will be caught in the blast. I suppose an autopsy might show you've been stunned, but who's going to look that closely at a couple of corpses who've been flattened like roadkill?"

"Why are you doing this?"

"With two more fatalities, the firm will either close or be sold to Marchetti Demolition. If Marchetti gets it, he'll probably hire me to run it. If it closes—well, PDI won't be competing with my company anymore. Either way, I win. It would have been so much easier if Sam had just left the company to me in the first place."

His selfish rationalizations revolted Kate, but there was no time to waste in hating him. No use yelling—there was too much demolition noise. Her radio was out of reach, and Donovan was down for the count. She was on her own. Luckily, Nick had to be within touching distance to use the stun gun. He was also complacent, sure he could take her whenever he wanted. If she could find some kind of weapon, she'd have a chance.

A sizable length of broken rebar caught her eye. Lying about fifteen feet to her left, it would make a formidable weapon, and could be wielded from a distance beyond Nick's reach. She began inching to her left. Nick mirrored her movements in a weird dance in which he drew ever closer.

Stalling for time, she said, "Have you had anything to do with the accidents that have been happening on so many PDI projects lately?"

"You're smart, Kate. Yeah, I've been behind most of

'em. Since I did the account work, I knew all of PDI's upcoming projects. I also know demolition people all over the country. It wasn't hard to find guys who didn't mind picking up a few extra bucks in return for playing pranks. Set a little fire, make a mistake or two in ordering or delivering explosives, or when operating equipment—no problem. I turned the gas on here myself. Dead easy."

"So you have a talent for low-grade industrial espionage. You're a good snake-oil salesman, too, but that doesn't mean you have the technical skills to run PDI. You were always a talker, not a doer. You'd probably bankrupt the firm in a couple of years."

"And you were always a smartmouthed little princess! Daddy's dear little girl, who could do no wrong."

Donovan's shaky voice said, "You're a slob technically, Nick. That's the real reason why Sam didn't leave you the firm."

Nick swung around, enraged. "You're the one who wasn't carrying your weight! Anyone can drill holes, but it takes talent to find and keep clients. I was the one who was indispensable, not you. But after I left, you poisoned Sam's mind against me, so that he refused when I asked to come back. You brought this on yourself!"

"Bullshit." Donovan rolled onto his side, his whole frame shaking with the effort. "You say that Sam didn't honor family, but he did. If you weren't his nephew, you'd have been out on your ass."

Kate had been taking advantage of Donovan's diversionary tactics to edge toward the rebar. As Nick furiously kicked Donovan in the ribs, she leaped for the length of steel and grabbed it in both hands. Three racing strides and she was close enough to strike her cousin. Using all her strength, she swung for the back of his neck, hoping she'd break it.

Hearing the whistle of steel slicing through the air, he turned in time to throw up one arm and block the worst impact. He staggered backward, then caught his balance and lunged toward her, the stun gun crackling with blue-white fire.

Oh, God, he was aiming for the rebar. Fearing that steel would conduct electricity dangerously well, she threw the heavy bar at him, then grabbed a piece of broken concrete and hurled it at her cousin's face. The rebar caught him at waist level, ironically bending him over so that the flying concrete missed.

Undamaged, he straightened. "Forget it, daddy's little princess. You never beat me in a fight in your life."

She bolted, moving parallel to the damaged west front. He raced after her. She scooped up a handful of grit and gravel and threw it behind her. Some struck Nick's face. "Christ, you little—"

It gave her the seconds she needed to get past him. Pivoting sharply, she raced toward the undamaged section of the building. With any kind of lead, she could outrun him, and just a floor below, there was help . . .

"Come back here, Kate!" Nick bellowed. "If you don't, I swear Donovan will be dead before you reach the next floor."

She stopped in her tracks. Then, heart pounding with terror, she turned to face her father's murderer.

40

Nick grabbed a crowbar from the floor and positioned himself above Donovan. "A couple of blows with this should crush his skull nicely. Though jabbing him through an eye socket might be more efficient. Kind of like killing a frog in biology. I remember you were too much of a sissy for that. Had to get your nerdy friend Rachel to do it for you. Shall I show you how it's done right now?"

His threat filled her with icy rage. She must think, *think,* or she and Donovan were both dead. "If you're going to murder us both anyhow, there's no percentage in me sticking around. It will just get me killed without helping Donovan."

He frowned. "You're right. It would have worked if I could take you both out with no one the wiser, but I blew it. Not much point in offing him, then getting arrested for murder. Besides, it's not as if I really want to kill someone else. Time to negotiate. How about I give you Donovan's life in return for silence? Promise that neither of you will squeal on me, and you can both walk away. We'll all pretend this never happened."

Did he think she was stupid enough to believe he'd let them go? Apparently. But as long as he was holding a crowbar to Donovan's head, he was in control. "All I have to do is keep quiet?"

"That's it. After all, Katie, I haven't done any real damage. Donovan will be as good as new in a few minutes, and Sam was going to die anyhow."

"That's true." Wanting to make this convincing, she frowned at Donovan and put a note of doubt in her voice. "I think I can persuade him to agree."

"Don't worry," Nick said confidently. "I've seen how he looks at you. You've got Donovan's balls in your pocket— he'll do any damn thing you want. So let's call it a wash, and get on with our lives. I wanted PDI, but I've missed my chance. My company is doing fine. I'll get my revenge by beating your brains out in the marketplace."

She looked into his dark eyes, and saw a stone killer. If she came within reach, he'd stun her, then set off a blast that would kill her and Donovan. He must think she was an idiot. Of course, she was only a woman, and he'd never taken women seriously.

Take advantage of that. "Okay, Nick, you've got a deal."
"Let's shake on it."

She moved forward slowly. She had to stay out of reach of the stun gun, keep him from hurting Donovan, and summon help. Her gaze flicked about the rubble-strewn site, looking for anything that might help her.

In a flash of lethal clarity, a plan formed. Her walkie-talkie lay about six feet from Nick. Five seconds with that, and every man in the building would come on the double.

As soon as she picked it up, Nick would come after her instead of threatening Donovan. She wouldn't have much chance if he were armed with a real gun or a knife, but the stun gun was designed for defense, not offense. She was willing to bet she could hold him off long enough. She *was* betting—and her stake was two lives.

She took the last few steps, forcing herself not to look at the radio. "You promise to leave me and Donovan and PDI alone in the future?"

"You got my word on it. I'll admit maybe I went too far, but Sam really hurt my feelings." He scowled at Donovan. "Keep this jerk away from me. He gets on my nerves."

His brief shift in attention was the best chance she'd get. She dived for the radio, hitting the transmit key even as she raised it to her mouth.

Before she could speak, Nick swung around with snakelike swiftness and knocked the radio from her hand with his crowbar. "You treacherous little bitch!"

Face contorted, he raised the stun gun. She spun away, but the contacts of the weapon caught her elbow in a glancing blow. A dazzling blue-white arc crackled wickedly, and stinging needles blitzed from the point of contact.

Left arm half-numb and half-tingling, she grabbed a chunk of concrete in her right hand. "Not so easy to use that nasty little toy if the person knows it's coming, is it? The only way you could take Donovan was by surprise.

He's ten times the man you are—that's why Sam wanted him to have the company."

As she'd hoped, the insult brought Nick forward like a charging bull. Rather than assaulting him directly, she smashed the concrete into the stun gun. It shattered in his hand, no longer a threat.

But she couldn't avoid the battering ram of Nick's solid body. He struck her in a punishing tackle, and she fell heavily to the ground, pinned beneath him. His hot breath hit her face as he snarled, "You filthy little slut!" He grabbed for her throat.

She drove a knee viciously toward his groin, but he rolled away and scrambled to his feet before she could connect. He spat out, "You'll pay for that before you die!"

He was between her and the column, in exactly the right place. Sure he had her now, Nick moved in for the kill. She forced herself to wait until he was leaning over her. Then she whipped up her knees, planted her boots in his gut, and kicked with all her strength.

His breath whooshed out as he hurtled backward— straight onto a rebar rod that spiked from the broken column. He screamed, a horrible, echoing sound, as the metal shaft emerged from his chest. For an endless, ghastly instant, he stared at her incredulously. Then blood gushed from his mouth, and his head fell limply forward.

Before Kate could even heave a sigh of relief, a grinding noise from above gave warning that the impact of his body smashing into the broken column had affected the stability of the fractured structure around them. She scrambled to her feet. "Patrick, we've got to get out of here!"

Her urgency pierced his haze, and he managed to feebly push himself to his knees. Her left arm was still numbed, so she used the other to yank him to his feet. Then she hauled his arm over her shoulders and began half dragging him to safety with a strength she hadn't known she'd possessed.

As they passed the column, a massive slab of concrete

fell behind them in a boom of shattering material and chok-
ing billows of dust. The impact knocked them from their
feet. Remembering that Donovan's hard hat was gone, she
threw herself over him, shielding his head.

The world darkened as something heavy smashed her
hard hat. A sharp-edged chunk struck between her shoulder
blades, followed by an avalanche of smaller debris.

Then silence—and the recognition of what she'd done.

Julia was dozing on the sofa when Donovan returned home,
but she awoke when he entered the living room. He kissed
her cheek. "How's Kate? I thought they'd keep her in the
hospital."

"You know how hospitals are these days—no overnight
stays unless the patient is at death's door. Kate was bruised
and disoriented, but no concussion or other serious damage.
She's been asleep since I brought her home." Her gaze went
over him. "You look as if you've taken as much punishment as she has."

He thought of the long hours of work after he and Kate
had been pulled out of the debris by Luther and the rest of
the crew. By the time Nick's body was recovered, he was
ready to work again. United in their desire to bring down
the building, his people had finished the explosives loading
in record time.

"I'm just tired. But the job is done—that damned can-
nibalistic building came down an hour ago." When the rest
of Concord Place was dropped, it would be at high noon
with TV crews and the mayor wearing a hard hat. For
Building Four, there had been only somber cops, firemen,
and PDI staffers. Donovan had taken a savage pleasure in
pushing the buttons himself.

"Good riddance to it." Julia got to her feet. "Time to go
home. Oscar will be wondering what happened to me."

"Why not stay here for the rest of the night? The guest
room is made up."

"I'd rather go home. In a few hours I'll have to go over

to Angie Corsi's house to see if there's anything I can do. Poor Angie. Both of us have lost our husbands in demolition accidents. It's a ghastly thing to have in common."

There was a lot Julia didn't know, but Donovan wasn't about to say more. Not until he'd talked to Kate.

Kate tensed when Donovan entered the master bedroom, tempted to continue to play possum. It was four in the morning according to the bedside clock, and decent citizens were entitled to be asleep. But she'd been awake for hours, and short of faking a coma, she'd have to face the world—and Donovan—sooner or later.

"Kate, are you awake?"

"I'm afraid so." The soft glow of a lamp illuminated his face, lined with concern and weariness. He was in his work clothes and decorated with dust and dirt.

He sat on the edge of the bed and took her hand. "Building Four is history. It . . . it didn't take long to dig out Nick's body. The city told us to blow that sucker to hell as quickly as possible, before someone else was hurt or killed."

"How are you? Did the stun gun do any damage?"

"I'm fine. It was the damnedest thing—sort of like being anesthetized. I was conscious, but floating. Almost totally passive. The effect cleared up in about half an hour, but by that time you'd been hustled off to the emergency room. I didn't tell anyone what happened, except that there was a ceiling fall. I figured I'd better talk to you since I'm vague on some of the details."

"Nick thought PDI should have come to him, and he was willing to kill us both to get it. He did kill Sam, orchestrated the job-site problems PDI has been experiencing, and personally caused the gas explosion at Concord Place."

Donovan swore. "I remember some of that, but thought I must have imagined what he said. It's so . . . so lurid. Not like real life. There's a terrible, ironic justice that Nick's own vandalism ended up causing his death."

"Nick wasn't killed by the ceiling fall," she said flatly. "I murdered him."

She tried to pull her hand away, but Donovan caught it between both of his. "Tell me what happened, *cara*," he said softly.

"I deliberately kicked him into a rebar spike. It went right through his chest."

"Jesus! No wonder you were in shock when they pulled us out of the rubble." Donovan lay down beside her on top of the covers and circled her with a protective arm. "But that wasn't murder, Kate. It was self-defense. I worked with Nick for years and most of the time he was okay, but he had a twisty streak. Once he decided that we had to die in order to save his sorry ass, the only choice was to fight back, which you did well enough to save both of us." He stroked her arm from shoulder to wrist, trying to warm her shivering body.

"But I *did* have a choice!" She remembered the rusty shaft emerging from Nick's chest in a gout of blood. Saw his familiar face, contorted by death and disbelief. Dear God, she'd done her job well, carefully plotting her actions, lining Nick up in front of the damaged column. Nick, her cousin, who'd attended all her birthday parties when she was small, and taught her how to play poker. Who had usually been fun. The magnitude of what she'd done made her want to vomit. "I wanted him dead, Patrick. *I wanted him dead*!" She began to sob with wrenching intensity.

He drew her into his arms. "Kate, Kate, that's hardly surprising under the circumstances. Don't blame yourself."

"I have to blame myself!" He didn't understand. She hadn't understood herself until now, when killing her cousin had ripped away her self-delusions with brutal clarity.

In that final skirmish, she hadn't wanted to wound or disable Nick—she had wanted to exact vengeance for what he'd done to Sam, for what he'd tried to do to Patrick and her. She had gone beyond self-defense to blood lust. "Ev-

eryone was willing to let me off the hook for stabbing you.
Tom, Rachel, even you. God knows I desperately wanted
to believe that the violence I committed that day really had
nothing to do with me. But it *was* me. I might have killed
you. Today, I did kill Nick."

He was silent for the space of a dozen heartbeats. "The
worst thing I've ever had to face was that I could, and did,
hurt the person I loved more than anyone on earth. Looking
into the ugliest corners of one's soul is . . . is hell."

"You confronted your dark side long before I did. I'm a
murderer, Patrick. My mother's nice, well-bred daughter
has a vicious streak a yard wide. I don't understand how
you can bear to be close to me."

"I should be upset that you had the strength to save my
life? I've always known you were strong, *cara*. Of course
you have a potential for violence. Just about everyone does
in extreme circumstances. Frankly, I think wanting to kill
Nick shows damned good judgment."

"You're accepting my homicidal tendencies far better
than I."

"That's because I love you, Kate. Always have. Always
will." Gently he pressed his lips to her nape, then enfolded
her more closely, his body heat dispelling her chill.

Ever since her mother had brought her back from the
hospital and put her to bed, she'd been lying awake, re-
playing the scene with Nick over and over in her head.
Perhaps striking back at him had been essential to save her
and Patrick—but the fierce exultation she'd felt when lashing out hadn't been necessary. The memory of it sickened
her.

Yet she could not deny that she'd felt that way. Dear
God, she'd spent her whole life denying her scarier emotions. Refusing to discuss the end of her marriage had been
partly to shield Patrick, partly for the sake of her own pride,
but most of all, a result of her sheer inability to reveal
something so deeply painful. To confront her anguish
would have meant tapping into the molten core of fear and

anger in her heart. The only way she could be in control was through denial. Not good. Disastrous, in fact.

Yet now that she accepted her shadow self, she felt oddly liberated. There was no joy in the knowledge of what she had done, but to protect someone she loved, she would do the same again.

It was clear now that she had been paralyzed not only by Patrick's potential for violence, but another, more secret fear of her own deepest emotions. Ironically, in the past weeks Patrick had demonstrated his ability to keep from going too far again and again. Though he would always have a temper, in her heart she knew he would never hurt her again. Her own dark side had been another matter. Instinctively she had feared that if she released those searing emotions, they would destroy her and everyone around her.

And now that she had faced that fear . . . "I love you, Patrick."

He became very still. "I like the conclusion, but I'm not sure I understand the reasoning."

"I finally figured out that I've been crippled as much by fear of myself as of you. Fear of how angry I was at you, at Sam, at the whole outrageous situation."

"All perfectly reasonable emotions, Kate. I've been scared of myself and my anger many times. Maybe it's human nature to be our own worst enemies. I've been working on my shortcomings for years. I'll bet you get your dark side sorted out a lot faster than I did." He pressed his lips to her forehead, her eyes, the sensitive spot under her ear. "Let's go back to the part where you said that you love me. I'd like to hear that again."

"I love you, Patrick. Lord, it's so good to finally admit it!" She clung to him, feeling whole for the first time since the early years of her marriage. No, better than that. At eighteen she'd been a girl with good luck and good instincts. Now she was a woman, bruised and scarred, but a lot tougher and wiser.

Another insight struck her. "You know, I've just figured

out why I love demolition so much. Apart from the adolescent kick, I mean."

"Another reason is needed?"

"I was raised to be a nice little lady who never showed anger," she explained. "Demolition was a terrific way to sublimate all the wild impulses that I couldn't use anywhere else. No wonder I wanted so much to work for PDI."

"Interesting. That must be part of the appeal for me, too. Except that I was angry and knew it, and needed a safe outlet."

And now, finally, they could find peace and safety in each other's arms. Kate closed her eyes and rested her head against his chest, soothed by the strong, steady beat of her heart. *Carissimo.*

"I love you, Kate." He pulled her close again. "And I'm the luckiest man in world."

She released her breath in a long sigh of pure relaxation. Home at last.

EPILOGUE

Julia inhaled the scented May air with pleasure. It was a perfect spring day, and she was as pleased as if she were personally responsible for the weather. After all, she'd done most of the rest of the organizing for Kate and Donovan's open house, and was now acting as a reception committee for latecomers.

She glanced through the den into the crowded living room. The house Kate had designed was excellent for entertaining, with good traffic flow from kitchen and den to living room and deck. Her redecorating was adding warmth to the impressive but rather empty spaces Donovan had built. At the moment Kate and Donovan were standing in front of the fireplace, laughing with Connie and Frank Russo.

Kate wore a long, flowing blue dress with embroidered panels that wouldn't have looked out of place at a Renaissance festival. As a mother, Julia had no qualms about thinking that her daughter looked breathtakingly beautiful. Beside her Donovan was more conventionally dressed in navy blazer and tan slacks, and looked good enough to eat.

Also in blazer and slacks, Tom ambled in from the kitchen. "I'd forgotten how lovely Maryland is in the spring. The woods full of dogwoods, azaleas blazing everywhere. Even California can't match Ruxton in May."

Julia slipped her hand through her son's arm. "Then you'll just have to come more often."

"To be honest, I've been thinking of entering a monastery in New Mexico. I've visited often, and every time I do, I wonder if I should stay."

"A monastery?" Her son, the monk? How had she and Sam produced such an otherworldly child? Yet the image wasn't hard to conjure up. Tom had always had a spirituality that was very rare. "I thought the Church was pretty rigidly antigay."

"This particular community feels that as long as the vow of celibacy is honored, it doesn't matter what a man did earlier in his life."

That made sense. "Are visitors allowed?"

"Oh, yes. Our Lady of the High Desert isn't a prison. You'd like it there. The New Mexico air and light have a purity that illuminates the spirit. There's . . . peace."

"If you say so. I'll certainly visit, if you're there. What would you do? Besides pray, I presume."

"The brothers keep busy. Tending the garden, baking bread, making wine." He grinned. "Designing Web pages."

"Seriously?"

"God's own truth. One of the brothers makes illuminated-manuscript designs that get used in Web pages. I suspect that my computer skills are one reason they're willing to consider accepting me. Monasteries have to pay their bills somehow."

Before he could say more, Sam's sister Maria and her husband Sean approached. "Tom, how the hell are you?" Sean boomed. "You should come home more often, if only for the crab cakes."

"They have crabs in San Francisco Bay, too."

Sean made a disgusted face. "*Not* the same thing." Working with the skill of a long-married couple, he and Maria carried Tom off to meet their newest grandchild. Julia watched them go, knowing she had a doting smile on her face.

Charles joined her from the kitchen. "Need another drink? That ice water seems to have lost its ice."

"Thanks, but I'm fine. I don't need anything more to be happy today."

"You can leave your post soon. The fatal hour is almost here."

"I'll wait a few minutes longer. After all, most people think this is just an open house, so a few guests are still trickling in." She smiled as Dinah stropped her ankles. "Besides, I've got the company of my grandcat here."

Charles's gaze went back to the great room, where Angela Corsi was now talking with Connie Russo. "I'm glad Angie came today. Since Nick's death, she seems more relaxed. Not happy, certainly, but better able to breathe."

Spring had been complicated, to say the least. But it had been a profound relief to learn that Sam hadn't killed himself. Matters had resolved themselves about as well as could be hoped for.

A slim young woman came briskly through the front screen door. Raine Marlowe. "Rainey, how wonderful!" Julia said. "I'm so glad you could make it."

"I missed Kate's first wedding, so I promised her that nothing would keep me from her second." Rainey hugged Julia. Today she had eschewed Hollywood glamour in favor of a simplicity that reminded Julia of the times when Kate and all of her friends would sprawl around the family room, weeping in unison as they watched *An Affair to Remember*. The good old days.

Speaking of Hollywood . . . "Did the Sexiest Man Alive come?"

"He's in Greece starting a new movie."

Just as well, perhaps. Julia would love to meet him, but Kenzie Scott's presence would definitely distract from the main event. "Go in and say hello to Kate. She and the rest of your gang will be delighted to see you."

Rainey walked down the three steps into the great room, and was promptly engulfed in old friends. It was good to have her back in Baltimore.

A Tibetan temple bell chimed, its mellow tone slicing

through the chatter. Julia quietly laced her fingers through Charles's. The main event had arrived.

Being able to outshout the noise of a demolition site had advantages, Donovan thought as he raised both arms and called out, "May I have your attention, please!"

As the happily chattering crowd quieted down, Kate emerged from the middle of her friends suddenly equipped with flowers in her shining hair and a bouquet in one hand. She looked like an exquisite medieval princess.

"I have a confession to make. This isn't just an open house. It's a wedding," he announced. "The only people we told in advance were out-of-staters who needed an incentive to come."

As laughter and whispers of excitement rippled through the room, the witnesses stepped forward, Tom Corsi to be best man and Liz Chen as maid of honor. "We didn't want a lot of hoopla, just the presence of those we love." He glanced around the room, thinking of that first wedding more than a dozen years ago. God, they'd been young. "We didn't want gifts, either. Many of you already gave once, which lets you off the hook for remarriages. Find yourselves a good viewing spot, and we'll proceed."

Laurel Clark, who played the hammer dulcimer, had set up her instrument in the corner earlier. Now she filled the air with exuberant Renaissance dance music as the guests rearranged themselves around the wedding party. Julia and Charles stood in the doorway to the den, since the three steps gave them a good view over the other guests. His dignified, once-and-future mother-in-law blew him a kiss.

The Methodist minister who would perform the ceremony, a Corsi family friend, had slipped from the room to put on his robes. As the Reverend Whittaker worked his way slowly toward the wedding party, Donovan dug in his pocket for the rings. He and Kate both still had their original wedding bands, with the date of the first ceremony engraved inside, so he'd taken the rings to a jeweler to have the new date added.

He handed the rings to Tom and Liz, then took Kate's hand. "Did you add the divorce date to the rings?" she asked. "It seems only fair to include the whole story for our grandchildren's sake."

He grinned, thinking how in the weeks since their reconciliation, she'd become the laughing, confident Kate again. "Nope. Instead I had an infinity sign engraved inside each ring." He raised their joined hands and tenderly kissed her fingers. "This time, *carissima,* it's forever."

"I now pronounce you husband and wife."

As Kate and Patrick kissed, Julia wiped her eyes. This time the two of them would get it right.

As she tucked away her handkerchief, Charles said quietly, "I love a wedding. How about if you and I do this after a discreet interval has passed? Say, a year or so from now."

Julia's pulse went into overtime. "I . . . I haven't really thought that far ahead."

"I have. The kids are right, second weddings should be simple. I keep thinking how lovely you'd look coming down the staircase in my front hall. That leaded-glass window always looks its best with a bride in front of it. Until and unless Rachel finds someone she wants to keep, you're the best bet my window has."

Julia bit her lip. Then, voice almost inaudible, she whispered, "Yes."

His expression lit up. "In case I haven't mentioned it, Julia, I love you."

"And I you, Charles." She sent a silent prayer of thanksgiving heavenward, for if ever a woman had been doubly blessed, it was her.

In front of the fireplace, Patrick had his arm around his radiant bride. "The last thing I want to say is how lucky I am. I was amazed that Kate married me once." He looked down into her eyes, his gaze as intimate as a kiss. "The fact that she's willing to marry me again is nothing short of a miracle."

"Patrick, as always, underrates himself," Kate said. "I've a confession to make, too. All of you nice, opinionated people who told me I should look hard at what I'd thrown away were absolutely right."

More laughter. When the levity faded, Kate said in a voice turned serious, "The one person who should be here but isn't is my father. Could we please have a moment of silence in memory of Sam Corsi? If not for him, none of us would be here today, and my life would be . . . incomplete."

The silence was absolute. It ended when Reverend Whittaker said, "Amen. And now, in the endless cycle of life, it's time to celebrate a joyful new beginning."

As a receiving line formed, Charles said, "When Sam insisted on writing that crazy will, I told him that in my professional opinion he was madder than a March hare. But damned if he didn't know what he was doing."

Julia tucked her hand into Charles's elbow. "I don't know if he was wise, or if he just got lucky, but there's one thing I'm sure of." She smiled through a misting of tears. "Somewhere, my dear, Sam Corsi is laughing."

AUTHOR'S NOTE

Domestic violence is wrong, wrong, wrong. That is inarguable, and no one should tolerate it. Yet life is seldom black and white as it unfolds, and good days and bad days are usually mixed together in a most confusing way.

Though the theme is difficult, in *The Burning Point* I've chosen to explore a fictional road less traveled because transformation and reconciliation are recurring themes in all my novels. When is it time to leave before a bad situation can turn catastrophic? And once trust has been shattered, can it be rebuilt?

As a very young wife, Kate rationalized the conditions that were gradually undermining her marriage. She believed that each violent incident was isolated and wouldn't recur. She knew that Donovan loved her, which surely meant their marriage was strong and sound. She was convinced that if she was just loving and understanding enough, everything would work out. Luckily, she learned better in time.

Donovan was never a bad guy, but he'd been raised with abuse, and his needs and his love were dangerously focused on Kate. Sometimes his behavior was appalling and he knew it, yet as long as Kate tolerated his actions, there was no incentive to change. Only after losing what he loved most in the world did he realize that he must make profound and painful changes in himself.

Although Kate and Donovan are fictional, they are modeled on real men and women who have successfully overcome troubled pasts and built healthier lives. Healing a destructive relationship requires more than love. There must also be compassion, wisdom, and emotional toughness. Kate and Donovan have all of those qualities, along with a great capacity for forgiveness. This is why together they are able to rebuild their relationship, and make it "stronger in the mended places."